THE RIVALED CROWN

USA TODAY BESTSELLING AUTHOR

HOLLY RENEE

PRONUNCIATION GUIDE

Marmoris: MAR-moris
Enveilarian: ON-veil-air-ian
Dacre: DAY-ker
Nyra: near-ah
Wren: ren
Verena: Vuh- rehn-ah
Kai: K ai h
Eiran: AIR-in
Veyrith: VAY-r-ih-th
Liya: LIE-ah
Elis: EE-l-ee-s

CONTENT WARNING

This series contains depictions of sexually explicit scenes, violence, and assault. It contains mature language, themes, and content that may not be suitable for all readers. Reader discretion is advised.

For Reagan, Ellie, and Arizona-
My sweet, powerful girls.
I love you endlessly.

CHAPTER 1
VERENA

A sharp, biting cold enveloped my body, stealing away every last bit of warmth. I shivered, my skin pressing against damp stone, my muscles stiff from the unforgiving surface beneath me. Every inch of the dimly lit room felt coated in a bitter chill, seeping into my bones until they ached. Even the chains that bound my wrists seemed to hold on to the cold, leeching the heat from my skin until my fingers had gone numb.

I blinked slowly, willing my eyes to focus. The space felt both vast and suffocating, its shadows looming and shifting with the faint beam of daylight that seeped through a small, barred window high above. The musty stench of iron and wet stone clung to my tongue, thick and stale.

I shifted slightly and the rattle of my chains sent a sharp clang reverberating through the silence. A lance of pain shot up my arms, the rough bindings digging into my raw skin. My shoulders screamed from the constant strain of being bound for what felt like an eternity, though it could have been only hours or even days.

A shudder ran down my spine as I struggled to push myself upright, my back scraping against the rough stone wall. Every part of me rebelled, stiff with pain, but I gritted my teeth and willed myself to keep going. Even the pain was better than the paralyzing sense of powerlessness that threatened to consume me.

The iron door loomed ahead, its surface streaked with rust as if it had been guarding secrets for centuries. The room remained eerily stagnant, the only movement coming from flickers of dust drifting through the taunting sliver of sunlight. I tilted my head, my gaze locking onto the narrow window. Even if I could stand, even if my legs would hold me, it was impossibly high. Another prison within a prison.

Despair threatened to settle in, curling around me like a vise.

"You're wasting my time, Verena." My father's voice echoed in my memory. *"Show me your power or you'll wish for death."*

His voice was always a weapon, sharper than any blade, cutting through my defenses with ease. He didn't shout. He didn't need to. The calm in his voice as he tore me down was more terrifying than his rage.

He wanted me to break.

A thick blanket of silence smothered the air, pressing against my ears, allowing my thoughts to spiral, faster and louder, until they tangled into an oppressive snare.

"You are worthless."

"A powerless heir."

Doubt slithered in like a whispering snake, its

venomous words seeping into my mind and poisoning my resolve.

I closed my eyes and reached for something, someone, anything to ground me.

Dacre.

His face came to me easily, as though my mind had carved every detail into my memory. His dark, unruly hair, the sharp angles of his jaw, the quiet, simmering intensity in his eyes. The way he looked at me, like he saw every part of me, the pieces I hid from the world.

I imagined his touch, rough but careful, the way his calloused fingers would trail down my spine, soothing and firm. I could almost hear his voice, deep and steady, grounding me in a way nothing else could. My pulse kicked up, warmth trying to push past the ice that had settled in my chest.

He would come for me.

He had to.

But doubt was like a shadow, hauntingly clinging to my every thought and refusing to let me find solace in the words I desperately held onto.

I forced away the memory of him on the docks, his hands outstretched, his face twisted in rage and desperation. The sound of my name torn from his lips, raw and broken, as the guards dragged me away from the ship that was meant for the two of us.

An agonizing ache swelled in my chest, thick and unbearable.

Where had they taken him? What cruel fate awaited him at the hands of those sailors? What had my father paid them in exchange for the betrayal? What reward would he offer for them to ensure I never saw Dacre again.

My mind raced with frantic images, each one more terrifying than the last, but I knew that wherever he was, he was far safer than if he had been here with me.

My father ruled through fear and fire. I had seen what happened to those who defied him.

And Dacre had done far worse than defy him.

He had helped me escape. I had been his enemy. I represented the thing he hated most. I was a threat to everything he stood for.

And still, he had chosen me.

Even after the betrayal, after learning my true identity, after every reason I had given him to turn away, he had protected me.

He had given me the most dangerous weapon of all.

Hope.

It flickered inside me, fragile and desperate. A single ember in the darkness.

My throat constricted. Panic clawed at the edges of my mind, but I clung to that ember like a drowning girl clung to driftwood.

Dacre would come, I told myself over and over again, the words becoming a desperate mantra as fear pulsed through me.

My thoughts were a raging battlefield, my mind and heart being pulled in opposite directions until I was on the brink of breaking apart. Clinging to the hope that he would come for me, I also whispered pleas to the gods that he would stay away.

For if he dared come for me, my father would never

allow him to escape with his life. He would wield Dacre as a tool, subjecting him to relentless torment while I was forced to watch. And it would break me, bending my will until I gave in completely, molding me into the very thing he desperately wanted me to become.

A sudden sound shattered the silence.

Footsteps.

Heavy. Purposeful.

Coming closer.

My heart pounded so hard I could feel it slamming against my ribs, as if trying to break out of its cage. Every muscle in my body tensed as I forced my spine straight, squaring my shoulders despite the sharp tug of my bindings.

The iron door let out a haunting groan, its rusted hinges screaming as it swung open.

Two figures entered.

Tall, hooded, their faces hidden in the shadows cast by the dim light.

My father followed them, his presence smothering the room like smoke and draining the air from my lungs.

One of the hooded figures stepped forward. "Is this her?"

The voice was smooth. Female. Calculating.

She crouched, drawing back her hood.

She was beautiful. Strikingly so. White hair framed her sharp cheekbones, her features precise, as if sculpted from marble.

But it was the scar running jagged along her jaw that caught my attention.

Old. Healed poorly. A wound that had once been deep.

Her eyes were milky white and flicked from the right to the left as if she weren't seeing me at all.

She was a sight.

I quickly shifted my gaze, taking in the other hooded figure, the one enveloped entirely in a cloak of deep black with my father's crest intricately embroidered on their chest in gleaming thread. They stood, unmoving, but I could sense their eyes fixed on me.

My father moved closer to the woman, his hand resting on the hilt of a dagger. "Yes. She's resistant. A flaw she inherited from her mother."

The woman's gaze flickered toward my father before settling back on me, but I glared at him, anger flaring in my chest.

"Interesting," she purred, and I looked back at her just in time to watch her gaze scan over every part of me. "She seems to have quite a bit more fight in her than you alluded."

She reached out, and I jerked back on instinct.

Her fingers brushed my skin, and a sharp jolt of magic surged through me, cold and invasive, prying into my mind like talons digging into flesh.

My back bowed involuntarily, a gasp escaping before I could stop it.

"She's shielding herself," she murmured, almost impressed. "Strongly, too."

"Try harder," my father snapped.

The woman pressed her fingertips against my temple, her brow furrowing in concentration. I gritted my teeth, summoning every ounce of strength I had left.

Dacre's voice whispered through my mind. His touch.

His promises. His presence. I clung to the memories, wrapped myself in them like armor.

A moment later, the woman swore under her breath and withdrew her hand, rubbing at her forehead. "This shielding is strong. I can't break through it."

Sweat beaded on her forehead as I stared into her eyes.

My father's jaw clenched. "Leave us."

The woman hesitated as she stood. "Your methods aren't working. You're weakening her body, but her power…"

"How much power can the girl have?" My father began rolling up his sleeves, and the tiniest whimper slipped past my lips. "She's been powerless most of her life, and she will remain powerless when I'm through with her."

The woman stood and retreated with the other who had accompanied her, but she hesitated near the door. "Allow me time with her, Your Majesty. I don't know what she was before, but she's not powerless now. I can't use my sight if you…"

"We do not have time for your gentleness," my father growled. His hand shot out, tangling in the back of my hair, yanking my head back so hard a strangled cry tore from my throat. My arms strained against the chains that bound me, pulling at my joints with a relentless pressure.

He leaned in, his breath warm against my skin. "You think you've won some small victory," he murmured, his tone deceptively soft, deadly. "But you haven't. You're weak, Verena. Just like your mother."

My heart raced as I stared into my father's cold eyes, searching for any hint of the man I once believed him to be.

But all that remained was a cold, calculating ruler consumed by greed and bitterness.

"My mother wasn't weak," I managed to say through gritted teeth, my voice trembling with anger.

His sneer deepened, twisting his features. "She couldn't handle the demands of being queen, nor could she provide me a suitable heir for our kingdom."

I clenched my fists, nails biting into my palms. "And the new queen?" I forced the words past the lump in my throat. "Was it the demands of being your wife that killed her as well?"

His hand cracked across my face before I saw it coming. The force sent me reeling, my vision blurring, and the metallic taste of blood flooding my mouth.

"You insolent fool," he seethed. The words dripped from his lips like venom, curling around me with suffocating intent. "It will be my demands that will seal your fate as well if you don't give me what I want."

He stepped back, exhaling sharply. His fingers traced the sharp edges of his jaw, a calculated movement, as though restraining himself from further violence.

"I don't know how to give you what you want," I lied, my voice breaking despite my best efforts. We both knew the truth. He could taste it in the air between us, thick with unspoken defiance.

His eyes darkened, a storm gathering inside them just before his fist collided with my temple.

Pain exploded behind my eyes. The hit sent me crashing to the cold stone floor, my bound wrists twisting painfully beneath me. The impact sent shock waves through my already bruised body, agony sparking every nerve.

Through the ringing in my ears, I could barely make out the voice of the woman who still stood at the back of my cell. "Your Majesty…" Her voice trembled, a hint of fear and concern laced within her words.

My father barely spared her a glance, his dark eyes locked on to me as he circled around me, his footsteps echoing menacingly in the confined space. "What?"

"I won't be able to detect her magic if she's barely alive."

His shadow loomed over me, stretching long and ominous in the dim candlelight.

"You have two days." His hand trembled as he wiped his hand over his mouth, leaving a trail of crimson on his skin. Whether it was his own blood from his split knuckles or mine, I couldn't tell.

"But for now, you leave her," he continued, his voice filled with a mixture of anger and disappointment.

His gaze dropped to where I lay, a broken thing at his feet. I prayed he wouldn't see the silent tears slipping down my cheeks.

"My heir would rather die with her mouth full of those rebels' secrets than kneel to the king who has spent his life shielding her from the cruelties of this world." He exhaled sharply, rolling his shoulders as though shaking off the weight of what I'd done. "She needs time to reflect on her choices and the consequences that come with them."

He turned away, his boots clicking against the stone.

A heavy slam echoed through the chamber as the door sealed shut.

I lay motionless, breath shallow, waiting for the ache in my ribs to dull. The pain was a living thing, clawing at my insides, demanding surrender.

I squeezed my eyes shut, lips moving in a silent prayer to the gods I had long abandoned.

The chamber swallowed time, its silence stretching, suffocating.

Darkness crept in, its icy fingers wrapping around my ribs. Each breath came slower, more labored.

Then, a whisper of movement.

A shift in the air.

My eyes snapped open.

The door stood slightly ajar, the flickering torchlight casting strange shadows against the wall.

I tensed. Someone was here.

My fingers curled into fists. "Who's there?" My voice came out hoarse, fractured.

No answer.

I scanned the corners of the room, my pulse hammering against my chest.

"Show yourself," I demanded, though my body was too weak to do anything if they meant me harm.

Another flicker of movement.

A shadow detached itself from the darkness.

I stiffened, instinct screaming at me to retreat, but there was nowhere to go.

Then, a familiar voice.

The figure that was still cloaked in all black moved toward me slowly, their cloak concealing their form and features.

"You look worse than I expected."

The hood fell back, revealing a face I had thought I'd never see again.

Warm brown eyes met mine, gentle and filled with something I couldn't name.

A sob clawed up my throat, thick and unbearable.

"What are you doing here?" I pleaded, raw with disbelief.

"I'm here for you, Nyra," he murmured the only name he had ever known me by.

Micah.

CHAPTER 2
DACRE

The ship let out a relentless chorus of creaks and groans, like a drumbeat that echoed my failure. The waves pounded against the hull, hammering home the same cruel truth: I had failed to protect Verena.

The iron shackles dug into my wrists, leaving behind angry red welts that burned with each movement. But the pain was distant, a mere background noise in my mind.

All that mattered was *her*.

The image of Verena being dragged away burned behind my eyes, her desperate screams swallowed by the crashing waves. Her name had been the last thing on my lips when they forcibly silenced me with a gag, as if trying to sever the bond that tied us.

But they had failed.

Hunched in the far corner of my cell, the thick stench of saltwater and unwashed bodies clung to me like a second skin. The damp air was almost suffocating, pressing in on all sides as I took shallow breaths.

My shoulders slumped, defeated, as I leaned against the cold iron bars.

Outside, a lantern swayed back and forth, casting golden light that danced across the rough wooden walls. But despite its efforts to illuminate the darkness, it only deepened the shadows in my mind.

I replayed the events over and over again in my head. I should have fought harder. Been smarter. I should have done something, anything, to keep Verena from being taken.

But instead, here I was, trapped in this wretched cell aboard this cursed ship while she...gods, I couldn't begin to imagine the horrors she was enduring.

My hands clenched into tight fists, my nails digging into my palms as the cold metal cuffs mercilessly bit into my skin. Her face haunted me even when I closed my eyes. The pain in my chest was overwhelming, a mix of guilt and anger that made it hard to breathe. But more than that, it was the void left by her absence that weighed heavily on me, a constant reminder of what I had lost and allowed to be taken away from me.

It was as though I could physically sense her, through the delicate and untested bond that tethered us together. A faint echo of her agony reverberated through my being, like a distant whisper brushing against the edges of my mind. It was nothing more than a feeling, a cruel trick of desperation, but I clung to it anyway.

"Verena," I breathed, her name escaping my lips like a whispered plea.

I clenched my teeth, forcing myself upright. I could not remain here any longer. Not while she was out there, hurt, alone, and at the mercy of her cruel father. The thought sent a surge of fury within me. It burned away the numbness that had settled over my limbs, igniting a fierce determination within me.

The guard stationed outside my cell was a hulking brute of a man, his arms crossed over his chest, a tarnished dagger clenched in one fist. He leaned against the damp wooden walls, his heavy-lidded eyes staring blankly ahead, as if the monotony of his job had dulled his mind.

I climbed to my feet on the damp floor and crouched low, my eyes darting back and forth as I surveyed the narrow corridor beyond the iron bars. The ship rocked and swayed beneath my feet, the relentless crash of waves against the hull masking any sound I made.

The plan forming in my mind wasn't perfect. It wasn't even good. But it was all I had.

The cold, heavy chains encircling my wrists clinked as I adjusted them, testing their weight and tension. Just long enough to move, enough to be useful.

"Hey," I called out, my voice hoarse and rough from disuse and lack of water.

He didn't react at first, his gaze fixed on some distant point. But when I called out again, louder this time, he finally turned toward me, annoyance flickering in his eyes.

"Shut it," he growled as his hand tightened around his dagger.

I didn't shut it.

I leaned casually against the metal bars of my cell, watching him with a bored expression.

"I'm going to be sick," I told him as I pressed my hands

against my stomach. "The wounds on my body. I think they are infected."

It wasn't a complete lie. My body did feel like it was fighting against itself, begging to be healed.

"You're going to have to wait until we reach land, and you've got days before we get there. The king ordered you as far away from his kingdom, his heir, as we can get you, and we've been at sea less than a day, boy."

I could see the muscles in his jaw tense as he clenched his teeth, his hand tightening further on his rusted dagger.

Come closer.

I hunched over farther, groaning until he cursed under his breath.

"The king wants you alive," he hissed. "He wants you questioned by the captain. He wants you tortured until you squeal like a pig about your beloved rebellion." He took an aggressive step toward me, his dagger now pointed in my direction. "The king rewards handsomely when he gets what he wants. Show me the wound."

I shifted my weight, ready to strike as soon as he was within reach. The pounding of my heart seemed to echo through the walls of my cell, each beat thumping loudly in my ears.

"Show me your wound," he snarled, his voice low and menacing as he stepped right up to the bars of my cell.

Before he could react, I lunged. The heavy chains around my wrists rattled as I wrapped them around his thick neck, yanking him forward with every ounce of strength I had left.

His dagger clattered to the floor as he let out a choked gasp, his hands flying to the chains, clawing at them.

The ship pitched violently, sending both of us stumbling. I held tight, using the bars for leverage as I pulled harder.

He struggled, his breath coming in desperate wheezes and his nails digging into my wrists as he tried to pry the chains loose.

I yanked again until his body jerked once, twice, before going limp.

I let him slump to the floor.

No hesitation. No mercy.

Dropping to my knees, I frantically searched his belt for keys. My trembling fingers finally found a ring of cold metal, and I pulled it free.

The first key didn't fit. Neither did the second.

Footsteps sounded from the deck above. I swore under my breath, fumbling with the keys and nearly dropping them.

Not now. Not when I'm this close.

Finally, on the third try, I felt a satisfying click as the key turned in the lock and the cuffs fell away from my sore wrists with a dull clank.

I exhaled sharply, shoving the pain in my wrists to the back of my mind as I jammed a key into the rusted lock of the cell door.

With the attempt of each key, the weight seemed to get heavier, and I cursed as I searched the hallway for any sign that someone had heard me.

The hinges groaned in protest as I turned the next key and heard the lock click open.

Slowly, carefully, I pushed the heavy door outward, its rusted edge scraping against the floor.

My pulse thundered in my ears as I stole a glance at the guard, still slumped over, his face slack in unconsciousness. Not dead. But close enough.

The passageway twisted and turned, lined with coils of rope, discarded fishing gear, and rusted tools. The ship rocked beneath me, the low murmur of voices from above filtering through the wooden planks overhead.

I kept to the shadows, my feet barely making a sound against the damp floorboards. Every step was calculated. Every breath was measured.

The stairs loomed ahead, steep and narrow. At the top, faint torchlights flickered, and beyond that, freedom.

A surge of resolve hardened my spine. I would not die here.

I took the first step. Then another. Each creak of the wood beneath me sent my pulse hammering, every sound a threat.

The voices above grew clearer.

"Captain wants us moving east by morning."

"Should be at the next port in…"

The words cut off as the ship gave a sudden, violent lurch.

Shit.

I threw myself against the wall, pressing into the shadows as a pair of boots appeared at the top of the stairs.

The man muttered something under his breath, adjusting his belt as he stepped down.

Closer.

I tried to reach for my power, but I was too weak. My strength leached from me in a way that left nothing for my magic.

As soon as he was within reach, I struck.

My arm shot out, catching him by the throat. His eyes bulged as I drove him backward, his balance lost on the uneven steps.

He barely had time to choke out a curse before I slammed his head against the railing.

Once.

Twice.

He slumped.

I caught his belt, easing him down the stairs as silently as I could before laying him beside the unconscious guard. No time to search for weapons. No time for caution.

I took the stairs two at a time.

The cold sea air hit me like a blade the moment I reached the top deck, salt and wind tearing at my skin.

The dark expanse of the ocean stretched in every direction, endless and unforgiving. The moon was bright overhead, silver light reflecting off the rippling waves, casting eerie, shifting shadows across the deck.

Two crew members stood near the railing, their backs to me, deep in quiet conversation.

I moved fast.

Silent. Deadly.

My fingers brushed against a length of rope coiled near the mast, and I pulled it free in one fluid motion.

The first man turned, brow furrowed. "Hey…"

I lunged, slamming my shoulder into his chest before he could finish the word.

He stumbled back into the other crew member, throwing them both off balance. Their swords were halfway drawn before I was already moving.

I didn't give them a chance.

The first man lunged, and I ducked, driving my elbow into his ribs before sweeping his legs out from under him.

The second man was faster, his blade whistled through the air, missing my throat by inches.

I twisted, grabbing his wrist and driving my knee into his gut. He choked on a curse as I wrenched the sword from his grasp and slammed the hilt against his temple.

He crumpled.

I turned back to the first man, now scrambling to his feet.

Too slowly.

I drove my stolen sword into his thigh. He let out a strangled cry, his legs buckling beneath him as he collapsed against the deck.

I didn't stay to watch him fall.

The ropes.

I grabbed the nearest coil, heart hammering as I knotted one end around the railing and hurled the other end overboard.

Below, the small lifeboat bobbed violently, ropes straining as it fought against the pull of the waves.

I peered over the railing, my eyes stinging from the sharp spray of saltwater. I swung my leg over, bracing against the slick wood.

A shout rang out behind me.

I pushed off, plummeting toward the waiting boat below.

The boat pitched hard as I hit the bottom, the impact slamming the breath from my lungs.

I barely had time to register the pain before I was moving again.

The ship loomed above, voices shouting in alarm, boots pounding against the deck.

I reached for my blade, gripping it tight. The last rope still held the lifeboat tethered. I had to cut it.

I sawed at the thick fibers, the blade slipping against the damp, sea-worn rope.

Come on.

A shadow passed overhead, and I looked up just as the captain leaned over the railing, his eyes wild with fury.

"Stop him!"

More shouts. More movement.

The sword in my grip dug deeper, slicing halfway through.

The boat rocked violently beneath me as another wave hit, sending cold seawater sloshing over the edge.

Footsteps thundered above.

I was almost there. Another slash…

The rope snapped.

The boat lurched, breaking free from the ship, and plunging into the churning waters below.

The impact sent me sprawling, my back colliding against the wooden bench. Pain flared through my ribs, but I didn't stop moving.

Above, the crew scrambled, their voices growing distant as the lifeboat drifted farther and farther away.

The sea had claimed me now.

Salt stung my skin, the frigid wind howling as I struggled to steady myself. The waves were relentless, crashing against the small vessel, tossing it about.

But I was free.

I grabbed the oars, my muscles protesting as I rowed, each pull sending fire through my exhausted limbs.

Verena.

The thought of her remained steady like a lighthouse in the storm.

Time blurred.

The sky darkened, then lightened again.

The hours stretched, my body numb with exhaustion.

My mind was as turbulent as the ocean. Fear, regrets, and desperate hope crashed and churned, threatening to consume me.

Her name echoed through my mind, a whisper against the roar of the sea.

There was a fragile thread that tethered me to her, and I clung to it as I rowed harder.

I forced myself to focus on the details of her face. The delicate freckles that danced along her cheeks. The warmth in her smile as she shared the story about her mother. I replayed those vows we spoke from her story on an endless loop inside my mind.

Each word held a weight and a promise that still lingered.

Until…the seabirds began to fly overhead.

Then a thin line of land appeared on the horizon.

Relief hit me like a blow to the chest, staggering and overwhelming.

I pushed forward, the last reserves of my strength pouring into every stroke of the oars.

The shoreline grew closer, the jagged cliffs rising from the sea like sentinels.

And then, I could see a few figures lining the beach, and trepidation filled me.

My father was still looking for me. My father who I had betrayed to save her.

My people who I had betrayed.

But I had no choice.

The boat scraped against the sand. I stumbled out, my legs nearly buckling as they met solid ground.

"Dacre!"

The voice was distant but achingly familiar. I lifted my head, my vision swimming.

Footsteps pounding against the sand grew louder until they were right beside me, and hands gripped my shoulders. The sand shifted beneath my weight as I struggled to focus on the face in front of me.

Kai.

He was speaking, but I couldn't make out the words.

Another voice.

"We'll find her."

Wren.

I tried to stand, tried to speak. "Where is she?"

But the world tilted.

Darkness swallowed me, and all I heard was Wren's voice carrying through the void.

"We'll find her."

CHAPTER 3
VERENA

P ain pulsed through me like a living thing, clawing at the edges of my mind, tormenting me with its insistent presence and leaving no room for coherent thought. Even the rough stone floor beneath me seemed to conspire against me, its rutted edges digging into my bruised and battered body.

I tried to take a deep breath, but my ribs screamed in protest.

A dry, raspy cough tore from my throat, the sound echoing through the chamber, mocking my weakness. It had been days since they had given me water.

Days since Micah had visited my cell.

Days since I feared I had imagined my friend.

Every inhale was a struggle; each exhale tasted of iron.

He won't break me.

I desperately repeated the words in my mind, clinging to them like my last thread of hope.

But even that thread was fraying.

Just like the edges of my father's control.

I closed my eyes and pressed my forehead against my knees, curling in on myself. Hunger gnawed at my stomach, twisting it into knots and making my vision blur.

I flinched as my father's voice cut through the thick, hazy air.

"Still clinging to your defiance, I see."

His heavy boots thudded against the floorboards, each step deliberate and precise. The room suddenly felt small, suffocating under his presence.

"I admire your resolve, Verena," he sneered, his words dripping with disdain.

I refused to meet his gaze, knowing it would only fuel his anger. But I could feel his eyes boring into me, dissecting every ounce of weakness.

The air grew heavier as he loomed over me. I braced myself.

His fingers clamped around my chin, a cruel grip that forced my face upward.

Fractured shadows cast over his features.

"Do you know what I admire most about you, my dear daughter?" he asked, his voice deceptively soft. "It's your unrelenting stubbornness." His grip tightened, nails biting into my skin. "It's almost…inspiring."

Then, he shoved back, my head cracking against the wall. A sharp gasp tore from my lips as pain flared through my skull.

"But stubbornness without purpose is useless," he continued, pacing like a predator. His voice turned cold, cruel. "You're clinging to loyalty that will only lead to ruin.

The hidden city?" He paused, waiting for me to look at him. "We've found it."

My heart lurched in my chest, pounding with a sickening intensity. "You're lying."

He smirked. Slow. Calculated. He was enjoying this.

"Let me assure you, Verena. My army is thorough," he said, mocking my fear. "Even that boy you were so desperate to protect couldn't stop us."

"No." A chill rushed through my veins.

My father crouched, his eyes glittering with dark amusement.

"No?" He tilted his head, watching me. "Do you think I'm lying? Do you think they're safe?"

My breath came in ragged gasps. *He's playing with you. He doesn't know. He can't know.*

"Tell me, daughter," he said, leaning closer, his voice almost tender. "What secrets are worth the lives of those you claim to care for?"

Dacre.

His face flashed in my mind, and I wasn't sure if it was the doubt my father was trying to weave or my own desperation, but I could have sworn I could feel him through that invisible tether, a rush of his longing whispering through me.

"You don't know where they are," I whispered.

"Perhaps," he said, straightening. "But are you willing to take that risk?"

The words sank into my skin like poison.

"Give me what I want, Verena." His voice turned deathly quiet. "Reveal your magic. Tell me everything you know."

The room tilted, the walls closing in as his threats wrapped around my throat like a snare. My breaths came faster, each one a shallow gasp as doubt gnawed at the edges of my resolve.

"I won't betray him."

"You have no choice," my father snarled, his hand wrapping around my throat.

I gasped, kicking, clawing, struggling.

"You're already betraying them all."

His fingers tightened, and my lungs burned, my vision spotted.

I clawed at his wrist, but he wouldn't let go.

"Keep your secrets," he sneered, "and they will die with you. Or embrace who you were always meant to be…" His grip squeezed, his breath hot against my ear. "And I will spare them."

I writhed desperately. I reached for anything inside me, my magic, remnants of strength, but there was nothing.

"The rebellion they are fighting for is dead either way, Verena."

My father's low, menacing chuckle filled the room.

Then, as if I were nothing more than a discarded doll, he threw me to the ground.

Pain exploded across my ribs. My arms, still bound in chains, twisted beneath me, sending jolts of agony through my shoulders.

I choked on a sob, my body trembling as I curled in on myself.

"Don't delude yourself into thinking you have any control here." His boots scraped against the stone as he turned away. "The princess of Marmoris." He tsked, but I didn't turn around to look at him. "As pathetic as your mother."

I bit down on my lip, tasting blood.

I wouldn't break.

"Excuse me, Your Majesty." There was a soft creak of the iron door before a guard stepped inside.

"What is it?" my father demanded, barely taking his eyes off me long enough to look at him.

"They have asked for you in the war room. It is urgent."

I barely registered the words. I was still gasping for breath, still trembling.

Then the guard stepped into the light.

Micah.

The breath froze in my lungs.

He stood rigid, dressed in the crisp uniform of the King's Guard, every crease and seam sharp and precise. The crest of my father's rule was stitched into the breast of his jacket, gleaming like a brand against him.

It was *wrong.*

"The sight," my father ordered, his voice impatient. "Bring her to see the heir at once. Time is of the essence."

Micah nodded once. "We'll fetch her immediately, Your Majesty."

My father turned to leave, his eyes lingering on me before he disappeared out the door.

I didn't breathe until his footsteps faded into silence. When I finally did, my lungs ached.

I looked back at Micah, searching for a trace of the friend I used to know, the boy I had once trusted. But all I could see was the crest on his chest. The weight of his betrayal.

"Why are you here?" My voice was hoarse, raw from screaming, from choking, from struggling.

Micah's jaw tightened. He hesitated. Then, finally, he spoke. "I didn't have a choice."

The words were quiet, but heavy, like an anchor pulling him under.

"Your father…" He stopped. Looked away.

Something flickered behind his eyes, guilt, fear, regret.

Then he whispered something that sent ice through my veins.

"My sister."

I had spent so many nights hearing him speak of her. The younger sister who had been ripped from his arms the night their parents had been killed. The only thing in the world he had ever wanted to protect.

"What did he do?" I barely recognized my own voice.

Micah shook his head and glanced back to the cell door.

My stomach churned, my heart slamming against my ribs.

"What do you want from me?"

Micah's gaze flicked back to me before he did the last thing I expected. He dropped to his knees before me, his trembling hand moving over me but not touching.

"I want to help you."

The words hung between us, fragile and uncertain.

I didn't believe them.

Not when he kneeled before me in that uniform. Not when my father had made a weapon out of everyone he touched.

"Help me?" My voice was barely above a whisper.

"How many of my father's orders did you follow before deciding that?"

Micah flinched before pressing his lips into a thin line. "I never wanted this."

My laugh was harsh, humorless. "And yet, here you are."

Micah's jaw locked. "You think this was a choice?"

I didn't answer him. I didn't think that either of us would like my answer.

A long silence stretched between us. Then he sighed.

"I've been looking for you since the moment I heard you were arrested."

I stilled.

"What?"

He ran a hand over his face, looking away. "I would never have let them take me alive if I hadn't been looking…" He cut himself off, shaking his head.

Regret was carved into his features.

"I'm sorry," I whispered.

He looked at me then, his gaze flickering over my bruises, my chains. The damage.

"For what?" His voice was empty.

"For lying to you. For not telling you who I really was." My voice was strained with guilt. The words felt like stones tumbling from my lips, each one heavier than the last. "You deserved the truth, Micah. About…everything."

Micah's gaze flickered back to the open door, as though expecting someone to burst in and drag him away. Then he looked back at me, and I saw it, the faint flicker of distrust in his eyes.

"I thought we were fighting for the same thing," he said

quietly. There was no malice in his tone, just a bone-deep weariness. "I thought I knew who you were."

It was a simple statement, but it cut straight to my core.

"I couldn't tell you." My throat constricted at my confession. "I didn't know who I could trust. I didn't even trust myself."

His shoulders stiffened, and I saw it, the weight he carried because of me.

"It doesn't matter now," he spat, his body seemed to be vibrating with tension. "None of it matters anymore."

I flinched at the bitterness in his voice. "Micah…"

"No one's coming for you, Verena." His words were a cold blade, cutting through the haze of my hope. It was the first time he had ever called me by my real name. His eyes were like steel, piercing and unyielding as they met mine. "Not whoever you left behind. No one."

His words twisted inside my chest.

"You don't know him," I managed to choke out, my voice trembling with the fear I couldn't hide. "He'll come for me."

Micah's expression didn't change, but something in his eyes made my stomach churn.

"Maybe he will," he murmured, "But will you still be here when he does?"

His hand lifted, fingers reaching toward my cheek. A touch I once trusted.

But my body reacted first.

I flinched back, pressing myself against the cold stone wall.

Micah froze then he stood, staring down at me for a

long moment. Like he wanted to say something else. Like he was waiting.

But I couldn't give him what he wanted.

Not forgiveness.

Not understanding.

Not when I was still choking on the betrayal.

He must have seen it in my face because his jaw tightened.

Then he turned away.

"I'll be back," he muttered over his shoulder, his voice hollow. "When I can."

The door creaked. Micah gripped the handle, starting to pull it shut, and that same creeping panic began to set in.

I had once cared for Micah deeply, I had trusted him when I had no one left in this world to trust, and I used to allow myself to dream of a day when he and I could have escaped this kingdom together.

But we were back exactly where we started.

Trapped.

"You should run."

The words escaped me before I could stop them.

Micah hesitated. His hand clenched around the iron bars. For a second, I thought he might listen, but when he looked back at me, something harder had settled behind his eyes.

"Running is no longer a choice."

The door slammed shut.

CHAPTER 4
DACRE

The rhythmic, constant dripping of water was the first thing I noticed. It echoed faintly against the cavernous stone, the sound bouncing inside my skull until I couldn't tell if it was real or just my own mind turning against me. I blinked my eyes open, struggling to adjust to the dim light, my head pounding in time with the steady drips.

The stale, musty air told me all I needed to know.

I was back in the hidden city.

Not as a leader. Not even as a soldier. As a prisoner.

The irony would've been amusing if it weren't for the iron cuffs locked around my wrists. I reached for my magic, but the iron simply burned against my skin. Truly a prisoner then.

A healer knelt beside me, his hands hovering over my chest. The faint hum of his magic prickled against my skin, a sensation that was both soothing and jarring, like a dull blade brushing too close. I recoiled instinctively, the motion making me groan in pain.

"Don't move," he ordered, his tone clipped.

I bit back the retort that rose to my lips.

I tried to piece together everything that had happened, the last moments that I could drag up through my memories. I had been with Wren and Kai, barely standing after they dragged me from the sea.

We hadn't made it far.

I had been in no condition to run, my body weak from exhaustion, my hands torn from gripping the oars for gods knew how long. Even Kai had been struggling under the weight of my near-unconscious form.

And he had been in no shape to take them all on when they found us before we reached the outskirts of the coast.

I had known the moment I heard the rustle of shifting bodies beyond the tree line that we were outnumbered. The torches flared first, illuminating the rebels who had become like family to me as they emerged from the dense brush, surrounding us.

It was our men. My father's men.

And they were there for us.

Wren had stepped in front of me, her bow half raised despite the way her hands trembled. Kai's dagger was already drawn, his stance tense, protective.

But we all knew the truth, it wasn't a fight we could win. Not in my condition. Not against so many.

Then, *he* had stepped forward.

The firelight had illuminated my father's face, the deep lines of his scowl, the grim determination in his gaze. He had been waiting for me.

And I had been too damn weak to stop him.

I had managed a single step forward, my body screaming in protest, before the first blow landed. A swift, precise strike to my side. I had crumpled to my knees, the world tilting as the pain had crashed over me like a wave.

Through the haze, I had heard Wren scream my name. Heard the sharp clash of steel as Kai fought back. But it hadn't mattered.

They hadn't been who my father wanted.

And I had already lost the one thing that he desperately needed.

Everything after that was a blur. The journey back, the weight of the chains, the cold of the underground tunnels.

Now, I was here.

And Wren and Kai weren't.

I gritted my teeth, my hands curling into fists as the healer's magic pulsed.

He was only trying to help, and it didn't matter that I had brought several members of our rebellion to his table for treatment. In this moment, I was simply a prisoner under his care, not the son of his leader.

Not someone he had once respected.

"You're lucky to be alive," he added, his voice taut.

"Luck had nothing to do with it," I rasped, my throat dry and raw.

The healer snorted softly. "No, just sheer stupidity, then."

His words held no malice, only the resigned familiarity.

I shot him a sharp look. "Where is my sister? Kai?"

He looked up at me, and he hesitated before he finally spoke. "They are both within the city." His magic thrummed harder as it moved over my ribs. "Your father isn't charging them with treason. He's reserved that honor only for you."

"They're safe?" I asked the only question I cared about.

"Yes." He nodded. "Both were a bit roughed up from when you were found, but they are safe. Your father is just watching them heavily. He questioned them about what they knew, but found them lacking."

Before I could respond, the heavy thud of boots echoed down the corridor, the sound growing closer with each step. My senses went on high alert, my body tensing despite the ache that screamed at me to stay still.

The door pushed open with an ominous creak.

The healer didn't flinch, his hand remaining steady above my chest. The faint warmth of his magic faded as he pulled away, as if he already knew his time was up. The air shifted, weighed down by something heavier than just another visitor.

My father.

"Leave us."

His words weren't a request.

Without hesitation, the healer obeyed, his footsteps retreating swiftly down the corridor. The absence of his magic left a cold emptiness in its wake. I forced myself up on my elbows, gritting my teeth as pain flared through my body.

My father stood before me, arms crossed, his expression a mask of disappointment.

"So," he said at last, his tone dripping with disdain. "The prodigal son returns. Dragged back in chains, no less."

I sat up slowly, the iron cuffs rattling as I shifted. "You better not have hurt Wren."

"Threats?" he asked, stepping farther into the room. "That's bold for someone who needs my help."

I clenched my fists, forcing myself to hold his gaze. "I am here because your men dragged me here. I didn't need your help."

He barked out a harsh, bitter laugh. "And what about now?" He looked me up and down, as if assessing the damage. "Whose help is it that you need now?"

I gritted my teeth, biting back the response that surged up my throat.

"You were supposed to help me bring back the heir, help me save *our* people." He shook his head. "You have defied me at every turn, and now you expect me to clean up your mess?"

"It's not my mess," I snapped back, my words heated. "This is yours. This rebellion was supposed to be about freedom, about justice, but all you do is use people as pawns, sacrificing them for your own ambition."

His jaw tightened, his expression contorting into one of barely contained anger. But he didn't respond immediately. Instead, he strode over to the small wooden table in the corner of the room, his fingers lightly brushing against the chipped edge as if he were trying to calm himself.

"You sound just like your mother."

The mention of her was a punch to the gut, a wound that refused to heal. I forced my breathing to remain even, my nails digging into my palms.

"She believed in this rebellion," I said, my voice steady

despite the fury bubbling beneath the surface. "In what it could be. Not in what you've turned it into."

His eyes narrowed as his gaze met mine. "Don't pretend you know what she believed," he spat. "You were barely more than a child when she died."

My teeth ached from clenching them together. "And yet, I remember enough." I looked down at myself, my clothes still covered in sand, dirt, and dried blood. "Verena is back in her father's hands. Mother never would have let that happen."

His expression darkened, but he said nothing.

"She wouldn't have been hunting her down and ready to hand her over as a bartering tool. She would have protected her," I pushed, my voice growing rougher with every word.

His fingers curled into fists at his sides. "You think she would've risked everything for the heir? That I should?"

"Yes," I answered without hesitation.

His expression twisted, something between frustration and exhaustion flickering in his eyes. "You're a fool," he said quietly. "You think war is won with reckless emotions? That peace comes without a cost?" He stepped closer, his gaze pinning me in place. "How much more are you willing to sacrifice for her? Our resources, our secrets. Your loyalty to her has cost us more than you can imagine."

"It's not about my loyalty to her," I said, though the lie was made evident by the way I searched for our thread of connection. I would have been loyal to Verena no matter the cost. "She's the only way this war ends."

He stepped closer, his expression unreadable. "What we're fighting for comes at a price."

"And that price shouldn't be her."

For a moment, we stared at one another in silence, but it was my father who finally broke first.

"You'll stay here." He turned on his heel, his voice cold and final as he headed toward the door. "Until you remember where your loyalties lie. Until you remember that the blood in your veins has been spilled by the blood of the very one you're trying to protect."

With a resounding thud, the door slammed shut behind him, leaving me alone, and I forced myself to take a deep breath. The air in the cell was stale, thick with dampness, but it wasn't the stench of captivity that unsettled me.

It was the certainty that my father had no intention of helping me save Verena.

I pushed myself further upright, my muscles stiff from disuse, my ribs aching from the fight aboard that ship. My wrists were raw from the bindings they used to drag me here, the remnants of saltwater stinging the torn skin.

He was wrong.

This wasn't a reckless emotion.

This wasn't some foolish attachment to a girl.

This was about *her*, about what she meant to this rebellion, to this kingdom. To me.

I had seen firsthand what she was capable of, the way she had fought even when everyone, including herself, had thought she was powerless.

And I would not let that be for nothing.

I would not let everything that she had suffered be for nothing.

She deserved far more than this kingdom had ever given her.

I rolled my shoulders, ignoring the pain that shot through them. I couldn't sit here and wait for my father to understand what she had already given, to come to the decision that she was worth protecting. I needed a plan.

The rebellion's prison cells weren't like the ones in the palace. They weren't made to keep enemies locked away for years. They were meant to hold traitors long enough for judgment to be passed.

And judgment was coming for me.

I knew they would be discussing me, that they would be trying to decide if I was still one of them.

I had bled for this rebellion. I had fought for it, killed for it, and now, because I had decided to fight for her, I had become their enemy.

But I wouldn't let them decide my fate for me.

I wouldn't let them decide her fate either.

CHAPTER 5
VERENA

The cell felt colder than before. Or maybe it was me —hollowed out, carved into something brittle and unrecognizable.

I curled into myself, pressing my forehead to my knees. I had been here too long. Too many days had bled together into one endless stretch of suffering. My thoughts had long ceased to make sense, fragments of the past and present colliding into one another, all merging into a singular, unrelenting torment.

Dacre's face burned brightest in the haze. His eyes, his voice, his promises. They haunted me, taunting me with a hope I couldn't afford to believe in. A hope that I still clung to and a thread of our bond that I had tricked my mind into believing I could still feel.

I had been strong in the beginning, had convinced myself I could withstand whatever my father threw at me. But doubt seeped in like a dense fog, coiling around my mind, wrapping itself around my throat until I could barely breathe.

What if Dacre wasn't coming for me?

"No," I whispered, the word escaping my lips in a soft, strained whimper. It felt like gravel scraping against my throat, as if saying it out loud somehow made it real.

But the thought lingered, relentlessly clawing at the edges of my mind.

Deep down, I knew that Dacre wouldn't give up on me, but the uncertainty and fear gnawed at me, whispering doubts in the darkest corners of my mind. He would try. Of course, he would.

But my father's power only seemed to grow as each day passed.

The rebellion had been fighting against him for as long as I could remember, and nothing about his reign had changed.

Me falling in love with Dacre didn't change that. It didn't give him any advantage. It had only given us hope, and hope was dangerous.

But it wasn't enough to overthrow a king.

I swallowed hard, forcing down the lump in my throat. As much as I wanted Dacre to save me, his determination could only take him so far.

My father crushed defiance beneath his heel before it ever had a chance to grow, and I was still here, locked in this cell, helpless to stop him.

The sound of the cell door groaning open shattered my thoughts. My head snapped up, and I winced as the sudden movement sent a spike of pain through my skull.

I hadn't even heard footsteps.

Terror coursed through my veins, gripping me in a way that was all too familiar. It twisted and turned inside me, burrowing in my chest, constricting my lungs.

I knew my father's footsteps, had memorized the deliberate thud and drag of his boots across the floor, and I braced myself for the inevitable.

But it wasn't him who stood in front of me now. It was *him.*

Dacre had come for me.

My breath hitched, hope cutting through the fog of exhaustion. He stood tall, his dark hair falling into his eyes as he stared at me.

"Dacre," I choked out, relief flooding through me so quickly that my vision blurred with tears.

He didn't reply. He simply strode toward me until he was kneeling before me on the cold ground, and without hesitation, I raised my still shackled hands and brought them to his face.

"I'm so sorry," he whispered against my palm, his voice breaking. "I should have been here sooner."

"It doesn't matter," I rasped, clinging to him as though he were the only solid thing in a world threatening to shatter. "You're here now."

His skin felt different beneath my fingertips. The lines of his jaw were softer, less defined. His lashes fanned against his cheeks, and he looked younger than anything I could draw from my memory. He felt unfamiliar.

The warmth of his magic, the silent hum that cracked beneath my skin when I touched him, was absent.

I felt…nothing. A hollow emptiness where there should have been a storm. Something was wrong.

Doubt slithered through me, slow and cold, unraveling the fragile moment I had just allowed myself to believe in.

My fingers trembled as I searched his face, waiting for something, anything, to feel right, but it never came. My fingers curled, withdrawing slightly.

"Dacre," I whispered, my voice barely audible over the rush of blood in my ears.

His gaze flickered, too quick, too uncertain, and he didn't look at me. My stomach dropped.

"How did you get in here?" My voice was hoarse.

"I had help," he murmured, reaching for the cuffs at my wrists. "We don't have much time."

We.

"Who is with you?" I pushed, forcing my voice to stay steady.

Dacre hesitated, just for a breath, but it was enough. "My father."

The words landed, and I froze. His father wanted to use me, to control me, but Dacre had chosen me. If his father was here, then Dacre had no other options left.

I swallowed against the weight pressing on my chest. "And Wren?"

The was a small flicker of longing on his face as I said her name, almost imperceptible, but I caught it.

I caught it because this wasn't Dacre. This wasn't him.

My pulse thundered in my ears as I pulled away, my shackles rattling against the stone floor.

"You're lying," I whispered, horror sinking its claws into my skin.

His lips parted, but he didn't answer fast enough. I saw it then, the subtle shimmer at the edges of his form, like heat rising from stone.

A distortion. An illusion. This wasn't Dacre. It was Micah.

My stomach turned violently. "Stop it." My voice wavered as I recoiled, rage and betrayal ripping through my chest. "How dare you?"

The illusion faltered, and Micah was kneeling before me, his face grim and unrepentant.

"You used him against me." My voice trembled. "You…"

Micah didn't flinch. "You need to wake up, Verena."

I shook my head, my entire body shaking. "You…"

"You're losing yourself," he cut me off, his voice calm, almost gentle. "Clinging to a fantasy that will get you killed."

My breath came in ragged, shallow bursts. "He's coming for me." My voice shook, and I hated how uncertain I sounded, how unsure I felt.

Micah's gaze darkened. "Even if he does, what then? You want to watch him be destroyed by your father?" His voice hardened. "You want to listen to him scream while you lay here helpless?"

"Stop," I rasped as a knot formed in my chest.

Micah pressed forward, his expression unyielding. "You're dying in this cell, Verena. And you're waiting for someone who might never come, who might not make it in time."

I shut my eyes, forcing away the images he was painting for me, but doubt was already taking root.

"I don't trust you." The words were cold, unwavering, a fragile shield I refused to lower as I glared at him.

Micah exhaled slowly, his expression unreadable, but his eyes, his eyes were tired. "But you trust him?"

I didn't answer. I didn't need to.

Micah's lips pressed into a thin line, and he looked away, as if gathering the strength to say what came next. "Even if he comes for you," he said finally, his voice quiet, dangerous, "what then? Do you really think that you can win?"

The words sent a chill through me, delving deep beneath my skin.

"You saw what your father did to you. Do you think he'll do anything less to Dacre?"

I tried to shake my head, tried to fight against the images his words forced into my mind, but they were already there.

Dacre on his knees. Dacre bleeding out on the cold marble of my father's throne room. Dacre gasping my name before his world went dark.

No. I refused to let that happen.

Micah must have seen the shift in my expression, because his voice softened, just slightly. "Verena, you have to see the truth," he said, leaning forward. "Your father doesn't lose. He never has."

I clenched my jaw, forcing my hands to still their trembling.

Micah reached into the folds of his uniform, pulling out a flask. "Drink."

I hesitated, my throat aching from thirst, but I no longer trusted him.

"It's water." He pushed it forward until he touched my hand.

The hesitation didn't last long because the need outweighed the doubt. The flask was cool against my palm, and the first sip was pure agony, a burn that scraped down my throat and sent a shudder through me. I coughed, nearly choking as my body struggled to adjust.

"Slowly." Micah's hand hovered near me, as if he might steady me, but he didn't touch me.

I took another sip, then another, my hands trembling as I lowered the flask. My breathing was unsteady, my heart hammering far too fast, and I clutched the flask tightly, the weight of it grounding me. "Why are you doing this?"

He didn't answer right away. Instead, he leaned back on his heels, his gaze fixed on the floor, his shoulders tense. "You think I had a choice?" His voice was low, his jaw tight. "You think this is what I want?"

His eyes flicked back to mine, something raw and sharp flickering beneath the surface. "I should have run instead of looking for you."

The words stole my breath.

"Your father would have never been able to take me if I hadn't been looking after you. He wouldn't be able to use us…" He paused and looked away from me, his jaw tightening until I could see the muscles shift and bunch beneath his skin.

Something cracked in my chest. "Micah, I…"

"It doesn't matter." He looked at me then, and I noticed the deep circles under his eyes. He looked…older. As if the weight of the world had settled on his shoulders and refused to let go.

"Where is your sister?"

He flinched, his body going rigid, and, for a moment, I thought he might leave, might turn his back and walk away. But instead, he leaned forward, his expression hardening. "Don't speak of her. Don't you dare fucking speak of her."

I swallowed hard, the weight of guilt pressing heavily on me.

"I'm sorry," I whispered as I shook my head. I couldn't wrap my head around what was happening, on how he could be standing in front of me so different than the man I knew. "I never wanted this for you."

Micah let out a soft, bitter laugh. "Well. Here we are."

Silence settled between us, stretching wide and forcing us further apart. I opened my mouth, to say what, I didn't know, but before I could, footsteps echoed from the hallway beyond my cell.

Micah stiffened, his head snapping toward the sound before he looked back at me, his fingers twitching at his side, as if he wanted to reach for me. Instead, his voice dropped to a whisper, low, urgent, uncertain.

"Your father won't stop." His hand lifted slightly, hovering in the space between us, as if he meant to touch my face.

I recoiled before I could stop myself, a sharp, instinctual reaction, and Micah froze. For the briefest moment, pain flashed across his face, then, just as quickly, it was gone.

"He's not going to stop, and if you keep defying him, you're only going to make things worse for yourself—and for them."

The mention of them sent a chill up my spine, and I shook my head.

"What will it take for you to listen to me?"

I said nothing, and Micah's hands curled into tight fists at his sides.

"Would you rather your father continues to torture you until every part of you I've ever known becomes unrecognizable?" He leaned closer, his voice dropping even lower. "Would you like for me to enter your cell late at night when you whimper Dacre's name in your sleep and make you trust me then?"

It felt like a slap. His words slammed into me even as I watched his eyes shudder, watched the way his face fell with regret. But it was too late.

"Get out," I spat, my voice shaking with fury as I looked at the stranger in front of me. "I don't want you here."

His gaze darkened. "You're not in a position to refuse, Verena." That regret slipped from his face, replaced instead with something colder. "Neither of us are." He hesitated for another second, shaking his head. "Your father will…"

"You did all of this for my father?" Panic flared in my chest, even though I already knew the truth. "For the man who took your parents?"

He flinched just as I saw another shadow step into my cell. I scurried back as fear consumed me, and something inside me snapped.

I hadn't been able to feel my magic since I arrived back at the palace, hadn't been able to find it no matter how hard I begged it to return, but I could feel power within me now, a violent storm churning and thundering beneath my skin.

My vision blurred, the world a dizzying whirlpool of light and darkness.

It was frenzied and out of my control, and I realized that this wasn't my magic at all. It belonged to another, and when it finally cleared, when I felt as if I could breathe again, I saw with horror what I had done.

The guard lay slumped against the far wall, his body unnaturally still, and a faint glow surrounded him, pulsing in time with my heartbeat, casting an eerie light in the dark room.

"What did you do?" Micah sounded as horrified as I felt.

But I couldn't answer him because I hadn't done anything. The power wasn't mine. The magic...

Cold, cruel laughter rang out from the doorway, and my head snapped up just as my father stepped inside, his eyes gleaming with satisfaction. "There it is."

I tried to scramble back from him, but my body wouldn't move. My limbs felt heavy, the energy inside me still humming, still burning beneath my skin.

"What...what did I do?" My voice trembled with the rest of my body.

"You took his power," my father answered, his smile widening.

"I didn't..." I squeezed my eyes shut and tried to control my ragged breath.

"You did." His words were dripping with triumph, and his eyes, gods, his eyes looked crazed as he said the next words. "A siphon is a rarity. A weapon."

I couldn't breathe. I shook my head, pressing my hands to my ears, trying to block out his words.

Tithe.

The word echoed in my mind over and over like a curse. My father was a siphon, and he used his power at every tithe to transfer the power that the people of this kingdom gave. At least, that was what he was meant to do. That was the history of the tithe that I had always been told.

The people sacrificed at the tithe, gave a bit of their own magic, and in return, the tithe gave back. It was meant to provide a balance that our kingdom no longer had.

A balance that the rebellion had been fighting for.

Siphoning was a power that was rare, a power that was necessary. That was what he had always said. It was a power that I had always been lacking. The power my father hated me for. The power that I didn't understand.

It was the power that he searched for in another heir, the power my mother had died for trying to give him.

And it had all been for nothing.

I bit down on my lip until blood flooded my mouth, and my nails dug into my palms as my chest heaved. I had stolen that guard's life, had taken it as if it had never truly belonged to him. I had siphoned his power, and I had no idea how I'd done it.

And that terrified me.

I tried to think about the times I had used my power since I had first felt it, thought of how I hadn't been able to feel it until Dacre, how I felt weaker without him, without our bond.

Had I been siphoning from him all this time?

Dacre. I let myself whisper his name in my mind over and over, my heart pounding so quickly that the rhythm ached in my chest, and for a moment, I felt him. A thread of warmth, fragile and distant, but undeniably there.

I clung to it, to him, like a lifeline. It didn't matter if I was imagining it, it was the only thing I had.

I had believed I was stronger with Dacre because of our bond, because we were mates, but now I feared what I truly was. I feared that I had become the one thing my father always wanted me to be.

I was a siphon. I was just like him.

I was powerless on my own.

"We move her tonight." My father's voice cut through my thoughts, sharp and decisive. "This is my heir." There was a sudden note of pride in his voice that made bile flood my mouth. "The heir to this kingdom doesn't belong in a dungeon. She belongs by my side, where I can watch her."

I heard the rustle of movement, felt rough hands gripping my shoulders, but I didn't fight. There was no point. It was no use.

The chains fell from my wrists with a loud clang, and I kept my eyes shut as they dragged me from my cell. I stumbled, my feet catching on something. I blinked my eyes open and wished I hadn't.

The guard.

My stomach lurched as I tripped over his limp legs, nearly falling, and the weight of what I had done crushed me.

I had killed him. The siphon inside me, the power my father had been searching for all along, had taken his life, and I had no control to stop it.

The hallway stretched before me, each step leading me deeper into a fate I didn't understand. A fate I didn't want.

The walls closed in, smothering me. I had spent a lifetime inside this palace, this very dungeon beneath me as I
slept, but now, after gods knew how long, my father was
taking me home.

To the cage that was far more opulent but a cage just
the same.

And I had never been more afraid.

CHAPTER 6
DACRE

The rebellion was a curse, one I'd been shackled to since birth. Every breath I'd taken had been in service to a cause that felt more like a cage with each passing day.

The realization hit me hard, winding through my chest until it made it difficult to breathe.

How had I never seen it before?

I had spent my life fighting for this rebellion, for my father's war, and suddenly, it was hard to remember what we had been battling for at all.

I shifted slightly, and the walls of my cell pressed in on me. Despite the chill seeping into my bones, I couldn't help but feel a strange sense of familiarity.

My fingers traced over the rough stone, over the walls that had surrounded me since I was a child. These caves had always been my home, the only constant in my life, and yet, I wasn't safe here anymore.

I tilted my head back, gazing toward the faint glow of

lanterns reflected on the cave walls, casting an orange and yellow hue. If I concentrated hard enough, I could almost conjure the sensation of the sun's warmth on my skin, reminiscent of my childhood days when I roamed these caves, enveloped in darkness with not a single ray of light penetrating through.

I allowed that imaginary sun to envelop me in its gentle embrace, and I could see Verena, her skin kissed by the same sun, her eyes sparkling with the same warmth.

My chest ached painfully at the thought of her, at the uncertainty of where she was. I told myself she was safe, tucked away in the comforts of her gilded prison, but that was a lie.

She was his captive, and yet, I clung to the hope that she had found some sliver of comfort in her imprisonment.

But hope was a dangerous thing, a double-edged sword, the only weapon I had left, and I wouldn't let it slip through my fingers. Without it, I had nothing left, and I refused to stop fighting.

I had been too late to protect her from all the harm that she had already endured, but I would fight, knuckles bloody and the word *traitor* branded into my skin, to make sure that she never suffered again.

Footsteps echoed in the hall, heavy enough to pull me from my thoughts.

I didn't move. I kept my head tilted back, eyes closed, waiting for whoever was coming. I prayed for Kai or Wren, but I knew better. It would be foolish to let either of them near me, and my father wasn't a fool.

The cell door groaned open, and I didn't allow my eyes

to blink open until the sound of his familiar, measured voice reached me.

"You're making a mistake."

Eiran.

He stood just inside the cell door, arms rigidly crossed, his piercing gaze locked on me. I didn't meet it. Instead, I focused on the cracks in the ceiling above, anything to avoid looking at him.

"I feel like I've heard this from you before," I muttered, voice dripping with sarcasm. "Perhaps it's time to try something new."

"You're choosing her over us," he accused, stepping farther inside. His words should have struck deep, just as he intended them to, and there was a time when they would have.

But now, it was just another reminder of how much we had changed.

"Over the rebellion," he continued. "Over the people we both swore to protect."

I finally met his gaze. Unflinching. Unapologetic.

"And who exactly have you protected, Eiran?" I asked, my tone sharp. "Being my father's mouthpiece doesn't make you a warrior. It makes you a puppet."

His jaw clenched, his composure faltering before his mask snapped back into place.

"This isn't a joke," he spat. "The council is done indulging your recklessness. You've endangered all of us, and you know it."

The mere mention of the council sent a wave of fury through me. My hands tightened into fists at the thought of those self-righteous cowards. They claimed to speak for the rebellion, but they were no better than my father.

I had once trusted them, but I didn't anymore. It didn't matter that our people had come together and voted for them as our head, that we had chosen to give them the power they now held.

This world had been cruel, this rebellion isolating, and the people I fought beside had long since forgotten what they were fighting for. The council had forgotten. They claimed to hate the king, the man who had stolen power from the masses, draining them dry with his tithe.

Yet, they were willing to let his daughter suffer under his cruelty.

I cracked my neck, trying to rein in my rage.

"What I know," I said finally, my voice low, "is that you'd sell your own father for a seat at the council's table."

"You mean my father that you attacked?" he sneered. "The man can't even walk without a cane now because of you."

A slow smirk curled on my lips. "I did you a favor then. One step closer."

Eiran's nostrils flared. "You fucking…"

"Let me be clear," I said, my voice like a whip. "I will choose her over every one of you."

Eiran's eyes darkened, his stance shifting slightly.

"Verena, Wren, and Kai are the only ones who have my loyalty." I took a slow step forward, the weight of my chains dragging across the stone floor. "I have spent my life fighting for this rebellion, but it's a rebellion that has forgotten what it's fighting for."

His jaw tightened until I feared it would snap, but I didn't stop.

"It's full of people like you who would rather watch the world burn than stop for a second to think…" I narrowed my eyes, letting the next words strike deep. "That Verena may be the very person who saves us all."

He scoffed, shaking his head. "You think she's our savior?" His voice was laced with mockery. "She's born of Marmoris, born of the king."

His lips curled in disgust. "Her blood is poison, just like her father's."

I cocked my head, studying him, and I wished like hell that my hands weren't bound. "And in the forest?" I asked, my voice deceptively calm. "When you were helping her?

Eiran stilled, but I saw it, the flicker of uncertainty.

"Was she poison then, too?"

"I know my place, Dacre." His voice was tight, his knuckles white where they curled into fists. "It's you and the heir who need to learn yours."

He took another step forward, chest heaving. "You were born to fight for your people, and she was born to die for that same cause."

His words tore through me, and before I knew what I was doing, I lunged. The chains snapped taut, yanking me back just before I could wrap my hands around his throat.

Eiran stumbled back, his face paling, and for the first time since he entered my cell, he looked truly afraid of me.

Good.

"Don't ever speak of her again." I growled out the words. "You do not decide her fate."

Eiran's eyes narrowed, but I could still see the fear in

them as they flicked from my face back to my fists. "You may have forgotten your duty, Dacre, but I have not."

"You can cling to your delusions all you want," he continued, his tone turning to ice. "But the reality is that in choosing her, you have become our enemy."

I let out a low, humorless laugh.

"And you will regret it." I looked him over, and I smiled when I noted the slight tremble in his hands. "I am not an enemy you want, Eiran, but for her, I will become whatever I have to."

His eyes narrowed, a glint of his hate for me cutting through the bitterness that clouded his expression. He took a step back, his hand instinctively reaching for the hilt of his sword. "You think you're invincible, Dacre." His voice was quieter now, but no less venomous. "But you underestimate the lengths your father will go to in order to ensure the rebellion's success."

I tilted my head, voice cold. "No." I let the word linger. "I know exactly the lengths he will go to, and I refuse to allow Verena to be another casualty in his war."

"Her blood in our soil will do nothing but strengthen our people," he spat out, and it was almost like looking at my father.

"Get out of my cell," I growled, and I could feel my power swirling in my veins begging for me to spill Eiran's blood across the very soil he spoke of. But I had no control here, not with these shackles wrapped around my wrists.

Eiran didn't budge. "You're not in a position to give orders, Dacre. You've thrown away every bit of power you once had here."

Slowly, he motioned toward someone outside, and I

braced myself as two others entered my cell. Both of them were men I had helped train for the sake of this rebellion.

"Good afternoon, boys." I nodded toward them as I watched them with wary eyes, taking in their hardened expressions and tense postures. One had a scar running down the length of his cheek, and I had been the one who tore off a strip of my shirt to stop the bleeding when one of the King's Guard had given it to him. *Grady.* "Are you coming to visit?"

Grady had enough decency to keep his eyes downcast, his brow furrowed and a slight frown on his lips. Neither of them answered me, instead moving closer with a sense of purpose that I recognized.

"No?" I looked back and forth between the two of them. "Neither of you missed me?"

Each of them took one of my arms and pulled me forward as I heard the jingle of keys behind me. I tried to remind myself that they were here on orders, not by choice. I had been in their exact positions so many times over.

They were rebellion soldiers just as I had been.

They unlocked my wrists from the chain that was bolted into the stone, but they left the shackles around them.

"Take him to the council," Eiran commanded abruptly.

I didn't fight them as they dragged me forward. Whatever the council had planned, it didn't matter.

Because I knew what I had to do.

The hidden city sprawled out before us, its stone-carved pathways twisting through the underground cavern like veins through flesh. Homes carved into rock, the low hum of lanterns floating above them, casting golden light across a city built in secrecy, in survival.

I had lived and bled for this place, and now I walked through it in chains.

The river that cut through the city was calm, too calm. I had never seen it so low, so dormant. People lined the streets, their voices hushed, their gazes darting toward me as I passed. Some wore pity in their eyes. Others, something colder.

But none of them looked surprised to see me bound and being led like a traitor.

A sour taste crept into my mouth. They had expected this.

The weight of their silent judgment pressed on me like a hand around my throat, but I refused to bow beneath it. They didn't know the truth. They didn't know Verena.

Our footsteps echoed down the corridors, growing louder, heavier until the council chamber loomed ahead. Its towering doors were etched with the rebellion's sigil, the symbol of a cause I had once believed in, a symbol that was branded on my skin.

The guards halted, forcing me to a stop. One of them reached for the iron ring of keys on his belt, his fingers fumbling slightly as he worked the heavy lock.

I exhaled slowly, forcing myself to stay calm. Because once I stepped through those doors, everything would change, and I would do everything within my power to make it change in my favor.

The council chamber was carved deep into the stone, its walls lined with torches, flickering flames that brought it no warmth. At the center of the room, a long, curved table loomed, surrounded by figures that I knew too well.

The council. The leaders of this rebellion.

The same people who had once trusted me, who had trained me, raised me, now sat in judgment, their expressions unreadable as I was dragged before them.

My father sat at the head of the table, his broad shoulders rigid, his weathered face unreadable. His gaze followed me, and I could feel his anger simmering beneath his skin.

Waiting.

One of the council members, Aelira, was the first to speak.

"Dacre." Her voice was calm, almost gentle, but there was no kindness behind it. "You stand before us today accused of treason."

Treason. The word should have shaken me, but I felt nothing.

"What do you have to say for yourself?" she asked.

I lifted my chin, meeting her gaze head-on. "Where is my sister?" I asked simply, ignoring her question.

"Wren is not your concern," my father answered, and I let my gaze slam back into his.

"We all see how you are willing to treat your son." I lifted my hands slightly, letting the rattle of chains ring out around us all. "I need to see with my own eyes that she's okay, that you haven't harmed her."

His jaw ticked. "My daughter did not betray her people. She simply made a poor decision to try to save her brother."

"And all I'm doing is trying to save my mate." I met him head-on even as murmurs rippled through the council.

The word settled hard into the room, and it seemed to draw the very breath from each of their lungs as they stared at me in disbelief.

"Mates are from storybooks." My father cocked his head slightly as if he could see through me, see the lies he believed I told. "And we have grown tired of your lies."

"She is my mate." I said each word slowly, letting them land as hard as I intended. "She is bound to me as I am bound to her."

"She is a witch." My father's voice rose. "Look how she has tricked your mind."

He motioned to me, and I felt the weight of all of their stares.

"You think she is your mate?" He laughed bitterly. "She is a weapon just like her father. She was created to destroy us all."

"I am bound to her," I said the words again, and the truth of them hummed within every inch of me as I raised my wrists. "I am tethered to her in a way that even these chains cannot stop."

My father ground his teeth together, his dark gaze tearing into mine. "The heir is a liability. She is not your mate."

Despite his words, you could hear the doubt crawling through the chamber. And doubt was a weapon that I could wield.

My father raised a hand, silencing them.

"You are here because you've betrayed us all. You've put us all at risk by allowing this foolish obsession with our enemy's daughter to cloud your judgment. You thought with your cock instead of your head, and you not only helped her get away, you attacked one of our council members to do so."

I saw Eiran nodding his head out of the corner of my eye, and for the first time since we walked in, I noticed that he had slid into one of the seats at the table. A seat that had been reserved for his father.

"And what of your obsession, Father?" I looked back at him. "You put us at far more risk than I ever could. This rebellion has lost what it used to stand for. You claim to hate the king, but I fear that you envy him."

My father stood suddenly, his chair scraping loudly against the ground as he slammed his hand against the table.

"That *man*," he spat the words, "killed my wife."

"And my mother," I reminded him. "And now, he's going to hurt my mate. He's going to torture her until he can make her into a weapon."

The silence that followed was deafening. My father's expression didn't falter, but his chest visibly rose and fell with each harsh breath.

"You've been blinded by a girl who will destroy everything we've built," my father growled, his voice thick with anger. "She turned you against your own blood."

I clenched my jaw, trying to keep my composure as the murmurs of disapproval rose from the council members around us.

"She didn't turn me against anyone," I said firmly, and looked away from my father to meet the gazes of the council members I had known my entire life. "She showed me the reality of our actions. All she wanted was freedom, yet we couldn't allow her to have that. Instead, you hunted her like she was a fucking beast to bring her back for the highest bidder. You are no better than the tyrant that we're fighting against."

The murmurs rose again, and my father slammed his fist down on the table once more, but it didn't silence them this time.

"You've made your choice, Dacre," he said through clenched teeth. "And now, you'll live with the consequences."

One of the guards pulled at my chains, as if he was readying to throw me back in my cell.

"You need me." The words shot from my lips.

"And what is it," Aelira asked, her voice drawing my attention back to her, "that makes you so sure of that?"

I didn't hesitate, didn't falter. "Because I know how to get into the palace." The silence stretched long and taut, a thread pulled too tight. This was the weapon they needed. "I know the location of the tunnels we've spent years searching for."

I could feel every gaze in the room land on me, some of them turning to look at each other in disbelief before they erupted. Murmurs turned to sharp whispers, voices clashing as they debated my claim, as if I weren't standing right in front of them.

My father said nothing. He simply watched me, and despite having to endure that look all of my life, it still unnerved me.

Eiran's voice cut through the noise. "And why," he asked, leaning forward, "should we believe you?"

I looked over at the fucking coward. "I have no reason to lie. You have me in chains, and I need to get into that palace."

Aelira exchanged a glance with my father, something unspoken passing between them before my father spoke. "Enough."

The room fell silent once again. He stood, slow and deliberate, his hands pressed flat against the table.

"You claim to know the way in," he said. "Prove it."

I held my ground, refusing to let him see even a flicker of my unease. "I will," I said. "But not before I get something in return."

My father's jaw tightened. "This isn't a negotiation."

I tilted my head, meeting his cold gaze with unwavering defiance. "Then kill me. Because without her, I am no use to you, no use to this rebellion."

My father's expression didn't change, but the flicker of doubt in the council members' faces told me I had struck where I needed to.

Aelira's eyes narrowed. "And what, exactly, is it you want?"

I let the moment stretch, ensuring they were listening, then, I spoke the only demand that mattered. "I will show you the location only when these chains come off my arms." I looked around to each of them. "I will get Verena back, and you must promise that she is not to be harmed."

The tension in the chamber shifted.

Eiran scoffed. "You expect us to agree to that?"

I turned my head toward him, my voice steady as steel. "You don't have to agree to anything."

I looked back at my father. "I've spent my life

bowing to the whims of this rebellion, and I finally have the intel you need to get to the king, to get what you've always wanted. Are you so willing to sacrifice Verena for this cause that you are unwilling to save her for it?"

My father's eyes darkened, the room seeming to constrict around us as his rage simmered. "Sacrifice is the foundation of the rebellion," he growled, his fists clenched at his sides. "Your mother, my wife, died for it."

He opened his mouth to finish, but I spoke before he could. "And if Verena dies for it, the way into the palace dies with her."

Aelira folded her hands on the table. "And if we spare her?"

I considered my words carefully before I said them. "If you let me save her, if you help me, then I'll take you inside. I will help you defeat the king."

My father watched me, and for the first time, he hesitated. It wasn't hesitation born of weakness. It was calculation. We both knew what I was worth, and we both knew what she was worth.

Even if he couldn't see Verena as I saw her, he knew the truth. She was the king's heir.

Eiran scoffed, crossing his arms over his chest. "You expect us to believe you'll just hand over the tunnels once she's here?"

I looked at them all, slow and deliberate. "Kai, Wren, and I will use the tunnel to get Verena back. I will show you the tunnel before we go in. I will trust your word on what will await us when we return."

Torrin finally spoke, studying me carefully from where

he sat at my father's side, a place he had been most of my father's life. "And if you betray us?"

I didn't blink. "Then you'll have every opportunity to kill me. Send as many warriors with us as you like until you get the information you want." I let my gaze slide back to my father. "But not him."

The room seemed to shudder at my demand.

Aelira exhaled, her gaze flickering between my father and me. "Your father…"

"I can't trust him," I answered honestly. "He would rather see Verena dead than at my side. He will betray me to get what he wants."

The smallest smile slipped over my father's lips, and I could practically see him calculating his next move.

"The council is meant to make decisions for this rebellion. Not him alone." I looked over each of them. There were only two left who hadn't spoken, and one of them had been one of Mother's closest friends. The only one who didn't bow to my father.

Liya.

I let my gaze settle on her as I spoke. "My mother would be ashamed of what we've become. She would be outraged that her death had meant nothing." I let my words sink in hard as her gaze shuddered, but I didn't look away. "Help me save my mate, and it will not be for nothing. Help me save my mate, and I will help us win this war."

She looked at me, truly looked at me, and there was such sadness reflected in her eyes. Liya had loved my mother, and in turn, I knew that she loved both Wren and me. And I was counting on that connection, on her loyalty to her friend. I was betting everything on it.

The whole room seemed to hold their breath with her before she finally looked away from me and stared at my father. "This council would never make any decision that wasn't in the best interest of our people, and if he truly knows the location of the tunnels as he says he does, it would be detrimental to us to ignore that."

"But…" Eiran started but clamped his mouth shut as she shot him a look.

"This is a risk, but it is one we have to take," Liya finished.

Eiran let out a low curse, shoving away from the table. "This is a mistake."

"And you are not on the council," she corrected him. "If your father is unable to vote then we will do so without him."

My father remained motionless, his face unreadable, but I could see the way his fingers still curled around the edge of the table. The tension in his jaw. He hated this.

"There isn't a single member of this council who would vote against the possibility of saving our people in a way we have fought for, for years." She turned back to my father, and she didn't look away from him as she said the next words. "And if Camellia were here, she would remind you that our children are why we fight. Her children are why she was willing to sacrifice everything."

My father stiffened, but his chest heaved.

Liya looked at me carefully. "You think Elis, your grandmother, followed your mother into this rebellion blindly? Why do you think she stays in that damned city." She pointed up toward the ceiling, and I knew what she meant.

After all this time, my grandmother had never moved to the hidden city, she had been unwilling to leave the capital.

"Your grandmother was not from Marmoris, Dacre. She came here as a young woman, a handmaiden to the princess of Veyrith. The princess to the last kingdom that stood against Verena's father."

The air seemed to thicken, pressing against my lungs. I had never heard this, never been told.

"She served Verena's mother," Liya continued, her voice steady. "And she watched firsthand as the King of Marmoris burned her kingdom to the ground."

My stomach twisted.

"This was never just our war, your mother's war," Liya whispered. "It was your grandmother's too." She paused, and nobody said a word. "And it is Verena's."

Her eyes searched mine, and I hoped she found what she was looking for because I would have given anything for them to give me what I was asking, for them to help me save her.

"All those in favor?" Her voice rang out, and I watched as four hands raised in the air, all except for Eiran and my father. But I didn't need either of their votes.

"We will move before the next moon." Liya looked away from my father, shaking her head. "You will take us to the tunnels, then the real war begins."

CHAPTER 7
VERENA

The scent of lavender hung heavy in the air, curling through the room like a whispered lullaby. It was suffocating, too sweet, too cloying. Once, it had been a comfort.

Now, it was a lie. This was not my home.

I traced a trembling finger along the windowsill, feeling the cool stone beneath my fingertips. The sun dipped below the horizon, setting fire to the sky, as gold and orange melted into the deep blue water of the sea.

My stomach ached as I watched the waves roll in against the shore. The sea felt as restless as I did.

As a child, I had dreamed of what lay beyond it, of places untouched by my father's power. Of freedom. But now, when I looked at it, I thought only of Dacre.

I had begged the gods for years to let me leave this place, to be free of its walls and whispered cruelties. And when I'd finally escaped, it hadn't been to freedom. It had been to war. To a rebellion that saw me as nothing more than my father's daughter.

But Dacre had been different. He looked at me like I was more than a crown, more than a weapon, and I had allowed myself to hope for things with him that I had never wished for before.

But that hope had slipped through my fingers like the sea slipped through the sand.

The water stretched out before me, vast and endless. White foam bubbled and frothed at the crest of each wave, taunting me with the fact that freedom was right before me, yet the roots of who I was kept me buried on land.

Buried in this palace.

My roots were buried deep in the very place I had prayed to the gods I would never return to.

A hollow ache spread through my chest, a heavy weight that no amount of rest or sleep would alleviate. I dragged myself away from the window and collapsed onto the silk sheets. My muscles tensed as I tried to force my eyes shut, knowing that sleep wouldn't bring me peace, but rather another battlefield in my mind.

But my body was too heavy with exhaustion to fight it, and the dream came swiftly, just like those waves crashing against the shore.

It was inescapable.

I was still in my room, but it was different. Shadows stretched long across the walls, flickering like candlelight. And beneath the thick perfume of lavender, I caught another scent.

Vanilla.

Familiar. Comforting. I turned, my heart pounding as I frantically searched the room, and there she was.

My mother stood at the foot of my bed, her emerald eyes soft and knowing. Her dark hair cascading over her shoulders, untouched by time.

I had spent years trying to remember the exact curve of her smile, the precise shade of green in her eyes. But now, standing before me, she was as vivid as the last day I had seen her.

"Come, Vee." Her voice was a gentle hum, threading through the silence like a melody I had almost forgotten.

I hesitated, my throat tightening. No one had called me that since she died.

She stretched out a hand, waiting for me to take it. I reached for her, desperate to feel the warmth of her skin, but my fingers passed through hers like mist.

She didn't seem to notice.

"Mama?"

"You found your power," she said, studying me as though she could see the magic curled beneath my skin.

I swallowed as I shook my head. "I don't know what I've found."

"It's been waiting for you," she murmured, lifting a hand to brush against my cheek. The touch sent a shiver through me, not quite there, yet somehow more real than anything I'd felt in what seemed like forever.

"We don't have much time."

The room shifted suddenly. The scent of lavender was gone, the sea breeze disappeared, and my nose burned as it was replaced with moss and earth and decay. Damp stone surrounded us, the walls pulsing with veins of gold, shimmering faintly like trapped starlight.

I didn't recognize this place, yet it somehow felt like a memory.

A well loomed in the center of the chamber. Dark. Pulsing. Alive.

A sense of unease crept over me as I tentatively took a small step forward. Whatever was in the well seemed to shift like a living creature, constantly pulsing between hues of gold and sickly green.

I took another step closer, and I could *feel* it.

My mother's hand, gentle yet firm, caught me by my wrist and snapped me out of the trance. She shook her head ever so slightly.

"What is this?" I whispered.

"The last of them," she said. "The last vessel."

A chill wrapped around my spine, and she exhaled as she stepped forward, pressing a hand against the well's edge.

"The vessel was never meant to be ruled by one kingdom," she murmured. "It was a covenant. A balance. Created by the five nations, each with their own vessel, each sharing magic freely across the lands."

She lifted her gaze to mine. "It was never meant to be hoarded. Never meant to be drained."

Dread settled in my stomach as my father's words echoed in my mind, the way he spoke of the tithe, of his right to take what he needed.

"What happened?" I asked, and my mother's expression hardened.

"Marmoris was not content with balance," she said.

"One by one, the other kingdoms fell. Their vessels lost. Until only this one remained."

I clenched my fists. "Father."

She nodded. "And the kings before him. But your father promised peace. He promised an alliance. And I believed him."

Her voice trembled.

"And so had my father." Her eyes searched mine. "We were the final two kingdoms, the two lands desperate to survive, and I thought that he wanted peace as badly as I did. He had convinced me with his words, with the way he made me fall for him."

She swallowed hard, and her eyes glittered with unshed tears. "I had loved your father, and I had believed in him. Until it was too late."

The truth struck like lightning.

"You were…" I swallowed.

She let out a slow, shuddering breath.

"The King of Veyrith," she whispered, "was my father."

Everything inside me went still. The world around me blurred, the glow of the vessel suddenly too bright, too sharp. I staggered back.

"No," I choked.

I had grown up hearing tales of Veyrith, whispered bedtime stories that she would tell me of a make-believe world that thrived and flourished. She would tell of their people, of their lore, and all that time, I hadn't known.

My mother had been their princess.

"Veyrith is real?" I asked, although I knew the truth; it hummed inside me, leaving no room for doubt.

"It was." She nodded, but her eyes shuddered. "But that

land was long ago turned to ash, its people a sacrifice my father never agreed to make."

I clutched my stomach, bile rising in my throat.

"Our vessel was failing, and our land with it." She glanced toward the vessel before us. "Marmoris had grown too powerful, the share of magic unbalanced between the kingdoms." She looked back at me. "I was betrothed to your father, to be his queen, and in return, the balance was to be restored."

But he lied. She didn't need to say it. I could feel the truth.

"He married you to take Veyrith's vessel," I whispered.

She nodded. "I loved your father, and I think a small part of him had loved me too. But his greed was more powerful than anything we ever had." She looked away from me, glancing down at the vessel. "After we were married, I was bound to him, bound to this kingdom. And he didn't falter in showing me who he truly was. He killed my father." Every ounce of longing and sadness disappeared from her voice as it was replaced with anger. "He killed him before he drained our vessel until there was nothing left of Veyrith. The land I loved became void of magic, and without it, the rivers slowed until the water dried up, the crops withered, and with them so did our people."

My father had built his empire on the bones of stolen kingdoms.

And even that hadn't been enough.

Her fingers trailed back and forth over the edge of the vessel. "My home was turned to ash, and this is the final vessel that remains."

The silence stretched between us before I finally forced myself to meet her gaze.

"You could have left," I whispered. "You could have run."

Her eyes softened. "No, my love." She reached out, her fingertips brushing the air between us. "I stayed because of you."

Tears burned at the edges of my vision.

"When I saw your power, when I realized what you were, I knew I had to protect you." Her hands trembled. "You were so young the first time you siphoned, younger than most discover their power. I was hiding behind your drapes as you looked for me. I could hear your little giggle, but then I felt it, the moment you got scared. You couldn't find me, and before I could tell you where I was, your power found me for you."

"I don't remember..."

"You were too young." She smiled. "But the moment I realized what happened, that I realized the amount of power that flowed within your tiny body, I knew that your father could never know."

Her words settled over me like a weight, and I looked back to the vessel, the magic within it shifting and writhing as if it were beckoning me forward.

"So, I hid it."

I sucked in a sharp breath. "You cursed me."

"I protected you," she said fiercely. "I did what the queens of Veyrith have done for generations."

I swallowed hard. "Why? Why would the queens need to hide their power?"

She exhaled and searched my face. "Because Veyrith

was a kingdom of balance. Of magic. Of power. And where there is power, there is always someone who seeks to take it."

Her emerald eyes searched mine, steady and unyielding.

"The queens of Veyrith were not just rulers. They were guardians of magic itself before magic turned against our lands and the kings sought to fix it. It ran through our blood, deep and untamed. And that power, if left unchecked, could be twisted, manipulated."

I shivered, thinking of my father, of what he had done. "So they hid it?"

"They did more than that." Her voice was solemn. "The queens of Veyrith wove a protection into the very bloodline of their daughters. A spell as old as the vessels themselves. It was meant to shield us, but that spell became watered down with time. Just as everything does. Our magic weakened, it became angry, and the very magic that had sustained us began turning against us all."

I searched her eyes, begged her with one look to tell me this was all a lie.

"You are not just the daughter of Marmoris, Verena. You are a daughter of Veyrith, the last daughter, and I bound your power to protect you. I bound your magic so it wouldn't awaken until you found safety in someone who wanted you to have power, but did not wish to use it."

Dacre.

The moment my magic had surfaced, I had been with him. I had felt *safe.*

I had been powerless until him.

My mother's expression turned sorrowful.

"I had already lost Veyrith. I would not lose you, too."

My throat tightened.

"And now?" I whispered. "Now that this protection is broken?"

Pain flickered through her gaze.

"Now, my love," she murmured, "your father will do everything in his power to claim you as his own. He will do the very thing that our magic rioted against that forced the kings to bind it to the vessels in the first place."

The vessel pulsed behind her, casting long shadows along her face. I could feel the anger she spoke of, feel the way it trembled with fury.

"The tithe was never meant to be a tool for power," she said. "It was meant to restore the balance within our magic, to pay the price for what we had destroyed. We gave back to our magic, to the vessels, but your father…he has twisted it."

A shiver ran through me, but I forced myself to ask, "How?"

She exhaled, pressing a hand to the stone. The gold veins beneath her fingers flared, illuminating the room in an eerie glow.

"The vessel feeds on sacrifice, the magic had demanded it," she explained. "For years, the people of all five kingdoms gave willingly to the vessels, and the vessels gave back to our kingdoms in return."

She shook her head gently. "But to wield it is something else entirely. It angered the magic, forced its rage to ravish through our lands, and first, the people of Veyrith paid for your father's greed. But now, it will take Marmoris. It will take him."

I sucked in a breath, and she quickly said the next words so quietly as if she feared the vessel would hear. "You must surrender something of yourself to wield it as your father has done. A piece of your soul. A piece of your life."

I swallowed hard. "Then how has he used it for so long."

"He has stolen what he cannot afford to give. Each tithe, the people of Marmoris suffer. They are drained, their magic stripped far more than they are willing to give, their lives shortened. But even that isn't enough."

The weight of her words pressed against my ribs, choking me as they cut off my air. My father had taken from his people, and still, the vessel demanded more.

"He realized too late," she continued, "that he could not stop."

"I don't understand." I shook my head, trying to grasp what she was saying. "Stop what?"

She met my gaze. "Dying."

A cold dread slithered through my veins.

"He siphoned from the vessel because he thought he could control it, but it has been devouring him from the inside out. His magic is not his own, it is borrowed, stolen, temporary. And now, it is running out."

I forced down the bile rising in my throat. "He needs more power," I breathed, thinking about how desperately my father had been trying to find power in me, how he despised me for being powerless. The way he had looked almost euphoric when I had siphoned the life from that guard.

"He needs an heir." Her gaze softened as she studied

me. "The vessel will not bind itself to just anyone. He needs someone powerful. He needs a siphon."

I clenched my fists, nausea rolling in my stomach.

"If I bind to it," I whispered, "if he forces me to take his place…"

"The vessel is corrupted." Her voice was pained. "It is angry, and I fear that it will never find balance again. It will run through you as it does him, and it will take from you."

I stepped back, shaking my head. "No."

"It will demand sacrifice," she whispered. "It will hunger."

I pressed my hands to my temples, my breath coming too fast. My father hadn't been torturing me out of cruelty alone. He was hunting, preparing. He didn't just want to be more powerful; he needed me to be powerful.

"In the other kingdoms, in Veyrith, were the kings bound to the vessels there?"

"No." She stepped closer, her hand brushing over mine. "But those vessels have been gone for many, many years, and your father, his greed, has turned the vessel into a weapon. He's turned it into a curse."

A sharp chill ran down my spine.

"He has already given too much of himself," she murmured. "And now the vessel is tied to him, it feeds off him, drains him, makes him desperate. But your father is no fool. He has been searching for a way to free himself from its grasp without losing what it has given him."

"How?" My voice trembled. "How will he do it?"

My mother let out a slow, pained breath. "The vessel will not simply let him go. It will not release him willingly after all that has been done."

I swallowed against the lump rising in my throat. "Then how…"

Her expression was sorrowful but unyielding. "To sever the bond, he must tether it to someone else. A willing sacrifice cannot be forced. That was the original magic of the vessels, a kingdom willingly giving, bowing before the magic. But your father has found ways to twist even that."

I shook my head. "I will never willingly take his place."

Her fingers clenched into a fist. "That is why he has spent so many years trying to break you."

The pieces were falling into place too quickly, slotting together with a sickening finality. The torture, the isolation, the pain, the fear. It had not been simply punishment. It had been preparation. To weaken me. To leave me with no choice but to become what he demanded.

I pressed a hand to my chest, trying to steady the erratic beat of my heart. "And if I am bound to it?"

Her gaze faltered. "Then you will be as he is."

Corrupted. Controlled. Changed.

A shudder racked through me.

"The vessel's hunger will become your own," she whispered. "You will feel it inside you, pressing against your ribs, sinking into your bones. You will crave magic. Crave power. And if you do not take it, if you do not siphon from others, you will wither."

I clenched my fists, nausea rolling in my stomach.

"You will be stronger than you have ever imagined," she continued. "You will feel it thrumming beneath your skin, a limitless well of magic at your fingertips. But it will never belong to you." Her voice grew quieter. "And the vessel does not share."

I sucked in a sharp breath, dread curling in my gut. "What do you mean?"

She turned to face me fully. "It will not let you leave. It will not let you disobey."

I shook my head violently. "No—"

"Your father controls the vessel because he has fed it for years. But if you take his place, you will be something different. The vessel will crave you. It will crave your power, your sacrifice, and your father will use that against you."

Her hands trembled as she reached for me, but I barely felt the ghost of her touch. "If you are bound to it, he will have power over you, Verena. He will never fully break his bond, and you will become the conduit between him and the vessel's power. He will not need to force you to obey, your own body will betray you."

My vision blurred as the walls of the chamber seemed to shrink around me. I was drowning. Drowning in him, in this place, in the future that was waiting for me.

"No," I whispered. "No, I won't."

Fear flickered across my mother's face, and it stole my breath. I grabbed her wrist, or at least, I tried to. My fingers passed through her skin as if she weren't there at all.

"Mama." My voice sounded so young, so weak.

The vessel pulsed behind us. It writhed in the anger that she spoke of, and the walls shuddered as if bowing before it.

"Verena." Her voice trembled. "There is a prophecy. It has been whispered through centuries, hidden in the bones of Veyrith. Your father fears it. He has buried it, burned it, tried to erase it. Just as he has erased history, erased the traces of what he has done."

A sharp, biting wind tore through the chamber, whipping around us like a storm. The vessel pulsed harder, and my mother's form flickered.

No.

Not yet.

"What does it say?" I begged, reaching for her. "What does the prophecy say?"

Her lips parted and her eyes softened as she took me in one last time. "You are a siphon, Vee, but you are also a daughter of Veyrith. There is power there."

"What power?" I frantically asked as I tried to reach for her, desperately tried to cling to another moment.

"Trust the tides, darling girl. They always know when to rise."

The wind howled harder, echoing in my ear, and then she was gone and the chamber shattered around me.

I woke with a gasp, my chest heaving. Lavender still clung to the air, but it was the smell of my mother that still enveloped me.

But everything else was gone. Her, the chamber, the vessel. They were all gone, but the words she had left behind still echoed inside me.

I shoved the blankets off my body, a tremor running through my fingers as I tried to steady my breath. It was just a dream, but I knew better.

This was a warning.

I pressed a hand to my ribs, wincing at the lingering ache. The room was suffocating, too silent, the heavy weight of the palace pressing in from all sides. I needed air.

I swung my legs over the side of the bed, ignoring the stiffness in my limbs, and pushed myself to my feet. Something wasn't right. The floor was too smooth beneath my bare feet. The silence was too thick. Everything felt shifted, like the dream had followed me into waking.

And then I saw it.

The bookshelf across the room, the gilded spines of ancient tomes that had been there all my life catching the flickering candlelight. But one was missing. A gap sat between two books, an empty space where something should have been.

I swallowed hard, scanning the floor, and my breath caught. A single book lay open near the foot of my bed, its pages curled at the edges, its spine cracked with age.

Chill bumps rushed over my skin as I slowly dropped to my knees and reached for the book with trembling hands. The moment my fingers brushed the cover, a sharp pulse of something cold and ancient curled through me. I flinched but didn't pull away. Instead, I turned it over in my hands, my heart thundering as I read the faded lettering on the cover.

Veyrith.

My mother had read it to me as a child, a collection of myths and old stories passed down through the ages, a book I once believed to be a mere fairy tale.

But it was a book from her own childhood, her home. It was a history buried beneath metaphor, hidden in poetry, and on the inside of the cover, scrawled in elegant ink, was a note in my mother's handwriting.

My breath hitched as I took in her script. It was rushed, smudged in places, as if written in fear rather than care.

If you have found this, then it is already beginning.
Read the words.
Find in them the truth.

I pressed my fingers over the ink, tracing the curves of each letter. My mother had left this for me. She had tried to warn me. It had been right in front of me all along.

Dread curled in my stomach as I turned the page. The book opened easily, as if it wanted me to find this place.

I quickly flipped through pages, reading the words etched within them that seemed to leap off the parchment as if they carried their own magic. It spoke of power, of balance, of harnessing energies long lost in time.

It spoke of the covenant, of queens and their people. It told stories of oaths made and promises broken, of temples in each of the five kingdoms that had once been sacred to the magic, temples where people had bowed before the magic of their land, temples that were now lost in time.

And there, written in a script that was not my mother's, were the words I was meant to find.

The prophecy.

When shadow swallows the golden throne,
And rivers run dry where magic has flown.,
The cursed shall rise with fate-bound hands,
A tethered soul to shifting sands.
Born of ruin, blood, and war,
Bound to take yet cursed to mourn.
The tideborn's gift, bound in chain,
To break the bond or bind again.

The room seemed to press in around me as I read them over and over. The words were scrawled in the careful, precise script. But on the margins, in ink far darker than the rest, was the handwriting I recognized.

My breath hitched as I looked beneath the first line at what my mother had written.

The shadow is already here.

A chill ran down my spine.

Beside the third line another word was scribbled, a single word.

Siphon.

My stomach twisted because she had known exactly what I was.

Her notes continued, fragmented thoughts scattered like pieces of a puzzle waiting to be solved.

Bound to take. *The hunger will not subside.*

Tideborn. *You are the tideborn.* She underlined the word three times. *The people of Veyrith are born of the sea. You are born of the tide.*

My fingers tightened around the edge of the page. She had left this for me, but it created more questions than answers. It created more fear.

I stared at the last line. Read it over and over again.

To break the bond or bind again.

To break the bond.

I flipped through the pages desperately, searching for more. But there were no answers, only riddles, poetic history, and a final note, written so faintly I almost missed it.

The sideburn's gift, cursed in the wrong hands. Wielded with intent, it can set the world right again. But beware, my love. Beware of the weight of fate.

The words blurred before me.

A tethered soul to shifting sands.
To break the bond or bind again.

The meaning struck me all at once. This was not just a prophecy about the vessel. It was about me.

I was not just my father's daughter. I was not just a siphon.

I was the choice.

I pressed a hand to my chest, as if I could still feel my mother's presence there, still feel the warmth of her words before she had vanished. But warmth had no place in this kingdom, and if I didn't find a way to stop my father, neither would I.

I closed the book, my fingers trembling over the worn leather cover.

The choice was coming.

And I didn't know if I was strong enough to make it.

CHAPTER 8
DACRE

The iron cuffs bit into my wrists with every step, the cold metal chafing against my skin. They weren't tight enough to cause serious harm, but the weight of them was a silent warning. I was only here because they allowed it.

Torrin walked beside me, his distrust an almost tangible thing. His hand never strayed far from the hilt of his sword, his narrowed gaze flicking to me at every shift of my footing. He might have been a councilman, but he was a soldier first. One who was loyal to my father, and he wasn't alone.

Liya moved a few steps ahead, her pace measured and steady. Unlike the others, she didn't keep a hand on her weapon or cast me wary glances, but she was here all the same. Watching. Weighing every decision I made.

She had been the only one who spoke for me in the council chamber, the only one willing to defy my father, but that didn't mean she trusted me.

Three other men flanked us, their stiff postures betraying their unease. These weren't just nameless warriors; they were men I had fought alongside, men who once followed me without question. Now, they watched me as if I were the enemy.

I clenched my fists, forcing myself to ignore the coil of anger tightening in my chest, but it was Wren's silence that gnawed at me most.

She moved next to me, her shoulders taut, her hands flexing at her sides as if she was moments away from reaching for her dagger. Her head was high, her expression unreadable, but I knew her well enough to see the battle raging beneath her cool exterior.

She had fought for this.

The moment we left the council chamber, Wren had been there. She had faced the council head-on, yelled at my father before anyone else could speak as she stood in front of me, guarding me from the very people we had always thought would protect us.

She had not been allowed to leave the hidden city since they had dragged us back, ever since the ambush, and she was not permitted to visit me at the cells. I hadn't been able to stop the small smile that curled on my lips when she slammed her finger into my father's chest and demanded that if he was going to treat her like a prisoner than he should lock her up at my side.

Her body had trembled as she had yelled, and I could see the weight she was carrying, the way she had thought she had failed.

I had been able to see it in Kai's eyes as well, when he

leaned against the wall and simply allowed Wren to tear into the council, into my father.

It had been Liya who finally stopped her, who had told her the plan as Kai wrapped his hands around Wren's shoulders and pulled her back from our furious father. They would be accompanying me to the palace, accompanying me in saving Verena, and Wren's eyes slammed into mine when those words slipped past Liya's lips.

But even now as we walked through the forest, careful with our footsteps and vigilantly watching the trees, I could practically feel the regret pouring off her, the guilt that threatened to eat her alive.

I knew it wouldn't stop until we got to Verena, until we pulled her from that palace and saw with our own eyes that she was okay. I knew because those same feelings gnawed at me, devouring me in a way that I couldn't escape.

But we were going to get her back.

Kai walked ahead of us, his long strides purposeful, hands buried deep in his pockets. His magic pulsed faintly in the air, the telltale hum of it barely perceptible. To anyone else, it might have gone unnoticed.

But to me, it felt like home.

Torrin's men were uneasy, their eyes darting into the shadows before quickly snapping back to me and Kai, watching us both carefully as we walked. But it was Torrin's stare that burned into me.

"You'd better not be lying about the tunnel," he finally said, his voice laced with suspicion he had no chance of hiding.

I clenched my jaw. "I'm not."

"Convenient, isn't it?" A sneer twisted on his lips. "That the king's daughter just happened to confide in you."

I stopped walking as a quiet, simmering anger curled inside me. I had expected the council's doubt, expected their distrust, but hearing the accusation out loud settled like iron in my stomach.

"She isn't just the king's daughter. Not just the heir." My voice was low and steady, but I could feel the weight of Wren's and Kai's attention shifting toward me. "She's my mate, and you're the one who agreed to come with us, Torrin."

Torrin narrowed his gaze, but he didn't stop walking. "You can dress it up however you want, boy, but that doesn't change what she is. I came because we need this tunnel. If you don't know where it is, I'll—"

"What will you do?" Wren cut in, her voice sharp, clipped, lethal.

She stepped in front of him, forcing him to a halt, and the air between them pulsed with barely restrained hostility.

"Go ahead," she continued, tilting her head slightly, her expression more deadly than I had ever seen it before. "Tell me exactly what it is you'll do to my brother. The man who has fought for this rebellion while my father and the rest of you have been blinded by your own greed."

Torrin's mouth opened, but nothing came out as he searched her face. I watched as his anger overtook him, as his body trembled, and his hand tightened on his dagger.

But Wren didn't seem to care.

"No?" When she got no response, she scoffed. "That's what I thought."

"Wren." It was Liya who spoke then, Wren's name a tense, gentle warning, but not one that she was willing to heed. My sister stared down Torrin a long moment before she finally turned on her heel.

The group fell into silence after that, but the tension didn't falter.

As the last rays of sunlight faded from the sky, a dark canvas unfurled above us. The stars emerged one by one, twinkling like tiny gems scattered across the velvet night.

We were close to the city edge now, close enough that I could feel my own trepidation snaking up my spine. It had been roughly two hours since we left the hidden city, the same two hours that we had traveled many times before to get here.

To the right was the familiar path we would have taken into the capital, and they paused as I led them left.

The air grew damp and heavy as we moved farther away from the city's main entrance. The tree coverage thicker as the sound of water echoed through the leaves long before it came into view.

The waterfall slowly flowed down into the pool below, its mist curling around us in a cool embrace. The water didn't rush; it didn't roar as it slammed into the waiting river. Instead, it glided over the rocks, trickling down moss and stone, as if it were desperate to meet the river once more.

You could see the erosion on the rocks where the waterfall normally raged, but those weathered spots were dry now, spectators to the way the water now perilously fell as if it were dying.

Torrin slowed his steps, and I could sense his hesitation without him saying another word.

Carefully, we navigated our way around the water, my footing slipping once on the slick stones, my heart racing with each step the closer we got.

Then I saw it.

The two trees stood where Verena had described them, their gnarled roots twisted and intertwined, thick with time and secrets. I stepped forward, reaching out my still bound hands to touch the roots, and a jolt of energy surged through my body, sudden and electric, sending a shiver up my spine.

"A kingdom torn in blood; a world turned to ash."

The words left my lips before I could stop them.

I could still hear her voice, soft and full of awe, as she whispered them to me, as they wrapped around me until they stole the breath from my lungs.

"What?" Torrin's voice snapped me out of my thoughts as he moved to my side, reaching forward to touch the same roots.

I didn't look at him. Instead, I dug my fingers into the damp earth, pulling apart the mass of roots until light from the moon could filter past their cover. I pulled harder, the roots snapping and breaking in my hands, until a small and unassuming opening emerged from the earth.

I dropped to my knees before it and cleared away the debris, my fingers digging into the soil, revealing tiny pebbles and dying leaves.

I coughed, the air musty and not meant to be disturbed, but then it gave way, revealing the larger opening.

The tunnel.

Torrin exhaled sharply, his breath catching in his throat as he took a step back.

"Holy shit," he murmured.

But before he could say anything else, Wren was at his back. Her dagger pressed firmly against his throat. His entire body stiffened, and it was far too late for him to grab his own weapon.

"Take off his cuffs," my sister commanded, her gaze staring straight ahead at the tunnel before me.

"What the hell is this?" Torrin's breath was ragged, but he didn't dare move.

The dagger in Wren's grip remained steady, the sharp point pressing against his throat, forcing him to still beneath her hold.

The rebellion's council had voted; they had agreed to give me what I asked for in exchange for this information, but Wren didn't trust them.

And neither did I.

Kai stood between Torrin's men and us, leaning against the stone with his own dagger drawn limply in his hands, his magic curling faintly in the air.

"Everyone calm down." Liya moved to step forward, but Kai's hand shot out, blocking her path.

Wren's voice was as sharp as the blade against Torrin's skin. "Take off his cuffs."

Torrin's fingers twitched, hesitating for a fraction of a second too long.

Wren didn't flinch. She pressed the dagger harder, just enough to bite into his skin. "Now."

Torrin muttered a curse under his breath, then fumbled in his pocket before producing a key. He didn't even try to meet my gaze as he held it out, and I extended my hands, the metal cuffs biting against my skin.

The key scraped against the lock, a grating sound that sent a shiver of anticipation through me, and then, a click.

The moment the cuffs fell away, I barely stifled a sharp inhale. Power surged beneath my skin, flooding through my veins like fire after a long winter. My magic.

Wren lowered her dagger but didn't step away from Torrin. She turned and pressed the blade into my palm instead. She trusted me to finish this.

I curled my fingers around the hilt, adjusting my grip as I studied Torrin's face.

"It's real," he murmured, barely more than a whisper. His gaze flicked to the entrance of the tunnel, the roots still peeled away like a wound in the earth.

I met his eyes then. "We'll take it from here, councilman."

Torrin hesitated, as did Liya. "Dacre." She tried to take another step forward, but Kai still didn't allow her to pass.

"This is what you wanted," I answered her and pointed my dagger to the tunnel. "And I've given it to you. I kept my promise."

Torrin looked back at her, and I wondered if he could see the hesitation in her eyes as I could.

"Wren, Kai, and I will go forward from here." I took a small step closer to the tunnel. "I don't trust any of you to go with us. I don't trust you with my mate."

"I made promises too, you know?" Her gaze shuddered, and absently I wondered if she was talking about the promises they made to me in the council chambers or the promises she had once made to my mother.

"And I expect you to keep them." I nodded to Wren, and she moved to my side, farther away from them and closer to the tunnel. "Once we have Verena, we plan to escape back through this tunnel. We plan to come back to the hidden city because we have nowhere else to go, nowhere else where I can protect her."

Kai moved then, grabbing a torch from one of Torrin's men, his grip unbothered by their protests. "We need this more than you."

I smirked at my friend despite the tightness in my chest, but then I returned my gaze to Liya. "Verena is not to be harmed."

She nodded once, and I tried to allow trust to bloom in my chest, but it wouldn't come.

"We're not staying here," Torrin spat as Kai passed him. "We're not waiting in hopes that you all make it out alive. We'll return to the hidden city, update our people."

Kai snorted. "You mean report back to his father?"

Torrin shot him a glare but didn't argue.

I didn't care what they did. Let them go. Let them run back to my father and tell him what we found. Let them tell him that his son had found the very thing he had been desperate to find.

It didn't matter. Verena was waiting.

She was my only concern.

I stepped forward, feeling the earth shift beneath me as I knelt at the tunnel's entrance. I placed a hand on either side, feeling an odd thrum through the stone, but I didn't hesitate. I took one last breath before I squeezed through the narrow opening, descending into the dark tunnel on my hands and knees.

The air inside the tunnel was thick and stale, pressing against my lungs like the weight of the past. I reached out, running my fingers along the stone as I moved forward, and let my magic ripple beneath my skin.

The walls were damp; old magic unlike any I'd ever felt before clung to them like whispers of something long forgotten. It wasn't strong, but it was there, lingering as if it were waiting for something, for someone.

Wren climbed in after me, a soft curse falling from her lips as the darkness swallowed her, but then there was a flicker of light as Kai followed, the torch still clenched between his fingers.

It only took a moment before the tunnel opened up, widening enough for us to climb to our feet.

Kai moved ahead of me, holding the torch high. His magic pulsed subtly in the air around him, the faintest tendrils of shadow curling against the stone as if sensing the way forward and searching for danger.

Wren trailed behind me as we moved, her breathing steady but sharp, her movements cautious.

It had been years since any of us had been in a tunnel like this. Not since we were children. Not since we believed that the rebellion was something untouchable, something good. When we had run through the hidden city, searching every alcove and hidden passage, typically hitting dead ends and coming home covered in mud.

I exhaled slowly, pressing my palm against the wall again. This time, I let my magic sink deeper. Heat licked against my fingers, the stone warming beneath my touch.

I frowned, pulling my hand back.

Kai paused ahead of me. "What is it?"

I hesitated, flexing my fingers before shaking my head. "Nothing. Keep moving."

Kai didn't look convinced, but he turned and pressed on.

The tunnel twisted, curling into a narrow passage that forced us to slow as we squeezed through. The dampness increased, our leathers becoming slick with the moisture, until finally, the tunnel gave way, spilling into an open cavern.

And it wasn't empty.

A towering stone statue loomed in the center of the chamber, its features worn by time. I circled around it until I reached the front, taking in the woman's face.

There was nothing particularly unique about the woman, every bit of her covered in a weathered bronze, but when I looked up into her eyes, I suddenly couldn't catch my breath. Long robes were draped across her body in bronze, her face forlorn, but it was her eyes that seemed to follow me, to see so deeply within me that my magic quivered.

Wren reached out and ran her fingers over the base of the statue, tilting her head slightly. "There's something carved here."

Kai lifted the torch higher, casting flickering light over the weathered inscription. I stepped closer, brushing my fingers over the ancient words, and it burned inside me like fire ravishing through a dry, thirsty forest.

I sucked in a sharp breath, trying to rein in the feel of it crashing through me.

Kai shifted beside me, his grip tightening around the

torch. The flickering light barely reached the cavern ceiling as he leaned closer to Wren.

And neither seemed to be affected by the statue, neither aware of what was happening inside me.

"A tethered soul to shifting sands." Wren read the words as she traced over them, each one slamming into me harder than the last until my knees threatened to buckle beneath me. "What does that mean?"

Wren glanced back at me, and her eyes widened as I shook my head.

"I don't know." I pressed my hand against my stomach, and I couldn't control the word that thrashed through me, tormenting me.

Verena.

My stomach twisted violently, bile rising in my throat. This was a warning.

"Are you okay?" Wren climbed to her feet, and I glanced at my sister, panic weaving through every inch of me.

"We need to get to Verena."

Kai lifted the torch higher, scanning the towering cave. "There."

I followed his gaze, a small, dark opening directly above the statue's crown. A way out. The tunnel stretched on, but we had no idea which way these tunnels led.

Wren took a step back, assessing the climb, before she steadied herself with her hands upon the statue. She lifted her foot, placing it against the woman's hand, and she appeared to be helping Wren as she climbed.

I held my breath as Wren reached the top, placing a foot on each of the woman's shoulders before she jumped.

Her fingers caught on the lip of the passage above, and she pulled herself up.

"Wait," Kai growled. "We don't know what's up there. I should go first."

"I'm more than capable, Kai." Wren groaned as she pulled herself higher, until the top half of her body disappeared from view.

Kai cursed under his breath, turning toward me. "Say something."

"To Wren?" I asked as I glanced between my sister's dangling legs and the statue. "I'd prefer not to be stabbed."

Kai shot me a glare but wasted no more time arguing. He followed her up, his movements slower, more precise. I tilted my head back, watching them disappear through the opening.

I stepped closer to the statue, and a cold gust of air slipped from the passage above. We weren't just going up. We were going outside.

I grabbed onto the statue, my magic crackling beneath my skin and colliding with the magic that pulsed within the statue as I climbed. The statue was slick with condensation, but every place my fingers touched, heat surged through the rock.

Verena. Her name whispered through me in a voice that wasn't my own. A woman's voice that called out for her until I reached for the opening, my skin slipping away from the stone.

It stopped immediately, my head feeling too quiet as I pulled myself the rest of the way up.

Wren and Kai were already crouched near the edge of the passage, our view blocked by twisting vines.

Wren turned, her eyes glinting. "You're not going to believe this."

I glanced past her, where her hands pulled at the trailing plant, and the capital city stretched before us, quiet and still beneath the stars.

We weren't in the palace yet. We were on the streets just outside my grandmother's house.

The night pressed against my skin, cool and filled with brine from the sea. The city was quiet, but that didn't mean it was safe. The palace loomed in the distance, its dark towers stretching toward the sky. Every step we took brought us closer to Verena, closer to danger.

We moved quickly, keeping to the alleys, avoiding the main streets. The tension in the air was thick, a silent warning none of us spoke aloud.

"Look." Wren's hushed whisper caught my attention.

I followed her gaze to the brick facade on one of the houses, and I stumbled on the cobblestone as I looked up, high above their door. A rebellion sigil had been painted in stark black against the worn brick. It appeared that someone had tried to scrub it away, fading it in certain areas, but the mark remained.

I could feel my heartbeat, hear it rushing in my ears, and I quickly looked away.

The rebellion had been raging for decades, a fight that had been happening even before I was born, and the flames of revolution burned bright throughout our people. But I had never witnessed something like this within the capital city.

"Keep walking." I pressed my trembling hand against Wren's back and pushed her forward as we turned a corner.

Her soft gasp filled my ears, and I pushed harder. An older man, whose hair was leeched of color and face lined with years of life, hung from the side of the building. His feet swayed in the air just above our heads, his neck turned unnaturally against the rope that held him, but it was his arm that had fear sinking through me.

His left sleeve was rolled up past his withered bicep, and there, just above his wrist, was the same mark that stained the brick.

I could feel Wren shaking beneath my hand, feel Kai's magic as he tried to keep it under control, but none of us stopped. We pushed forward until my grandmother's house emerged before us.

It was small, tucked between two other brick buildings, the familiar glow of light seeping from the front window. It should have been comforting.

Instead, nothing but unease curled in my gut.

I hastily climbed the three wooden steps, my boots landing too loud against the worn planks. I rapped my knuckles against the door, counting the seconds in my head until finally, it opened.

My grandmother stood before me, eyes widening. "Dacre." Her voice held more trepidation than relief.

I never showed up here unannounced.

Her gaze flicked behind me, taking in Wren's and Kai's rigid postures, the way Kai's hand hovered near his weapon and the way Wren was still looking back at the man that neither of us knew.

Then, without another word, she stepped aside, motioning us in, and the warmth of the house swallowed me whole. Trinkets and books filled every available space, the scent of vanilla and old parchment curling in the air. It was painfully familiar.

An ache formed in my chest like it always did, an ache for my mother.

"What brings you here tonight?' She smiled as she moved to the window and calmly slid the curtains closed.

I started to pace, running my fingers through my hair. " We don't have time to explain everything, but we need—"

Movement. I stilled just as my grandmother's face slid past me, and I followed it.

And then, I saw him. A man sat at her small dining table, his posture tense, his eyes locked on to mine. I hardly recognized him; it had been years since the last time we saw one another.

I reached for my dagger on instinct. "Micah?"

He nodded once, wiping his hand over his mouth where crumbs of bread had lingered. "Hi, Dacre."

"Micah." Wren breathed his name as she passed me, heading straight for him.

He smiled at her as he stood, but it didn't reach his eyes. She wrapped her arms around his neck, and he buried his head in hers as if breathing her in.

Kai shifted beside me, his magic thrumming slightly harder than before.

"Where have you been?" Wren asked as she squeezed him tighter against her. "It's been years, Micah."

"I know." He nodded, and I glanced over at my grandmother who was carefully watching me, too carefully.

She wrapped her wrinkled hands around the back of one of her dining chairs, her bony fingers clenching tightly to the wood. "Why are you here, Dacre?"

Micah went rigid against my sister, but he didn't pull away.

"I've come for Verena," I answered hesitantly. "The king has taken her back. He has her."

There wasn't an ounce of shock in her silver eyes as she watched me. "I know." She nodded and pressed one of her hands to her stomach, patting there as she spoke. "The tides have risen."

I looked to Kai, but he shrugged his shoulders as he still stared at Wren.

"We have to get into the palace." I turned back to my grandmother. "We used the tunnels to get here, but I'm not sure which one leads into the palace."

"I can help," Micah spoke as he finally released Wren. He was still looking down at her, his fingers pushing stray pieces of hair behind her ear. "I can get you into the palace."

He turned to face me fully then, and I sucked in a shocked breath as Wren no longer blocked my view of him. He stood there in my grandmother's kitchen wearing the uniform of a guard, a king's guard, and on his chest, the king's crest. A symbol of his power embroidered in gold thread. Worn only by the guards sworn to his service.

My blood turned to ice.

Kai stepped forward, his magic crackling around him, and he reached for Wren, jerking her away from Micah. "What the hell is going on?"

"This is where you've been?" My voice clapped like thunder. "Your loyalty is to the king?"

"No," Micah started, but I didn't believe him. The truth was in front of me, the uniform covering his body until he became one of them instead of one of us. "I am not loyal to the king."

"It sure as hell looks like it." I lifted my hand, motioning toward him.

"Stop," my grandmother's voice commanded, but I was too busy watching him.

"I am his prisoner, just as she is," he spat, running his fingers through his hair. "I don't have a choice."

I took a step forward, closing the gap between us, and my power felt desperate within me. "You always have a choice, and it looks like you've made yours."

Kai shifted, his body blocking Wren slightly, and the only sound in the room was Wren's slow, measured breathing.

Micah didn't move. He didn't flinch. He just stared at me, jaw tight, and when he spoke, his voice was quieter. "You don't understand."

I curled my hand into a fist, feeling my magic pushing against my skin, as out of control and confused as I felt. "Then make me."

Micah exhaled sharply, his gaze never leaving mine. "The king has my sister."

He let his words sink in as Wren gasped, but I knew of no sister. When Micah had lived with my grandmother years ago, there had been no talk of a sister, no talk of anyone.

I turned to my grandmother. "I thought you said that he was brought here on a ship, fled from his kingdom with nowhere else to go, no one to help him when you found him on the streets."

I remembered it vividly, the first time we had come to

visit my grandmother with our mom, the two of them exchanging notes between their hands, intel for the rebellion that my grandmother somehow knew, and Micah had been here. I had felt sorry for him then, pitied him, and the tale my grandmother had woven about his past.

"He did." My grandmother nodded, not an ounce of regret in her tone. "He came from my kingdom, the kingdom of my mother before me. The kingdom of Verena's mother before her."

Her words slammed into me as I searched her silver eyes. "And his sister?"

"She was taken the day we arrived," Micah said, his voice now laced with fury. "My feet hit the sand, and they pulled her away screaming." His gaze shuddered, haunted by his past. "I didn't see my sister again until two days after Verena was arrested."

"I don't understand." I looked back and forth between the two of them.

"I made promises to Verena's mother, to our queen," my grandmother started before glancing back at Micah. "And after your mother was killed in that raid, after Verena managed to escape, I knew that I had to do something."

I tried to suck in a breath, tried to calm my thundering heart, but it was no use.

"She fled to the streets, and the moment I saw her, I knew that her father would have her back within days if she was on her own."

My gaze slid back to Micah, to the way his jaw worked. "You were the one on the streets with her. That's the reason you were suddenly gone from here, why she let us believe you ran."

I looked at my grandmother, and the bitter taste of betrayal coated my tongue.

"I asked this of Micah," my grandmother insisted. "He protected her on the streets until his protection wasn't strong enough anymore. And when she was arrested by the guards, I feared what they would do with her once they realized who she was. I made the queen promises," she demanded, her voice louder than before. "I sent Micah searching for her, only to find that she had already been taken by the rebellion, by you."

"That doesn't explain this," Wren finally spoke, and she was staring at Micah, unable to look away from his uniform.

"I was arrested while trying to find Verena." His hands shook at his sides as he balled them into fists. "And that's when I saw her inside the palace, my sister." He looked up at me then, and all I could see was rage. "They had taken her off that ship and straight to the king. She was far too young." He shook his head. "A royal courtesan."

Bile flooded my mouth, but he didn't stop.

"I screamed for her, begged for them to take me in her place."

Micah's eyes were unfocused, his body tense, like he was no longer here but back in that moment.

"The guards didn't listen." His throat bobbed. "But the king…"

The room seemed to constrict, and I could feel Kai's barely restrained magic as if it were moving around me.

"What did he do?" Wren's voice was careful, quiet.

Micah let out a slow, shuddering breath. "He laughed and made me watch as he paraded my sister in front of me.

He had her sit on his knee as he ordered his guards to drag me to the dungeons." Micah's voice dropped lower, his next words hoarse. "I was desperate, mad with rage, and I said the very thing that I never should have."

The world felt like it had stopped spinning because I already knew what he was going to say.

"You gave him Verena."

Micah flinched.

"What did you tell him?"

He didn't want to answer at first; he swallowed hard, his jaw trembling as he clenched it.

"I told him that I had been with her on the streets. That I protected her." His voice was weak. "That I had been the one who gave her the rebellion mark."

Everything inside me went cold. The rebellion mark. The one carved into Verena's skin.

Kai swore softly, Wren sucked in a sharp breath, but I couldn't look away from Micah.

"I didn't mean to." His voice broke. "I tried to fight him after that. I did. But he knew exactly what to say, exactly what to do, to make me—"

I forced my voice to stay steady. "And what did he do to get your loyalty?" I motioned to his uniform.

Micah swallowed hard. "The king made me a deal."

There it was.

"He promised to let my sister go if I helped him with Verena. Helped get her back, helped break her."

I exhaled slowly as I stared at him. I was going to kill him. It didn't matter that he had done what he did for his sister; it didn't matter to me what I would have done if I had been in his place. I couldn't see past his betrayal of Verena.

"Does Verena know?" My fists curled at my sides, nails digging into my palms until I felt my skin break. "Does she know how easy it was for you to betray her?"

Micah recoiled. "You think this has been easy? You think this is what I wanted?" Micah's eyes widened, and I saw the desperation there, the torment. "You're not the only one who has ever loved her, you know, but what would you have done if it was Wren?"

The room shrank around me, the walls pressing in as my magic surged.

"Don't you dare speak of loving her as if you have the right, as if you aren't the one who fucking betrayed her." My words sliced through the room like a blade I desperately wished to wield. "Don't you dare speak of Wren."

"Where were you?" Micah shifted uncomfortably. "She spoke of you when he still held her in the dungeon, cried out your name when I'm not even sure she realized she was doing so. You damn me for what I've done, but where were you as she begged?"

I could see black at the edges of my vision. "You were there when he tortured her?" I took a step forward, even as my chest felt like it was caving in at the image he had just painted in my mind. "You stood there, and you did nothing to stop him?"

I shot forward, the table scraping across the floor as I dove for him, wrapping my hand around his throat and slamming him against the wall.

"He knows," Micah cried out, looking to my grandmother, and that only fueled my anger more. "He knows that she's a siphon, that her magic was bound inside her."

I tightened my hand around his throat, watching as he struggled before I looked to my grandmother. "What does he mean?"

"The king is a siphon," she started, her gaze latched on to my hand that was still wrapped around Micah's neck.

I already knew this. We all did. It was what made him so powerful, so dangerous. He didn't just wield magic; he took it, drained it, bent it to his will.

He demanded magic at the tithe, magic that was meant for balance of our kingdom, and he stole it.

"This is what he's been searching for, what he's tried to force her to become, why he wanted another heir."

My grandmother nodded.

I forced my voice to stay even. "Why didn't she know? She has spent her life thinking she was powerless. How did she not know?"

"Because it was hidden." Her expression didn't waver. "The queen and I bound her magic inside her so he couldn't use her. "

Wren's breath hitched, and my hand flexed against Micah.

"When she was still small, before she could even understand what she was." My grandmother nodded once more, and when she moved, it hit me how fragile she appeared.

"He wants her for the vessel." Micah struggled to speak against my hand, and I dropped him, taking a step back, and looking at the two of them as if they were complete strangers.

"What vessel?"

My grandmother hesitated.

"Tell me," I barked, and her silver eyes darkened.

"There were five vessels in the beginning. Five different kingdoms bound to control the magic they angered, but the one in the palace, it's the only one left. It was meant for balance, to control the tithe."

Kai straightened beside me, his entire body going rigid. "What happened to the others?"

"Destroyed." Her voice was quiet. "One by one."

"By him." I already knew the answer.

She nodded. "And Veyrith was the last one. The last kingdom that stood against him, but our kingdom fell just like the others."

The kingdom the queen's family had once ruled. The kingdom my grandmother had once called home. That Micah had.

I shook my head. "Why? What does he gain from destroying them?"

My grandmother's gaze steadied on mine. "Power."

My stomach twisted violently.

"It's the same thing he gains from being bound to the vessel, the thing he will gain if he manages to bind Verena."

The word settled like a curse.

Bound.

"I don't understand."

"The king siphoned from the vessel, siphoned the magic and the tithe that was given by the people of this land. But he took too much, demanded too much, and the vessel demanded in return.

"He's powerful, but at a cost. And that cost has finally

become too profound." She exhaled and ran her hand over her neck. "The vessel is killing him."

"He will bind Verena to it to save himself."

The realization slammed into me, cold and brutal.

A tethered soul to shifting sands. The words on that statue suddenly drummed through me, ringing in my ear.

The war we had been fighting wasn't just against a tyrant. It was far worse.

I turned toward the door. "We leave now."

Micah exhaled sharply. "Dacre, wait—"

CHAPTER 9
VERENA

P ain at my father's hand had become a constant presence in my life, like an old, unwelcomed companion.

It no longer came in sharp, sudden bursts; instead, it clung to me like a stubborn stain, sinking so deep into my skin that I could never scrub it away.

He was tearing me apart from the inside, forcing my power to the surface, demanding that I siphon, that I yield to what I was.

But for the past few days, he had left me alone.

It should have been a relief, but it wasn't.

The absence of his cruelty was its own kind of torment, a silence thick with unspoken threats. He was waiting. Preparing for something worse.

I curled into myself on the massive bed, staring at the carved canopy above. I barely had the strength to move, to breathe. Even after the healers had come and gone, they hadn't been able to take away the pain.

My father hadn't wanted them to.

"I need her strong," my father had instructed. "Heal her, but don't let her forget."

And they had.

My body was no longer broken in the way it had been before, but I was fraying.

And Micah hadn't come back, not in days, not since I siphoned.

I squeezed my eyes shut and forced myself not to think of the guard's face. It had haunted me for days, the life absent from his eyes, his body limp against the stone floor.

The palace was still, but beyond the walls, I could hear the city. The muffled hum of life carried on as if nothing had changed. As if I was not here, trapped in this room like an animal waiting to be led to slaughter.

I would have given anything to be back there. To feel hunger gnaw at my stomach instead of this.

I was unraveling. My magic thrummed inside me now, as desperate to escape as I was, and tendrils of chaos pulsed within me, threatening the scraps of sanity I had left.

I felt hollow as I thought of what my father had called me, of what I knew I was, but it was my mother's words that haunted me.

"Beware of the weight of fate".

The words staggered through me and my stomach lurched violently.

I didn't want to believe her words. I wanted to revolt against them, even when everything inside me knew she was telling the truth.

But her truth felt too late. She knew of my power, knew

of the consequences I would face, yet she hadn't prepared me for what was to come.

She should have stolen me away, boarded a ship, and sent us sailing past the coast until my father could no longer see us.

Until he could no longer touch us.

And anger tore through me because she hadn't.

I wavered between fury and longing, torn apart by the fear that she had failed me, yet aching for her presence, hoping she would slip back into my dreams and never let me go.

The heavy wooden door of my chambers creaked open, pulling me from my thoughts, and I hated how my next breath slipped from my lips different from the ones before it.

I didn't move, didn't flinch.

I kept my eyes on the canopy above as his presence smothered the air, like smoke creeping into my lungs. His boots scraped against the marble floor as he stepped closer.

I counted his steps, bracing for what was to come.

"Sit up."

The words were soft, deceptively so, but I didn't move.

A sharp inhale, the sound of fabric shifting, and then, his hand wrapped around my ankle, yanking me down the bed. I gasped when my knees slammed into his, but he didn't stop. He fisted his hand in my hair, pain searing across my scalp as I was wrenched upright.

"I gave you days to rest." His voice was quiet, almost thoughtful. "Yet, here you are, still wallowing."

I clenched my jaw, swallowing against the nausea curling in my gut, and his grip tightened.

"Do you think I am a cruel man, Verena?"

The question sent ice through my veins. It was a trap, a test, and I knew better than to answer him. Instead, I forced my body to remain still, to keep my expression as blank as his.

He sighed, as if disappointed. "You think I do this because I enjoy it." He released my hair abruptly, and my teeth slammed together. "You think I take pleasure in your suffering."

He bent his knees, lowering himself until his eyes were level with mine, and the urge to look away from him was overwhelming.

"I do not enjoy it, Verena, but I will do whatever is necessary to make you into what you were meant to be."

A shiver ran down my spine. I had heard these words before, a hundred different times that had fallen from his lips, but now, they carried a new weight.

"Get up."

I buried my hands into the sheets. "Where are you taking me?"

"I won't ask again." He reached forward, his hand brushing against my cheek, and I jerked away from his touch. "You will not defy me."

Tears welled in my eyes, hot and stinging. I could feel my magic building inside me, but I had never felt more powerless.

"Please," I cried, and he touched me again, his hand sweeping away the hair that was stuck to my lips.

There was a sharp knock at the door, and I looked away

from my father to watch Micah hesitating near my door. He didn't look at me, refusing to meet my eyes.

Something was different about him.

His shoulders were stiff, his posture more rigid than usual, and there was a red mark at the base of his throat, a fading imprint of fingers.

"Take her," my father demanded as he stepped back, running his hand over his mouth.

Micah hesitated for half a breath before he crossed the room in two long strides.

"Don't," I whispered as he reached for me. My voice was raw, trembling. "Please, Micah, don't."

But he did.

His hands closed around my arms, firm but careful. His touch was not cruel, but it didn't matter. Without a word, he hoisted me against him, the rough fabric of his uniform pressing against my skin, and a tear trailed down my cheek.

Micah's grip was steady, but it didn't matter. I fought him anyway. I twisted, dug my nails into his forearms, anything to slow my descent into whatever nightmare awaited me.

But Micah did not let go. He barely reacted as a sob clawed up my throat, and I slammed my fists into his chests.

"Verena," he growled my name under his breath, so low that I thought I imagined it, but when I looked up into his wide eyes, they bore down on me, warning me.

I stopped fighting as he pulled me across the room, the cold floor biting into my bare feet, but sobs still racked through my body.

The hallways stretched endlessly before us, twisting

into familiar corridors I had once known so well. My father walked ahead, his pace unhurried, and he didn't look back to know that we followed.

Servants bowed as we passed, and not one of them met my eyes. There wasn't one of them who even glanced in my direction as my cries echoed off the walls.

We reached a heavy metal door, and I knew exactly where it led. My father didn't stop, and another guard scurried forward, opening the door to the dungeons before he could reach it. Micah stared straight ahead, and he didn't look at me, even as I clung to him, even as I whimpered against his arm.

Step by step, we descended farther into the darkness until we reached the dungeons that I had grown to know too well, but my father didn't stop. We passed cell after cell before we turned a corner, and my stomach lurched violently.

The stairwell ahead of us was different from the rest. Older. Uneven.

"Please," I begged, but no one was listening.

Micah's fingers twitched around my arm, as if bracing himself, and I felt it too. The air changed the moment we stepped over the threshold. It was heavier, venomous, alive.

I had felt it before; I had known it from my dreams.

"No!" I dug my feet into the unforgiving ground as my body trembled with another sob, but it was no use.

The first step was cold, and the second was even colder. By the time we reached the tenth, the temperature had dropped so low that each breath burned in my lungs, but still, we went deeper.

Down and down, farther than I had ever been before.

The stone walls pulsed. At first, I thought it was my own unsteady breathing, my own erratic heartbeat hammering too loudly against my ribs, but the walls themselves seemed to breathe.

Micah's grip on me tightened as a massive, dark iron door appeared before us. A heartbeat that was not my own thundered in my ears. The vessel knew I was here, and it was waiting.

We passed through the door, and Micah's hand tightened against me before he finally let me go. Vaulted ceilings stretched high above us, and torches lined the walls, their flickering glow lost against the unnatural light spilling from the center of the room.

The vessel.

The massive well looked just as it had in my dream, like a wound in the earth that pulsed and churned. That same sickly green glow flowed within the vessel, flickering between shades of black and gold, as if the magic inside was constantly shifting, constantly struggling against itself.

A slow exhale drew my attention away from the vessel. Across the chamber, half cloaked in darkness, stood the Sight. Her robes pooled around her feet, her hood drawn back so the sharp features of her face were revealed, her white hair glowing like moonlight.

She did not move. Did not speak. She only watched.

And then, the vessel whispered.

A sharp pang shot through my chest. The pressure increased, the air thickening until it pressed against my lungs. My father was speaking, but I couldn't hear him.

Because the vessel spoke to me now. Not with words.

With need.

With hunger.

With pain.

A sudden, searing heat licked up my spine, curling beneath my ribs. My knees buckled, but Micah caught me before I hit the floor.

I gasped, my fingers clutching at his arms, my vision swimming. The whispers grew louder, twining through my mind like vines creeping through cracks in stone.

Its pain merged with my own, blurring the lines between us until I couldn't remember who it had belonged to before.

Then whispers inside the vessel turned to something else. A pull. A desperate, clawing need. My body arched involuntarily, my magic surging toward it, toward the hunger waiting inside the well.

It wanted me. It thirsted for my power. It was trying to take, and my magic suddenly recoiled.

A low, keening sound filled the chamber. It was coming from me. I gritted my teeth, trying to resist, trying to hold myself together, but my body was weak.

I was weak, and my magic...

It was unraveling, slipping out of my grasp like sand through open fingers.

A sharp pain shot through my chest, stealing my breath away. My vision blurred and tunneled as I gasped for air.

I found myself moving closer to the vessel, my own movements outside of my control, and my fingers dug into the cold stone edge, anchoring myself as my body trembled uncontrollably.

I tried to recall what my mother had told me, tried to

think of anything except the overwhelming urge to press my hand into the vessel. I wanted to feel it across my skin, inside my veins.

I clamped my eyes closed and tried to block it out.

But another voice cut through the air, soft but unmistakable. I opened my eyes and turned my head sharply, my movements feeling unnatural.

The Sight.

Her lips moved, whispering words too faint for me to hear, but her eyes, milky and unfocused, seemed to stare through me, her head tilting ever so slightly.

"What did you say?" my father demanded. I had almost forgotten that he was in the room. I could no longer feel his presence. I couldn't feel my fear.

The Sight lifted her head fully, but she didn't look to the king.

"The tideborn." Her voice was soft, eerily detached.

A chill wrapped around my spine.

My mother's voice echoed in my mind, the prophecy, her notes scrawled in the margins.

The tideborn's gift, bound in chain,
To break the bond or bind again.

The vessel seemed to pause. It held its breath along with me as we watched her.

"What does that mean?" My father's voice rang out, but the Sight didn't acknowledge him and neither did I.

"Born of two kingdoms," she murmured. "Bound to take, yet cursed to mourn."

The vessel whispered then. It grew urgent and louder, curling around me like unseen hands. I swallowed hard, feeling the pressure in my chest building with each passing moment, drowning out everything else.

"Please." Tears ran down my face as I pleaded with her, my voice raw and desperate, but I didn't know what I was asking.

She blinked, and whatever force had overtaken her seemed to fade. She swayed slightly, reaching for the stone wall behind her as if steadying herself.

My father took a slow, measured step toward her. " What was that? What did you see?"

The Sight finally met his gaze, but her expression remained void of emotion. But I couldn't hear her words as she spoke. I was waning, buckling under the overwhelming weight of the vessel's power.

But then a tiny spark ignited in the air, triggering a shift in the atmosphere around me. A warmth circled in my chest, steady and strong, cutting through the hazy fear that consumed me.

I sucked in a deep breath, my pulse racing as I blinked and looked around. But every eye was still on the Sight, my father's face reddened and filled with rage.

I pushed against the vessel, trying to force the other-worldly magic out of my chest as the other feeling took root.

The magic that pushed inside me now was like warm honey pooling within me, slow and steady, a quiet strength in the chaos. It wrapped around me, not pulling, not taking —only shielding. It was different from the vessel's hunger. It didn't want to consume me. It wanted to keep me whole. It wanted to keep me *safe*.

It was my bond. It was my mate.

I didn't know what was real inside me and what was an illusion, but I couldn't bring myself to care. I could feel him, and nothing else mattered at that moment.

My own magic twisted inside me, not in pain this time, but in recognition.

Dacre was fighting.

He was coming for me.

My fingers curled against the stone, and I could feel bits of it crumble beneath my touch.

"Verena!" my father shouted my name, but I barely heard him.

Instead, I clung to the only thing keeping me tethered to myself.

And in a whisper, so soft it barely passed my lips, I breathed his name.

"Dacre."

CHAPTER 10
DACRE

The sun had just begun to set when the capital shifted into something else entirely.

By nightfall, the city moved with a different rhythm, slow and fevered. The capital was alive in the way all dying things were, clinging and desperate.

The streets, once bustling with the shouts of merchants and beggars, had grown quieter, but not empty. Never empty.

The king's guards patrolled in thick rotations, their torches flickering like the last remnants of a world the king was burning to the ground. There were more of them than there had been yesterday, and that was a problem.

I tugged at the stiff collar of my stolen uniform, trying to ignore the suffocating weight of the fabric against my skin. The crest embroidered on my chest made my stomach churn, but Micah had been right. This uniform, this guise, it was the only way we were getting inside the palace.

Still, it made my skin crawl.

"Do you see them?" Wren's voice was barely more than a whisper. She crouched low beside me, her fingers hovering just above the handle of her dagger as her eyes scanned the streets.

Kai was just behind us, blending into the shadows of the alleyway. His magic hummed softly in the air, weaving an illusion around us, a simple stretch of empty cobblestone where our bodies should have been.

A well-placed distraction, one that had kept us hidden thus far, but Kai couldn't hold it for much longer.

Magic never came without a cost.

I exhaled slowly, watching the guards move in pairs along the perimeter of the palace gates. Micah had given us everything we needed: rotation schedules, blind spots, weaknesses in their patrols. He had spent enough time as a guard to know the weak points, enough time at the king's side to know where the cracks were in his defenses.

But there were more guards on patrol now than he said there would be, more guards than I had ever seen before.

Something was wrong.

"There are more than Micah said," I murmured.

The guard presence had doubled. Tripled. They weren't just patrolling. They were bracing for something.

A sharp, icy shiver raced down my spine as the thought consumed me. Despite everything Micah had done, I had still let him become part of our plan to get to Verena.

I had ignored my instincts, buried them deep, and now they resurfaced with a vengeance.

What if Micah had given us the wrong information? What if he led us into a trap?

"They're on edge." Wren's muttered words mirrored

the unease that crept through me. "Something has them spooked."

Kai shifted beside us, his magic pulsing. "Then we use it."

His voice was steady, but I could see the way his fingers flexed. He was already preparing to push his magic further than he should.

"Not yet," I cautioned.

He let out a sharp exhale but nodded.

We needed to move. The plan was already set. We had mapped it out last night, traced every step through the tunnels beneath the city after my grandmother convinced me how big of a fool I was to try to charge into the palace.

If we could get inside undetected, we'd have a fighting change.

And a chance was all I needed.

I swallowed the dry burn in my throat. My bond with Verena pulsed faintly in my chest, a tether that refused to break.

She was alive.

I could feel it with every beat of my heart, but she was suffering.

And I was running out of time.

The passage was still hidden beneath a thick curtain of ivy at the edge of the city's perimeter.

I hesitated for only a breath before I gripped the lip of the opening and dropped down into the dark.

My boots slammed into the unforgiving ground, sending a jolt of pain through my knees.

The silence engulfed me, only the sounds of Wren and Kai landing beside me broke it.

The statue loomed in the darkness, its stony eyes watching us. Watching me.

I ran my fingers along its weathered surface as we passed, and I wished I hadn't as that same feeling from before coursed through me. This place felt like a grave.

We moved quickly, our footsteps muffled against the damp ground as we followed the tunnel forward. I could hear a steady drip of water echoing off the walls, creating an eerie symphony that seemed to follow us.

My heart raced as I took a deep breath and pushed forward. We walked for what felt like an eternity, before finally, a faint light flickered ahead.

We were close.

I crept forward, pressing myself against the stone as I peered through the opening. A corridor stretched ahead, silent and empty for now. With a slow exhale, we pushed forward.

Micah told us that Verena had been moved from the dungeons to her room, which meant we needed to go up.

But as we reached the end of the hall, I froze. A figure stood in the shadows, his uniform identical to mine.

A palace guard.

I motioned for Kai and Wren to stay back. My heart pounded as I stepped forward, every muscle in my body tense, ready to spring into action.

The guard didn't move, but his gaze was fixed on me with an intensity that made my skin prickle.

Micah had said nothing about a guard being on patrol here.

"Who goes there?"

I continued forward, refusing to falter as I kept my

voice steady. "Just patrolling the lower levels. Everything is secure."

The guard's eyes narrowed. "You're not supposed to be down here."

"I was about to say the same of you." I moved closer to him, and I mentally tallied the weapons on my body. "Who approved you for this patrol?"

There was a flicker of uncertainty then came his anger. "You little…"

I didn't let him finish before I charged.

My dagger found its mark between his ribs with ease. The blade slid in clean, and he gasped, a strangled noise escaping his lips. I pressed my other hand over his mouth, shielding the sound as I lowered him to the ground. His eyes were still open, glazed with shock.

I didn't look away, even as his breathing stopped, and I didn't allow myself to feel even a flicker of remorse for taking his life.

Wren crouched beside me, fingers wrapping around the hilt of my dagger as she pulled it free. She wiped the crimson blood on his tunic, meeting my gaze.

"We need to move." Kai reached down and gently wrapped his hand around Wren's arm before pulling her back to her feet.

I nodded, feeling my heart race as I stood, releasing a slow exhale through my nostrils.

I swallowed hard, the sudden taste of iron thick on my tongue.

Verena was close. I could feel her.

We reached the final door, a massive slab of iron that

bore the weight of time and wear, and I wrapped my fingers around the cold handle and pulled.

Its hinges groaned in protest, the sound loud and bouncing off the dungeon walls that stretched before us.

The hall was cold and dark as we stepped inside, empty, but then I felt it, her magic. It pulsed like a second heartbeat beneath my skin, curling through me, pressing against my ribs.

"What's wrong?" Wren gripped my arm and tried to force me to look at her. But I shook off her touch and darted through the rows of cells, searching frantically for any sign of Verena.

My heart pounded in my chest, threatening to cave it in, as I scanned each cell, my palms growing slick with sweat. The dank smell of metal and mold filled my nostrils, but I could still taste blood on my tongue.

"Verena is close," I hissed. "I can feel her."

My breath came in ragged gasps as I whipped around, searching for any sign of her.

"Where is she?" My voice was sharp, panicked.

Kai's footsteps echoed behind me as he backtracked. "I'm going up into the palace. Micah said they had moved her to her room. If she's not down here…"

I was barely listening as I scrambled to find her, but then, a scream.

Muffled, distant, but unmistakable in its terror.

My entire body wrenched, my magic snapping tight like it had been hooked and dragged forward.

Verena.

The sound of her scream tore through me, and I was

running before I could think. Kai and Wren were at my heels, their weapons drawn.

Another scream. This time closer. Down. She was below us.

I ran harder, shoving the door open and tearing down the stairs.

The thick, metallic scent of blood filled my senses, almost causing me to retch as I gripped the rough wall for support.

I gritted my teeth, forcing my body forward down the narrow staircase that creaked beneath my weight.

Her scream came again, this time closer. It fueled a fire within me as we reached the bottom of the staircase.

"Dacre." Her voice was so weak, so broken.

But I heard it, and I did not stop.

CHAPTER 11
VERENA

I was drowning, engulfed by an unrelenting wave of agony.

It pressed against me, dragging me under, deeper and deeper, until there was no light, no breath, no escape.

All I could feel was the vessel.

Time blurred in this darkness; seconds stretched into hours, hours into eternity, broken only by the relentless cycle of torment.

The vessel coiled around me like a venomous snake, tightening its grip with each passing moment. It fed on my suffering and drained my magic until there was nothing left to take.

But somehow, it found more.

I screamed until my voice was hoarse, pleading with my father to make it stop. *I begged him.*

But mercy wasn't a trait my father possessed.

He hardly glanced at me while my lips split and started to bleed; he didn't seem to hear me even as my throat grew raw and shredded from the screams that now lingered as silent echoes in my mind.

I wanted to fight against this, against him, against the way I seemed to meld with the vessel, my very bones aching until they no longer felt like they were my own. But I had no fight left.

The floor beneath my knees was unforgiving, cold stone biting into my skin with every movement I made, but it was the silence that crawled beneath my skin and laced every inch of me with fear that I couldn't escape.

Because the silence meant he was waiting, waiting for me to beg again, for me to give into what he wanted.

But I didn't know what else I could give him, what was left of me that he hadn't already taken.

The vessel still pulsed before me. I could feel it, a monstrous thing that breathed in tandem with me, its hunger curling inside my chest. It was alive, ancient, unrelenting, and it wanted me to bend to its will.

The force of it was tugging at my magic, twisting it with relentless intensity, its threads gradually unraveling me with each ragged breath we shared. I could feel its invasive presence as it compelled my magic outward, allowing my siphon to gently brush against each person in the room. It was as if we were cautiously sampling their magic, savoring the unique taste of each individual, calculating precisely what it intended for me to absorb to appease its insatiable hunger.

It was as if my very being had been reduced to a dwindling flame, flickering and fading with each passing moment. The vessel rushed through me like a wind, plucking at the threads of my magic, unraveling me bit by bit.

"She's close," my father mused, his voice a quiet, calculated thing, as though he were watching an experiment unfold before him. "Verena, let go. Let the vessel take care of you."

I turned to look at him, my movements so swift my vision seemed to lag behind. I fixed my gaze on my father, on the man whose blood ran through my veins, a river of history that bound us in our fates.

The vessel paused, reluctant to reach out, but I urged it forward, compelling it to sweep over his skin until I could feel the power that dwelled within him, the very magic that he had passed down to me.

I needed to see for myself, to discern how much like him I had already become.

But the moment we touched him, I recoiled.

It was a visceral assault on my senses, like sinking my teeth into rotting fruit, its blood and decay flooding my mouth. His magic didn't feel like anything that I recognized, there was no reflection of the power that pulsed with me.

He was a vacant shell, a husk of a man, with blackened bones.

He felt like *death.*

Micah stood rigidly by his side, his posture portraying an unsettling stiffness, while an overwhelming wave of pity washed across his face as he gazed down at me. The power inside me churned restlessly as I took in the familiar features of someone I had once cared for so deeply.

I felt a serpentine chill weave through me as my hatred

rose, dark and menacing, to the surface, and the vessel purred inside my veins, lapping up my anger as if it was the very thing it had been craving all along.

And that feeling inside me, it did nothing but fuel the surge of loathing I felt for Micah at what he had become. The leverage my father held over him was irrelevant as he stood there, a silent sentinel beside my father, as if his allegiance was undeniably pledged to him, and the sight seared a permanent mark of betrayal into me.

Just as he had been the one to mark my skin with the rebellion sigil what felt like an eternity ago.

He had told me then that it would protect me, but he lied.

We were nothing but two traitors whose fates were undeniably linked, but we were as lost today as the day we had found one another.

I forced myself to look away from him, and I pushed my trembling hands against the stone. Bolts of agony lanced through my body, but I forced myself to lean back, bracing my weight against my palms until I could look my father in the eye.

I refused to give in to what he wanted, but he was going to take it either way. Even if my body shattered beneath me or the power tore me apart. He would get what he wanted, but it would not be given willingly.

The moment I raised my head, my father's eyes glinted with dark amusement.

"Still fighting it?" His voice held a dangerous edge as he stepped forward, his boots dragging across the floor.

My body screamed at me to stay down, still trembling

from what I had seen within him, but I would not bow before him.

He was no king of mine.

"Isn't this what you wanted?" I rasped, my hands shaking visibly against the stone.

His expression flickered, his lips pressing into a thin line as he tucked his hands into his pockets and leaned against the vessel without a trace of fear. "I've been ashamed of you, Verena." He cocked his head and watched me for a reaction. "The heir to the greatest kingdom in the world, and she turned out as useless as her mother."

I jerked back, flinching as if I could protect myself from his words, but pain ripped through my body.

"A weak, pitiful thing that would bring ruin to this kingdom."

The vessel beneath my trembling hands seemed to throb with a vibrant, almost palpable intensity. Its surface quivered and shimmered in response to the storm of emotions churning within me. I couldn't discern whether it was my fury that fueled its relentless energy or if my inability to maintain control had somehow become the sustenance it craved.

"You don't have to be." My father squatted before me until he stared directly into my eyes, so close that I could reach forward and touch him. "You're trying to control it, but you need to relent. Give in, Verena, and I can show you power like you've never dreamed."

He reached his hand out, skimming his fingers over mine, and his mouth dropped open with a sigh as his eyes rolled closed.

"It calls to you," he murmured, his words almost euphoric. "It knows you as it knows me."

"I am nothing like you." There was no conviction in my voice because I could feel it, the way I was changing. "You are going to destroy us just as you did Veyrith, and our people hate you for it. The rebellion…"

His pupils flared until the inkiness leached every bit of color from his narrowed eyes before his magic lashed out at me, slamming into my chest.

I hit the ground with a sickening thud and the breath was knocked from my lungs. I tried to scramble to my knees, but another wave of power crashed into me, searing against my skin like fire.

I choked on ash.

My father crouched before me, gripping my chin between his fingers and forcing me to look up at him. His touch was like flames and his magic unfurled along my skin as if he were staining me with his corrosion.

"You've always been a foolish girl," he sneered, his voice laced with cruelty. "Clinging to false hope, to people who abandon you so willingly."

I tried to twist free of his hold, but his grip only tightened, threatening to crack my jaw.

"They can't save you," he taunted. "And they won't. People only love you when you have power, Verena, and the vessel will give you more power than you've ever dreamed of."

I clenched my teeth, trying to block him out.

"You talk of Veyrith, but it will be you who brings ruin to Marmoris. You are fighting me, fighting the vessel, and in doing so, you will damn them all."

His grip tightened, and my teeth ached as if they were on the verge of cracking. "Give in to the vessel, Verena. Give in or you can watch as the kingdom burns at your hand."

Heat seared my chest. It started as a flicker, a small, pulsing ember, barely noticeable beneath the pain.

But then it grew.

"I'm not capable of what you want." It wasn't a lie. I could feel the vessel destroying me from within, eating at my very soul. My mother had said he needed a siphon, that he needed someone powerful, and I felt more powerless now than I ever had before.

Powerless to the agony that ate at me, but something else surged inside me, a heat, fierce and wild, slicing through the suffocating pull of the vessel like a blade against taut rope. It didn't demand, didn't take. It reached for me. Steady. Unyielding. **A lifeline.**

I gasped as it wrapped around my ribs, burning through my veins with a desperate kind of fury, anchoring me when everything else was unraveling.

Dacre.

I felt him. Not a fleeting thread at the edges of my mind, not the ghost of a bond I feared had been severed. Real. Solid. Here.

A shock wave of warmth surged through me; a force so fierce it nearly knocked the breath from my lungs. His presence roared through my veins, fighting against the vessel's grip, fighting for me.

A strangled gasp tore from my throat, my body trembling under the weight of it, of him. He wasn't just close. *He was here.*

And my father knew something had changed. I could see it in the way his gaze sharpened, the way he frantically looked over my features as if trying to find it.

He leaned in, his breath ghosting across my face like poison. "I will break you, Verena. Just as I broke your mother."

Magic crashed into me before I could brace for it. A searing tide, violent and relentless, dragging me under, splintering me apart. Pain shot through my body, sharp as shattered glass, and a scream wrenched from my throat.

It was unnatural, the way his magic hit me. Not like a force striking from the outside, but something ripping through me from within. Like his power wasn't his at all, but something stolen, something pulled from the same source that was trying to devour me.

The vessel.

It was his tether, his lifeline, and I could feel it now, the way he needed me.

I was like a channel, a link that let him take from the vessel without it taking from him, a siphon carved from his own flesh.

He was wielding my pain, my magic, the vessel, and turning it against me. Every ounce of suffering, every drop of agony that seeped into my veins from the vessel, he was feeding from it, drinking it in, and twisting it into a blade aimed straight at me.

My body seized, every nerve raw and flayed open as his magic pushed through me, siphoning everything I had left to give. I choked, my fingers clawing at the stone beneath me, but there was nothing to hold on to.

Because I wasn't just breaking, I was being consumed.

The warmth in my chest staggered, faltered, and, for one terrifying second, it flickered out.

Panic surged with the pain, wild and destructive. *No.* I reached for it, for him, for the one thing that still felt real as my father's power tore into me like talons sinking into flesh. I would not lose him.

I sank my nails into the bond, digging deep, desperate. Focusing on nothing but Dacre. Only him. His magic curled against the tattered edges of mine, a wildfire against the cold.

It was him and me, and it was the only thing I allowed myself to focus on.

He was the only thing I wanted to feel when I finally broke.

The ground groaned beneath me, a deep, guttural sound that rattled through the stone like the castle itself was coming apart. The very walls shuddered, trembling under an unseen weight, as if something far greater than us had been set into motion.

Something unstoppable.

"Dacre." His name slipped past my lips, a breathless, desperate thing. A prayer. A plea. A promise.

And then the world exploded. A deafening blast ripped through the chamber as the door exploded outward, shards of stone and splintered iron sent flying like shrapnel. A shock wave tore through the room, a force so violent it sent cracks splintering across the floor beneath me, stretching out like jagged veins.

Dust and debris billowed into the air, swallowing the chamber in a choking fog of ruin.

The guard barely had time to react before a blade

flashed through the haze, cutting through flesh like parchment. A sharp, wet gasp, his blood pooling across the broken stone.

And then, through the wreckage, through the smoke, I saw him.

Micah was already moving, his blade flashing as he tore through the chaos. But my father turned just as Dacre dropped his guard to the ground.

Dacre's dagger was still dripping red and glinting, his chest heaving, his body taut with fury. His eyes locked on to mine, searing, wild, alive, and something inside me shattered.

There was no hesitation. No thought. No fear.

Just power.

Magic detonated from my chest, a raw, untamed storm. The walls trembled, torches sputtered, the air itself seemed to fracture under the force of it. A blast of energy roared outward, tearing through the chamber.

My father barely managed to lift his arm before the blast slammed into him, sending him careening across the room. His body collided with the vessel, the impact so violent that a deafening crack split the air. The vessel shuddered in response, its eerie glow flickering wildly.

Dacre was already lunging for me. A snarl on his lips. Blood in his teeth.

Micah turned to Dacre, his blade flashing in the dim torchlight, his posture rigid with deadly intent. "Get her and go!" he shouted.

But my father was already climbing back to his feet.

Blood dripped from my father's mouth, and still, he smiled. The fury pouring from him was a living thing, slithering through the air like a snake coiling around its prey.

I tried to move, tried to stand, but my body betrayed me.

A jagged bolt of pain ripped through my limbs, locking them in place, my muscles trembling and useless. I gasped, but even that felt like too much effort. My vision fractured at the edges, dark spots clouding my sight.

I had used too much magic, too fast. My father had drawn too much power from me, from the vessel. Gods, the vessel, it was still there, drinking me down to the marrow. It was pulling, pulling, pulling, devouring everything I had left, dragging me to the edge of nothing.

"Verena!" Dacre's voice slammed through the haze, sharp and desperate.

I forced my head up, searching for him, my heart a frantic, stuttering thing. His eyes were wild, blazing with a fear I had never seen before. He reached for me, but before he could touch me, my father moved. Faster than I had ever seen him move before.

A black current of magic lashed from his palm, cutting through the air like a whip of pure darkness, magic that I had seen fall from my own hands before.

It struck Dacre in the chest, hard, brutal, merciless, and the impact sent him flying. He crashed into the stone wall with a sickening crack, his body folding in on itself, his breath ripping from his lungs in a choked grunt.

My world fractured.

"Dacre!" His name tore from my throat, raw, broken, the only thing I could still feel.

But he didn't move.

My father barely spared me a glance as he advanced on Dacre, slow and measured, a predator savoring the kill. His lips curled into a sneer, but his posture was too relaxed, too composed.

But I could feel it, I could feel his rage.

It coiled through his veins like black poison, a deadly, creeping thing, waiting to strike again. He was pulling it from me, the magic to kill my mate.

"You've come a long way just to die," my father mused, rolling his shoulders, as if this was nothing. As if Dacre wasn't worth the effort.

But Dacre finally moved. He shoved himself off the wall, staggering just for a second before he snarled like an animal. Murder burned behind his gaze, hot and feral. His dagger gleamed in his grip, its tip still wet with blood. His own blood dripped from his nose, from the corner of his mouth, but he didn't care.

Because he wasn't looking at my father. He was looking at me.

And there was something primal in his eyes. Something reckless and unyielding.

He was going to kill my father; he was desperate to end him.

But he was going to fail.

I knew it, felt it.

The power inside me swelled, a pressure so vast, so crushing. My father was pulling harder now, ripping at the vessel with a hunger so vicious it felt like the very walls of the palace might collapse under the weight of his greed.

More. More. More.

He was drawing too much, and it was enough to tear this place apart, to shatter stone and bone alike.

Enough to kill Dacre, and I couldn't let that happen.

Dacre lunged. A flash of steel, a blur of motion, a death sentence carved in the air.

The room detonated into chaos. I tried to move, tried to scream, tried to reach him, but I had no control, the vessel's power coiled around my ribs like iron bindings as it flowed through me and into my father.

Dacre's dagger collided against my father's blade, the impact sending a burst of sparks skittering across the stone. But I could see it, feel it.

My father was toying with him.

No, no, no.

Magic crackled through the air, a suffocating storm of power that made my skin prickle and burn as I forced myself onto my knees. I could barely track their movements, their figures weaving between light and shadow, the clash of metal a brutal symphony.

Dacre was fast. But somehow, my father was faster.

Every strike, every vicious thrust of Dacre's dagger, every deadly arc, my father countered with ease. As if he had been waiting for this fight.

The power rolling off them shook the chamber. The torches lining the walls flickered wildly, shadows twisting and writhing like specters against the stone.

A dagger whistled through the air, a silver streak aimed for my father's throat. My father shifted, dark magic bursting from his palm, and the dagger hit the ground with a sharp clatter.

Another dagger flew through the air, faster than the last, and a strangled sob tore from my throat.

Kai's gaze flicked back to the guard before him, to the guard who now charged against Wren. They had come. They were fighting.

Kai's hand moved like smoke catching in the wind, and another dagger soared through the air, but magic collided with steel as the dagger didn't meet its mark.

Dacre's movements turned desperate, sharp and brutal, a warrior refusing to fall.

But I could feel it, the shift inside me, the sickening pull of my father's power as it bled through me, siphoning from me.

His hunger slid down my throat, a taste that wasn't my own. It coated my tongue, like the moment before a beast strikes, when hunger becomes certainty, when the kill is inevitable.

I could already taste his satisfaction, the ruin, the power.

And I knew if I didn't move, if I didn't stop this, Dacre was going to die.

Dacre staggered, his body folding as his knees slammed into the stone. The sound cracked through me, louder than any thunder, sharper than any blade.

I couldn't bear to watch. I would not lose him.

With every ounce of strength I had left, I clawed my way up, my hands slipping against the cold, unforgiving ground. My breath came in ragged gasps, shallow and trembling, my body a battlefield of agony.

But I couldn't stop.

Not when Dacre was still fighting for me. Not when the

bond between us strained, screamed, a raw wound torn wide open.

A distant shout cut through the haze, followed by the roar of boots pounding against stone. There were more guards. A wave of them. I could hear their steel hissing from their sheaths, could feel the death they carried rushing toward us.

Micah cursed violently, darting forward to intercept them, his blade a flash of silver as he cut down the first guard to reach the doorway.

I froze.

Micah.

He moved like a man possessed, blade carving through flesh without hesitation, without mercy. Not for my father. Not for the king he was sworn to protect as a part of his guard.

A sharp, bitter taste coated my tongue. He showed no loyalty to my father, and my mind staggered under the weight of it.

He had been standing beside my father, watching, guarding, but now he was killing for me.

The hate I had clung to curled in on itself, twisting into something else, something sharp-edged and uncertain.

"Wren!" I screamed for her, my voice shaking, raw.

She was already moving, already sprinting toward me. She dropped to her knees, her hands skimming over my face, my shoulders, searching for injuries even as she trembled.

"We have to go." Her voice wavered, but her grip on me was strong, urgent. "Come, Verena. We have to get out."

A laugh slithered through the room, cold and tainted with amusement. The sound wrapped around me like a slow-working poison, seeping into my pores, winding into my lungs.

"Foolish." My father's voice was silk and steel, a quiet thing that promised devastation.

He lifted one hand, palm open, poised to strike, while the other pressed firmly against the vessel. He was still tethered to it, still taking. I wasn't giving him enough.

A violent wrenching tore through my chest, a force so brutal it felt as if my very soul was being unspooled from the inside out. The vessel, my father, ripped into me, an unrelenting pull that sent ice flooding through my veins. He was taking everything.

A jagged scream caught in my throat as my body lurched forward.

Magic, black and violent, exploded outward. I barely had time to see it coming before the force of it slammed into Wren.

Her strangled gasp hit the air as she was flung backward, her body colliding hard into Kai's. They crashed to the ground in a heap of tangled limbs, and the sharp, wet sound of impact sent nausea curling up my throat.

The room fractured into chaos. A wall of guards surged into the chamber, their footsteps thundering against the stone floor. Micah still fought near the doorway, his blade a silver blur, desperation etched into every strike. He was fighting, cutting them down, but there were too many.

"Shit, Wren." Kai had Wren's head in his hands, his fingers pressing against the deep gash at her temple, blood slicking his palms.

His magic curled at his fingertips, but I could see it, the trembling, the way his body sagged with exhaustion. He was too drained. And Wren wasn't moving.

The world fractured around me, spinning too fast, tilting at an angle that sent me reeling. I couldn't find my footing, couldn't find my breath. I was drowning in the chaos, in the blood, in the screams.

And they were fighting for me.

I saw Kai's hands slick with Wren's blood. I saw Micah outnumbered, the guards slamming into him now from every side. I saw Dacre, still on his knees, breath ragged, pain twisting his features.

They were fighting, and they were losing.

Dying.

A sound ripped from my throat, raw and feral, a scream that wasn't just pain, wasn't just rage. It was terror. The storm inside me was snapping, convulsing, the magic twisting, desperate to be free.

I fought it, fought to hold it in, but it was too wild. Too much. It burned, crackling against my ribs, pushing against the fragile barriers of my body until I thought I might shatter.

I squeezed my eyes shut and tried to control it, tried to tame it.

My nails bit into my palms until the skin split, my teeth sank into my lip, copper flooding my tongue, but still the magic didn't obey.

It roared.

A surge of raw, electrifying energy erupted inside me, bursting through every fiber of my being like a dam breaking and unleashing a raging torrent. It flooded through my veins and consumed me completely until I could no longer tell where the magic ended and I began.

My body thrummed, the power inside me pulsing, seething. It licked up my spine, curled around my ribs, and settled into my bones, a symphony of fire and fury.

And still, I let it consume me.

I opened my eyes, and the world blurred in heat and rage. My father stood just beyond Dacre, smiling. His cruelty dripped from him like poison, his pleasure thick in the air, feeding off the torment he had crafted.

And Dacre was on his knees, bleeding, gasping, reaching for me.

Panic and fury ignited inside me, fusing into something uncontrollable. Power swelled, raged, howled for destruction, for vengeance.

My father's hand lifted, fingers curling into a fist, aimed at Dacre.

Another scream tore from my throat, feral, broken, unstoppable. "No!"

Dacre was closer to me now, so close, but I couldn't reach him. I couldn't stop this.

I reached out for him, a sob tearing from my lips, and a raw, uncontrollable force erupted from my chest, a storm of unbound, raging magic. The entire chamber convulsed, the ground cracking beneath me.

The air shook as the magic swallowed everything, sending everyone in the room flying.

Through the chaos, my gaze snapped to the Sight. She stood unmoving, untouched by the devastation, her white hair gleaming like a specter in the dark. Her eyes were glassy, distant, as if seeing something none of us could.

A whisper curled through my mind. *A tide, a choice, a reckoning.*

But I had no time to decipher its meaning, no time to dwell on the destruction I had wrought, because Dacre was still on the ground.

His pain lanced through our bond, a raw, visceral thing, and I pushed myself up, my legs trembling beneath me as I staggered forward. The vessel shook with every step, a furious, writhing beast inside me, but I didn't care.

I called out to it, not as a prisoner, not as a pawn. I demanded that it bow before me, that it bend to my will.

The air was thick with smoke, the sting of burning magic curling in my throat, but I barely registered it. Because the moment I stood, my father struck.

Dark power slammed into me, crushing, suffocating, wrapping around my throat like iron chains. He was still trying to control me, still trying to own me, but I wasn't his to command.

Not anymore.

"That's it, Verena." His voice was a ragged, breathless thing, but still, he smiled.

He leaned against the vessel, one arm wrapped around his ribs, his breathing uneven, but his eyes never left me.

Studying me. Weighing me.

"You feel it now, don't you?" he murmured, almost reverent. "What you are? What you can be?"

Something inside me twisted. I wanted to hurt him. *Gods,* I wanted to watch him break the way he had broken me. I wanted to take Dacre's dagger and carve him apart, piece by piece, until there was nothing left but the wreckage of a man who had spent his life taking.

"Look what you're capable of," he said, voice dripping with approval. "Feel how powerful you've become."

The magic inside me preened at his words, basked in them, and bile rose in my throat.

This was what he wanted. This was what he had always wanted. To twist me into something he could use. To make me love the power the way he did.

Once, I might have given anything to be this girl, to be the heir he had always wanted, but that girl was dead.

Magic roared through me, writhing, as if it couldn't decide who it belonged to, who I belonged to.

But it slowed as we felt him. A sharp, searing pulse through my bond. Dacre's desperation cut through me like a razor, slicing through the storm inside me, dragging me back from the abyss.

I snapped my gaze toward him just as he staggered to his feet, blood staining his skin, his face twisted into a snarl of rage.

"I'll kill every one of them." The words slithered through the air, and everything inside me froze.

I turned to my father, my pulse a deafening roar in my ears as I tracked his gaze, not on me, not on Dacre.

On them, Wren and Kai.

Kai was hauling Wren to her feet, his hands steady, but his eyes locked on to my father with pure, unfiltered rage. His lip curled back, teeth bared, like a wolf ready to tear out his throat.

"Don't fucking touch them." The words ripped from me, low and guttural, a snarl that barely felt like my own. I moved before I could think, shifting just enough to block his view of them, a silent threat.

His eyes slid past me as if I were nothing, and they landed on Dacre.

"Him, then?" He tilted his head, thoughtful.

His hands rose, one toward Dacre, the other toward my friends. Smoke curled from his fingertips, thick and black, dripping like oil. "Rulers must make hard decisions, Verena." His voice was almost gentle, deceptive. A father teaching a lesson to a child. "Sacrifice becomes a necessary evil."

The words twisted through me. Not them. Not him.

They were not a sacrifice I was willing to make.

My magic crackled, violent and untamed, scorching through me in a frenzied, brutal surge, and I didn't hold it back. Didn't restrain it. Didn't let him speak another fucking word.

I let it loose. A vicious, feral wave of power—mine.

It slammed into him with a force that sent him hurtling back, his body crashing into the vessel, hard enough that taste of ash flooded my mouth as I felt his bone snap.

The guards staggered, hesitated, and I felt it. Their fear. I could taste it, could feel it seep into the air like smoke. I fed on it.

"You will not touch them," I said, and my own voice felt wrong. Deeper. Rougher. Something more.

I rolled my neck, feeling the raw power licking up my skin, wrapping around my bones like a flame. And my father laughed.

Low, breathless, but not as calm as before. There was something else beneath it now. A crack in the foundation.

But still, he smiled.

"I can feel it," he murmured, bracing himself against

the vessel, steadying himself like a man gripping on to the last threads of his own power. "The way you have responded to it, and it to you."

I bared my teeth. I wanted to snarl, to spit my denial, to force him to choke on his own words, but he was right.

I could feel it slipping through my ribs, whispering through my veins, weaving itself into the marrow of my bones.

Not my father's power, not my own. The vessel's.

It wanted me. It was still taking, still pulling, whispering, begging—*stay, stay, stay.*

"No." My voice wasn't steady, wasn't sure, but I said it anyway as my stomach turned.

I shook my head, tried to shake the thing inside me loose, and my father's smile widened.

"Do you feel your pain fading?" He straightened, pulled himself up fully. "Think of what it could do, what we could do together."

I blinked. The pain that had once torn through me like razors, the agony that had stolen my breath, I could hardly feel it anymore, could barely feel anything except the way it moved within me.

Strong arms wrapped around me, pulling me back, and Dacre's breath was at my ear, warm, urgent.

"Verena," he murmured, and I could barely hear him. "We have to go. Now."

The bond between us roared back to life, a fierce tug-of-war against the vessel's hold. I was being pulled in two directions, my mind splitting, unraveling, caught in a haze of power and need.

A dagger flew through the air, the blade sinking into my

father's shoulder, and he let out a snarl of pain as my gaze snapped to Kai.

Dacre didn't wait for the impact to settle. "We're leaving!" he barked, but Kai was already moving, already lifting Wren, heading for the door.

The power inside me paused. It slowly pulled against me, but Dacre didn't give me a choice, didn't give it a choice.

His arms tightened, his grip unrelenting as he lifted me from my feet.

I sucked in a breath. The vessel was screaming, humming, begging. I could still feel it reaching for me, its claws in my skin, its voice in my head.

I couldn't control it, couldn't break it.

There were so many guards, so many obstacles that kept us locked in this palace, and I could feel the weight of them pressing in, a force we couldn't outrun.

Micah was still fighting, blood slipping from a wound on his arm. Kai's magic flared, a last-ditch attempt as he took out another guard, his exhaustion written in the slow drag of his stance.

They were all tired. They weren't going to make it out. We weren't going to make it.

Something inside me coiled, twisting tight, too tight, and then, Dacre's hand was on my face. His thumb brushed my cheek, calloused and warm, his grip steady, grounding.

"Verena."

A whisper.

A plea.

I locked on to him, on to the bond between us, on to the only thing keeping me from losing myself completely.

And I did the only thing I could do. I let go.

Not of myself. Not of him.

But of the vessel's hold.

And in its place, my own magic answered.

It ripped free from my chest, an explosion that sent the entire chamber quaking. Stone cracked, torches winked out, and the guards were flung back, their swords clattering against the stone.

Even Kai was sent to his knees, his hands bracing against the floor before he pushed himself up, reaching for Wren.

Dacre tightened his hold, his arms unrelenting as he sprinted toward the stairs.

The chamber trembled behind us, the vessel raging like a violent sea.

Micah was at our backs, Kai and Wren ahead, leading the way through the falling debris.

I looked back.

And the last thing I saw was my father.

Still on his knees, blood dripping from his nose, and his gaze locked on to mine.

His rage.

His hatred.

But beneath it—

A flicker of something else.

Fear.

CHAPTER 12
DACRE

The weight of Verena's body in my arms was all I could feel, all I could breathe, all I could think about as we ran.

She was too still. Too limp.

Her head lay slack against my shoulder, her body frighteningly light, her breaths shallow and uneven. I pressed my palm against her chest, needing to feel the rise and fall, needing proof that she was still breathing. But the magic beneath her skin was erratic, thrashing one moment, terrifyingly faint the next.

I had seen her fight. Had seen her break free of her father's grasp, had watched her unleash magic powerful enough to crack the very foundation of the palace. But now, that power felt like it had turned on her. She was slipping through my fingers.

Not again. Not this time.

"Faster," I snarled, my legs burning as I pushed harder, lungs straining with every breath. Wren and Kai were ahead, moving like shadows through the crumbling halls, but I didn't dare take my eyes off Verena.

The walls trembled, groaning under the weight of what she had done. Dust rained from the ceiling, choking me as we ran, and behind us, the deep, earth-rattling roar of stone breaking swallowed everything else.

My hands shook, holding on to her like she was the only thing anchoring me to this world.

Her magic pulsed again, wild and restless, as if it didn't know whether to die out or erupt. The sharp flicker of it sent a tremor through my fingers, and she whimpered softly against my chest.

It was a small sound, fragile, pain-racked, and it gutted me.

Her magic moved beneath her skin, flickered hot and cold, shifting unpredictably, as if it didn't belong solely to her anymore.

I gritted my teeth, a cold weight settling in my chest. *What had he done to her?*

Her father had spoken of the vessel, of how Verena had responded to it and it to her. I had seen its power as it rolled across the surface, seeming to devour everything in its path. It was like it was devouring her, coiling inside her like a living nightmare.

But what I hadn't felt until now was that it hadn't just taken from her, it had left something behind.

A scar. A presence. Something that didn't belong.

I couldn't begin to imagine the agony she had endured. The way he had torn her apart piece by piece, the way the vessel had tried to reshape her into something else.

A sickness curled in my gut.

She had fought against him, fought against what he wanted, but even now, even after breaking free, she wasn't entirely free.

I glanced at Wren. Her fingers clutched her side, blood seeping between them, but she didn't falter. Kai kept close to her, his arm a quiet anchor at her back bearing most of her weight, his magic still thrumming faintly in the air, a dull, pulsing heartbeat against the quiet.

Her gaze flickered to Verena. I saw it, the fear, the weight of everything that had happened.

I wasn't the only one shaken.

"How much farther?" I forced the words out, but my throat felt tight. The storm inside me hadn't settled. It had only grown darker, heavier. A violent, relentless thing.

"Not far," Micah said from behind me, his voice strained. "Just down this hall, then right into the tunnels."

I barely looked at him as my grip tightened around Verena, holding her closer.

We had to get her out. Now.

We tore around the corner, desperation sinking into our bones, and then we stopped short.

Half a dozen guards blocked the hallway, swords glinting under the uneven torchlight. The air shifted instantly, thickening with the promise of violence.

"Shit," Wren cursed, and she didn't hesitate to pull her dagger from its sheath.

The first blade swung, catching the light as it arced toward Kai and Wren. Kai surged forward, magic crackling like lightning as he threw up a shield just in time. Micah was already moving, ducking beneath a swinging sword and driving his dagger deep into a guard's gut.

The air sang with the whistle of a blade slicing toward Micah's throat. He barely had time to jerk sideways, the steel grazing past his ear.

"Fucking traitor," the guard spat, fury twisting his face as he lunged again, blade aimed to kill.

Micah caught his wrist mid-strike, his grip unrelenting. His dagger plunged deep, twisting with a brutal precision that sent the guard's breath stuttering out in a choked gasp. Blood seeped between Micah's fingers as he yanked his blade free.

Another guard surged toward Wren, sword raised, but Kai was already moving.

Magic roared, a wave of power slamming into the guards, and they staggered back, steel scraping against stone.

But it wasn't enough.

They were already recovering, charging at us again.

I refused to let Verena get caught in another fight. Not after everything she had already given. Not after everything they had taken from her.

With a snarl, I lowered her carefully to the ground, pressing one final, steadying hand against her chest before I turned. My dagger was already in my hand as I twisted, just as a blade came slashing toward me.

Steel screamed against steel as I caught the strike, shoving back with brutal force.

"You're not taking the heir from the palace," the guard growled, his voice dripping with venom. The word heir slid from his tongue like a curse, like Verena was nothing more than a title, a pawn in a game her father was playing with all of our lives.

Red-hot rage ignited inside me.

I shoved hard, forcing his blade wide. My knee drove into his ribs, cracking against bone. He gasped, staggering back, and I didn't hesitate. I twisted behind him, catching the back of his neck in an unyielding grip.

"She's not your fucking heir," I snarled into his ear, my voice laced with pure fury. "She's my mate."

The guard jerked just as my blade carved through his throat. There was a wet, gurgling gasp, a spray of blood, before his body slumped, lifeless, and I let him fall.

Another lunged at me, and I turned at the last second, my dagger snapping up to catch the blade meant to split me apart, the force vibrating through my bones.

The guard's blade scraped across my shoulder, slicing through fabric and skin, pain searing like fire licking through my veins. I gritted my teeth and ignored the pain, ignored the warm trickle of blood running down my arm.

I had fought a thousand battles before this, had faced worse odds, had spilled more blood than I could count, but this was different.

This wasn't a fight to survive.

I was fighting for her.

For Verena, who lay limp against the stone, her breaths shallow, too faint, too fragile.

For Wren, who bled freely from the gash along her ribs but fought like she didn't feel it, her dagger flashing, her jaw set with ruthless determination.

For Kai, who had pushed himself beyond exhaustion, his magic flickering at his fingertips like the last embers of a dying fire. His skin was pale, his breath ragged, but still, he fought.

This was my family.

And I would burn the world for them.

I would give everything.

Micah cut his way toward the tunnel entrance, his blade carving through flesh with brutal efficiency. Another guard lunged for him, but he pivoted sharply, dodging the strike before plunging his dagger into the man's side.

There were only two left between us and the tunnels, but the weight of time pressed against me, each second stretching, suffocating, closing in like a tightening noose.

Behind me, Verena let out a broken, breathless gasp, and something inside me snapped.

I turned so fast the world blurred. My hands found the nearest guard, fingers locking around his skull. Before he could react, I slammed him into the wall. Bone shattered beneath my grip, the sickening crack reverberating through my body. He crumpled, lifeless, before I had even registered his death.

The last guard turned toward Wren, and he didn't see me coming. I moved in the space between heartbeats, my fingers brushing the nape of his neck, warm, living flesh, before I wrapped my hands around it fully and twisted. His spine snapped beneath my hands. A chilling, final sound that I felt through my whole body.

I let him go and turned back to her, already moving before his body hit the ground. I dropped to my knees, gathering Verena back into my arms, curling her against my chest as if I could shield her from everything that had already been done.

My chest burned as I pushed forward, sprinting for the

tunnels, the weight of her in my arms grounding me, even as everything inside me begged to break apart.

"Move!" I snarled, my voice razor-sharp. Wren glanced at me, her concern flickering in the dim light, but I didn't stop. *Couldn't stop.*

We barreled into the hidden passage, Micah at the lead, his breath coming fast and uneven. The damp stone walls pressed in around us, our footsteps muffled yet urgent, swallowed by the darkness that stretched ahead.

The palace, the battle, the screams, it all faded behind us, the only sound now the shallow, uneven breaths rasping against my throat.

I bent my head, pressing my lips to the crown of her head, trying to anchor myself in the warmth of her skin, the fact that she was still breathing. Still here.

"We're almost there," I whispered, barely recognizing the rawness in my own voice. I needed to heal her, to check her for every wound her father had inflicted, to ensure that she was still whole. But we couldn't stop. Not yet.

The tunnel stretched endlessly before us, longer than I remembered, each step dragging, each turn pressing like an iron weight against my ribs. My patience thinned to a fragile thread. I wanted out. I wanted distance. I wanted her safe.

I wanted to be able to breathe.

Micah slowed as the tunnel constricted, the walls pressing in, the air thick with damp earth. I gritted my teeth. We were moving too slow, the tunnel too tight. It was all too fucking dangerous.

The passage funneled into a narrow throat of stone, forcing Micah onto his knees. He crawled forward, vanishing into the darkness ahead.

I exhaled sharply and jerked my chin at Wren. *Go.*

She hesitated for only a fraction of a second before dropping into the tight space, following him. I reached the tunnel's mouth just as Micah turned back, his hands extended toward me. Toward Verena.

"I've got her," he said, and my grip tightened around her, a sharp, instinctive refusal clawing up my throat.

No.

Micah's jaw tensed. "You're going to hurt her." His voice was steady, but there was an edge to it now, something taut beneath the words. "Just hand her to me until you can get out."

I didn't trust him. I would never trust him again, but I wasn't blind. I was too big for the tunnel. I couldn't carry her through without jarring her already battered body.

Every muscle in me screamed against it, but I forced myself to move.

Carefully, so fucking carefully, I lifted her, my hands reluctant as I placed her into his waiting arms. He gripped her firmly, and I scrambled out after them, my chest tight until I had her back, until she was in my arms again.

Micah exhaled sharply, but I didn't look at him. I didn't care about whatever thoughts lurked behind his dark, unreadable eyes.

I only cared about her.

I turned my gaze and took a deep breath as Kai emerged from the tunnel.

We were out, but we weren't safe. The priority now was

to reach the hidden city. My father's mistrust weighed heavily, but the hidden city was the only place I had where I stood a chance in keeping her safe.

"You're going back to the city?" I asked Micah, trying to think back to the plan we had made the night before.

He nodded. "I need to warn the others," he said. "The rebels in the city need to know what happened tonight. The war..." His gaze flickered to Verena. "It's coming faster than any of us thought."

"My grandmother..."

"I'll have her with me," he assured, his voice tinged with urgency. "She's no longer safe in the city. She never has been."

"Thank you." I gave him a stiff nod and adjusted Verena in my arms. "We'll see you in the hidden city."

Micah glanced at Verena before he looked to my sister, and his features were tight with regret as he disappeared into the darkness.

Kai muttered a curse, glancing back toward the tunnel. "We should keep moving. We need to get as far away from the capital as possible."

I didn't argue.

We were all bleeding, all exhausted, and Verena...

She hadn't spoken, had barely moved since we left the palace, and that terrified me.

So I held her close and let the world blur past us as we ran.

Branches tore at my skin, brambles slicing through my already torn uniform, but I didn't stop. The only thing that mattered was the weight in my arms, the shallow rise and fall of Verena's breath against my chest.

We didn't stop, even as Wren whimpered, and Kai lifted her in his arms. We kept going, and by the time the hidden city came into view, my legs were threatening to give out.

There should have been dread as we entered the city, but the sight of it sent a wave of relief crashing over me.

They were waiting for us.

Figures stood near the entrance, their weapons raised, expressions wary as they caught sight of us emerging from above ground. A murmur rippled through them, and then they shifted, some stepping forward, others stepping back as if uncertain whether to let us through.

Then Liya was there, pushing past the others, her face pale as she took in Wren's injuries, the blood staining my uniform, and the limp weight of Verena in my arms.

"Get the council," she demanded, panic creeping into her voice. "Now!"

The tension was instant, sharp, the air thickening around us.

I pushed past them all and moved to the street, the stone beneath me unforgiving as I slowly lowered Verena from my arms. I barely noticed the crowd pressing in, barely heard the whispers, the shuffling of boots as the people of the rebellion gathered around us.

The only thing I could hear was her shallow breathing.

I gently laid her down before me, my hands pressing against the cold stone as I hovered over her.

"Verena," I rasped, but she didn't stir.

The bond between us flickered, a dim thread, barely there. Her magic was still unsettled, thrumming erratically beneath her skin. She was alive, but I had no idea how badly her father had hurt her.

I brushed the damp hair from her face, my pulse thundering in my ears. Then, I pressed my hands to her ribs, to the fragile, struggling rise and fall of her chest, and I reached for my magic.

Golden light flickered at my fingertips. A sharp gasp rippled through the onlookers, but I ignored their unease. I poured my magic into her, coaxing warmth back into her skin, urging her body to heal, to fight.

"Come on, Verena," I whispered, my forehead pressing against hers. "Come back to me."

I focused on that bond that had tethered us together from the start. I pressed against it, begged it, and then—a spark.

A sharp, sudden pull.

My magic twisted as her body tensed, her back arching off the ground as her breath came in a shuddered gasp. A violent pulse of energy lashed out from her, slipping through that bond I had just been focusing on, and suddenly, the magic that I had been feeding into her was no longer mine to give.

My body seized as a force stronger than anything I'd ever felt surged through me, ripping my magic away in brutal waves. I gasped, but I couldn't move, couldn't breathe.

She was taking from me.

Siphoning.

A strangled noise escaped my lips as my limbs weakened, my vision darkening at the edges. The warmth I had been feeding into her bled from me now, and I could hardly register the shouts that rang out around us, the gasps, the distinct ring of weapons being drawn.

Liya staggered back, eyes wide with shock. A murmur rushed through the rebels like wildfire.

I couldn't turn, couldn't even lift my head, and I barely registered Kai cursing, barely heard Wren shouting my name.

All I could feel was the crushing, suffocating drain of my magic leaving me, slipping through my fingers like water I couldn't hold on to.

Until Verena's eyes flew open.

A sharp, broken gasp wrenched from her throat as she came back to herself, her magic snapping back, pulling away as if it suddenly feared me, and then she met my gaze.

The horror on her face hit me like a dagger to the gut.

"No…" The word trembled past her lips, and her magic snapped like a severed cord under her command.

I collapsed forward, catching myself before my body crashed into hers. I felt hollow, drained.

She was waking up to chaos, to the weight of her power pressing down on everyone around us, to the entire rebellion watching.

Verena scrambled back on trembling limbs, her movements frantic and unsteady. Her breathing was ragged and uneven as she stared at me with her eyes stretched wide in terror. She didn't look away from me.

"Dacre," she choked out, her voice quivering with fear.

"It's okay," I rasped, forcing myself upright. My limbs felt like lead, my head spinning, but I didn't stop. "You're okay."

Her hands curled into fists against the stone, and she shook her head wildly. "No," she insisted, her voice a mixture of disbelief and certainty. Her eyes darted around us, wide and frantic. "I *took* from you. I…"

"Verena, stop." I reached for her, brushing my fingers lightly against her, and she flinched.

Something splintered inside me as I watched her.

Her magic quivered in the air between us, wild and erratic, like a beast that had broken free of its chains. She was still too weak to control it, and I could see it in her eyes. She was terrified of herself.

She was caught in a battle between her power and her fear, and all I could do was watch as it tore her apart.

"You didn't mean to," I murmured, carefully keeping my voice steady and soothing. I started to reach out for her, my hand moving slowly through the air, but I hesitated and pulled back when I noticed the fear grow in her eyes. "We'll figure this out. Together," I assured her, my words a promise as solid as the ground beneath us.

"She's dangerous!" The words hit like a blade to my spine.

Verena flinched, curling further into herself. Her breathing was ragged, her hands trembling against the stone as if she were trying to make herself smaller, as if she could disappear beneath the weight of their stares.

"She's just like the king," another voice carried through the street, and the dam broke, rushing over us all.

Fear seeped through the gathered rebels, their hesitation souring into something worse. Their whispers turned to murmurs, their murmurs to voices.

"She siphoned from him."

"She took his power."

"She's a siphon. A true siphon."

"Like him."

Like him.

I heard the words, felt them pulse through the crowd, rippling outward in an unstoppable wave.

They feared her.

Not just my father, not just the council, not just the warriors who stood closest to us gripping their swords. It was all of them.

I saw it in Liya's sharp inhale, in the way she took half a step back. I saw it in the way Kai shifted, his body tensing, his gaze darting between the rebellion leaders like he was bracing for the inevitable. I saw it in Wren, the way her bloodied hands curled into fists like she wanted to reach for her daggers even though she was in no state to do so.

Verena could feel it too.

She turned her head slowly, her wide, shattered eyes flickering over the faces of the people before her. The people who had no idea how badly she had suffered to fight against her father. The people who now looked at her as if she were a monster.

I reached for her, no hesitation this time, no care about the fear she had over hurting me. I pulled her back against me, shielding her, curling my body around hers as if I could somehow protect her from the weight of what had just happened.

She had fought against her father, against the vessel, against the very magic that belonged to her.

But this was the battle she could not win.

Because the rebellion wasn't looking at her like she was one of them. They were looking at her like she was him, like she was her father's heir after all.

The words I wanted to say stuck in my throat, useless. Nothing I said would stop the way the fear festered. Nothing I said would undo what they had seen.

And then, through the murmurs, through the suffocating weight of fear pressing in on us from all sides, I saw him.

My father stood at the back of the crowd, standing just beyond the others, and he watched.

His gaze wasn't on our people. It wasn't on the council, or even on me.

It was on her.

He was staring at Verena as if he were already calculating his next move.

As if he had just seen something that changed everything.

As if he had just won.

CHAPTER 13
VERENA

The hidden city wasn't the same, or maybe I wasn't.

The first time I walked through these caves I had been a prisoner. A stranger in a rebellion that wanted nothing to do with me.

But now, I was something worse.

I was a threat.

The weight of a thousand eyes pressed against me, their whispers curling through the cavern walls like creeping ivy, and I could feel it, the way they looked at me, the way they watched every breath I took as if my next inhale could steal the air from their own lungs.

Because I had taken from Dacre. I had stolen from him, siphoned his power, drained him in front of them all.

I hadn't meant to. *Gods, I hadn't meant to.*

But I didn't have control. My magic had reached out on its own, had sunk its claws into him, ripped him open and drank him dry.

And I had let it happen.

I curled my fingers into his shirt, pressing my forehead against his shoulder, just to feel the rise and fall of his breath. Just to prove to myself that I hadn't ruined him the way my father had ruined everything else.

His heartbeat was steady. Solid.

Mine wasn't.

I sucked in a sharp breath, but it did nothing to steady me. Because I wasn't steady. I was breaking, and the city, it knew.

Dacre's grip on me never loosened. Not when we stepped deeper into the city. Not when the shadows of the rebellion closed in, their faces twisted with suspicion.

They didn't trust me, and he didn't trust them.

I could feel it in the way his arms tightened around me, the way his body shifted to shield me from their stares. I could see it in the sharp cut of his gaze, the way he scanned the streets, the way his fingers flexed against my skin, ready to draw steel at the first sign of danger.

The city wasn't the same, and I knew, it wasn't just because of me. Dacre had lived here his entire life. These were his people, his warriors, the ones who had once followed him without question.

But now they watched him with barely veiled suspicion in their eyes. They looked at him like he was a traitor.

He had chosen me, and in doing so, he had lost everything.

A hollow ache bloomed in my chest, sharp and all-consuming. I had stolen from him. Not just his magic. Not just his strength. I had stolen his home. His rebellion. His family.

And for what?

For a girl who had siphoned from him in front of them all, a girl who had taken what wasn't hers, a girl they would never trust.

A girl who was dangerous.

I dug my fingers into him, gripping the fabric of his shirt tightly between my fingers, and I looked up at him. I really looked at him, and for the first time since I had woken, I saw what my absence had done to him.

Dacre had always carried war in his bones, but this was different. He looked hollow. His eyes, the ones that had once burned with defiance, with life, with reckless confidence, were dull now. Distant. As if he had been trapped in some kind of torture from the moment I was taken, never truly sleeping, never truly living, just waiting.

Waiting for a moment that may have never come.

The sharp angles of his face were sharper now, his skin drawn tight over cheekbones that had once been carved with golden warmth. There was a fading bruise beneath his jaw, and the faintest tremor in his fingers where they held me.

Dacre didn't break, but he had unraveled.

And I had been the one to pull the thread.

A slow, aching pressure built in my chest, winding tight around my ribs. I had given so much, endured too much, but so had he.

And I had stolen even more.

I could feel it in the air around me now, the way the city itself recoiled.

It had always been alive, a quiet hum of existence beneath the ground. Warriors training, children laughing, people living despite all that my father had taken from them.

But tonight, the streets were still. Not hushed with reverence. Not holding their breath in relief.

They weren't celebrating our return. They were waiting.

Every shadow we passed felt like it held eyes. Every figure lingering in doorways and alley corners tensed as we moved through the streets. Not one person spoke. Not one person stepped forward. No one called out Dacre's name, not as a leader, not as a brother, not as a friend.

And I knew this wasn't just wariness. It was fear.

They weren't just looking at me. They were looking at what I had done, at what I had become.

Dacre's arm tightened around me, his grip sure and steady, but I could feel the tension in his body, a barely restrained storm, ready to break as we reached the large doors, already open and waiting.

The chamber inside was crowded with rebellion leaders, and the tension snapped into place like a snare. The moment they saw me, the moment they saw Dacre shielding me, the air curdled with anger, uncertainty, fear.

They didn't speak, not at first. But I heard it, the shuffle of boots as they edged closer, the sharp exhales, the clench of fingers around weapons. The weight of their eyes pressed into my skin, burned hotter than the bruises on my body.

I tried to stand on my own, tried to will the weakness from my limbs, but the moment my feet touched the ground, my knees buckled. Dacre's hands were on me instantly, steadying me before I collapsed. His touch was grounding, but it did nothing to stop the slow, creeping horror unfurling inside me.

They had watched me siphon from him. They had felt my power lash through the air, had seen how easily I took from him, drained him.

They had seen what I was.

And I had seen it, too. Felt the way my magic had hooked into him, desperate, insatiable, unwilling to let go.

They were afraid of me, and for the first time, I was afraid of me too.

Dacre pulled me firmly against his broad chest, every inch of my body melding into his warmth. His arm encircled me with gentle possessiveness, his hand resting securely on my stomach. He leaned down to place a soft, lingering kiss on my shoulder. It was a tender gesture, a kiss for everyone to witness, a silent declaration in front of them all.

One that I didn't deserve.

"She's a siphon!" The words struck like a blade, sharp and merciless, and I flinched. My body curled in on itself before I could stop it, as if trying to make myself smaller, as if I could somehow shrink away from the truth of the words.

"He'll come for her." Torin stepped forward, his face a mask of fury. I barely knew the man's name, had only seen him a few times. "He'll come for his heir."

It didn't matter that he hadn't shouted it. It didn't have to be loud to hit like a war drum.

Gasps. Footsteps scraping back. The murmur of voices swelled into a roar, the whispers turning to accusations, the uncertainty into something sharper.

Torin wasn't alone.

"Did you feel it?" another voice rang out. A woman's voice, raw with disbelief. "I did. She was taking from him —taking—"

"She drained him," someone else hissed. "If she can do it to him, she can do it to any of us."

"She'll bleed us dry, just like her father."

The words should have been impossible to hear over the chaos, but somehow, they sank in, lodged deep.

I dug my nails into my arms, as if that alone could keep my power contained, as if I could hold it all together before it spilled out of me again. But I could feel it, recoiling against their words, as desperate to hide as I was.

It wasn't just fear in their voices now. It was anger. Disgust.

Dacre's father stepped forward, and the room seemed to close in. His eyes found mine instantly. He wasn't just looking at me. He was weighing me. Measuring. Calculating.

A verdict in search of a trial.

And it didn't matter that I hadn't spoken a single word. He had already decided my fate. His gaze flickered once to Dacre. Then, back to me.

"You've brought war to our doorstep." The words hit like the lash of a whip.

The murmur of the crowd snapped into silence. The finality in his voice split through the room like a fault line.

Dacre stiffened. His grip on me tightened, his body locking around mine like armor.

"She can't stay here."

A woman moved before Dacre did. Her light hair glinted in the firelight as she stepped forward, placing herself between Dacre and his father, her sharp gaze flicking between them.

"And what, exactly, do you propose we do with her?" Her tone was even, unreadable. But there was a warning beneath it. A quiet blade waiting in the dark.

Dacre's father barely spared her a glance. "You know what must be done, Liya."

The room reacted first. A ripple of movement, a sharp inhale, the subtle shift of warriors tightening their stances.

"You mean to use her?" Liya pressed. "You're going to tell your son that after everything he just risked for her, after everything he's done, you would slit her throat like a lamb and hold her out for her father to feast?"

Dacre's hand left my waist, and he was moving before I could stop him. His father didn't flinch, but the room did. Several people took a step back. Liya didn't move at all.

"You gave me your word," Dacre growled as the space between them shrank. "I gave you the way in and you swore she would not be harmed."

Dacre slammed his hands into his father's chest, and he stumbled back, knocking into the stone wall. But Dacre didn't stop. His hands fisted into his father's leathers, his voice low and lethal.

"I gave you no such promises." His father's voice was steady, but it was impossible to miss the way he clenched his jaw or the blood rushing to his face in fury. "That was them." He nodded his head toward Liya, but Dacre didn't turn.

"You were the one scouring the kingdom for her not too long ago. It was you who was willing to do whatever it took to get her back." Dacre shoved him harder against the wall.

There was movement at my side, and I flinched before I saw Wren step forward, lining herself up with me. She looked awful, blood coated her clothes and splattered on her face, but she was standing at my side, staring straight ahead at her brother and father without wavering.

"I was willing to fetch the heir from the damn forest!" their father bellowed, his face a mask of fury. "But you, you have done far worse. You risked this whole rebellion to save that girl."

He spoke of me as though I were invisible, as though his piercing gaze didn't scrutinize every detail of my being, absorbing every fragment of vulnerability I couldn't conceal.

"That was before we knew what she was."

"She is my mate." The words cracked through the chamber like a thunderclap. Undeniable. Unyielding. "I'd risk every one of you to save her." Dacre's voice was steel, forged in fire, honed by war. "I'd risk everything."

My heart lurched, an uneven stutter in my chest, as the words settled over me like a death sentence. He had already risked everything.

The moment he found me in the forest, the moment he tore me from that palace, the moment he held me in his arms and whispered my name like a vow, he had made his choice.

And I was destroying him for it.

The bond, our bond, flared. It roared to life inside me, sudden and all-consuming, seeping into every fraying thread of me. Warm. Steady. *Him.*

My stomach curled violently, my hands trembled as I pressed them against my ribs, as if I could push the bond back, bury it, sever it.

He was standing here, daring them all to strike him down just so I could keep breathing, so he could protect me at his side.

I couldn't do this. I couldn't do this to him. Not again.

I staggered back, my body locking up as panic tore through me. I felt like I couldn't breathe, like the bond was pulling at me, pushing into me, trying to settle in a body that didn't deserve it.

I barely noticed the way the chamber erupted, the murmurs turning to shouts, a fevered, frenzied pitch of voices clamoring over each other. The council was no longer afraid. They were enraged.

"Then you are no son of mine," Dacre's father hissed. His voice was quiet, deadly. But the rage behind it was a blade unsheathed.

Dacre turned slowly, and I saw it.

The way his body went eerily still. The way his fingers twitched, like they ached for steel. He was one breath away from war with his own people, and I was one breath away from breaking.

Dacre was too close. His warmth pressed into me, steady, unrelenting, an anchor in the storm. The only solid thing in a world I was slipping through, and I couldn't handle it.

My pulse thundered. My hands shook. I couldn't breathe.

I jerked back, panic crashing over me in a violent, suffocating wave, but Dacre didn't let me go. His fingers wrapped around my arms as he pulled me in. His body coiled around mine, iron and heat, locking me in place, refusing to let me slip away.

"Verena." His voice was low, quiet, barely more than a breath, but I felt it everywhere.

I shook my head, pressing against his chest, desperate to pull away, to make space, to make the bond stop digging its claws into me.

"Verena." This time, his voice was insistent, his grip firmer. "Breathe."

I couldn't. *I couldn't.*

"She's dangerous," someone snarled. "Look at her."

I flinched. I already knew. I knew what I was, what they saw when they looked at me.

Dacre moved so quickly. One second, he was holding me, the next, he was turning, his body snapping toward the voice with lethal precision.

"She is not her father." The words slammed into the room, slammed into me, and everything stopped.

The shouts cut off; the whispers fell silent.

"She is not him," Dacre repeated, and this time, his voice trembled with rage.

His father scoffed. "She's his heir—"

"She was his prisoner," Dacre snarled.

Something deep inside me cracked. The words lashed through me, carving through the panic, cutting deeper than anything else in the room.

Dacre's chest heaved, his fists clenching at his sides. "You think she is dangerous? You think she is a monster? Then look at her. Look what he's done."

He turned to me with his jaw tight, his eyes dark. "You're asking me to choose between this rebellion and my mate, but I already chose. I wouldn't care if it was poison that runs through her veins, I will still choose her."

I stiffened, my gaze snapping up to search his face.

"You've doomed us all," his father spat, drawing my attention back to him. "You brought a dying flame into a forest already burning, and now you expect us to just hope she won't damn us all? You want us to pray to the gods that she won't do to us what we all witnessed her do to you?"

"I won't..." I said suddenly, my voice hoarse and raw. "I didn't mean to."

The room went silent, and I looked around the room at the leaders who stood there with nothing but distrust on their faces.

I stepped around Dacre, ignoring the way he tensed, ready to pull me back.

"I know what my father has done to you, to your people," I said, my voice quiet but steady. "I cannot change my past, or who my blood belongs to."

I turned slowly, giving my back to Dacre's father and the rest of the council. My hands were shaking as I reached for the hem of my shirt, as I pulled the fabric up, as I bared the wreckage carved into my skin.

"This is who I am to my father." My whole body trembled, yet I held on to my shirt, refusing to let it fall. I wanted them to see it all, the landscape of scars etched into my skin over the years. Some were pale and faded, mere whispers of past pain, while others were freshly healed, their edges still pink and tender.

And then there were the wounds that still wept with blood, raw and angry, as if the hurt was too deep to ever fully close.

Gasps. Curses. Someone made a strangled noise in the back of the room.

The room moved around me, stepping closer, stepping away, crowding in and recoiling all at once.

Wren made a choked sound, and I looked at her, allowed myself to take in her sorrow. Her eyes were fixated on my back, transfixed by the raw agony etched into it, and I hated that I had to allow her to see it.

I looked away from her as my chest ached, but Kai was almost worse. His expression was a tempest of fury, his features twisted into a mask of barely contained rage.

But it was Dacre who I could hardly stand to look at.

His body went rigid as the color drained from his face, and he looked like he was about to collapse under the weight of what he was witnessing. His eyes flickered over each scar, and I could almost see the gears turning in his mind as every bit of his guilt set into place.

My arms ached with the weight of holding my shirt up, with the weight of all the eyes scraping across my back.

I let them look. I let them see the truth.

"Your father did this to you?" The voice wasn't sharp this time. It wasn't angry. It was Liya. She was watching me, her expression haunted. She wasn't looking at the scars. She was looking at me.

I nodded. Just once before I let my shirt fall back into place, as I forced myself to meet their stares.

"You're right to fear me." My voice was raw and quiet. "I don't trust myself, either."

I swallowed hard, my throat tight, my ribs locking around my lungs. "If you think I will hurt you, if you think I will be your ruin, then imprison me."

"No." Dacre's voice wasn't quiet. It wasn't soft. It was a growl of pure, unrelenting fury.

His grip locked around my wrist, not hard, not cruel, but unshakable.

I didn't turn to look at him. I couldn't. "Do whatever it is you need to do, but don't send me back." I looked up at his father, met his eyes when I wanted to do anything else. "I'd rather you slit my throat than send me back to him."

Dacre was breathing too hard against me. His hands were shaking.

"No." This time, his voice was softer, only for me, and I finally looked at him. His eyes burned, flickering gold in the torchlight. "You did not go through hell just to be treated like this."

"Dacre…"

"No." He cupped my jaw, tilting my face up toward his, forcing me to really look at him. His fingers pressed against my skin, gentle but firm. "You are mine."

"She will stay in the cells until the council decides her fate."

I barely had time to register his father's words before Dacre's hand slipped away from my face and he moved like a shadow. His hand shot out, fisting his father's leathers, and he jerked him forward until their noses almost touched.

Weapons unsheathed in a sharp chorus of steel that sang through the chamber, but it didn't matter. The moment they saw Dacre's face, the absolute, undiluted rage burning in his eyes, no one moved.

"If you put her in a cell," Dacre snarled, his voice thick with something dark and dangerous. "If any of you lay a single finger on her, I will burn this city to the ground."

And this time, no one doubted that he would.

I didn't let go of her until the door was shut behind us, sealing us away from the world outside.

Even then, my grip only tightened.

Even when I heard Wren and Kai step away, giving us space, I could see the worry covering my sister's face. Even when I felt the tension still gripping this city like a noose, its people watching, waiting for a sign that they were right to fear her.

Even when I could still hear my father's voice fighting to lock her away, his fury a blade at our backs, and Liya, the only voice of reason, cutting through the chaos. Even when I knew it wasn't a victory, just a temporary reprieve, a battle stalled but not yet won.

I didn't care.

I had her in my arms, and after everything she had endured, after nearly losing her, losing us, I refused to let her go.

Not now. Not ever.

I held her against my chest as I walked deeper into my room. It was dimly lit, with the fire in the lantern reduced to a flame that appeared to be losing its life. The scent of leather and old parchment filled the air, familiar but suddenly foreign.

This wasn't where I belonged. Not anymore.

She was.

Verena barely stirred in my arms, her breath featherlight against my throat. Her fingers had twisted into the fabric of my shirt, clinging desperately as if fearing I might vanish if she didn't hold on tight enough.

I knew I should speak, say something to ease the weight pressing down on us, but words felt futile. What could I possibly say that could erase what had been done? What could I utter that would undo the terror that lived in her eyes since I found her in the chamber, broken and bleeding?

There was nothing.

I lowered us both onto the edge of the bed, the mattress dipping slightly under our weight.

She let out a soft noise, something between a sigh and a whimper, and my grip on her tightened instinctively.

I pressed my lips tenderly to the crown of her head, needing to feel her warmth, her presence, to anchor myself in the reality of her being here.

"Verena," I finally murmured against her hair, my voice barely rising above a whisper.

She shuddered, just a faint tremor that rippled through her, but I felt it.

Her delicate fingers flexed gently against my chest, but she didn't lift her head.

I ran a slow, tender hand down her spine, feeling the sharp edges of her bones, the places where her body had wasted away under her father's cruelty.

I clenched my jaw so tightly it ached.

I had been too late.

She was here, she was alive, but I had still been too late.

"I need to get you cleaned up," I said softly, brushing a kiss against her temple. "I need to make sure there are no other wounds that need to be healed."

Her breath hitched, but she didn't answer, she simply clung harder to me.

I stood, cradling her gently against me, as I moved us to the bathroom. I shifted my hold, carefully lowering her to her feet, and forced myself to pull away.

It nearly killed me.

Verena stared at me, her eyes wide with uncertainty, with *fear*. Her gaze flicked around the small room as I quickly started the bath, filling the tub with steaming water and oil.

The room quickly filled with the scent of clove as steam rose from the water.

When I turned back to Verena, she hadn't moved and her eyes were still haunted. Her hands were clasped tightly in front of her, her shoulder drawn tight, as if she were trying to shrink into herself.

I inhaled deeply, steadying myself before lowering to my knees in front of her. My fingers gently reached for the worn, tattered edges of the shoes on her feet.

She stiffened.

"Verena." I lifted my gaze to hers, making sure she was here with me, not lost in the memories. "It's just me."

She swallowed hard, the motion visible in the tense line of her throat. "I know," she replied, but her voice was fragile. It was small.

I waited.

I would never rush her.

Her hands trembled as she reached out, gently resting them on my shoulders. Her fingers felt cool and hesitant as she steadied herself before cautiously lifting one foot. I quickly removed her shoe, the worn leather slipping off easily, before she lifted her other foot, allowing me to do the same.

The room was quiet, filled only with the sound of the rising water.

I reached for the ties of her trousers, deftly loosening them and sliding the fabric down her legs.

As she stepped out of them, her legs came into view, revealing the tapestry of bruises in various stages of healing, painting a silent story of pain on her skin.

I stood up, the gravity of her pain threatening to crush me.

Her hands shook visibly as she reached for her shirt, fingers fumbling with the hem before she slowly lifted. The fabric inched its way up her stomach, and I shuddered at the state of her skin. She moved it higher, the shirt gliding over her ribs and chest, until it finally slipped past her shoulders and over her head. She let it fall to the floor, the fabric pooling around her feet.

Angry red marks crisscrossed her flesh, wounds still

healing, while dark bruises bloomed like storm clouds against her too pale skin.

A slow, controlled breath escaped my lips.

I reached for her, carefully sliding one arm behind her back and the other beneath her knees. With a gentle lift, I cradled her against my chest, feeling the warmth of her broken body against me, and I moved closer to the bath, where steam rose in soft tendrils from the water's surface.

Slowly, I lowered her, allowing her feet to dip into the warm water.

"Tell me if it's too much," I murmured softly.

She responded with a small nod, her eyes meeting mine.

I let her body sink fully into the water, which rose to drench me up to my shoulders. She sighed softly as I cradled her head and laid it back against the tub's edge.

I started running a cloth over her arms, gently wiping away the layers of dirt and remnants of dried blood.

I hated how fragile she felt beneath my touch, how easily I could feel every ridge of her ribs, every sharp angle where there used to be softness.

But she allowed me to care for her.

She let me have this.

I worked in silence, watching her, studying her face and the way she bit the inside of her cheek every time the cloth passed over a particularly tender spot.

I could barely contain the torrent of anger that surged within me, a seething fury that boiled over with each fresh scar or wound I discovered. It felt like a wildfire raging through my veins, consuming every rational thought and leaving only a blistering heat in its wake.

I gently brushed the cloth over the wound at her side, and she sucked in a sharp breath, her body jerking away from me instinctively.

I immediately dropped the cloth. "I'm sorry."

She shook her head, her eyes betraying the storm of emotions despite her words. "You didn't..." she managed, though her breath was uneven and ragged. "I'm fine."

But she wasn't.

I lifted my hands, gathering what magic I could still feel within my fingertips. "Let me finish healing you."

"No." The word was sharp, sudden.

She snatched my wrists with trembling hands, her grip feeble yet frantic. Her eyes met mine, wide with panic. "No, Dacre. You can't. I might..." The words faltered on her lips.

She couldn't even say it, but I knew.

I could see the fear etched into her features. She feared that she might take from me again.

My chest constricted as I gently pried her fingers from around my wrists. "You won't," I assured her.

Her response was a silent shake of her head, breaths fast and shallow, hands trembling as they curled into fists under the water. "I won't risk it."

The fear in her eyes pierced me, a reflection of my own guilt.

I cupped her face in my hands, tilting her chin so she had no choice but to look at me. "You won't hurt me," I insisted. "I trust you."

Her eyes blazed with uncertainty, a storm of emotion swirling within. "I don't trust myself."

I leaned in and kissed her, the action driven by instinct rather than thought. There was no hesitation, just an overwhelming need to bridge the gap between us.

She softened into me instantly, her hands moving to my shirt and clenching the fabric like a lifeline.

I needed her.

Needed to remind her of what we were, that this bond between us was stronger than her fear.

She melted into me as I deepened the kiss, her fingers trembling as she clutched at me with a mix of urgency and uncertainty. Her lips parted beneath mine, soft and desperate, a silent plea for something neither of us could put into words.

I slid my hand up the back of her neck, threading my fingers through her damp hair as I pulled her closer, needing her, needing this—needing to feel her warmth, her life, after so many nights fearing what I had lost.

Her breath hitched, a delicate gasp, as I dragged my lips over the corner of her mouth, tracing a path along her cheek until I could whisper against her skin, "You are not your father."

A shudder ran through her, a ripple of emotion, but she didn't pull away.

I pressed my lips against the delicate skin beneath her ear, letting my lips linger there for a heartbeat. "You will never be him, Verena."

Her hands tightened in my shirt as a ragged breath slipped from her lips.

I kissed her again, gently, reverently.

I wanted to pull her into me, wrap myself around her

until she forgot what it meant to be afraid. I wanted her to forget everything until she only knew this, only knew me.

But when I felt her shift, her body stiffening, I forced myself to pull back.

Her eyes were wide, haunted, her breathing still unsteady.

She was still drowning in that fear.

I ran my hands slowly down her arms, then took her wrists in mine, holding them between us, letting her feel the steady beat of my pulse. "I trust you," I said again, softer this time.

Her eyes flickered to my wrists, as if she could still see the place where she had once siphoned from me, where she had drained me without meaning to.

I knew she would never forgive herself for it.

"Come here," I murmured, shifting so I could brace my arm behind her back, supporting her weight. "Just let me hold you."

She hesitated.

Then, slowly, she moved toward me, pressing her forehead against my shoulder, her breath warm against my throat.

I let out a quiet exhale, wrapping my arms around her, one hand smoothing down her back. She was too thin, too fragile, but she was here.

She was here.

And I would give everything to keep her that way.

Her fingers tangled in my hair, pulling me closer as she sighed into me, a sound that sent a slow ache curling through my chest.

When we finally pulled away, I let my forehead rest against hers, our breaths mingling.

"I love you," I whispered. I couldn't hold it in any longer, couldn't risk not getting the chance to tell her exactly how I felt.

She let out a shuddering breath, and when she spoke, her voice shook. "I love you too."

I needed more.

I needed to feel every part of her.

I lifted her from the tub, her damp skin pressed against me as I carried her back into the room. She didn't fight me, didn't even hesitate. She just pressed into me as if she belonged there.

I set her down on the edge of the bed, reaching for the towel, and wrapped it around her gently, tucking the fabric against her shoulder. She clutched it tightly, her hands barely peeking from the folds.

Her skin was still damp, the ends of her dark hair curling as water dripped from them. She looked small. So small.

And I hated it.

I knelt before her again, my hands resting on her knees. "Come here," I murmured, gently tugging her toward me.

She listened.

She slid forward, letting me press between her thighs, her body pressing into mine until I could wrap my arms around her, until there was no space between us.

Until there was only us.

She buried her face in my shoulder, her hands fisting in my shirt. "I don't want to close my eyes."

I exhaled sharply, pressing a kiss to the top of her head. "Then don't."

She let out a soft laugh, but it was hollow, empty.

I hated that too.

I pulled away just enough to tip her chin up, forcing her to look at me.

"We made it back," I said, my voice steady. "You're safe. And I will burn this fucking world to the ground before I let anything happen to you again."

A flicker of something passed over her face, something fragile. "I know."

I let my forehead press against hers, closing my eyes. "Then let me hold you while you sleep."

She hesitated.

But then, she nodded.

I stood, lifting her with me, and she let me. Let me settle her in the center of the bed, let me climb in beside her, let me pull the blankets up around us.

She pressed into my side the moment I lay back, her fingers resting lightly against my chest, feeling my heartbeat.

I ran a slow hand down her back, pressing a kiss to her forehead.

I could feel the tension in her body, the lingering terror that clung to her even now.

So I held her tighter.

I pressed my lips against her hair, against the crown of her head, against her temple, willing her to feel me.

"I've got you," I murmured. "I'm not letting go."

She exhaled softly, the breath fanning across my throat.

Slowly, her body relaxed, her breathing steadied.

Her hands pressed against my chest, her fingers curling into the fabric of my shirt.

I kissed her forehead once more, lingering.

Then, finally, finally, sleep pulled her under, and I stayed awake, holding her, watching over her, because I would never let anything take her from me again.

CHAPTER 15
DACRE

I didn't want to leave her.

Not when she was still asleep in my arms, not when every breath she took felt like a silent war against everything she had endured.

But I had to go.

Because while she lay curled beneath the blankets, safe for now, the rebellion was deciding what fate they would allow her.

As if the choice was ever theirs to make.

I shifted carefully, peeling myself from the bed, but the moment my warmth left her, she stirred. Her fingers twitched against the fabric of my shirt, grasping blindly, as if reaching for something just out of her reach.

"Dacre…" Her voice was rough with exhaustion.

"I'm right here." I brushed my lips over her temple, breathing her in, trying to stop the ache in my chest. "Go back to sleep. I will be back soon."

She blinked slowly, fighting it. "Where…?"

I ran a hand down her spine, grounding her. "I need to speak with the council," I murmured, running my lips along her cheek. "Wren and Kai are going to take you to the springs once you're ready to wake."

Her lips parted, a sliver of panic flashing in her eyes.

I cradled her face between my hands, forcing her to look at me. *To see me.*

"No one will take you from me." I searched her eyes, watched as her pupils flared at my words. "No one."

She stared at me for a long moment before slowly nodding.

I exhaled, resting my forehead against hers. "Wren will be with you the whole time."

She swallowed hard, and her magic stirred beneath my fingertips. "And you?"

"I'll find you the second this is over."

I didn't wait for her to reply. I couldn't, or else I wouldn't leave at all.

I kissed her before I walked away from her and pulled my bedroom door open. I looked back at her one last time to remind myself that she was safe, to try to stop the burning desire to never leave her side again.

Wren and Kai were already waiting outside, their faces grim.

"She's still sleeping," I said, my voice tense. "Do not leave her side."

Wren nodded, already reaching for the door. "We'll be with her."

Kai's eyes met mine, sharp and knowing. "We'll keep her safe. You handle the council."

I moved through the halls with sharp, purposeful

strides, but I could feel the city watching me with every step I took. The air felt different today, tighter, thinner. The weight of a thousand unspoken fears pressed into the walls. The council wasn't the only ones waiting for a verdict.

They all were.

She wasn't one of us. She was his heir. She was dangerous.

I could feel the words, feel their fear, whispering through the city, and I clenched my fists, forcing my pace steady. I had never wanted to be my father's son. But tonight, I needed the power that came with it.

Verena was the daughter to the king, and I, I was the son to the rebellion leader.

Verena was not their prisoner, and I would make sure they knew it.

The closer I got to the chamber doors, the sharper the tension wound in my gut. I swept my gaze around the corridor, searching for any sign of my grandmother. Of Micah.

They were supposed to be here. Micah had promised to bring her.

I hadn't wanted to place trust in him again, not after what he had allowed to happen to Verena in that palace, but he was the only choice I had.

I needed my grandmother in the hidden city. I needed to leverage the way they all respected her, to use her against my father in a way that only she could provide.

He was the rebellion leader, but my grandmother, she was something else entirely. She had served the queen, served this rebellion, and she had lost her daughter to the cause.

And if Micah was lying, if he had betrayed us—

I exhaled sharply through my nose, forcing the thought away.

Micah had too much to lose. His sister was still in the king's hands, and he knew that this rebellion was his only chance of getting her back.

I still didn't trust him, and I would never forgive him.

But I needed him.

And right now, I needed my grandmother more.

I reached for the chamber doors, my jaw set, my pulse a slow, steady war drum in my chest.

The moment I stepped inside, the talking stopped. Not gradually. Not in murmurs that faded into silence. The moment my boot crossed the threshold, the room silenced like a blade severing sound itself.

I had their attention, their fear, and I welcomed it.

I let the door shut behind me, the sound echoing through the cavernous space. Familiar faces turned to stare. Some I had fought beside. Some had trained me. Some I had bled with.

Now, they looked at me as if I had already betrayed them. As if siding with Verena had already signed their death sentence.

Good. Let them be afraid.

If they feared me, they wouldn't touch her. If they feared me, they would know that I would do whatever it took to keep her safe.

My father stood at the center of the chamber, waiting. His expression was carefully neutral, but I saw the triumph in his eyes. He had already won them.

The council had been divided, but I could see it, the

way they leaned toward him, their expressions wary but persuaded. He had already started his work.

But it wasn't just the council who was packed into the chamber now. My father had brought others who would aid in his cause, elders and soldiers alike. All of them loyal to him, all of them fearful of her.

"We must discuss what is to be done about the heir," Enora, one of the elders, spoke first.

Heir. Not Verena.

I clenched my jaw so hard it ached.

"She's a liability," my father said smoothly, stepping forward, his voice calm. Calculated. "Her magic is unstable as we all witnessed last night, and her father will do whatever it takes to get her back."

A murmur rippled through the room, and I let it settle before I spoke. I knew their arguments, knew their fears, and my father had probably spent the entirety of the night helping those fears fester while I held Verena and tried to make hers disappear.

"The king is desperate." My voice was like iron. I let my words settle, let them cut through the thick tension strangling the room. "And we all know what happens when men become desperate." I looked to my father. "They make poor decisions. They make mistakes."

I took a slow step forward, sweeping my gaze over the council. "I've given you the location to the tunnels." My voice was calm, but the edge beneath it was sharp. "Verena has more knowledge of the palace than all of us combined. She can help us."

A few of them shifted uncomfortably.

My father tilted his head, watching me carefully. "That

is exactly my point, boy." His voice was smooth, even. "Do you really believe he's just going to let her slip through his fingers so easily? She knows the palace, she knows the king, and he isn't going to allow his secrets to stay hidden in the rebellion that wants him dead."

He let the question linger, let the weight of it sink in before his gaze flickered over the room.

"And worse," he continued, his voice soft but dangerous, "what happens when she wants to go back to him?"

A murmur rippled through the room, and I felt the anger in my chest crack like wildfire.

"You dare suggest that she—"

"I suggest," my father interrupted smoothly, "that her loyalty is not so clear-cut." He turned his attention back to the others. "Tell me, Dacre, are you so blinded by your feelings for her that you don't see the truth of what she is?"

My hands balled into fists as I shifted, trying to control the anger that grew with every word he spoke. "The truth is that she is not your prisoner."

I wanted them to hear me, to let what I said sink into the very marrow of this rebellion.

"She is not your enemy," I continued, letting my eyes sweep across the chamber. "She is not a weapon. She is not a siphon to be locked away, or a blade to be pointed at her father. She is a girl who barely escaped with her life. A girl who has suffered more than anyone in this room can begin to imagine. She is not him."

No one spoke, they didn't move, but my father smiled. Slowly.

"You say she is not him," he murmured, his voice quiet, taunting. "But she took from you, didn't she?"

My muscles locked, and his smile only grew.

"We all saw it, Dacre. We felt it when she siphoned from you. We felt the way she stole the life from your body until there was almost nothing left." His eyes shuddered, and for the slightest moment, I thought I could see fear in his eyes. Not for himself, for me. "Tell me, did it feel different than what her father has done to us our whole lives? Did it feel like she was protecting you in the way you are dying to protect her?"

No. It had felt like drowning in her. It had felt like being consumed.

A few of the council members nodded, their eyes dark with unease, as my father's words spread through them, fermenting their fears until they became more potent with each passing moment.

"She didn't mean to," I snarled. "She would never—"

"She would never?" My father laughed, cold and callous. "Don't treat us as if we're fools, Dacre. We all witnessed what she did. What will stop her from doing it again?"

I stepped forward, my rage barely leashed.

"You're all so focused on fearing her," I growled, letting my own magic crackle at my fingertips, "that you've forgotten who the real enemy is."

I let my gaze sweep the room, let them see the fire in my veins, the truth written in every inch of me.

"The land is already dying," I continued, my voice hard as stone. "The rivers slow, the earth wilts beneath his rule. You think you can hide in these caves forever? You think you can outlast his cruelty?"

I pointed to the ceiling, to the kingdom that lived above

us. "Walk outside this city. Look at the land. It is rotting. It is withering beneath his magic, beneath the vessel."

A few murmurs rippled through the room. They knew. They had seen it too. We had all seen it for years.

And still, no one moved. No one spoke.

They just sat there like fucking cowards as if their silence somehow negated the truth, but then the doors opened, and they could hide no longer.

"You fear her power, but I do not."

The council turned, shocked gasps ringing out around us as my grandmother stepped through the chamber doors with Micah at her back.

Her eyes were twin mirrors, reflecting like the cool glow of the moon, and her gaze was unflinching, piercing through the chaos and landing directly on my father.

And he was watching her back, his gaze fixed intently on her as she moved farther into the room until she could look upon each and every person inside.

"You say you fight for this rebellion," she said softly, but there was a knowing lilt in her voice. "You say you fight for freedom, but you are afraid of the only one who can truly stop him."

She turned her head, sweeping her gaze across the council. "The king will not stop. He will bring Marmoris to ruin just as he did with the others. He will devastate your home just as he did with Veyrith."

"This has nothing to do with a forgotten land." My father bristled. "We are not fighting for Veyrith."

"You should be." My grandmother's gaze snapped back to my father's, and he flinched. "Verena is the last daughter of Veyrith, but there were many daughters before her."

She took a step forward.

"The queen."

Another step.

"My daughter."

Her voice sharpened.

"Me."

A slow, tense silence stretched through the chamber. Not one of us daring to utter a word. "I watched Veyrith die," she continued. "I watched the land beg for mercy beneath his rule. I watched as he took and took and took until there was nothing left to give."

She stared at my father, so close to him now that she could reach out and touch him if she chose to. "And you think hiding in these caves will save you?"

She took another slow step toward him, and he recoiled, the sound of his boots stepping back away from her echoing for us all to hear.

"You will starve beneath these stones," she murmured. "You will rot in the darkness, just like the land above you."

It was as if she had poured a bowl of molten lead into the room, each word heavy and thick as it landed and coated the air with an oppressive weight. She turned back to the council with a somber grace.

"You do not have to trust her," she said simply. "You do not even have to fight beside her, but you will fight for her. Because she is the only future you have left."

The chamber shifted. A ripple of unease spread through the council as my grandmother turned, her presence filling the space like a tide rolling into the shore.

She did not look at me. She did not look at my father.

Her gaze locked on to the rebels who had barely seemed to breathe since she arrived.

"She is his heir, Elis," my father roared, but she moved as if she hadn't heard him.

"That is not what she is." Her voice was quiet, but it commanded the attention of every soul in the room.

My father scoffed, his nostrils flaring. "Then tell us, what is she?"

My grandmother tilted her chin, her silver eyes gleaming like steel in the torchlight. "She is the tideborn."

The word slammed into me like a strike to the ribs.

Tideborn.

The word had been written on the statue beneath the capital city, in the ruins that led us into the palace, in the whisper of stone carved long before we were born.

A tethered soul to shifting sands.

It was a warning etched into the bones of the past. My blood ran cold as the words whispered in my mind.

Verena had been written into fate long before any of us knew her name.

"The king has spent his reign trying to rewrite the prophecy, to bury it beneath his rule," she urged. "But we are the only ones who have forgotten. The land has not. The sea has not. The vessel has not."

She turned, meeting my father's glare with something sharper than defiance.

"You call her dangerous." She let the words settle. "But that is because you know the truth. This war does not end with you. It does not end with this rebellion. It ends with her."

A profound silence settled deep into the chamber,

enveloping the space with an eerie stillness. It was not the silence of agreement; it was the heavy, oppressive silence of fear. I could feel it wrapping around the rebellion leaders like a vise.

They had devoted their entire lives to waging a war they believed they could win, a war that had not accounted for fate.

My father sneered. "Prophecies are for fools and kings desperate to hold their thrones."

My grandmother did not flinch. She did not waver.

"The king believes in this prophecy," she murmured. "Why else do you think he kept her alive?"

"What prophecy?"

My grandmother looked at me then, stared into my eyes as the words began falling from her lips. "When shadow swallows the golden throne, and rivers run dry where magic has flown. The cursed shall rise with fate-bound hands, a tethered soul to shifting sands."

Everything inside me stilled. I couldn't find my breath, couldn't stop the crushing weight of her words.

"Born of ruin, blood, and war, bound to take yet cursed to mourn. The tideborn's gift, bound in chain, to break the bond or bind again."

The words slammed into me like a hammer to stone.

My magic lurched. It coiled tight in my chest, like something ancient was twisting inside me, something that had been waiting. Waiting for *her*.

The bond flared. Not gently. It roared. A crack of heat racing through my ribs, searing through my veins like wildfire.

My breath locked in my throat, and for a moment, all I could breathe was her.

The prophecy wasn't just words. It was a thread, stitched into the very fabric of this war. It was woven into Verena's blood, into the magic that I felt writhing beneath her skin.

It had been waiting for her.

"The tide has already begun to rise." My grandmother's voice felt like it was whispered through a fog.

I clenched my fists at my sides, forcing myself to breathe, to steady my pulse, but the bond between us was still deafening inside me. It pulled at me, weaved within me, as if it knew.

The room shifted, murmurs rising again, uncertainty growing like a storm on the horizon. I met my father's gaze, felt the weight of the choice ahead. He saw it too.

This was no longer his rebellion.

This was hers.

"We either rise, or we drown."

CHAPTER 16
VERENA

The air felt different here.

Heavy.

Every breath I took pressed against my ribs like an invasive weight, a reminder of the expectations that now rested upon me.

The rebellion had allowed me to stay, but I wasn't safe.

Not from the whispers. Not from their eyes, tracking my every movement, waiting for proof that I was exactly what they feared me to be.

A monster.

The word had not been spoken aloud, but I heard it in every murmured conversation that stopped when I entered a room. I saw it in the tension that stiffened their spines whenever I walked past.

I wasn't one of them, and I never would be.

I would always be a part of my father, a part of the man that they hated, that they fought against.

I was a new monster born of the one they knew.

The realization settled deep in my chest, curling cold fingers around my lungs as I stood in the training room, a place that had become my constant since returning to the hidden kingdom only days ago.

A single torch flickered at the edge of the space, illuminating Kai's sharp features as he stood before me. His expression was unreadable, but his posture was relaxed, hands clasped behind his back as he observed me.

To my right, Dacre's grandmother sat on a smooth, flat stone. She was calmer than I had expected, her presence deceptively quiet. But there was something unshakable about her. A force.

A strength that had nothing to do with her small, frail size.

"Again," she said.

I exhaled, forcing my focus back to the task at hand.

The stone in front of me was small, barely the size of my palm. It was an easy target. Lifeless. Safe. I reached for it, or at least, I tried.

The magic in my veins flickered, twisted, resisted. It wanted more. Not a stone. Not something that had nothing to give.

A sharp pulse slammed into my ribs, and I gasped as I fought to reel it back.

"No," Dacre's grandmother murmured, watching me closely as she gently shook her head. "Focus on the stone."

A shudder ran through me, my irritation building. "My magic doesn't want the stone," I bit out.

She said nothing, just continued to watch me, and my stomach turned as I pulled my gaze away from her and pushed against the force inside me, urging it toward the object, forcing it to take.

A spark of energy jumped from the rock. A flicker. Then, nothing.

My knees trembled, threatening to buckle, but I pressed my hand against the cave wall before they could.

"You're pushing too hard," Kai said, his voice steady, even. "You need to feel your magic, let it settle inside you. You can't force it."

I clenched my jaw, wiping a thin layer of sweat from my forehead. "It doesn't want to take from things that don't have life."

Dacre's grandmother hummed in agreement. "That's because it isn't what it was meant to do."

"Then why try?" I argued, every bit of my frustration evident. "Why waste our time?"

"Because you must learn control."

The answer was simple, brutal, and I hated it.

My fists clenched at my sides, while I tried to force down the biting remarks on the edge of my tongue. I was *trying*. But they didn't understand what it was like to have spent a lifetime believing you were powerless, only to discover you had the capacity to hold more power than you ever wanted.

To hold a power that you wish you didn't have at all.

A power that stole.

I could feel that very power moving inside me, and a muscle jumped in my jaw. "I can't do this."

"You can," Dacre's grandmother answered immediately. "You just don't want to."

I lifted my gaze to hers. She didn't flinch, didn't soften.

"I want to control it," I whispered, and I could feel my blood rushing to my face, could hear it in my ears. "Of course I do."

"No." She shook her head, but her silver eyes didn't leave me. "You want it to go away."

The words punched through me like a blade, my magic coiled inside me, watching her, and I turned, desperate to stop the feel of it inside me.

The training had taken its toll. I had already given too much today, and my body and mind were paying the price.

Fatigue enveloped me, and I didn't know how much more I could take before I lost control, before I did something I would regret.

"Verena." Wren's voice had me snapping my head up to look at her.

I hadn't even heard her come in.

She stood at the entrance, arms crossed over her chest, watching me with an expression I couldn't quite decipher. Not pity. Not fear. Something else.

I exhaled sharply. "I need air."

She didn't try to stop me as I pushed past her, but her footsteps followed. We walked in silence through the shadowed corridors, the stone walls rough and jagged. I wanted to run my hand against them. I wanted to feel the rock dig into my palm, to feel the pain of what it would do to my skin. I wanted to feel anything other than this power.

"You're doing better than you think."

I let out a hollow laugh as I pushed stray hair out of my face. "That's not what it feels like."

"It never does." Her words were soft, almost sad, and I looked at her, really looked at her.

She was staring straight ahead, her face carefully neutral, but there was something tight in her posture, something rigid.

It made my chest feel like it was caving in. "I'm sorry. For everything that's happened."

Her steps faltered, but she didn't look at me. "You don't have to apologize."

"I do." I stopped and turned to face her fully, forcing her to meet my gaze.

"I know that I lied to you," I admitted. "And I know I'm not easy to trust."

Her throat bobbed as she swallowed, then, finally, she exhaled. "You had to lie to keep yourself safe," she murmured. "I don't blame you for that."

It hit me then what she had seen, what she had watched me take from her brother, and I didn't blame her for hardly being able to meet my eyes. I could barely stand to look at myself. "And for what I did to your brother." I looked away from her and bit down on the inside of my cheek. "I can't tell you how sorry I am for that. If I scared you…"

"Verena, stop." My name snapped from her lips, and she reached out, her hand wrapping around my bicep. I hated the way I flinched at her touch. I loathed the way I knew she felt it. "I'm not scared of you."

Her words slammed into my chest, making it difficult to breathe.

"I'm the one who is sorry," she said hesitantly, and my gaze snapped up to her.

"Wren—"

"I should have known." Her voice broke. "I am your friend, and I should have known that something wasn't right. I should have been there for you, so you didn't feel like you had to leave in the middle of the night alone."

I shook my head, but she didn't stop.

"If I had been a better friend…" Her hand on my arm tightened, and I could see her guilt eating at her. "You would have never gone back to your father."

I flinched, but I couldn't look away from her eyes, at the way they bored into me. "He would have never been able to touch you, never been able to give you those scars."

I could practically see the memory in her eyes, the way she had looked upon my back, the way it haunted her.

I reached for her, taking her trembling hands in my own, and Wren blinked as if startled. But she didn't pull away. Instead, she stared ahead, her jaw tight, her shoulders squared in a way that made her look so young. So broken.

I had spent so much time drowning in my own pain, in my own fear, that I hadn't stopped to consider how much I had hurt the people who had cared about me.

How much I had hurt *her*.

"Wren," I said softly, squeezing her hand, "I made my choices. Not you."

Her throat bobbed as she swallowed, but she still wouldn't meet my gaze.

"I should have seen it," she whispered. "I should have noticed how much you were struggling, how trapped you felt."

I didn't answer because we both knew the truth. I *had* felt trapped. I *had* struggled, and I *had* left her behind when I ran.

I had left her, and I had never really stopped to think about what it must have been like for Wren, to wake up and realize I was gone. To be left behind without a word, without an explanation.

"You are my very first friend in this world," I whispered. "Even when I didn't realize I needed one."

Her fingers tightened around mine, and they were the only thing keeping me from drowning.

"I thought I was doing the right thing," I admitted.

She inhaled sharply as she studied my face. "By leaving?"

"After Dacre found out who I really was, after your father did, I thought I had to do it alone. I thought I could..." I broke off, looking down at our hands. "I thought I could make things better if I could get out of this kingdom."

Her voice was barely above a whisper. "But it made it worse?"

I didn't answer because we both knew the truth.

Silence stretched between us before Wren let out a slow breath.

"You're back now," she said, her voice softer.

I nodded. "I am."

"Do you regret it? Not making it out of the kingdom?" she asked.

The question hit me like a punch to the ribs.

Yes. *I regretted everything.*

I regretted leaving Wren behind that night, regretted the lies, the pain, the choices that had led me to my father's feet. I regretted who I had become in that palace. I regretted what I had done to Dacre, what I had taken from him.

But more than all of that, I regretted that I had failed.

That I had fought so hard to be free, fought to escape,

fought to run, and in the end, I had been dragged back and remade into something I didn't recognize.

Something that took.

Something that I didn't know how to stop.

I sucked in a sharp breath, my fingers twitching against hers.

"I don't know who I am anymore," I admitted. The words were a raw thing, scraped from the deepest, most fractured part of me. "I thought I was doing the right thing by running, but all I did was bring myself back to him. And now…" I let my head drop back against the cave wall, my eyes squeezing shut. "Now, I fear myself as I once feared him."

"Verena…"

I looked back at her, let her see the depth of fear in my eyes. I didn't hide a single trace of it. "They all fear me." I motioned to the city around us. "And they are right to do so. I am just like him."

I let the words fall from my lips, the words that I had hidden inside myself and didn't dare speak.

"How can you say that?" She stepped closer, her warmth seeping into my cold. "I saw what he did to you. I saw you on that chamber floor. I saw the way you fought against everything, against him, against what he wanted to make you." Her eyes searched mine. "You are nothing like him."

I swallowed hard, my throat tight. I didn't believe her, but I wanted to. *Gods, I wanted to.*

"I'm a siphon." I let out a slow, shaky breath.

"I know." She didn't tell me I was wrong. She didn't tell me there was nothing to be afraid of. She just stood before me, solid and unmoving. "And I don't care what you are. You are my friend, and that is all that matters."

I let out a slow, shuddering breath and nodded, just once, and she returned the gesture, a flicker of understanding passing between us.

Then, as if sensing I couldn't take any more, she exhaled sharply and bumped her shoulder against mine. "Come on," she said, her voice lighter, though the weight of our conversation still lingered between us. "Let's go find Dacre before he kills someone in your honor."

A small, startled laugh escaped me. It wasn't much, but it was real.

This was real.

Wren grinned, looping her arm through mine as we started walking again, her presence grounding me, making it easier to breathe.

The city stretched around us in shadowed tunnels and dimly lit corridors. It was quieter now, the late hour settling over it like a hush, but that tension still lingered in the air, that ever-present watching, that whisper of fear that followed my every step.

But Wren didn't hesitate as she led me forward, her grip solid on my arm, her steps confident. Like she didn't care what they thought.

Like she knew where I belonged.

And right now, she was leading me straight to him.

We turned a corner, stepping into a wider street near the underground river, and the moment we did, I heard his voice.

"Whatever you think you know, I promise you, you

don't." Dacre's voice was sharp, barely leashed fury crackling in the air around him.

Wren sighed. "I was joking about finding him before he killed someone, but I think I might have been right."

We picked up our pace, rounding the corner just in time to see Dacre facing off with Eiran. A cold rush of something sharp lurched in my stomach.

I hadn't seen Eiran since that night in the woods, since the moment I realized he had been using me all along.

He looked the same. The same light brown hair, the same unreadable face, but now, standing before Dacre, I saw him for what he was. *A coward.*

And Dacre looked ready to tear him apart. His jaw was clenched so tightly I thought his teeth might crack. His hands curled into fists at his sides, knuckles white and straining against his skin.

Wren cleared her throat loudly. "Are we interrupting something?"

Dacre's gaze snapped to mine, and just like that, the tension in his body shifted. He didn't say a word. He just moved.

Three long strides and he was in front of me, his hand finding my wrist, his fingers wrapping around it with a grip that was firm but careful. Always careful.

"Are you okay?" His voice was quiet, soft, but still carried that sharp edge of anger, as if he was barely holding himself together.

I swallowed hard, feeling the warmth of his touch seep into my skin. "I'm fine."

His gaze flicked over me, scanning for any signs of harm, any proof that I wasn't fine. His hands followed, skimming over my arms, my waist, my ribs. His magic curled against mine, searching, checking.

I wanted to push it away.

And the way he looked at me told me that he knew, but he didn't stop. He brought my wrist up to his lips, pressing a kiss against my hammering pulse.

"She did well in training." Wren leaned against the wall, picking at her nails. "Better than she gives herself credit for."

Dacre's eyes lingered on mine, searching for answers I didn't think he'd find, before he nodded. Then, slowly, he turned back toward Eiran, but his hands didn't leave me.

"We're done here."

Eiran's eyes flashed with annoyance before he hesitated. "Verena…"

"Don't you dare fucking speak to her." Dacre's voice was a whip crack, low and dangerous. "I said we're done."

"I just wanted..."

"To what?" Dacre asked, turning to face Eiran again and tucking me behind his body. "Tell her how you wanted to abandon her in that palace with her cruel father? How you didn't care what happened to her, even if you had been able to hear her screams, you still would have left her there?"

My body went rigid, and I hated how weak I felt, how useless.

Eiran's face was impassive. But I saw it, the flicker of guilt when my eyes met his. "I am sorry, Verena."

A deep growl ripped from Dacre's chest, and Eiran turned before he could say anything else, disappearing into the shadows.

Dacre exhaled sharply, his fingers tightening around my wrist, before he turned and tucked some stray hair behind my ear. I leaned into his touch without thinking.

"Eiran's a damn creep." Wren shuddered, crossing her arms. "I'd like to tell him exactly where he can shove his fake apology."

Dacre's fingers laced through mine, wrapping around me. "Come with me."

I didn't fight him. I didn't want to.

"Yeah, sure. I'm good. You two go," Wren said sarcastically, but when I looked back at her, she winked.

"We'll see you later, Wren." Dacre didn't stop; he didn't slow his steps as he led me forward.

"Yeah, yeah. I guess I'll go find Kai and give him hell about something."

I smiled at that as I followed Dacre, but the moment we were alone, my mind reeled. Seeing Eiran again had rattled something loose in me. I hadn't thought of him in weeks, hadn't wasted a single breath mourning the friendship I thought we had before he had proven otherwise.

But now I was hit with it all over again, how little he had cared for me, how willing he was to turn me over to Dacre's father.

How I was nothing more than exactly what they wanted me to be.

Dacre's hand tightened around mine as we climbed the stairs toward his room. He didn't slow, didn't speak, didn't let go, and the moment the door shut behind us, the tension in his body snapped.

His breath left him in a long, slow exhale, like he had been holding it in since the second I walked onto that street. His shoulders were rigid, his muscles taut beneath his shirt. I could almost see the frenzy of emotions beneath his skin, like dark clouds gathering before a storm.

I could feel his restless magic through our bond.

"You're angry," I murmured.

His gaze snapped to mine, and they were so dark, *so alive.* "Of course I'm angry."

I stepped closer, placing a hand against his chest, feeling the erratic rise and fall of his breaths beneath my palm. "Because of Eiran?"

"Because of everything," he admitted, his voice rough and edged with frustration. "Because of him. Because of what they say when they think you're not listening. Because no matter how many times I tell them, they still don't understand that you are not a threat to them."

I let my fingers curl into the fabric of his shirt, feeling his warmth beneath it. "I am a threat."

His jaw tightened, a muscle twitching beneath the skin. "Not to them," he insisted, his eyes dark with determination.

I shook my head slowly, strands of hair slipping over my shoulders. "I'm a threat to everyone. Even you. Especially you."

His hands settled on my waist, steadying me. "Not to me," he murmured, his fingers pressing into my hips with a tenderness that sent a shiver down my spine. His hands were so gentle, so careful.

I lifted my chin and searched his face.

"Stop," I whispered. *I begged.*

His brows knitted together in confusion. "Stop what?"

"If you really don't fear me, then stop treating me like I'm going to break."

Something flickered in his gaze, a shadow of hesitation, a glimmer of uncertainty.

"Verena…"

I stepped closer, until there was barely any space between us, until I could feel the heat of his body against mine, feel his heart hammering within my own chest.

"Everyone is treating me differently," I murmured. "Like I'm broken." My throat tightened. "I don't want that from you."

His fingers flexed against me.

"You've been through hell."

"And I'm here with you now."

His hands shook, and I took the smallest step back, putting a breath of space between us.

"I know what I did." I looked away from him; I could barely stand to look him in the eye as I said it. My mind was racing, my warring emotions flooding me. I wanted him to reach for me, to stop being so careful with me, but I also wanted him to never touch me again, to never risk what I was capable of again. "I'm scared of myself." Another step back. "I'm scared to touch you."

His breath caught, a sharp intake of air that sent a chill down my spine, then he moved so quickly I didn't have time to stop him. I didn't have time to think.

His hand shot out, his fingers wrapping around the back of my neck, and he tugged forward until any space I created between us was gone. Then his lips crashed against mine with no hesitation, no caution.

His other hand slid up my back, wrapping around my

shoulders as if he could pull me inside him, as if he could undo the distance that had ever existed between us.

I melted into him, pressing closer, gasping as his tongue swept over mine. He swallowed the sound, tilting his head to deepen the kiss, his fingers curling into my hair, tugging just hard enough to make my breath catch.

I could feel him everywhere, his touch, his heat, his unshakable presence grounding me even as he was unraveling me at the same time.

But then his hands were moving, tracing down my back, gripping my waist, guiding me toward the bed.

He didn't stop kissing me.

I could feel the warmth of his chest against mine and the hardness of his arousal against my stomach, and I whimpered as his teeth grazed over my neck. My entire body was on fire, every nerve alight with need. His hands were everywhere, moving over my skin as if he were trying to memorize the feel of me, igniting sparks of pleasure that coursed through me.

His touch seared my skin; his teeth drew a deep ache low in my belly.

I clung to him, lost in the emotions and sensations that were crashing over me. Every touch brought an intensity that threatened to consume me.

There was only him and me. Nothing or no one outside of those doors mattered at that moment.

Dacre lifted me effortlessly, and I wrapped my legs around his waist as he pressed my back against the wall.

He met my gaze, and the hunger in his eyes matched the fire in my veins. I arched into him, craving more of what he was giving me, more of this feeling that reassured me that I was here with him, that I was no longer alone and desperate for escape.

Dacre's lips trailed down my neck, his teeth grazing over my skin as he moved lower. A moan escaped my lips as his hands slid under my shirt, the warmth of his touch igniting a wildfire within me. He growled against my skin as his hands kneaded and clutched at me.

I tightened my legs around him, pulling his hips impossibly closer to mine, and his touch became more frantic.

"You drive me insane," he murmured, his voice a low, gravelly rumble that sent shivers down my spine. One of his hands slid beneath my ass, gripping firmly as he lifted me higher against the cool, hard surface of the wall. His head dipped, and I felt the warmth of his breath against my skin as his lips trailed a languid, reverent path over my stomach. He continued upward, his lips brushing softly over my scarred ribs, lingering with a gentle, almost sacred devotion.

I was utterly consumed, enveloped in a haze that left me helpless against him.

His touch was maddeningly soft yet intoxicatingly intense, sending waves of pleasure through my body. He pushed my shirt up higher. His eyes locked on to mine, desire staring back at me, then, slowly, he ran his tongue over my nipple almost teasingly.

I inhaled sharply, the breath catching in my throat, and before I could exhale, he had already taken my nipple into his mouth.

"Oh gods," I whispered, my voice a soft plea as I pressed my head back against the wall. My fingers instinctively tangled in his hair, digging my fingertips into his scalp as if anchoring myself as he dragged his teeth over my sensitive flesh.

He moved lower once more, running his lips along my stomach as his hand reached the waistband of my pants.

His fingers, deft yet trembling, untied them with ease before he gently set me back on my feet. Slowly, he slid my pants down my legs, followed by my underwear, leaving me bare before him. My shoulders pressed against the wall, while my shirt remained hitched up, my breasts heaving with every breath I took.

I stood there in a daze, lost in the way he was looking at me, until he fell to his knees before me.

His hands wrapped around the backs of my calves, and he slowly, achingly dragged them up until he reached the backs of my knees.

"The rest of the kingdom will fall to their knees before you, Verena." He leaned forward and pressed a kiss just below my belly button before he stared up at me. "But please allow me to be the first." Another kiss, this time on my right hip bone. "Allow me to show you how you should be worshipped." The next kiss was on my left hip bone, and my hips surged forward, desperate for more. "Allow me to show you where I will gladly spend the rest of my days if you let me."

I sucked in a breath feeling the heat radiating from him as he knelt before me, his hands still clasped around the backs of my knees, his breath warm against my skin.

He pressed another kiss just above my pussy, and I gasped as my fingers tightened in his hair until he groaned.

"Tell me, Verena." He ran his tongue along the inside of

my thigh, his nose skating over my pussy. "Tell me what you want."

"I want you." My voice was breathless but sure. "I've always wanted you."

His eyes were dark with desire as they met mine, and he didn't hesitate as he lowered his head and ran his tongue along the length of my pussy. A shudder ran through me as pleasure shot straight to my core, and I dug my nails into his scalp.

"Dacre," I moaned his name as he rolled his tongue against me.

He tightened one of his hands behind my knee, lifting until he placed it over his shoulder, widening me before him, and I barely had time to adjust before he sucked my clit between his lips.

"Fuck," I cried out as my leg threatened to buckle beneath me.

He wrapped his hands behind me, gripping my ass, and he pulled me forward until there wasn't an inch of space between him and my core.

Waves of pleasure washed over me, making me moan and writhe against the wall. I clung onto him for support, my fingers pulling at his hair as he consumed me with his mouth.

I was lost in the way he was touching me, begging him for more, while pushing his head away when I thought I couldn't handle another moment.

"Please," I begged breathlessly, desperate for release. "Please let me come."

He sucked my clit back into his mouth, this time harder, and I clamped my eyes closed as my magic roamed under my skin as desperate for him as I was. It felt reckless, uncontrollably so, and suddenly, I wanted him to stop.

"Dacre, wait." I pulled at his hair, but he wasn't listening. "Dacre, my magic."

He looked up at me, his gaze dark and as out of control as I felt.

"It wants you." I shook my head trying to explain something I didn't understand. "I'm scared I'll take from you again."

He swallowed, his Adam's apple bobbing in his throat, my arousal still coating his lips.

"Take anything you want, love." One of his hands snaked around my hip until it pressed against my lower stomach. "Take from me until I have nothing left to give. I am devoted to you. Everything I have is yours to take."

He pressed hard on my stomach until my ass hit the wall, and I had no room to escape.

"Do you hear me, Verena?" He was watching me so carefully, so intensely. "I am drowning in my want for you, and there is no room inside me for fear. Take from me, touch me. Feed your body with what yearns for you. I would ruin every part of me to give to you."

I turned my head slightly, looking away from him, from his words.

"Look at me," he demanded, and I couldn't deny him. "I am yours, and you are mine. There is nothing beyond that. No fear between the two of us."

"But…"

He cut me off by leaning forward and nipping at my pussy.

Dacre pressed his lips to my inner thigh again, slower

this time, reverent. His breath was warm, his touch firm but gentle, grounding me when I felt like I was unraveling from the inside out. His hands, strong and sure, gripped my hips, holding me steady as his lips traced a slow, agonizing path along my skin.

My magic curled inside me, restless, eager, wanting.

But I was terrified.

It had taken from him before, drained him without my control, without either of our consent. What if it happened again? What if I lost myself in this, in him, and when I came back to my senses, I found him weakened beneath me?

What if I couldn't stop it?

"Dacre," I whispered, my fingers tightening in his hair, my chest rising and falling with shallow breaths. "I don't trust myself."

His gaze snapped up to mine, dark and wild, his lips still glistening from me. "Then trust me."

His hands slid higher, pressing into my waist, his fingers flexing as if to remind me that he was here, that he was unshaken. "I have never feared you, Verena. And I never will." His voice was rough, steady, a vow carved from stone. "You are mine." His grip on me tightened. "And I will not let you go another second thinking you are anything different."

I sucked in a sharp breath, my vision blurring for just a moment.

I was shaking as his hands smoothed up my thighs, tracing over my skin like a prayer. He was looking at me like I was something sacred, something holy, and it made me ache to the point of pain.

"I need you," I whispered, the words tumbling from my lips before I could stop them. "I need you, Dacre."

His jaw clenched, and his eyes flickered with something raw.

"Then take me," he murmured. "Take what you need."

A shiver ran through me, a tremor of fear and want that coiled inside my chest. Without another word, I reached for him, pulling him closer to me, and he didn't hesitate. He dove back into my flesh like a man starved, and I gasped as he easily brought me back to the brink.

His hands were everywhere, pleasure followed, and I could barely hold myself upright when he slid a finger inside me. He curled it forward slowly before sliding it back out and in again.

"Dacre."

"Do you like that, Verena." He pumped his finger into me again before adding a second. "Do you like feeling me inside you?"

I nodded my head, the pleasure rushing through me making me unable to form words.

"You're so fucking wet," he growled and pumped his fingers into me harder. "I want to feel you come against my mouth then again around my cock. I want to feel every part of you as I remind you of who you are, of who you belong to."

Dacre's words were like fuel to the fire inside me, flaming the desperation that coursed through me. My hips bucked against him as he stretched me with his fingers and flicked his tongue against my clit.

"Please," I gasped, unable to hold back any longer. "Please, Dacre."

"Come for me, Verena," he murmured against my pussy before he pressed his mouth firmer against me, his hand moving quicker.

I couldn't stop it then, couldn't control the pleasure or my magic as it raced through me. I fell over the edge as I screamed, and I clung to Dacre as I fell, crying out his name over and over.

"That's it," he hummed against me. The vibrations sending jolts of pleasure laced with pain through my body.

He held me tight as I shook against him, waves of pleasure still pulsing through my body. He pressed a soft kiss to my thigh, his hands soothing over my skin as he slowly lowered my leg.

"Are you okay?" he asked softly, his hands running down the outside of my thighs.

I nodded as I slowly came back to myself and blinked open my eyes.

Black magic filled the room; it surrounded us, and I knew that it was mine. This magic, this chaos, it belonged to me.

"Dacre." My voice shook as I looked him over, scouring his face to see if I had hurt him.

"You're incredible." He groaned before pressing another kiss on my belly and rising to his feet. "I have longed for you since the day they stole you away from me. I have begged the gods to make me strong enough to get you back."

I moved away from the wall slowly, my body still trembling from the intensity of my orgasm. Dacre reached for me quickly, steadying me, and I gasped as his hands moved over me, devoted and sure.

"I have hungered for you for every moment that I searched for you, and now that you're here, I will never have enough power to let you go again." He leaned forward, his lips pressing soft, searing kisses along my collarbones, up my throat, until his breath was hot against my ear.

"It was you," I whispered. "You are the only thing that kept me alive, the thing I clung to desperately through our bond whether I was imagining it or not. I only had you, and it was the only thing I needed."

His mouth paused against my skin, his fingers pressing into me.

"I will not be able to be gentle once I'm inside you," he rasped. "I am weak for you, utterly wrecked, and I cannot be careful with you right now."

"Then don't." My fingers dug into his back, my nails raking down his spine.

A low growl rumbled in his chest, and then his mouth was on mine again, fierce and claiming, and I felt myself give in, felt the last of my walls crumble.

This wasn't careful.

This was desperate.

This was need, raw and all-consuming.

He didn't care that my power surrounded us, dark and out of my control, and suddenly, I couldn't bring myself to either.

Dacre's hands were everywhere, pressing into me, guiding me, worshipping me in a way I had never known I needed. And gods, I did. I needed this. I needed *him*.

I arched into him, and he let out a rough breath, his

fingers trembling against my skin as he whispered my name like a curse, like a plea.

I needed him inside me, filling me. I needed him more than I had ever needed anything before.

With a deep groan, Dacre lifted me up and carried me to the bed, laying me down across his crumpled sheets. He quickly stripped off his clothes, and I joined him, pulling my shirt the rest of the way off.

Dacre's breath was ragged as he hovered over me, his gaze raking over my bare skin like a man seeing sunlight after years in the dark. His hands roamed over my ribs, up my sides, tracing every dip, every scar, as if memorizing me all over again.

His fingers trembled slightly, though not from hesitation. From restraint.

"You have no idea what you do to me," he rasped, his lips grazing my jaw, his voice thick with something raw.

I arched against him, the heat between us unbearable. "You do the same to me."

With a deep growl, he crushed his mouth to mine, the kiss desperate and unrelenting. His hands moved with newfound urgency, pressing into my skin, claiming me in a way that sent a fire through my veins.

His name was a gasp on my lips, a plea and a command all at once. He answered without words, his body aligning with mine, his grip tightening like he feared I might vanish beneath him.

But I wasn't going anywhere.

I had already been lost once. I had been torn apart, shattered, but Dacre would piece me back together with every whispered vow, every desperate touch, every moment where he refused to give up on me.

I needed this, needed him, to remind me that I was still here. That I was still me.

"Dacre," I whispered, pressing my forehead against his as he shuddered.

His hands trembled against my skin, his control fraying at the seams.

"I love you."

My words were a lifeline, anchoring me in a world that had spent my entire existence trying to rip me apart.

His eyes met mine, and they were so dark, so lost in us. "And I love you."

And then I felt him push inside me, slowly at first, stretching me with every inch until he filled me completely.

The room became filled with our ragged breaths, the sounds of our bodies moving together. The world around us fell away. There was only him. Only us.

The rebellion, the war, the prophecy, it all faded into nothing in that moment. Here, in his arms, I was not a weapon. I was not a pawn in a war of kings and traitors.

I was his.

And he was mine.

He leaned back, settling on his knees between my thighs, and he lifted my hips in his hands as he rolled his own against me over and over.

"So beautiful," he murmured as his eyes roamed over me and one of his hands found my clit. He rubbed small circles over my sensitive flesh, and I watched as bit by bit his control slipped, and he began moving faster inside me. "So perfect."

He reached back, lifting one of my legs in his hand, and he pulled it forward until my thigh was pressed against my stomach, opening me wider for him. He kissed my knee as he pushed into me, even deeper than before.

I clung to him, my nails digging in his skin as I tried to pull him closer to me. His name was a mantra on my lips, the only word I could form as the pleasure he gave me clouded my mind.

He gently nudged my leg to the side, skillfully flipping me over onto my stomach as his cock slipped out, leaving me gasping with a soft moan as his hands explored the curves of my ass.

"Hips up, love," he commanded, with a deep, barely controlled voice, and I obediently lifted myself onto trembling knees, keeping my head and chest pressed against the soft bed, feeling the cool sheets against my face.

I arched my back, pressing myself against him as he ran his lips down my spine. His fingers traced patterns on my skin, lighting up every nerve ending in their wake. And then his touch shifted, becoming more urgent, more desperate.

He gripped my hips, pulling me back against him as he thrust inside me once again. I cried out, reveling in the feel of being completely filled by him.

He set a punishing pace, his hips meeting mine with a force that made the bed shake beneath us. Every movement sent waves of pleasure coursing through me, building and building until I felt like I was going to explode.

But he didn't stop.

His hands slipped beneath my chest, and he lifted me until I was sitting upon him, and he rolled his hips once more.

Our bodies were slick with sweat. His touch was enough to send me spiraling, my body tensing as pleasure built inside me. He was relentless, his fingers moving back to my pussy and working tirelessly against me, his mouth on my neck in a bruising kiss.

The pleasure was almost unbearable, and I couldn't stop the moans that spilled from my lips as Dacre pushed me closer and closer to the edge.

I could feel him getting close too, his movements becoming more frantic as he chased his own release.

"You are mine," he growled against my neck just as his hand came down in a gentle slap against my pussy. "This pussy is mine."

I nodded frantically, everything that I had was his and his alone.

"Say it, Verena." He nipped at my neck as he spread his fingers open, spreading me and feeling the spot where his cock slid in and out of me with his hand. "I need your words."

"I am yours," I gasped. "Always yours."

He slammed into me harder this time, and I could no longer control it. I fell over the edge, crying out his name as my pussy clamped down around him.

"Fuck," he hissed against my skin, thrusting harder and harder until he came inside me with a roar.

My knees gave out beneath me, and we collapsed on the bed, Dacre careful to not let his body crush mine. I could feel my heart pounding in my chest, and only the sound of our heavy breathing filled the room.

Dacre's hand was on my back, gently rubbing circles as he caught his breath. I snuggled closer to him, feeling content for the first time in a very long time.

"Are you okay?" he whispered, pressing a kiss to my forehead.

I nodded. "I am."

I buried my face in his shoulder, my chest rising and falling with uneven breaths. His arms tightened around me, his lips pressing against the crown of my head.

"I love you," he murmured, the words slipping from his lips like a promise. "I don't care about the prophecy. I don't care about the kingdom." He pulled back just enough to cup my face, forcing me to meet his gaze. "You are all that matters."

I let out a shuddering breath, clinging to him with everything I had, and I kissed him again, hard and desperate, needing him to understand, needing him to feel what I couldn't put into words.

I had been so fearful, but he was still here. Still whole. Still mine.

And if I was a storm, then he was the one thing unshaken in its wake.

I had spent my entire life running, from my father, from my past, from the power that lived inside me, but not anymore.

I wasn't running.

I was his.

CHAPTER 17
DACRE

Verena slept in my arms, her breath steady against my skin, but I could not close my eyes.

The world outside this room wanted to tear her apart, and I would not let it.

I traced slow, absentminded circles on her back, my mind reeling with the weight of what was coming. The rebellion, the war, the inevitable bloodshed that loomed like a blade above our heads, her power. It all pressed against me.

But here, in this bed, with her wrapped around me, I could pretend, just for a moment, that none of it mattered.

Except it did.

And it always would.

Verena stirred, shifting closer to me, pressing her face against my chest as if she could sense the storm raging inside me.

I tightened my hold on her, clinging to her for as long as I was allowed.

She was mine, and no one, not the rebellion, not the king, not even fate, would take her from me.

She let out a soft sigh, her lips brushing against my skin. "You're thinking too loud," she murmured, her voice thick with sleep.

I exhaled sharply, pressing a kiss to her temple. "I'm sorry. Go back to sleep." I traced my fingers over her face, pushing some hair off her cheeks.

She tilted her head back and blinked her eyes open until they met mine. "Tell me what's wrong."

Everything.

The word was right there, lodged in my throat, but I couldn't bring myself to say it. Instead, I reached for her hand, lacing my fingers with hers. "I need you to promise me something."

Her brow furrowed. "Dacre…"

"Promise me," I interrupted, my voice rough, desperate. "No matter what happens, you won't hide any part of yourself from me, even if you fear it."

Her lips parted, her expression softening, and she hesitated for a long moment. "I won't."

"Swear it," I demanded, tightening my grip on her hand. "Swear that no matter what they say, no matter what anyone thinks, you won't let it come between us."

She inhaled sharply, and for a moment, I thought she might argue. But she pressed her palm flat against my chest, right over my heart. "I swear."

Something inside me unraveled at her words, but it wasn't enough. It would never be enough.

But I wanted to believe her.

I needed to.

She moved closer, her fingers pushing into my skin. "I trust you, Dacre." Her voice was barely above a whisper, but it was enough to shatter me. "I trust you to not let me lose myself."

No one had ever trusted me before. Not like this. Not in a way that felt sacred.

And I could feel it through our bond, the truth in her words, the way she breathed differently when she was with no one other than me. She had so much fear, but even the overwhelming feel of her worry couldn't smother the feel of her want for me, her *love*.

"I want to marry you." The words left my mouth before I could think, before I could stop them. But I didn't regret them. Not for a second.

Verena's breath caught, her body going still against mine. "What?"

I swallowed, my heart pounding as I lifted her hand and pressed my lips to her knuckles. "I want you, all of you, and I don't want politics or war dictating what we are to each other. I want to choose this. Choose you."

Her eyes searched mine, wide and unguarded, as if she was trying to decipher whether I meant it.

"I want you as my wife," I murmured, my voice hoarse. "Not because it's expected. Not because of the rebellion. But because I love you. Because we were bound before either of us even understood what it meant. We are bound by fate."

A sharp breath rushed past her lips, and she sat up, clutching the sheet to her chest. "Do you know what you're asking?"

I trailed my hand down her arm, feeling the warmth of her skin beneath my fingers. "Yes."

"Dacre..." She bit her lip, her brows knitting together. "Marriage isn't just a ceremony. It's..."

"Sacred," I finished for her. "And I am choosing you. Over everything."

Tears lined her lashes, and for a moment, I thought she might refuse. Part of me thought that maybe she should have. The idea was mad, it was reckless, and it felt like the only thing that either of us could control.

Our fates had taken away our choices in almost every aspect of our lives, but not this. Not her.

"Yes."

A shudder ran through me, my grip tightening around her. "Say it again."

"Yes," she repeated, her voice steadier this time. "I'll marry you."

For a long moment, I could only stare at her, my pulse roaring in my ears, my magic stirring beneath my skin as if it, too, had been waiting for this.

And then, suddenly, a memory surfaced, one I hadn't thought of in years.

My mother's voice, soft and sure, whispering in the dark.

"A true vow is not just words, my love. It is a tether, a bond as old as the land itself. To speak it with your soul is to be bound, not by laws or men, but by the gods themselves. That is the power of love, it does not bow to kings."

She had told me that on the night my father had returned from a raid, bloodstained and weary, too hardened by war to remember the softness in my mother's eyes.

"It is the only thing that is freely given, and when it is, Dacre, it is the most unbreakable thing in the world."

My mother had loved my father, even when he was difficult to love, even when Wren and I questioned whether or not our father was worth what she was willing to give.

She loved my father, and she had given her love willingly.

I swallowed hard, my chest tightening with a sudden, aching realization.

These vows, this love, they were the one thing in my life I could freely give.

And it belonged to her.

I let out a breath and pulled her into me, my lips finding hers in a kiss that felt like a vow in itself.

A promise.

She melted into me, her hands tangling in my hair, her body pressing against mine, and gods, I wanted to lose myself in her all over again.

I pulled back just enough to meet her gaze. "We'll need witnesses."

"Wren and Kai," she answered instantly.

The two people I trusted, that I loved. My family. *Our family.*

I pressed my forehead against hers. I breathed her in. I let my magic thrum through our bond until she was the only thing I could feel, until I knew that she could feel me. "We should do it before you can change your mind."

Her lips twitched, and I felt her nose scrunch against mine. "I'm not changing my mind."

Neither was I.

But I still climbed out of bed and pulled Verena to her

feet. She laughed softly as I tossed her clothes to her and quickly pulled my pants up my legs.

"Get dressed." I laughed as I pulled my shirt over my head before strapping on my leathers.

She did as I said before the two of us snuck out of my room.

We crept down the hall, the weight of what we were about to do settling between us like a secret only we could hold. Verena's fingers curled around mine, her grip tight, her warmth grounding me in a way I hadn't realized I needed.

I had never been this sure of anything in my life.

We stopped in front of Wren's door, and I knocked, hard.

"One minute," she called out, her voice rushed and slightly panicked. When she opened the door, she barely cracked it enough to let us see inside. "Is everything all right?"

"Yeah." I nodded, Verena's hand tightening in mine. "But we need you. Can you hurry and get dressed?"

"Yes, of course." She shook her head as if she were trying to shake away the fog of sleep. "I just need a minute."

"We're going to go get Kai."

"Wait." She said it so quickly that my gaze shot up to meet hers. "I'll get him." She quickly recovered. "Then I'll meet you downstairs."

Verena and I made our way down the hall as Wren closed her door, and Verena chuckled.

"What?" I asked. My heart was racing; it had been ever since she had opened her eyes this morning.

"You do realize that Kai is in your sister's room right now, right?" She glanced behind us, and I stopped in my tracks to do the same.

"What?" I asked again, but Verena just grinned mischievously at me before she pulled me to the end of the hall.

"Leave it," she murmured as we reached the first step. "I could feel their urge to rip each other's clothes off the first time I saw them together."

"What?" I looked behind me at my sister's closed door, and I tried to imagine what Verena was saying about my sister and my best friend. "That's my sister."

"So?" She pulled me down a couple more steps. "You're her brother."

We reached the bottom of the stairs and made our way toward the door leading outside. I opened the door as I looked up the stairs one more time, but Verena pulled me into her as the cool air hit my face.

"Leave them alone," she whispered against my mouth. "They are about to witness our wedding, and they don't even know it."

"Okay, okay." I nodded and wrapped my arms around her.

We stayed that way, holding on to one another, and Kai and my sister finally came out the door. I eyed them both warily, but Verena quickly slapped my chest.

Wren and Kai both looked disheveled and bleary-eyed, but Wren smiled at us as they joined us outside. "What's going on?"

"We need witnesses," Verena said, her voice steadier than I expected. "Will you be that for us?"

"Witnesses?" Kai's eyes finally met mine. "For what, exactly?"

I swallowed hard, keeping my eyes on my best friend. "For our vows."

Something flickered across his face, surprise, then understanding. He stepped forward, standing a little taller as his gaze met mine.

"It would be an honor."

Something in my chest tightened. I nodded once, unable to say more.

Wren glanced between us, her brows drawing together as if she were trying to decipher something unspoken between Verena and me. Then, she exhaled and clapped her hands together.

"All right," she said, voice lighter, though something unreadable lingered in her expression. "Where are we doing this?"

"I know just the place," I murmured, glancing toward the cavernous path beyond the training grounds. "Not far from here."

Verena's fingers tightened in mine, and I turned my hand over in hers, letting my thumb brush over her knuckles.

I looked at Kai. "Do you still remember the tunnels that lead to the ruins?"

His brows lifted slightly. "You want to do this there?"

"Yes."

Wren frowned. "What ruins?

Kai shifted his weight, exchanging a glance with me before he turned to her. "The old temples of the first kings."

Recognition flickered across her face, followed by something heavier.

"It will be just us," I continued, my voice softer. "No one goes there. It will just be you and me."

"And us," Wren interjected, and my chest swelled as Verena laughed.

"Yes," I admitted, nodding to my sister. "And them."

Verena's smile reached her eyes, and I swore I could have stared at it for the rest of my life.

"Okay," she whispered. "Then lead us to the ruins."

We moved quickly through the streets. The city was still quiet, most of the rebellion still locked in sleep. No one noticed us as we slipped past the warrior barracks, through the training hall, and toward the tunnels that would take us deeper underground.

Verena was tucked into my side, a smile still ghosting her lips, and I couldn't stop glancing down at her. She was going to be my wife.

We turned a sharp corner, I barely stopped in time before we crashed into someone standing in the hall.

My grandmother.

She stood before us, her silver eyes piercing in the dim light, as she glanced around at the four of us. It was as if she had been waiting for us, as if she had known.

Verena shifted uncomfortably beside me, and I tightened my hold on her, refusing to let go. My grandmother's gaze flickered over our joined hands before shifting to Wren and Kai behind us.

Then, without hesitation, she asked, "Do you know the weight of what you are about to do?"

The question settled over us like a heavy fog, pressing into my skin, into my bones.

I swallowed. "How…"

"Yes." Verena's answer came at the same time as mine, and my grandmother didn't answer me. She was only looking at her.

Something flickered in my grandmother's expression. Not hesitation, not disapproval. Something quieter. Something knowing.

She exhaled through her nose, slow and measured. "Then you will need someone to guide the binding."

Verena's brow furrowed. "Guide?"

My grandmother nodded, stepping forward, her skirt rustling against the stone floor. "I was bound to my mate long before this war began. I know what must be done."

She rolled up her sleeve, revealing the faintest trace of an old mark, a circular brand of fading gold on the inside of her wrist, the ink long faded but still visible.

Verena inhaled sharply, her free hand pressing against her own wrist as if she could already feel it forming.

I had never seen a brand like that before, had never even seen my grandmother's, but mates were rare.

"You are the heir to both Marmoris and Veyrith. This is more than just a vow." She met Verena's eyes, and her expression softened, just barely. "This is a soul-binding, the kind that has not been done in generations."

My pulse thundered, but I held Verena's gaze.

"We still want this," I said firmly.

Verena swallowed hard. "We do."

My grandmother nodded once, slowly, then turned on her heel, gesturing toward the tunnels.

"Then we must go. The temple is waiting."

The tunnels twisted beneath the city, cutting deeper into the rock, spiraling into the dark. The farther we walked, the cooler the air became, the scent of damp earth thickening with every step. It should have felt suffocating, the weight of the stone pressing in around us.

But it didn't. It felt open. Vast. Like something was waiting.

The flickering torch in Kai's hand barely cut through the thick shadows, but it was enough to reveal the widening of the tunnel, the faintest whisper of water running in the distance.

Verena moved closer to me, her hand clutching mine. She felt it too.

Magic.

Not mine. Not hers. But something ancient, something woven into the very walls around us. Something I had never felt before when Kai and I had come here as kids.

The tunnel gave way to a cavern, the air cool against my skin, the silence absolute, and as we stepped beyond the last stretch of stone, the ruins came into view.

A large temple stood at the center of the cavern, cradled by the underground river, the remnants of its three towering spires reaching toward the jagged ceiling above, stretching for the light that barely reached this deep beneath the city.

The stone was worn, cracked with time, but even in its decay, it was beautiful. The carvings along the pillars were still somewhat visible, intricate lines of text and imagery wrapping around them like vines, whispering of the past.

Verena sucked in a breath beside me, and I turned to

her, watching as her gaze swept over the temple, her expression full of awe.

She knew this place, or at least, part of her did.

My grandmother stepped forward, her hands wrapped in the fabric of her skirt, lifting it up as she walked.

"This was once a place of worship," she said, her voice reverberating around the cave. "Before Marmoris, before the rebellion, before the world we know now, this temple was built for something else entirely."

Verena inhaled sharply, and I felt the faintest tremor in her hand.

Wren shifted beside her, her head craned back as she looked around. "I've never even heard of this place."

"This place has long since been forgotten," my grandmother murmured.

A chill swept down my spine. "Wren, you've been here before."

Her gaze snapped to me. "What?"

"Our mother used to bring us here," I said, my voice low and thick with emotion. The memories came flooding back, threatening to overwhelm me. "Whenever my father was too hard on me, when he was too busy training me to be a warrior rather than his son, Mom would grab Wren and me by the hand, and we would sneak down these tunnels."

Her eyes narrowed, and I could practically see her searching her mind for the memory.

"You were young." I took another step forward, moving us closer to the temple. "And after Mom died, Kai and I used to come here when we'd get too stuck in our own heads."

Kai stepped forward, running a hand over one of the stone pillars, his brow furrowed as he looked at my grandmother. "How do you know of the temple?"

My grandmother's gaze didn't waver. "This temple is from the first kings. All five kingdoms had one." She moved to the bottom step. "These temples were where we honored the magic, where we honored our land."

"I think I read about this." Verena was staring at the temple, taking it in as if she had seen a ghost. "My mother brought..." She hesitated, swallowing hard. "I found a book in my room about Veyrith."

The weight of her words settled over us, heavier than the cavern ceiling above.

For the first time since we'd stepped into the cavern, something flickered in my grandmother's eyes. Something old. Something lost.

"She came here once," she admitted. "When she was first crowned queen, after your father had ripped her away from our home."

Verena's fingers tightened in mine, but she said nothing.

My grandmother lifted her chin, her silver eyes scanning the temple as though she could see something the rest of us couldn't.

"She was not alone."

Verena's breath hitched beside me. "What?"

My grandmother turned toward her, the weight of something unspoken pressing into the space between them. "Your mother," she murmured, "was not the only daughter of Veyrith to step foot in this temple after it had been abandoned."

A shiver ran down my spine as my grandmother looked at me, and I knew the answer before she spoke.

"My mother," I rasped.

The words felt heavy in my throat, like I had just unearthed a secret buried deep beneath my ribs.

The air inside the cavern shifted, and Verena's free hand came up to her chest, her fingertips pressing lightly over her heart as if she could feel it, the weight of the moment pressing into her bones the same way it was pressing into mine.

"They were here together," my grandmother murmured.

Verena turned back toward the temple, staring up at the worn stone, the cracked spires reaching for the ceiling like they had been frozen mid-prayer.

It felt like the world had stopped turning.

The Queen of Marmoris.

The wife of the rebellion leader.

Two women, from opposite sides of history, from opposite worlds, standing in this very spot, looking up at this very temple.

"I don't understand," Verena whispered, her voice barely more than a breath.

"Both your mothers came from Veyrith just as I did." She glanced back and forth between us. "And neither of them ever forgot what they lost, what they stood to lose."

She turned to Verena, and something aching was hiding in the depth of her eyes, something sad.

"This was where your mothers knelt side by side," she whispered, "whispering to gods who had long since turned their backs. This was where they begged for peace, where they mourned the war they could not stop."

Verena's nails dug into my palm.

This wasn't just a forgotten temple. Not just a place of worship.

And now, all these years later, we stood where they had stood, fighting a war they had prayed to stop.

A hush fell over us. The weight of the past pressed into the stone beneath our feet, and I could feel it, something shifting in the air, something awakening.

Verena's breathing shallowed beside me, and I turned my head just in time to see her lips part, her eyes darting across the temple walls. Her fingers twitched in mine.

And then, she pulled me forward.

Her steps were slow, deliberate, as if something unseen was guiding her. She lifted a hand, tracing the worn carvings at the temple as we moved up the steps. The stone was smoothed only by centuries of time. The carvings had been worn down, nearly illegible.

We moved farther into the temple, and I brushed my own fingers along the edges of an inscription. The moment I touched it, magic shuddered through my veins.

"Dacre." Verena's voice trembled.

Verena stilled beside me, her other hand wrapping around my forearm to steady herself as she spoke the words aloud.

"When shadow swallows the golden throne, and rivers run dry where magic has flown."

The cavern pulsed with power.

My stomach clenched as the words etched themselves into my mind, my soul, my bond with her.

"The cursed shall rise with fate-bound hands, a tethered soul to shifting sands."

She turned to me, her eyes wide, glassy with understanding.

This temple was not just sacred. It was part of the prophecy, and it had been waiting for us.

A silence settled over us, heavy, breathless, absolute.

The air inside the cavern felt different now, thick with something I couldn't name. I felt her magic shift first, a pulse like an exhale, rippling through the space between us. Then, mine responded.

A slow, deliberate pull, an undeniable force drawing us closer.

Her eyes were wide, her chest rising and falling in uneven breaths. "This was never just a temple," she whispered.

I swallowed against the tightness in my throat, the words carved into stone still burning behind my eyes.

She turned to my grandmother. "You knew."

My grandmother watched us carefully, her silver eyes calculating, measuring, deciding. "I knew the prophecy," she admitted. "I knew this temple had been forgotten to war and greed, but I did not know how it would respond to you."

I clenched my jaw, but I couldn't deny it. I could feel it responding. It was as if the very walls of the temple recognized us, recognized her.

A shudder rippled down my spine as our bond tightened, not just a thread between us, but something weaving us together, pulling, binding.

"Dacre," Verena whispered my name, her voice laced with something between fear and awe.

I lifted her hand to my lips, brushing my lips along her

knuckles. I didn't know what this meant. I didn't care if fate had written this moment long before we were even born.

This wasn't just fate's decision. It was ours.

I turned back to my grandmother and steadied my voice. "Tell us what to do."

The temple breathed around us, the silence stretching, expectant.

My grandmother lifted her chin, her silver eyes flicking between us. "Stand before the altar."

Verena and I stepped forward, our footsteps echoing against the worn stone. The closer we got, the heavier the air became.

Kai and Wren took their places behind us, quiet but unwavering. Our witnesses.

My grandmother moved closer, standing before us now, her presence as steady as the stone beneath our feet. "This ceremony is not of Marmoris. Nor of Veyrith. It predates both." She exhaled slowly. "It is a binding older than kingdoms, older than kings."

Verena swallowed hard, her fingers trembling in mine.

"Are you ready?" my grandmother asked softly.

Verena didn't hesitate. "Yes," she whispered.

Her voice sent a shudder down my spine, and I squeezed her hand. "Yes."

My grandmother nodded once, her shoulders straightening. "Then kneel."

I dropped to my knees without hesitation, the stone cold against my skin. Verena followed, our hands still clasped between us.

"The vows you speak here will not only bind your

fates," my grandmother continued. "They will bind your magic. Your souls. Once spoken, they cannot be undone."

Verena's breath hitched, but she didn't look away from me. She wasn't afraid of this.

She was afraid of herself.

I reached up, brushing my fingers against her cheek, anchoring her back to me. "We are already bound," I murmured.

Her lips parted, and I could feel it, the way the magic curled around us.

My grandmother stepped forward, lifting a small dagger from the folds of her cloak. The blade was old but well cared for, its edge honed to a deadly sharpness, the hilt wrapped in worn leather. The faintest trace of script was etched into the steel, almost imperceptible beneath the glow of the altar.

"A blade from Veyrith," she murmured, her voice steady. "Forged in a time before kings, before war."

She turned it in her palm, studying the edge as if remembering something long forgotten. Then, she met Verena's gaze.

"You must offer freely," she said softly. "Not because of the prophecy. Not because of fate. But because you choose this."

Verena's breath caught in her throat, her lips trembling, but slowly, she reached out.

"I choose this," she whispered.

Verena's gaze flicked to mine. I could see the storm in her eyes, the thousand emotions fighting for space, but there was no hesitation.

She handed me the blade, the metal warm against my skin, before she extended her hand, palm up. *Offering.*

My throat tightened, but I pressed the blade against the center of her palm, just deep enough to draw blood. She didn't flinch.

I held the blade out to her, and she slid the hilt into her hand before doing the same to me.

My hand shook as I reached out for her, and our blood met when our hands clasped between us, mingling, merging.

The air around us shuddered.

"The vows," my grandmother instructed, and I swallowed hard. I already knew the vows. We both did.

And I didn't waver. "A kingdom torn in blood."

Verena's lips parted, and I saw it, the memory flickering behind her eyes. We had spoken these words before. In that inn. In what felt like another life.

She had been taken from me, but she had fought, we both had. And now, fate had led us back here.

"To ruin and ash," she whispered, her voice shaking.

I let the next words roll off my tongue, anchoring us in something deeper than fate.

"But with my soul, I thee worship."

Magic pulsed through the ground beneath us. A tremor. A promise.

Verena's lips trembled, and her hand tightened in mine, sealing us in blood.

"But with my soul, I thee worship," she echoed.

The temple roared to life. The worn symbols beneath our knees flared with golden light. A low pulse bled through the cracks, illuminating the letters carved into the stone.

I gasped as the magic surged, wrapping around us like an unseen tether.

Verena shuddered. I could feel her magic twisting with mine, coiling, settling, weaving us together so tightly that we would never be undone.

My grandmother inhaled sharply, and I heard Wren curse under her breath.

Because as our blood mingled, as the magic recognized the vow we had just spoken, something burned against my skin.

I sucked in a breath as searing heat shot through my wrist. Verena cried out, her fingers tightening around mine. A mark was branding itself into our flesh.

"True mates are rare," my grandmother murmured, almost to herself. Her fingers ghosted just above Verena's skin, as if afraid to touch the mark now seared into her flesh. A circular brand of gold ink, the same one forming on my own wrist. "Many claim the bond, but few ever bear the mark.

Verena was shaking, her breath unsteady, her eyes wide as they flickered between her wrist and mine

"What does it mean?" she whispered. But even as the question passed her lips, I could feel it settle inside her, her love, her devotion, her desperation for me.

My grandmother exhaled slowly, her trembling hand moving back. "It means there is no undoing this. Not force, not time, not war, not even death, will break what has been bound here tonight."

She lifted her gaze to mine, something almost reverent in her eyes. The words settled between us, sinking into my bones, weaving themselves into something deeper than I could understand.

There is no undoing this. The thought should have frightened me. Instead, I felt whole.

Verena was staring at her wrist, her fingers hovering just above the mark as if she was afraid to touch it, and her magic flickered in the air between us, restless, shifting, as if it, too, was struggling to understand what had just happened.

I reached for her, curling my fingers around hers, feeling the heat of the brand still settling into our skin.

Her eyes snapped to mine, wide and searching.

I lifted our joined hands, brushing my lips against her wrist, against the mark now etched into her skin.

She sucked in a sharp breath, and I could feel the rapid beat of her pulse, the slight tremor in her fingers.

"Are you okay?" I murmured.

She didn't answer right away. Instead, she turned my wrist over in her grasp, running her fingers along the edges of the ink as if she could trace the weight of fate itself.

Then, finally, she whispered, "You are mine."

A sharp ache bloomed in my chest.

I tilted her chin up, forcing her to see me, to see the truth in my eyes. "And you are mine."

Her lips parted, her gaze flickering over my face, and I could feel it, the shift. Something inside both of us had changed, settled, like a key turning in a lock that had been waiting to open for a long, long time.

CHAPTER 18
VERENA

The door shut behind us with a quiet finality, sealing us inside.

My heart was still racing. My pulse thrummed against my skin, magic shifting restlessly beneath the surface, curling through my veins like smoke. The words we had spoken still echoed inside me, settling into places that had been untouched until now.

We were married.

Soul-bound.

There was no taking it back.

And I didn't want to.

Dacre stood in front of me, his eyes fixed on me with a deep intensity. His breathing was slow, deliberate, each inhale and exhale a testament to his patience. He was waiting for me.

His hands were clenched at his sides, his knuckles white. He was holding himself back.

I swallowed hard, my fingers still trembling as I

reached up to brush hair away from my flushed face. The air around us was thick, the magic moving inside me almost suffocating.

"I feel...different," I confessed as I met his gaze.

He tilted his head slightly, curiosity gleaming in his eyes as he stepped closer. "How?"

I grappled with my thoughts, searching for the right words to capture the swirling emotions within me. For so long, I had imagined that this moment would come with unmistakable clarity, that when I finally married, when I belonged to another, it would descend upon me like a tangible weight.

A collar around my throat, binding me.

But there was nothing about him that made me feel caged.

I felt...*steady*. Anchored in a way I had never been before.

"Lighter," I murmured, "and heavier. At the same time."

Dacre's lips twitched, the barest ghost of a smile. "You feel..."

"Whole." I finished it for him as I let out a shaky breath.

His eyes darkened, and he reached for me then, his fingers grazing the new mark on my wrist before wrapping fully around it. His grip was firm, grounding, as if testing whether or not I would pull away.

I didn't.

I wouldn't.

I stepped into him, letting my body press against his,

my hands flattening against his chest, feeling the steady thud of his heartbeat beneath my palm.

We had touched before. We had burned for each other before. But this was different.

There was no uncertainty.

No desperation driven by fear, no frantic grasping to hold on to something before it slipped away.

I wasn't running anymore.

I was done running.

I lifted my chin, my lips parting as I whispered, "Kiss me."

Dacre didn't hesitate.

His mouth met mine with a slowness that sent a shiver down my spine. This wasn't like before. It wasn't wild or frantic. It was something deeper. More intentional.

His hands smoothed up my arms, over my shoulders, until they cupped my face. His fingers trembled slightly, just enough for me to notice.

He was nervous.

Not because he didn't want this, but because it meant something.

And gods, it *did*.

I let out a soft breath against his lips, and he exhaled too, like he had been holding it in. I threaded my fingers into his hair, tugging him closer, and when he deepened the kiss, my knees nearly buckled.

Dacre groaned softly, one of his hands sliding down to press against my lower back, holding me up. The other remained at my jaw, his thumb stroking along my cheekbone, slow and reverent.

He was worshiping me, and I let him.

There was no one else whose adoration I craved, no other that I wanted on their knees before me.

My magic stirred at the same time his did, but it didn't struggle or rebel. It didn't lash out or resist.

It didn't take.

I felt it before I understood it. The shift. The moment where there was no more me or him, only *us*.

His power didn't just press into mine; it settled inside me, a second heartbeat, a breath drawn between us. It curled around my ribs, warm and sure, like an oath whispered against my skin.

And I knew.

We had always been tied together.

I gasped against his mouth as I felt him, *truly felt him*, in a way that rendered all previous moments pale and lifeless in comparison.

He broke the kiss just long enough to rest his forehead against mine, his breath coming in ragged, uneven breaths. "Please don't fear me, don't fear us."

"I don't." I shook my head and tried to make him understand. "Not anymore."

His fingers traced a delicate path along my jawline, tilting my head back, his eyes searching mine with an intensity that seemed to pierce my soul. "Can you feel me?"

I nodded frantically, my heart pounding in my chest. He was like a blazing sun, the only thing I could feel, the only thought that occupied my mind. "Yes."

"What does it feel like for you?" he asked, his voice thick with want that told me he could feel me just as I felt him.

"Like I'm not alone in my own skin anymore," I finally answered, feeling the truth of my words resonate deep within me.

Dacre's breath caught, an audible hitch, and his hands flexed against me.

"Verena," he breathed, my name a tender caress on his lips.

I didn't let him finish. I kissed him again, my arms wrapping around his neck as I pressed my body fully against his. He let out a sharp exhale against my lips, his hands sliding to my hips, holding me with a grip that bordered on painful.

His mouth moved over mine slowly, like he was savoring every second, tasting me in a way that sent heat pooling deep in my stomach.

But there was something else, something I had never felt before.

Like I was *safe*.

Not just with him, but *within myself*.

There were more dangers against me than ever before; I was more of a danger to myself than I had ever been, but somehow I felt the safest and most sure in this moment.

Dacre's hands trembled ever so slightly as they slipped beneath my shirt, his fingers grazing along the bare skin of my waist. His touch was warm, almost devout, as he skated over my skin.

He wasn't just touching me.

He was learning me as if the two of us had never touched before.

As if every brush of his fingertips, every press of his lips, was not just a rediscovery, but a revelation. The bond between us hummed with something ancient, like we had been remade, rewritten, tethered in ways neither of us fully understood.

He broke away from my lips, trailing featherlight kisses down my jaw, along the curve of my neck. Each press of his mouth was unhurried, like a prayer against my skin.

A soft gasp fell from my lips as his mouth found the tender spot where my pulse throbbed insistently against my throat. He lingered there, his warm breath fanning over my skin, sending a shiver down my spine.

Then he breathed, "I love you."

I froze.

Not because I didn't believe him.

But because I did.

The words settled inside me, taking root like a tree as they found their home. His words were embedded inside me; *he* was entrenched.

I clung to him with a newfound urgency, my fingers pulling at his hair, my chest rising and falling as I tried to find my voice.

"I love you too," I whispered, my voice shaking with something raw, something untamed. I had said the words before. I had thought about them before. But this was different.

This time, I was *giving* them.

Not like a whispered prayer to an indifferent god, not like a shield to protect myself from the fear of losing him.

I was giving them like a vow.

Like a part of my soul that I was surrendering to his keeping.

Dacre groaned softly, his hands gripping my waist possessively, his forehead pressing against my collarbone.

I could feel him not just in our magic, but *something deeper*. I felt him in my bones, in the way my power melded into his, in the way the air pressed against my skin.

This was not just a marriage.

It was a claiming.

A choosing.

It was utterly intoxicating, a heady mix that enveloped me, as if I were submerged in what we were together. It was a depthless ocean in which I found myself willingly lost, the currents pulling me deeper, yet I had no desire to rise to the surface ever again.

His fingers traced the curve of my waist, achingly slow, as if he were mapping constellations on my skin. His lips followed, lingering and dragging heat wherever they touched.

"Verena," he murmured against my skin, his voice thick. "I want all of you."

"I'm yours."

A tremor ran through him, a visible shudder that seemed to ripple from his very core. Then, he was kissing me again, his lips capturing mine with a fervor that was demanding as his hands roamed up my back.

He pulled back slightly, his eyes searching mine, dark with something deeper than desire. "Show me."

A challenge. A plea. A promise.

This wasn't survival.

This was something more, and I would give it to him.

I would give him everything.

I grasped the hem of my shirt with trembling fingers

and swiftly lifted it over my head. His hand extended toward me, and he gently brushed his knuckles along the soft, weighty curve beneath my breast, sending a shiver through my body.

The moment his hands slid over my skin, I felt it, our magic rising in tandem, swirling between us. The torches flickered, their flames bending toward us as if drawn by the pull between us.

I gasped as a crackle of energy sparked between our bodies, the very air around us thickening with something unseen, something *alive*.

Dacre's breath hitched. "Gods, Verena."

I shuddered at the sound of my name on his lips, at the raw worship in his voice. At the way our magic wasn't fighting anymore. It was emblazoned.

"Dacre," I breathed, uncertain if I was calling him back to me or pleading for him to take more.

His hand trembled as he traced my skin, the heat of his palm a brand against me. He wasn't rushing. He wasn't even breathing. His eyes darkened, hunger flickering in their depths, but there was something else there too, *awe*.

"My wife," he rasped, as if tasting the name in his mouth, memorizing the way it felt on his tongue.

And it settled deep in my core.

He kissed my collarbone, slow and unhurried, his breath hot against my skin. His lips lingered, pressing into the hollow of my throat, over the frantic pulse beneath my jaw.

"You're beautiful," he murmured, his voice thick. "Gods, Verena, you're..." His voice broke off into something inhuman, something feral, and a shiver ran through me.

He stood there, eyes dark and unreadable, his fingers now hovering inches from my skin as though he needed to memorize this moment before he touched me again.

I swallowed hard, heat dripping through me.

His breath fanned over my skin as he leaned in, close enough that his lips almost, *almost,* grazed my bare shoulder.

"Let me look at you," he rasped. It wasn't a request; it was a plea.

His hands smoothed over my waist, then lower, and I gasped as he sank down in front of me, my hands shaking at my sides, unsure if I could bear the weight of what he was doing.

He bowed his head slightly, his dark hair falling over his eyes, his breath shallow as his hands spanned my waist, his thumbs pressing into my hip bones like he was trying to steady himself.

And then, *gods.*

He pressed his lips against my stomach.

A soft, trembling kiss, *worship* woven into the way his mouth lingered against my skin.

We had done this before, been here only the night before, but this felt completely at odds with anything that had happened before now.

A broken sound slipped from my lips, something fragile and ruined.

His fingers flexed against my sides as he kissed me again, lower this time, just below my navel, his lips dragging over my skin.

"Dacre…" My voice was barely a breath, barely anything, because I was unraveling.

"Look at me," Dacre whispered.

I forced my gaze down, my chest rising and falling too fast, my skin burning beneath his touch. He was still kneeling, his hands sliding to the backs of my thighs, his thumbs brushing soft, soothing circles there.

When I met his eyes, I nearly collapsed.

Devotion.

Not desire, it was devotion staring back up at me. Like I was the only thing he had ever wanted. The only thing he would ever need.

His hands smoothed up, palms moving over my ribs, slow and aching, before he pressed another kiss to my stomach. "You are the most powerful thing I've ever held."

Something inside me broke. Not in fear. Not in hesitation. In *need*. In understanding.

Because no one had ever *looked* at me like that before. No one had ever *wanted* me like this, not just my body, not just my power.

Me.

"Dacre." My voice cracked, my fingers threading into his hair, *pulling* him closer because I needed him, needed *more*.

He let out a ragged breath, his lips parting against my skin, warm and trembling. His hands flexed against my hips, his grip tightening like he was anchoring himself.

His forehead pressed against my stomach, and his breath stuttered before he exhaled sharply.

"Verena," he rasped, his voice scraping against the quiet between us. "I—"

Whatever he was going to say, whatever words had formed on his tongue, they never came. He didn't need them.

Not when I could feel him.

His magic curled through mine, weaving tighter, until I didn't know where his power ended and mine began. It wasn't consuming. It wasn't suffocating. It belonged.

We belonged.

I shuddered, my fingers tightening in his hair, and when he lifted his head, his eyes locked on to mine with something raw, something unbreakable.

I reached for him, my fingers brushing along his jaw, tracing the sharp angles, the shadowed lines. His skin was hot beneath my touch, his pulse thundering in his throat.

He turned his head, pressing a kiss against my palm. His hands then glided down with deliberate slowness to the waistband of my pants. With care, he unfastened them, the quiet sound of the fabric shifting filling the room. He eased the pants down my legs, their texture cool against my overheated skin as they slipped away.

Then finally, finally, he lazily rose to his feet. His nose brushed against my skin, tracing a gentle path with each inch he ascended, drawing in my scent, unraveling me with every breath, until he finally stood to his full height before me.

He was no longer gentle in the way he kissed me. He was frantic.

The kiss was heavy with every unspoken promise, every unyielding devotion, pressed between us in the heat of his lips.

His hands smoothed up my sides, slowly, achingly, like

he wanted to make sure I knew this wasn't just need, wasn't just hunger.

It was him choosing me.

His fingers brushed the bare skin of my back, dragging over the curve of my spine, his touch so careful, so certain, and then he sighed into me, his entire body coiled tightly against me.

Our power surged again, pushing outward, wrapping around the room. The torches along the walls flickered wildly in response, their golden light stretching.

But Dacre wasn't paying attention to them. He was only looking at me as his hands skimmed over my skin, his thumbs brushing reverent paths over my ribs, my waist, until his thumb reached my lips.

He paused.

I could feel the silent question in the air between us, the way he waited, the way he gave me the space to pull away.

I didn't.

Instead, I reached forward, curling my fingers over his, and guided his thumb into my mouth.

His breath caught, his chest rising and falling unsteadily, and he closed his eyes for just a moment, like he needed to gather himself before he lost control completely.

Dacre exhaled slowly, his breath warm against my cheeks. He hadn't moved. He hadn't pushed.

But gods, I could feel it, the tension, the restraint in every line of his body, in every tremor of his hands against my skin.

I sucked his thumb into my mouth, my lips closing around it, and rolled my tongue slowly over his skin, tasting him.

He exhaled a ragged, uneven breath, a sound that was both a reaction and a warning.

"Verena." His voice was laced with caution.

I lifted my chin, allowing our eyes to lock, as I let his thumb slide back out of my mouth, only to draw it back in with a deliberate, teasing motion. He watched me carefully, he drank me in, let me fill him, let me break him open.

His hands shook as he withdrew his thumb from my mouth. The slightly calloused pad of his thumb traced roughly over my bottom lip, leaving a thin trail of moisture along the curve of my mouth.

Our magic swelled, a pulse, a breath, a pull that felt like it was dragging us deeper into each other. My skin burned where he touched me, but it wasn't fire.

It was power, raw and unfiltered. It wasn't trying to take. It was giving.

Dacre's hands moved to my hips, his fingers pressing intricate paths into my skin. He was still fully clothed, still holding back, but I could feel everything.

His magic was inside me, curling through my veins, through my bones.

I gasped, my head tipping back, and he caught me before I could fall, his arms winding around my waist, holding me steady.

"I feel you," I whispered, my hands fisting into his shirt, my chest heaving.

Dacre's lips parted, his gaze dark and wild. "I know."

He reached for my hand, lacing our fingers together, and, gods, the moment our palms touched where we had tethered our blood to one another, the room shuddered, the black smoke of my power ravishing every corner.

And suddenly, I could feel inside him.

I felt his devotion, his worship, his need, not just for my body, but for this.

For us.

The bond was like an invisible thread weaving us together, tethering us, binding us tighter than flesh and bone ever could.

A tremor racked through Dacre's body, and his hands tightened on me with a desperate urgency as he leaned in closer, the warmth of his breath cascading over my exposed neck.

"Verena," he whispered, my name tumbling from his lips like a prayer. "I think…I think I just…"

He didn't finish. He didn't need to.

Because we had both felt it.

The bond.

It snapped into place with an almost audible click, settling deeper within us, resonating with the rhythm of a second heartbeat.

I was his.

And he was mine.

Dacre slowly leaned back, his fingers brushing my cheek, trailing down my neck, over my bare shoulders.

I reached for him, my hands urgent, tugging at his shirt, and he let me pull it over his head in one swift movement.

My breath caught at the beauty of him.

There were so many scars that marred his skin. They crisscrossed his flesh, some faded with time, others still fresh, like a living testament to every battle he had ever endured.

My fingers brushed over the ridges and raised marks,

feeling the texture of his past etched into his skin, and he stilled.

We were both so scarred, our bodies bearing imprints of the wars we had waged and had been waged on us.

He wasn't breathing, but I didn't stop.

I dragged my fingers lower, down his chest, over his ribs, down to the deep scar that slashed across his stomach, and then, without thinking, I leaned forward and pressed my lips against it.

Dacre sucked in a sharp breath. His entire body tensed beneath me.

And then, slowly, so painfully slowly, his hands slid into my hair, cradling the back of my head.

I slid my tongue from my mouth, brushing it against his skin, savoring the taste, tracing the rough texture of his scars with a deliberate, lingering caress.

Then, I kissed him again. Lower.

Soft, slow, worshipful.

Like I was memorizing him too.

Dacre made a wrecked, guttural sound, and when I finally pulled away to look up at him, his eyes were wild, his breathing wanton. His fingers tightened in my hair until pain lanced through my scalp and moisture pooled between my thighs.

"I need to be inside you," he growled. "I need to fuck you until there is no one left in this kingdom who will question who you belong to."

I whimpered, the ache in my body becoming worse with every word he spoke.

He grabbed my hips and lifted me, carrying me toward the bed. He laid me against the mattress before he slotted himself between my legs and pressed against me with a force that almost knocked the breath from my lungs.

He was claiming me, leaving a mark upon me that could never be erased, and gods help me, I would willingly surrender everything I was to him.

Dacre hovered over me, his weight braced on his forearms, his breath rushed as his gaze raked over me. His eyes were dark, searching, as his fingers skated over my ribs, slowly, so unbearably slow, tracing the contours and curves of my body.

My breath caught as he grazed over the curve of my waist, the dip of my hip.

My body was quivering beneath his.

Dacre's forehead dropped against my breastbone, his chest heaving.

My hands tangled in his hair, my lips parting on a whimper as his hand brushed over my thigh, and he groaned, his restraint snapping like a bowstring.

The slow, measured control he had clung to fractured as his hands gripped my thighs, spreading me open beneath him.

I gasped into his mouth at the feeling, the solid weight of him pressing between my legs, and something desperate and wild unfurled inside me.

"Dacre," I whispered, his name a demand, a breaking.

His hand slid up, fingertips grazing the underside of my breast, and I shuddered.

"You have no idea," he broke off, his lips hovering over mine, his voice a wrecked rasp. "No idea what you do to me."

I did because I felt it.

His need. His devotion. His magic, tangled with mine, curling through my body, twining around my spine.

I reached for him, my fingers brushing the waistband of his pants, and he stilled. I sat up, pressing my palms against his chest, feeling the rapid thud of his heartbeat beneath my fingers.

He was a warrior.

He was dangerous.

But here, with me, he was trembling.

"Dacre," I whispered, pressing more firmly until he leaned back. "I am your wife," I reminded him. "And as such, I'm going to fuck you."

He growled, and I pushed harder until he fell to his back on the mattress.

He licked his lips as he watched me settle on his thighs, watched me bring my hands to the waistband of his trousers and sloppily tug them down his hips until his cock was exposed.

I looked up at him, and there was an ocean of vulnerability reflecting back at me. No armor, no walls, no defenses. Just him. Just me. Just us.

And I wanted to worship him.

I tucked my hair over one shoulder as I leaned down, my lips brushing against the head of his cock, and his hips surged forward.

"Tell me," I whispered as I ran my tongue down the length of him. "Tell me what you want."

He groaned, his hands fisting into the sheets at his sides. "You," he said hoarsely. "I want you."

I wrapped my hand around the base of him, slowly

stroking up and down his length as my other hand dug into his thigh.

"And what else?" I asked as I searched his eyes, opening my mouth and sliding the head of his cock into my mouth.

His hips jerked forward again involuntarily, and I moaned as he slipped farther into my mouth. I felt so needy, so wet, and I knew that he could feel my arousal against his legs.

"I want you to ride me," he said firmly, his voice laced with his need.

I whimpered as a ripple of pleasure coursed through me.

He reached down, his hand gently wrapping around my chin as he guided my mouth off his cock and pulled me to him.

Without hesitation, I positioned myself over him, and I jerked when the heaviness of his cock bobbed against my clit.

Dacre was shaking beneath me, his eyes dark and filled with desire as I lifted up onto my knees. His hands grabbed my hips, fingers digging into my skin as he guided me down onto him.

I moaned at the feeling of him sliding inside me, filling me completely.

"Fuck," Dacre groaned, his hands gripping tighter as I began to move.

I rode him slowly at first, savoring every inch of him inside me. But soon, the need for more took over, and I began to move faster, my body rising and falling against his in a steady, desperate rhythm.

Dacre's head fell back against the pillows, his breathing coming in gasps as he watched me with hungry eyes, and I could feel our magic moving inside us, amplifying our pleasure and tightening the connection between us.

"Harder," he groaned, and I complied eagerly.

I allowed my hands to climb up my body, and I gripped my breasts in my hands, rolling my nipples between my fingers as he slammed harder inside me.

"Touch your pussy," he commanded, the gentleness in his voice gone. "Show your husband exactly how you like to be touched."

I let one of my hands trail down my body, reaching between my legs to touch myself. I was already so wet and swollen, and the moment my fingers touched my clit, a jolt of pleasure shot through me, forcing my hips to slam down on his.

Dacre's eyes were locked on me as he continued to thrust up into me, his pace growing faster and deeper. I moaned loudly, arching my back as I rubbed circles over my clit.

I could feel my orgasm building inside me, and I knew Dacre was close too.

"Let me taste it." Dacre's hand wrapped firmly around my wrist, and I watched, entranced, as he guided my hand to his mouth. The warmth of his breath brushed against my skin before he slid my wet fingers between his lips, closing his eyes as he tasted me.

A deep, satisfied groan escaped him as he cleaned my arousal from my fingers, and I was so engrossed with watching him that I barely noticed the subtle shift of his hands, which had found their way to my hips.

He lifted me off his cock in one move, sliding me up along the length of his body, and he positioned me, my pussy hovering so close to his awaiting mouth.

My body lingered above him, suspended in a moment of anticipation, before his strong arms enveloped my thighs, pulling me down forcefully until every inch of me was pressed against his hungry mouth.

His tongue eagerly explored me, flicking back and forth, tracing patterns on my sensitive flesh, sending waves of pleasure shooting through me.

The feeling was overwhelming, my thighs spread open completely, and Dacre brought his hands to my pussy, rough and eager, spreading me open farther as he sucked my clit between his lips.

It drew a gasp from deep within me and I slammed my hand down on the mattress as I threatened to topple over.

Dacre continued to greedily devour me.

"I told you to ride me," Dacre growled against my flesh. "That means my face too, love."

I leaned back, looking down into his eyes, and I began to writhe against him, unable to hold back.

His tongue was relentless, swirling around my clit, dipping into me and exploring every inch of my aching flesh.

My hands gripped his hair, pulling him closer as I begged him for more.

Dacre groaned against me, the vibrations sending shock waves through my body. One hand moved to grip my hip, holding me steady as he continued to devour me with an intensity that left me breathless.

He slid two fingers inside me, curling them until my back arched and my hips jerked.

"That's it," he spoke against my pussy before rolling his tongue over my clit once more. "Come for your husband," he growled. "Come on my mouth."

I couldn't hold back any longer, the pressure building inside me reaching a peak I couldn't resist. With a loud cry, I came undone on Dacre's tongue, my body shaking as waves of pleasure washed over me.

Dacre continued to devour me, his hands gripping my hips tightly as he rode out my orgasm with me.

As I finally started coming down from the high, he quickly flipped me over and settled back between my trembling thighs.

He wasted no time in thrusting into me once more, his movements rough and primal as he chased his own release. My body was still so sensitive, but it responded to each thrust with a mix of pleasure and pain.

It was overwhelmingly intoxicating, too alluring to resist, and my magic surged across every inch of my skin, crackling with energy, as if it were yearning to draw him deeper into me.

"You feel so good." Dacre's hands pressed against the inside of my knees, and he pushed them open until I had nowhere to hide from him.

He kissed me deeply, the taste of me still on his tongue, before he leaned back and watched the way his cock slid in and out of my body.

"You were made for me," he growled. "This pussy was made for me."

My pussy clamped down around him, and his eyes slammed shut for a moment as his hips faltered.

When he opened his eyes again, they burned with a primal hunger and his hips set a brutal pace that had me crying out.

His fingers found my clit again, this time much gentler than before, and he rubbed the slowest circles over it that were in complete contrast to the way he moved inside me.

It was too much, it was maddening, and I feared that I was going to lose myself completely in the feeling.

"You're going to be a good girl, aren't you?" he asked, and I nodded my head, even though I had no idea what he was asking. "That's right. Be a good wife and come again for me. Come on your husband's cock with this pretty pussy."

I cried out as our bodies moved together, the room filled with our grunts and moans, mixing with the sounds of flesh slapping against flesh.

It only took a few more thrusts before I was surrendering to Dacre's commands, my body clenching around him as I came, this time far more intense than before.

My magic surged like a wild, untamed beast, insatiable and hungry, and a loud growl ripped from deep within Dacre's chest as he came inside me.

Dacre kissed me like he was drowning, like I was air, salvation, home all at once.

I couldn't breathe. I couldn't move, and yet, I had never felt more alive.

"Verena," he gasped, his voice raw, broken.

I turned my head, my lips brushing his ear.

"I'm here," I whispered. "I'm yours."

His body shuddered, finally relaxing, and his lips found mine again. This time, slower.

We lay tangled together for a long time, our bodies slick with sweat, our magic still humming through the room like the remnants of a storm.

His head rested against my chest, listening to the unsteady thud of my heart, and his hands still wrapped around me like he couldn't bear to let go.

Dacre let out a slow, contented sigh as he rolled over and pulled me with him until I was pressed against his chest.

The world outside was still waiting. The war, the rebellion, the prophecy, the vessel.

It would all come for us soon enough.

But here, in the space between battle and destiny, there was only this. Only him. Only me.

Only the vow we had spoken and the bond that had answered.

And nothing, not fate, not kings, not gods, could take that from us now.

CHAPTER 19
VERENA

I woke up feeling different.

Not just the dull, satisfying ache of muscles well-used, or the lingering warmth where Dacre had touched me, but something deeper, something that could not be seen or measured.

Something that settled inside me. Shifted. Rooted.

I was no longer just a weapon to be won, a pawn in a war I never asked to fight. I was no longer a girl struggling to survive a kingdom that had already decided what she would become.

I was something else entirely, and the realization did not unnerve me.

It calmed me.

Because with Dacre, I was more.

I felt it in the way my magic hummed gently beneath my skin, no longer a wild, writhing thing that demanded more than I was willing to give.

It belonged to me, and I to it.

And we were *his.*

I lifted a hand, my fingers trembling slightly as I turned my wrist, staring at the golden mark that had bound me to him. The ink was still fresh, the skin beneath it still tender.

We had spoken the vows. We had chosen each other.

And for the first time in my life, I had chosen myself.

The lanterns in Dacre's room flickered softly, their gold light dancing across the stone walls. I exhaled and lifted my fingers toward the flames. They bent toward me like a silent offering, as if the magic inside them recognized the shift within me.

Dacre stirred beside me, his breath warm against my shoulder, his arm still wrapped possessively around my waist. I lingered there, staring at him, committing this version of him to memory. His dark lashes resting against his skin, his brow furrowed slightly, even in sleep.

He was so vulnerable like this, when the rest of the world had been shut out, when it was only me and him.

My husband.

I wished to stay in this moment forever, to live in this space where he had sheltered us from the rest of the world, but reality slipped in, demanding my attention.

I carefully shifted out of Dacre's grasp, but his fingers twitched in his sleep, reaching for me, even in unconsciousness.

I reached for my shirt, slipping the fabric over my head, my movements slow, careful. I could still feel the way his hands had traced my skin, still feel his mouth on me, and even now, my body ached for him as I finished dressing and slipped on my boots.

I glanced back at him, hesitating, before quickly grabbing a scrap of parchment from his desk.

My hand shook slightly as I wrote the words: *I'm with Kai. I'll be on the training grounds.*

I was not running from him, not running from us, and even though I felt stronger, I still feared that I wouldn't be able to control my power when I needed it most.

And everything inside me knew that no matter what happened, no matter what came, I would need it.

The narrow streets of the city were still shrouded in early morning quiet, the usual hum of rebellion life only just beginning to stir. I moved carefully, shoulders tense, my fingers brushing absentmindedly over the mark on my wrist. The soul-bond had settled inside me, and yet, my body still hummed with the aftershocks.

Like something was still shifting. Like something was still waking.

I reached the training caves and found Kai already waiting. He leaned against the stone wall, arms crossed, a dagger twirling between his fingers. The faint light of the torches caught the sharp angles of his face, the cool calculation in his dark eyes.

His gaze flicked over me once, then twice.

Not in the usual way he assessed an opponent, not like he was looking for a weakness. This was something else. Something careful.

"I wasn't sure if you'd want to train today," he said, his voice unreadable.

I rolled my shoulders, the weight of my power shifting inside me, like a second pulse. "I feel more ready to train today than ever before."

Kai didn't move. He only studied me. Too long. Too quiet.

Then, finally, he straightened.

He flipped the dagger in his palm with practiced ease. "All right, then." His voice was lighter but not relaxed. "Let's get to work."

Kai held out a training sword, and I reached for it without thinking, my fingers tightening instinctively around the worn hilt.

The moment my skin met the leather, something stirred inside me. Not violently. Not like before. Not a force I was battling against.

It was there. *Waiting.*

A presence I could feel thrumming in my chest, buzzing beneath my skin. It wasn't demanding. It wasn't trying to take.

It was listening.

I exhaled sharply, shifting my stance as I tested the weight of the sword.

Kai was still watching me, but not like a sparring partner. Like someone who knew exactly what had happened last night and wasn't sure how to feel about it.

"The soul-bond," he finally said, tilting his head. "It settled."

It wasn't a question.

I tightened my grip on the sword, leveling my gaze with his. "Yes."

Kai hummed, flipping his dagger once more. "And?"

And?

I tried to find the right words, to explain the shift, the difference, but I didn't know how to make him understand.

Before, my magic had been like a storm, violent, unpredictable, impossible to contain. It lashed out when I was afraid. It took when it was desperate.

But the storm had settled.

It was now a shadow at my back. Not demanding. Not lashing. Just...there.

"I'm not fighting it anymore," I admitted as I moved the sword from one hand to the other.

Kai's brow furrowed slightly, and there was something about Kai that I couldn't explain. Something about him that told me he saw far more than anyone else. "But you're still afraid of it."

My stomach twisted. I hated that he could see that.

"I'm not afraid of it." I shifted my stance, bringing the sword up between us. "I'm afraid of what happens if I let go of it."

A slow exhale. A sharp nod. He understood.

"Then let's find out," Kai murmured, and before I could react, he struck.

Kai's blade came fast. Too fast. My instincts flared, a warning flashing behind my ribs. Danger. Threat. Move.

But before I could even think, my magic moved for me. It struck out, hungry, violent, fast. A blast exploded from my chest, an invisible force that lashed through the cavern like a whip.

Kai staggered back and let out a sharp, clipped grunt, and I watched in horror as blood trickled from his nose.

I hadn't even touched him. I had barely moved, and yet, his blood was on me.

"Kai." My voice cracked as I took a step toward him,

but he lifted a hand, not to block me, but to stop me from speaking.

My stomach twisted. My pulse roared in my ears. I had done that.

I thought I would be able to stop it, to keep it locked inside, but my magic had broken past my grip like a flood through a crumbling dam.

Kai exhaled slowly, rolling his shoulders before swiping the blood from beneath his nose with the back of his hand. "That wasn't control."

"I...I didn't mean to." My throat was closing. Panic threatened to take over.

Kai finally looked at me then, and something sharp and knowing flickered in his gaze.

"I know," he murmured.

That somehow made it worse because it hadn't mattered.

It hadn't mattered that I didn't want to hurt him. It hadn't mattered that I had tried to keep it buried. It had still acted on its own.

Just like it had with Dacre. Just like it had with my father.

I took another step back, my pulse erratic. "I can't—"

"Yes, you can," Kai interrupted, his voice steady. Certain.

I shook my head because he wasn't listening. "You don't understand."

"I understand," he said, tilting his head and watching me carefully. "I understand that you're still trying to suppress it, and I understand that's exactly why it keeps winning."

I exhaled sharply, my stomach twisting violently. I knew he wasn't wrong. I had spent so much of my life thinking I was powerless, and the moment I found it, I had tried to pretend I wasn't this, tried to bury the truth of what I was so deep that no one, not even myself, could reach it. But my magic had never needed permission to take. It had never asked. It had only waited. Waited for me to break.

Kai flipped his dagger in his hand again, his grip tightening. He was waiting and watching me in a way that made me want to run.

I swallowed hard. "Again."

His gaze flickered over my face before falling to my hold on the sword. "Are you sure?"

I wasn't, not at all, but I lifted my sword, adjusting my stance, forcing my feet to steady beneath me. I didn't want to hurt him, but I needed to learn to control myself, to control my magic.

"Again," I repeated.

Kai's face shifted, something like approval, like recognition, flashing behind his dark gaze.

And then, he moved even faster than before.

His blade shot out, the edge of it gleaming in the flickering torchlight, and I reacted. Not with my magic. Not yet.

I sidestepped, just barely, his dagger missing me by the width of a breath. His weight shifted, his body turning too fast, and the hilt of his blade came for my jaw.

I lifted my sword, too slow. Kai struck, and pain cracked across my face, snapping my head to the side. I stumbled, my vision blurring. My heartbeat slammed against my ribs, and my magic surged forward in response.

I gritted my teeth, fighting it back, and when I looked back up at Kai, I could see it, the way he was holding back, the way he carefully planned his attack with enough force to pull my magic forward.

I planted my feet, blinking through the ache in my jaw, and forced my body back into position and waited.

Kai watched me carefully, cocking his head so slightly I almost didn't notice. "You're still holding it in."

I didn't answer. I couldn't because he was right.

I was trying to stop it. Trying to keep it locked away, trying to suppress it because I didn't trust myself with it.

Because I knew what it could do. I had felt what it had done to Dacre.

But Kai didn't give me time to dwell. He lunged again.

I swung my sword, blocking the strike this time, my blade locking against his. Sparks cracked against the metal, but so did my control. My magic roared.

It slammed against my ribs, demanding release. I nearly let it. I nearly lost it again.

Kai paced in front of me. "You are a siphon, Verena, and that doesn't just mean you will take from others. Your magic will take from you as well if you allow it."

Memories of being in that room with the vessel surged through my mind, coursing through my body as my stomach rolled. I had felt it then, the overwhelming feeling as my own power intertwined with that of the vessel, threatening to consume me entirely, threatening to take what I wouldn't willingly give.

I clenched my jaw, feeling the muscles tense beneath my skin, and I shifted my stance once more. "Again."

Kai didn't give me a chance to change my mind before

his dagger sliced toward me again. I twisted, barely dodging, my back slamming into the rough stone wall behind me.

I had no escape, nowhere to go.

But he didn't stop. He pressed forward, unrelenting, giving me no time to breathe. No time to think.

The tip of his blade angled toward my throat, and I brought my sword up in a blind strike.

The impact sent a jarring vibration through my arms, but it wasn't enough.

He spun, his body moving like smoke, and the hilt of his blade crashed into my shoulder. Pain tore through me.

I stumbled, falling against the wall, and my magic swelled.

It wanted out. It surged forward, straining against me

I squeezed my eyes shut, forcing myself to breathe, to hold it back.

"Get up, Verena."

My magic screamed. A violent pulse slammed through my ribs, clawing its way up my throat, desperate to be free.

I lunged at Kai, throwing out my sword on instinct, but my grip was weak, my muscles burning from exhaustion. I didn't come close to landing a hit.

The tip of the sword slammed against the ground, sparks flying around us, and my control slipped. My vision blurred.

I was back there with the vessel, trapped in that room, my magic being ripped from me, poured into something that devoured and devoured and devoured.

I couldn't stop it.

The power in my veins snapped. I felt it break loose.

A violent, shuddering crackle of black mist curled from my fingertips, creeping outward, reaching, searching for something to take.

Kai cursed, stumbling back, his hands raised as if he could shield himself, but I could barely see him anymore.

Everything was fading. I was fading.

The magic wasn't mine anymore. It was something else. Something hungry. Something unrelenting.

I gasped, fighting for air, for clarity, for control, and then I felt it. A sharp, searing warmth flared against my wrist.

I sucked in a breath, my entire body jolting as my wrist burned. I looked down at the golden symbol etched into my skin that now glowed.

Steady. Solid. A heartbeat against my own.

It wasn't just a mark. It was a tether.

A tether to Dacre. To who I was. To who I wanted to be.

I clamped down on my magic with everything I had. I forced in a breath, fighting for clarity, for control, for myself. The golden glow of my mark pulsed in sync with my heartbeat.

Dacre. I could feel him.

Not just in my thoughts. I felt him in my bones. Like the moment we had spoken our vows and the bond had sealed between us. It was as if he was whispering my name from somewhere deep inside me.

The black tendrils of my power stilled, and I reached for it. I willed it to listen.

The dark mist curling from my fingertips didn't lash outward. It didn't take. It waited.

And when Kai moved again, when his blade came for

me, my magic whispered through my veins, curling through my limbs like mist. His dagger moved toward me, and just as it was about to pierce my skin, I sidestepped, moving faster than I ever had before.

It was as if I too became a mist in the air, a part of the black smokiness of my magic.

Kai's eyes widened in response, but I didn't hesitate. I twisted, lifting my sword in my now steady hand, and brought the edge down against his chest, halting just a hair's breadth before making contact.

Kai went rigid before me, and the cavern was enveloped in an echoing silence, broken only by the sound of our breathing. I met his gaze, and all I could see was his disbelief staring back at me. He had been expecting me to fail, to lose control, and I had expected it too.

I forced another slow breath through my lungs, my magic settling, twisting into something calmer. Something that was mine.

Kai's lips parted slightly. "You…" He hesitated, shaking his head, like he couldn't quite make sense of what he was seeing. "You controlled it."

I swallowed hard, feeling the weight of the moment press into me.

A slow, deliberate clap echoed through the cavern. It was not a mockery, not approval, but something else. Something colder.

Dacre's grandmother stepped forward from the shadows, her silver gaze locked on to me.

"You finally reached for it," she murmured. "But can you wield it?"

My heart slammed against my ribs. "I just did."

She tilted her head slightly, almost...amused. "No, child." She took another slow step forward. "You controlled it once, but you need to command it."

Kai's shoulders tensed. "She's already pushed herself enough today."

Dacre's grandmother turned her sharp gaze toward him, her face unreadable. "Leave us."

Kai's jaw ticked. His fingers flexed around the hilt of his dagger, his instincts battling his respect.

"Go, Kai. I'm fine." I nodded toward the mouth of the cave where she had just entered.

He hesitated for a long moment before his nostrils flared and then his gaze flicked to me for a single look before he started to move.

Dacre's grandmother stood motionless near the mouth of the cavern as she waited for Kai to pass, her gray hair pulled back in a tight bun, accentuating the sharpness of her features. Her eyes were piercing, carrying the weight and clarity that only came with a lifetime of accumulated wisdom.

She looked almost ethereal, as if she belonged in a world far different than our own.

Her sharp, calculating gaze absorbed every detail in the vast room before her eyes swept over me, lingering for much longer than was considered polite. And once Kai disappeared from view, she narrowed them, those eyes of molten silver.

"You still do not understand, do you?" she asked, her voice quiet as she moved, stepping closer to me. "What you are. What you could be."

I swallowed hard, my pulse thudding in my ears.

"You are not just a siphon, Verena." She took another step forward. "You are not just an heir to a throne." Her gaze flickered downward to the golden mark on my wrist. "And you are no longer just a girl with power bound inside her."

A chill slithered up my spine.

"You have never been powerless, but you have been trapped. But you are free," she murmured. "The only question now is what you will do with it."

Her fingers twitched at her side, and before I could react, a silver tendril of magic lashed toward me.

I gasped, my power instinctively slamming against it, meeting force with force.

A sharp crack split the air, the stone beneath me trembled, but Dacre's grandmother only nodded. "You fight like your father."

The words landed harder than any sword, and I went rigid, my pulse spiking. "I am not my father."

She lifted her chin. "Then stop wielding your magic like he does."

Something hot rushed up my throat. "And how would you have me wield it?"

Dacre's grandmother exhaled, her expression unreadable. "Like your mother did."

My stomach dropped. I swayed slightly where I stood, my body vibrating with something I didn't understand.

"My mother never fought," I said, my voice hoarse.

Dacre's grandmother's silver eyes burned. "Didn't she?"

Silence slammed into me because I knew. I had always known.

My mother had fought when she gave up her kingdom. She had fought when she defied my father. She had fought when she bound my magic away to protect me.

She had fought for me.

I inhaled sharply, feeling the magic inside me shift.

"I am not my father," I said again, my voice stronger this time.

Dacre's grandmother tilted her head slightly. "Then prove it."

I lifted my chin, and I did. I reached for my magic, not with fear or hesitation, but intention. The power that had once clawed at my ribs now curled into my palms, coiled around my bones. It was mine. It had always been mine.

I exhaled sharply and released it. Not in a wild burst or reckless destruction, but in command.

A tendril of dark energy spiraled from my fingertips, striking exactly where I willed it to go. The stones along the cavern floor cracked, not from chaos, but from precision.

Dacre's grandmother's silver eyes gleamed. She lifted her hand, and another strike of silver magic lashed toward me. I didn't fight it. I didn't panic. I let it come, and when it reached me, I took it.

My fingers twitched, and my magic swallowed hers whole, controlled it, molded it. I twisted my wrist, and the energy changed.

It didn't shatter the ground. It didn't destroy. It danced in my hands. Obedient. Steady. Mine.

Dacre's grandmother's lips parted, and then, so slightly that I could have imagined it, her head dipped with respect.

"Good," she murmured. "But this is not the only power you command."

My breath hitched, and I felt it before I saw it. The warmth curling beneath my skin, steady as a second pulse. The golden glow that singed on my wrist.

Dacre's grandmother's eyes burned into mine. "Call it."

My pulse thundered.

"Call it," she repeated, sharper this time. "Summon the strength you tethered yourself to."

My stomach tightened, feeling the golden heat pour into my lungs, pressing into the edges of my mind. I reached for it, not a gentle warmth or a flicker of power, but a searing force. It poured into me, branding itself into my very bones.

It was not consuming, not demanding. It came willingly.

Dacre's power flooded into me, and I gasped, my knees nearly buckling beneath me as my magic roared in response.

The bond ripped through me until I could feel the steady beat of his heart slamming against my own. I was overwhelmed by the unwavering presence of him, even though he was nowhere near this cavern.

The raw weight of him filled every corner of me, like sunlight pouring into a dark room, and I felt everything.

His focus.

His hunger.

His desperation to be at my side.

I reached for him, and the moment I did, I could feel him reaching back.

Verena. His voice wasn't spoken. It was within me. A

whisper pressed against my mind, curling around my throat.

My fingers twitched, and the magic surged higher, crackling against my skin like an electric storm. The golden light at my wrist flared, blending with the darkness of my own power, merging in a way that should have been impossible. The cave pulsed with energy, shaking beneath the weight of the connection stretching between us.

Dacre's grandmother saw it too. The silver light of her own magic faltered, and then she spoke, her voice steady despite the undeniable shift in the air.

"You have called him," she murmured.

I was shaking. Everything inside me trembled. Not from fear but from power.

The bond between us had never felt so visceral before.

I swallowed hard, forcing my pulse to steady. "I'm still here," I whispered, more to myself than to her.

Dacre's power curled into mine in response. *I know.*

The torches along the walls dimmed all at once, like the cavern itself was exhaling. The shaking stilled yet the bond didn't fade. It anchored into mine.

Dacre's grandmother was silent for a long moment before she took the smallest step forward and struck again.

I was so focused on the bond, on the way it consumed me, that I didn't have time to see it before the force of her power slammed into me, knocking me to the ground. I gasped as my back hit the stone, magic writhing inside me, on the verge of unraveling completely.

"Get up." Her voice was razor sharp.

I forced myself to my feet, my lungs heaving, my power still burning beneath my skin.

Dacre's heartbeat pounded against mine, a steady drum in my ribs.

He felt me. He was coming for me.

I forced my shoulders back, locking my knees to keep them from trembling, and Dacre's grandmother tilted her head.

"Your mother," she murmured, "gave up everything for you."

The words cut like a truth that had always been inside me, waiting to be spoken aloud.

Dacre's grandmother exhaled, slow and measured. "She gave you this." She nodded toward my wrist, toward the mark still glowing. "She gave you him."

She paused, and all I could hear was my blood rushing in my ears.

"She gave you the choice to decide what you would become."

My throat tightened. My mother had bound my power, not just to hide it, to protect me, to protect this.

The power coursing through my veins, the strength sinking into my bones, the bond thrumming beneath my skin.

She had bound me until I was ready, until I could wield it myself, until I could choose.

Dacre's grandmother moved again, too fast, too powerful. She was a phantom in the dim cavern light, her movements sharp and lethal in a way I hadn't expected from someone of her elderly appearance. I barely caught the flick of her wrist before another arc of power crackled through the air.

Desperation took over, and I threw up my hands,

relying more on instinct than any skill, and my magic responded.

It surged through me like a raging river, coiling around me like an eager serpent ready to strike at my command.

Then, pain erupted, searing and tearing through my connection with my power.

The force of her attack crashed into me, sending me skidding backward across the cold, unforgiving stone floor. I sucked in a sharp breath as my back collided with the cavern wall, the impact rattling my bones.

"She believed in who you would become. She prayed to the old gods and the new, her hopes weaved into every plea, that when her daughter ascended to rule this kingdom, she would do so with a courage that surpassed her own and possess a strength that could bring an entire kingdom to its knees."

A profound silence enveloped us as I climbed to my knees, the atmosphere around her shimmering with the raw intensity of her magic and the weight of her words.

I pushed off the ground and dusted the dirt from my hands.

"Are you to be that queen?" She cocked her head just as another brilliant wave of silver light surged forward.

My magic crackled beneath my skin like a thousand tiny storms. My breath slowed, becoming as calm and as rhythmic as the rise and fall of the ocean's tide.

I forced my hands to steady.

A deep, throbbing pulse of power radiated out of me, colliding with the tendrils of magic she had directed toward us. It crashed into her power before it could reach me, but instead of blocking her power, instead of pushing it away, I took it.

The searing heat of her magic melded into mine, like a molten current merging into an already raging river.

Her eyes narrowed, the faintest glint of approval flickering across her face.

She moved again, but this time, I was ready. I planted my feet firmly into the ground, feeling the solid stone beneath me as I braced myself to meet her head-on.

Her power struck like a weapon that had been honed for centuries. Mine rose to meet it, raw and untempered.

A magic that was not solely mine, but somehow mine completely.

Heat pulsed relentlessly against my skin as our magic clashed violently, silver light spiraling into the power that coiled in my veins. The force of it sent jagged cracks snaking across the cavern floor beneath us, while dust billowed up in swirling clouds.

She barely faltered as she pressed her assault forward. A flick of her wrist, and daggers of pure energy formed at her fingertips.

My breath hitched, but I steeled myself, forcing an unwavering steadiness to take hold.

This was nothing like sparring with Kai. He had challenged me, pushed me to the brink to hone my control, but this was a different beast entirely.

Her fingers moved with a speed that was unnatural, twisting in a blur that caught the light, creating a fleeting glint that danced in the air.

Attempting to block her advance was impossible. Dodging it was futile.

A violent shock of power rippled through my body, like a wave crashing against the shore. It reached for hers, like it was grasping for air, hungrily devouring the raw energy she hurled at me. The sheer force of mine and Dacre's power made my pulse falter, my skin burn, but I held steady until she stilled, watching as the last remnants of her power fused into me.

Her eyes widened in surprise, and I braced myself for what she would do next.

But she did something I wasn't prepared for, something I didn't expect.

"You are no longer the girl your mother and I hid away," she declared, her voice resolute.

The words hit me with a force stronger than even her power had been, causing a sharp exhale to leave my lips and a deep burn to form in my lungs.

"No. I am not."

She nodded once, almost to herself. "And you will fight?" She watched me carefully, like she was looking for someone she used to know, looking for any parts of my mother that still lived within me. "For your kingdom, for your bond?"

Dacre's pulse slammed into mine. I breathed in. Steady. Strong.

Then I lifted my chin. "Yes."

She reached for the wall beside her, her fingers pressing against the rough stone, steadying herself, and her breath left her in a slow, measured exhale.

Then she lowered herself carefully, her bones trembling as she bent her knee and let it land gently on the ground.

I tried to breathe, tried to force breath into my lungs, and when her eyes met mine again, they burned into me.

"Then I will fight at your side, Verena. I will fight for you as I once fought for your mother."

She pressed her palm to the cavern floor. "You are not just an heir, not just a warrior."

A whisper of her power rippled through the stone. "You are the last daughter of Veyrith. The next Queen of Marmoris.

Then, ever so slowly, she lowered her head. "You are the ruler that will unite us all."

CHAPTER 20
VERENA

The cavern walls still pulsed with energy, the ancient stone humming with the remnants of magic. My breathing had steadied, yet my body ached with an exhaustion that reached deep into my bones.

Every muscle burned. Every limb trembled.

The power I had wielded, the control I had found, had taken everything, but it had not broken me.

I ran my still trembling fingers down my arms, shaking a fine layer of dust from my skin as I made my way toward the mouth of the cave. My steps were slow, my body weak, but something inside me felt stronger.

Dacre.

The thought of him sent a sharp ache through my chest. His pulse still pounded against mine, steady, relentless, an echo inside me. He was looking for me. He had felt me. He knew.

A flicker of his warmth pressed against me, and I felt desperate to get to him.

The lantern light from outside the cave beckoned me forward, guiding me toward him. Toward home.

I picked up my pace, ignoring the way my limbs protested, ignoring the pain that ached through me, but just as I rounded the final bend in the tunnels, my body tensed.

Micah stood at the mouth of the cave waiting for me.

His posture was deceptively casual, one shoulder propped against the stone wall, arms crossed over his chest. But I saw the tension in the way his fingers curled slightly against his bicep, the way his gaze tracked me, flicking over my sweat-dampened skin, the bruises already forming along my flesh.

A shiver ran down my spine, and I clenched my fists.

Micah had been a shadow in my life—someone I had trusted once, someone who had helped me when no one else would. But he had also been there, standing in the corner of that cell, of that chamber, watching as my father tore me apart.

And he had done nothing.

"You look different." His voice was quiet.

I exhaled sharply, squaring my shoulders and willing myself to let the sudden fear of seeing him take hold. "I am different."

A muscle in his jaw ticked. His gaze flickered downward, landing on my wrist. On the golden mark that bound me to Dacre.

His throat bobbed. "I saw what you did in there."

I stiffened, and magic curled in my chest, restless. "Were you watching me train?" I asked, my voice sharper than I intended.

Micah held my gaze. "I wanted to make sure you were okay."

A bitter laugh slipped from my lips. "And?" I challenged, my fingers flexing at my sides. "What did you find?"

He pushed off the wall, stepping toward me with slow, careful steps. "Verena, I'm sorry."

I went still, cold, and I could almost feel it the moment Dacre felt it too, as if he could sense my fear, my anger.

"Don't you dare." My voice was a warning, a blade unsheathed.

He halted abruptly as if my words created an invisible barrier that stopped him from moving another inch closer. "It's true. I never wanted this to happen. I never imagined this is where we'd end up."

I shook my head, trying to find my words, but finding them trapped beneath a rising tide of my anger.

"You remind me of the girl you were trying to run away from." His voice was quieter now, his eyes studying me in a way that sent ice down my spine.

I knew the girl he spoke of. Not the girl from the castle he had watched wither away. Not the girl who had been locked in a gilded cage, waiting to be broken by powerful men.

He meant the girl from the streets.

The one who had fought to stay hidden, who had fought to survive. The one who had never wanted power, never wanted war. The girl who had only wanted to be free.

My hands curled into fists at my sides, my knuckles turning white.

He had no right to talk about that girl anymore.

"You stood by and did nothing while my father tore me apart," I whispered, my voice shaking with barely contained fury.

Micah's body tensed. He swallowed hard. "I know."

The admission knocked the air from my lungs.

I had braced myself for excuses, for justifications, for a desperate attempt to rewrite the truth. But instead, there was only the weight of his guilt.

Micah exhaled harshly, shaking his head. "You think I don't hate myself for that? For every moment I stood there just...watching? I had no choice, Verena."

"You always have a choice," I spat back, my voice a whip cracking between us. "You could have helped me."

His eyes met mine, unflinching. "I did once."

The breath left my lungs, but I wanted to scream.

"I helped you," he continued, voice raw. "I took care of you in the streets. I taught you how to hide, how to survive." His voice broke, and he clenched his fists like he could force himself to stay steady. "And for what? For you to fall right back into his hands, for you to fall into this damn rebellion that you never wanted any part of?"

His expression twisted, as if the words tasted like ash in his mouth.

Micah looked away, staring at the wall as if he could see the past etched into the stone. "They tore me apart too, you know," he confessed. "The night that you were arrested, the night that his soldiers took me in..." He swallowed hard as if he could barely force the words from his lips. "The things your father did to me...I wasn't strong enough. I wasn't..." He cut himself off again. "I told them things I shouldn't have. About you, about us hiding."

My stomach turned.

"You gave me up."

Micah flinched, just barely, but I saw it.

"Yes," he admitted, and I could hear the agony in that single syllable. "Your father ripped the truth from my lips even when I tried not to let it out. I told him that you had run, that you had been living inside the city the entire time. I told him about the rebellion mark I had given you as a last-ditch attempt to save you if the rebellion were to find you."

Instinctively, I wrapped my fingers around my left wrist, my thumb brushing over the ink Micah had burned into my skin all those years ago.

He took a step closer.

I jerked back before I could stop myself, my body reacting on instinct, as if he were still the man standing in my father's palace. As if he were still the one who had stood by while I screamed.

Micah froze, and for a moment, neither of us spoke. The cavern felt too small, the air too thick.

"I..." My breaths came too fast, my ribs tight around my lungs.

I had spent so many nights knowing Micah as my safe haven. But now, now I didn't know who he was anymore.

The boy who had protected me in the streets.

The man who had betrayed me in the palace.

The ghost who stood before me now, full of regrets.

Micah's throat bobbed, and he took the smallest step back, like he had just realized what had happened. Like he had seen the flicker of fear in my eyes and couldn't bear it.

"Verena." Micah exhaled heavily, his gaze flicking

away, like he couldn't look at me when he said what came next.

"I wasn't just some boy who found you in the streets." His voice was quieter now, like he was forcing himself to say it out loud. "I wasn't just your friend."

Something inside me stilled.

"What?"

Micah hesitated, his fingers twitching at his sides before he let out a slow breath, like he was bracing himself for a blow. "I was meant to protect you, and I failed her."

His words didn't make sense, and I let out a sharp, disbelieving laugh. "What the hell are you talking about?"

Micah's jaw clenched. "Your mother," he said slowly, carefully. "The queen and Elis." His eyes flicked past me to where I had just left Dacre's grandmother. "They entrusted me with you."

The cavern tilted, and my stomach clenched violently, my pulse roaring in my ears. "No." I shook my head, stepping back. "No, that's not—"

"That's the truth," he cut in, his voice steadier than mine. "I am from Veyrith, Verena."

I barely heard him.

Everything inside me twisted, it rebelled against the words coming out of his mouth.

I had believed that Micah and I had been two lost people who had found each other in the wreckage of our lives, and that we had protected each other.

But it had been a lie from the beginning.

I wasn't his friend. I wasn't his family.

I was a duty. A responsibility. A burden.

"You were watching after me," I whispered, my voice so small. "This whole time, you were just—"

Micah's throat bobbed. "I didn't want to tell you," he admitted. "Because after a while…" His brows pulled together, his voice raw. "You became my family."

It wasn't enough.

It would never be enough to erase the betrayal burning through my veins, setting fire to everything I thought I had known.

I stared at him, at the boy I had trusted with my life, the boy who had helped me find my first real taste of freedom.

And he had been sent to watch over me.

Micah watched me carefully, reading every emotion flickering across my face. "I was barely more than a child too, Verena. They asked me to look after you, but I never truly understood why. Not until I realized who you were."

I let out a sharp breath. He had always known. He had known the whole time.

I hated the way my stomach twisted, hated the way my chest ached.

"I trusted you." The words were a whisper. A hollow, aching whisper.

Micah's hands curled into fists at his sides. "I know you did, and I'm sorry."

I let out a sharp exhale, my eyes burning. "Why are you telling me this now?"

His expression shifted, his jaw tightening, his body so rigid that he looked like he wasn't breathing.

"My sister," he said, his voice raw, wrecked. "Verena, I have to go back for her."

I blinked, the fire in my veins roaring hotter. "What?"

Micah's fingers twitched at his sides, his throat bobbing as he swallowed. "The king still has her." His voice wavered, just slightly. "Your father has her. I don't even know if she's still alive."

Something in my chest cracked. I had spent so long trying not to care about what happened to him, trying to sever the part of me that still felt anything when it came to Micah.

But this was different because I knew what it was to be trapped in that palace. To feel the weight of my father's cruelty like his hands were constantly wrapped around my throat.

"Micah, you can't go back there."

"I don't have a choice." His voice was low, almost desperate. "I left to help get you out, because Dacre had come and I couldn't stand to watch it anymore. He was killing you." He exhaled sharply, his hands shaking. "He agreed to let her live, only as long as I was compliant, only as long as I'd help him break you. And if I don't go back soon, Verena, she won't survive."

My throat tightened painfully, and magic thrummed within me, aching and angry. Every bit of control I had just felt in that cave disappeared.

"I'll do whatever it takes. I'll lie, I'll steal, I'll—" *Betray me.* "I can't lose her."

I had spent so long hating him, resenting him, but he didn't have a choice.

Just like I hadn't had a choice.

The realization curled through me, unwelcomed. Micah and I had walked different paths, but they had still led us both to the same place.

To a prison neither of us had ever truly escaped from. Everything I thought I had known about Micah, about us, had unraveled before my eyes, leaving behind something raw and exposed.

He had been sent to protect me. He had known what I was before I did. He had lied, but he had also suffered.

I forced myself to breathe, trying to shove away the weight pressing against my ribs, the emotions clawing at my throat. "Then why are you here?"

"Because despite what you might think, I believe in you." His expression twisted, something sharp flashing behind his eyes. "I already watched Veyrith burn. I watched my parents wither away with it."

Another lie. Another thing I thought I knew about him but didn't.

"You're the only one who can stop him, Verena," he said, his voice rough. "But I need you to know, I need you to understand, that if I have to choose between saving her or saving your rebellion—" His fists clenched at his sides. "It won't be a choice."

Silence stretched between us, and he took a step back, then another. His eyes lingered on me for a long moment, and when I didn't say anything, he turned, walking away.

I swallowed hard, forcing down the tangled mess of emotions clawing at my throat. "Why didn't you tell me?" I called after him. "Why didn't you find me the moment you arrived here and tell me about her?"

Micah paused just before the cave curved out of sight, his shoulders stiff. He didn't look at me at first, didn't turn until the silence stretched so thin I thought it might snap.

Then, finally, he glanced back.

"I let him torture you." His voice was quiet, rough. "I stood there and did nothing while you screamed."

A breath shuddered through him, his hands curling into fists at his sides.

"I didn't want to add another burden for you to carry," he admitted, his throat bobbing as he swallowed. "Another thing to break you."

His gaze lingered on mine for only a second.

Then, he was gone.

CHAPTER 21
VERENA

I moved through the streets, my steps dragging and my mind racing. Exhaustion had sunk into my bones, from the training, from Micah, but I ignored it.

Because I could feel Dacre moving closer.

The mark on my wrist thrummed, faint and steady. A tether stretched between us, pulling me toward him even as my mind churned with everything that had happened. My mother's sacrifice, my father's cruelty, Micah's lies, and the weight of the rebellion pressing down on my shoulders like a blade poised at my throat.

My fingers curled around my wrist, the golden mark now hidden beneath my sleeve. I didn't want any of them to see it. I wasn't ready for the rest of the rebellion to question us or murmur their opinions or fear over what it meant.

It was still ours for now. Our bond, our marriage, and our secret.

And I wanted to keep it that way.

I weaved between the rebels who moved about the city.

The whispers followed me like they always did, like they had from the moment I stepped foot back into this place.

I terrified them, and there was nothing I could do, nothing I could say that was going to change that.

I walked faster, my breath unsteady, my body still humming with the remnants of magic. But no matter how much distance I put between myself and the training grounds, I couldn't escape the weight of what Micah had said.

"Another thing to break you."

I squeezed my eyes shut, trying to push the words away, but they clung to me.

Micah had been placed in my life by my mother and Dacre's grandmother. He had known the truth about me before I had. He had watched me struggle, had watched me starve, had watched me suffer, all the while keeping that secret buried inside him.

And then, when my father had dragged him back into the palace, when he had broken him down, he had betrayed me.

But he hadn't been given a choice.

The thought unsettled me, twisting something inside me.

I inhaled sharply as the warrior building came into view, the heavy doors looming in front of me. I was close now.

Dacre was close.

I could feel him searching for me through the bond. I could feel the steadiness of him, the way his presence coiled through me like it could protect me.

I reached for the door, but before my fingers could

graze the handle, a voice drifted through the air. Low. Sharp. Familiar.

Dacre's father.

I froze. I hadn't seen the man since they had decided to allow me to stay, hadn't wished to face him, but now, something inside me stirred at the low hum of his voice that was filled with frustration.

Slowly, I turned toward the sound, following it through a narrow path to the door of a small building carved from the stone, and that was where I saw them. Five men huddled around a worn wooden table, each of them dressed in their well-worn leathers.

Dacre's father sat at one side, his hands braced on the table, fingers curling against the edges of the map spread before him. The tension in his shoulders and sharp set of his jaw told me everything I needed to know.

This wasn't just idle conversation. This was strategy. This was war.

I took another slow step forward, keeping to the shadows, my body pressed against the cool stone wall.

"...too dangerous," one of the men said, his voice heavy with unease.

"She is the rightful heir," another countered. "The only heir much of this kingdom will accept."

"By name alone," Dacre's father retorted, his fingers dragging over the map. "We do not need a queen, and we certainly don't need one who is half of the king before her. Part of this kingdom may only accept her, but the other half will forbid it."

My heart slammed against my ribs.

Another man let out a quiet scoff. "Like it or not, your

son seems to believe otherwise, and our people are watching him. They are watching her. If they choose to follow her…"

"They won't," Dacre's father interrupted, his voice final, cold.

"And if they do?" The second man's words were carefully weighed, a subtle challenge hanging in the air.

Silence stretched between them, and I could hear my own breathing trembling in the stillness.

Then, slowly, Dacre's father straightened. His movements were stiff and controlled. "Then we make the choice for them."

My magic flared, and the mark on my wrist burned as if it were being branded into my skin all over again.

"What are you suggesting?" one of the men dared to ask.

Dacre's father hesitated for only a heartbeat, a moment that seemed to stretch into eternity before he spoke. "We remove her before she becomes a bigger threat than she already is."

I had known that they didn't trust me, that they feared my power, but hearing it spoken so plainly, hearing the decision settled in his voice—

I forced my breathing to remain even. Forced my magic to stay locked beneath my skin.

I had spent my entire life feeling like a prisoner, first in my father's palace, then in the rebellion's distrust, and now in their fear of what I was becoming.

But I was done letting them control me.

I was done hiding.

My life had been ruled by men who thought they could

decide my fate for me, but my fate wasn't theirs to control. It never had been.

Then, I stepped forward.

The moment my boots scraped against the stone, every head in the room snapped toward me.

I let the silence stretch, let them feel my presence before I reached for the only open chair and dragged it across the floor. The sound was deafening. Jarring.

Slowly, I sat down beside Dacre's father.

He didn't flinch, didn't look away, but I saw the slight shift in his body, the way he angled himself forward, blocking part of the map from my view.

I tilted my head, letting my gaze flick lazily over the table. "What's that?" I asked, my voice smooth, even.

"It's not your concern," he answered quickly. Too quickly.

"I'm nothing more than a dying heir, according to you." I leaned back in my chair, crossing my legs and resting one ankle on my knee as I met his gaze. "What could you possibly have to hide from me?"

Dacre's father didn't move. "Careful, girl," he murmured, his voice quiet, dangerous. "You have no idea the game you are trying to play."

I shifted in my seat, leaning forward slightly until our gazes locked. "And what game is that?"

His jaw tightened, but I didn't stop.

"Is this the game where I bleed for my kingdom while you remain hidden below it?"

His nostrils flared. "Excuse me?"

"You think you know what's best for this kingdom, but have you even looked upon it in the light of day?" My voice sharpened, and my magic stirred. "Do you even know what it is you're fighting for anymore? Who you are fighting for?"

One of the men inhaled sharply, but Dacre's father's cold eyes didn't waver from mine.

"You put too much faith in stories, girl. They've filled your head and made you believe that you're something that you're not." He leaned forward with his elbow pressed against the table, and he studied me intently. "Prophecies are the desperate prayers of those who don't have the strength to carve out their own future."

My magic hadn't stopped moving inside me, and for a moment, I wanted to unleash it upon him, to make him feel exactly what I was. "Those prayers, are they the same ones your wife uttered when she wanted a better future for your people, for her children?"

His expression faltered, and for the first time, I saw a crack in his mask.

I leaned forward slightly, mirroring his position. "Your wife, a daughter of Veyrith, just like me. A woman of the same kingdom as my own mother. A woman who fought against the same king as my own mother. That doesn't feel like some silly story to me. That feels like fate."

His jaw clenched, and I could practically see the way he pulled my words in and crafted his response in his mind as if he were sharpening a weapon. "Your mother did nothing to fight the king. She did nothing to stop the war." He ran his teeth over his bottom lip as he watched me, and I could feel the eyes of all the other men as well. "You speak of fate, but both of those mothers are dead. Both of them died at the hands of *your* father."

My voice was quiet, measured, but the magic inside me was not. "And your hands are clean?" I looked down at his hands before me, and he clamped them into fists. "My father will die for what he's done." The words settled into me. They slammed into my chest as I felt the truth of them in my bones. "And what price will you pay?"

His jaw locked, but he didn't speak.

The men around us shifted, their unease crackling in the air like an impending storm.

Then, footsteps echoed from behind me.

I didn't turn. I didn't have to. I felt him the moment he stepped into the room, the moment the tension around me shifted, the moment that thread between us pulled taut.

Dacre.

His fingers wrapped around the back of my chair. His lips brushed against my shoulder, the touch featherlight, but it sent a sharp shiver down my spine.

And I knew, even before I saw his face, even before I looked up at the men still watching us, that everything was about to change.

CHAPTER 22
DACRE

I had been making my way toward the training grounds when I felt it.

The mark on my wrist burned, a low, insistent hum, pulling at something deep inside me.

Verena.

I didn't know how to explain it, but it felt like something was wrong, like she was calling me forward through our bond.

I had never felt anything like it before, and when my mark had burned, when it had seared my skin, I could hardly catch my breath.

Wren and I had been scouting the perimeter of the hidden city when I felt it. Carefully watching the forest edge for any sign of Verena's father or his guards, but there had been none. I hadn't scouted once since we had arrived back in the hidden city, had relied on my father's intel alone, but when I had found her note this morning, when I slipped past the training grounds and saw her with Kai, I needed to see for myself.

I needed to calm the nightmares that I was creating in my mind that he was coming for her.

But then our soul-bond slammed into me, almost knocking me on my ass, and the mark on my wrist, it hadn't quit burning since.

I got back underground as quickly as I could, and I cursed as I had to push through people in the streets. I moved faster, my boots striking the stone with sharp, echoing steps. The closer I got, the stronger the feeling became. Not just the pulse of the bond, but something else. Something colder.

Voices drifted toward me from a narrow side street. Low, weighted, familiar. The feeling in my mark became stronger as I slowed.

Then I heard his voice.

My father.

I moved closer, keeping myself hidden in the shadows, my breathing steady despite the storm rising inside me.

"Prophecies are the desperate prayers of those who don't have the strength to carve out their own future."

My body went still. The words were laced with derision, dismissive in a way that made my blood run hot, but before I could even process them, another voice cut through the space between us.

Hers.

"Those prayers, are they the same ones your wife uttered when she wanted a better future for your people, for her children?"

I couldn't move. She was in there. She was with him, and she was talking about my mother.

"Your wife, a daughter of Veyrith, just like me. A woman of the same kingdom as my own mother. A woman who fought against the same king as my own mother. That doesn't feel like some silly story to me. That feels like fate."

I could feel her so powerfully in our bond in that moment, feel her anger and the way her magic wanted to escape. The way it made mine thrum to life in a way unlike I had ever felt before.

"Your mother did nothing to fight the king. She did nothing to stop the war."

My father paused, and I moved closer, looking into the room. There were other men in the room, other members of the rebellion, but none of them spoke. They were all looking at her.

"You speak of fate, but both of those mothers are dead. Both of them died at the hands of *your* father."

My father's words knocked the breath from my lungs, or maybe that was her. I couldn't tell the difference, couldn't tell which one of us was reacting, which one suddenly couldn't breathe.

"And your hands are clean? My father will die for what he's done."

Her words dripped from her lips like poison, and I realized that I had never heard her say them before. The king was her father, and I wanted to destroy him for what he had done. But there had always been fear in her voice when I heard her speak of him before, but I heard no fear now. I felt nothing but her rage.

"And what price will you pay?"

My father didn't answer immediately. The shocked silence stretched between them, and I wasn't willing to wait for his response.

I stepped forward, and the moment my boots hit the stone, she felt me.

Her back straightened, her fingers flexing just slightly where they rested on the table.

She didn't turn, didn't acknowledge me, but she knew. I could feel it in our bond that she knew.

And my father knew it too.

His sharp gaze flicked toward me, his jaw tightening at my presence. I moved with slow, deliberate steps, my eyes never leaving his as I crossed the room. The tension in the space thickened, the men around the table watching us like cornered prey.

I reached Verena's chair, curling my fingers around the back of it, letting them feel the weight of that small, possessive gesture. Letting them see it.

I leaned down and brushed my lips against her shoulder, and a shudder passed through her, so slight I almost couldn't feel it.

But she still didn't turn to look at me. She didn't need to.

She was still looking at my father, and so was I. I stood behind her, and I didn't speak.

I let the silence stretch, let my father feel the weight of my presence behind her, let him understand that this was not a fight he was going to win.

Verena tilted her head slightly, her fingers pressing against the table, as if she, too, was waiting, waiting to see if my father had anything left to say.

She had been challenging him.

She was the one holding his gaze.

Gods, she was magnificent.

Finally, I moved, slow and controlled, and I reached forward for her hand. She laced her fingers in mine with no hesitation, and I traced my fingers over the fabric of her sleeve, where I knew the golden mark of our soul-bond still burned beneath her skin.

"Please," I drawled, looking directly at my father. "Don't stop on my account."

My father's expression barely changed, but I saw it, the way his jaw ticked.

He was seething.

The other men shifted uneasily in their seats, their gazes flickering between my father and me, as if waiting for one of us to speak.

"No?" I laughed, but there wasn't an ounce of humor. "So there was a reason I wasn't invited to this meeting."

My father leaned back in his chair, his weathered eyes fixed on me. "There are conversations that no longer require your presence, son."

The name brushed against me, but I let it slide away, let it mean nothing.

I wasn't the little boy who still feared his father.

"But they require hers?" I asked, dipping my chin toward Verena.

Something sharp flickered in his gaze, but he masked it quickly. "She came of her own accord."

Verena looked up and my stomach tightened as her lip formed into a smile. "It's true." She nodded and her eyes

finally met mine. "I rudely interrupted them after over-
hearing them discuss my future."

"We were discussing the future of the rebellion." My
father tapped his fingers once against the table, his control
barely leashed, before his gaze flicked toward Verena.

"And? What was it you decided again?" A tense silence
settled at her question.

The fucking cowards.

"Ah, right," she continued as if they all weren't holding
their breath. "There was a bit of back and forth over
whether your people would ever accept me." She glanced
up at me again before quickly looking back to my father.
"But ultimately it was decided that your father here would
just take that choice away from them."

I exhaled slowly, a long, deliberate breath, as I traced
my free hand along the rough wood on the back of her
chair, each carved edge distinct beneath my palm.

The sensation grounded me slightly, cut into my mind
as I tried to maintain a sliver of composure in the face of
what she had just said.

But as I looked at my father, I knew that it was no use.

"You should get together with my father," Verena said
casually as her hand tightened against mine. "He has a lot
of experience in not allowing his people to have a voice. He
could give you some pointers."

My father's face contorted in rage, his brow furrowed,
jaw clenched, and eyes narrowing into fiery slits. His carefully crafted facade of calm control shattered, revealing the
true emotion boiling underneath.

"You believe you are the future of this kingdom?" he

spat, looking at her as if she weren't worthy of even sitting in front of him.

She didn't hesitate. It was as if she hadn't even noticed his anger. "I know I am."

I let my fingers tighten against the back of her chair.

My father exhaled through his nose. "Because of some prophecy?"

Verena tilted her head slightly, and she looked so powerful in that moment. So regal.

"Because it's her fate," I answered before she could. "You can fight it all you like, but Verena will be the next Queen of Marmoris."

One of the men spat out a curse, but I didn't stop.

"She is the heir to our kingdom. She is the heir to Veyrith, and fate has chosen her."

My father scoffed. "Fate." The word was laced with disdain, falling from his mouth like it was something foul. "I do not kneel for fate, nor for a girl who barely understands the power she wields." His eyes narrowed on Verena, and I stiffened. "You think I fear you? That I fear what you might become?" His gaze flicked to me. "I only fear that my son is too blind to see what stands before him. A curse, not a queen."

Magic snapped inside me. The bond roared to life, my mark burning, a silent response to the insult he had dared to utter.

"No one in this rebellion will follow you, none of them will bow."

Verena only smiled. A slow, lethal thing before her hand slipped out of mine, and she leaned forward until she was only inches away from my father. "Your son already bows for me."

A sharp inhale cut through the room. Someone cursed under their breath.

Fuck. She is going to drive them mad.

"We will never have her as our queen." He looked up at me, ignoring her completely. "No matter what happens, no matter what she gives. I'd rather have her head on a pike than wearing the crown."

The words rang through the room like a war cry, a declaration that could not be undone, and I snapped. I moved around Verena's chair, shielding her as I advanced on my father. His chair scraped loudly against the floor as he tried to retreat, but his efforts were futile.

My hand shot forward, seizing his shirt in a firm grasp. I pulled him toward me with a force that left our faces separated by only a breath.

Then the words tumbled from my lips, the ones imbued with the potential to alter the course of everything. Like a stone cast into a still pond, they rippled outward, carrying with them the weight of what we had done.

"You are my father, but if you dare speak of my wife like that again, I will slit your throat and paint this city in your blood."

The silence that followed was so intense it seemed to press against my ears until they threatened to rupture.

I lifted my other hand and jerked up my sleeve, allowing the mark that glowed against my skin to be right in my father's view.

"I don't want you to so much as look at my mate," I

growled as the mark glowed brighter, our magic between us raging to lash out at him.

My father's fury was no longer hidden. He seethed as he stared up at my mark. "You think tying yourself to her will change anything?" he hissed. "You think it will make her fit to rule?"

I let out a laugh that was low and mocking. "It changes everything."

Verena moved then, standing from her seat and sliding into my view with all the grace of a queen.

And gods, she looked the part.

I turned back to my father, watching as his rage flickered just beneath the surface, barely contained, barely leashed. *Good.* Let him feel it. Let him choke on it.

"This rebellion was built on the idea that we carve our own futures," I said, my voice ringing through the cavern. "That we are not ruled by the whims of tyrants who take what they want and discard the rest." I let my gaze sweep over the men at the table, then landed back on my father. And then, I twisted the knife deeper.

"But here you sit, deciding Verena's fate like she has no say in it. As if she isn't standing right in front of you, fighting harder than any of you ever have."

A few of the men looked away, shame flickering across their expressions. But not my father.

"She is dangerous," he spat. "And you are blind."

"I see clearer now than I ever have." My voice dropped, and I lifted my wrist higher, letting the golden mark shine in the torchlight.

"The tides have already turned," I said. "The storm you feared is already here."

My father's face twisted, and the men around the table refused to meet my gaze.

"She is my fate, my future," I said quietly, my words sharp as a blade. "And I serve only her."

I turned slightly, lifting my chin, letting the weight of my words press into the room. Then I stood to my full height and reached for Verena. She fell into me easily, her hand wrapping around mine, as we turned our backs to all of them and began walking out of the room.

But then I slowed, and I looked back over my shoulder. I had once respected every man in this room, and I had followed their commands as if they were gods.

But no gods stared back at me now.

"Your future queen is leaving," I said firmly, and I felt Verena stiffen beside me. I felt her magic take in my words and slither back as if it, too, were waiting to see what I would do. "Kneel."

A beat of silence before my father's laugh rang out. His hands curled into fists, his knuckles stark white against his skin.

But one by one, the others stood.

They all hesitated, their gazes flicking between Verena and my father, before the first finally dropped to his knee.

Verena tugged at my hand, but I didn't look away from them.

Another knelt to the ground.

And another.

Verena inhaled sharply beside me, but she did not speak as the last man finally dropped to his knee.

Every man except one.

I looked down at my father. Still sitting. Still furious.

His body was stiff, his shoulders locked in rigid defiance. He would never bow to her. I knew it without ever having to hear him say it.

"Careful." The word poured from his lips. "You're in my hidden city, in my rebellion." The fury that filled his gaze could have burned through stone, but I didn't care.

I turned away from him, and I lifted Verena's hand to my mouth. I pressed a kiss to her knuckles, slowly, reverently.

Then I looked back at my father one last time before I led her from the room.

CHAPTER 23
VERENA

The city had been restless for days.

It wasn't something tangible, not something I could see, but I could feel it, a hum in the streets, a shift in the way people moved. Conversations were quieter, glances sharper, tension settling like dust in the air.

I had spent the last few days training, forcing my body through exhaustion, forcing my magic into submission. But no matter how hard I pushed myself, I couldn't shake the feeling that something was coming.

And I wasn't the only one who felt it.

Dacre had been speaking with scouts more frequently, his patience thinner than usual, his fingers twitching toward his sword before he would draw back. I could feel it through the bond, through the way our magic curled around one another, restless and waiting.

War was coming faster than either of us wanted to admit, and when Dacre had left our room this morning to scout, I knew in my gut that we weren't going to like what he found.

Now, as I walked toward the training grounds, panic flooded me. I hadn't seen him since he'd been back. It was Wren who had told me that he had called a meeting, Wren whose features carried the same worry that I felt.

I walked into the cave that had started to feel like my second home, and it was already full.

Dacre stood near the far wall, his arms crossed over his chest, his expression hard as he surveyed the rebels before him. His grandmother stood at his side, silent and still, her silver eyes sharp beneath the torchlight.

To the right of the room, Liya leaned against the wall, her gaze flicking toward me as I entered.

The cave was filled with more rebels than I had ever seen in one place before. Several of the older members of the rebellion stood together, their postures stiff, their hands curled into fists at their sides. But others, the younger rebels, the ones who had grown up with Dacre, they stood closer to Dacre, their wary eyes watching the others.

A clear divide.

A divide that I had not noticed before now.

A murmur passed through the room as I moved toward Dacre. I felt the weight of their eyes settle upon me, some with hatred, some with open distrust, and others with apprehension.

But for the first time, I felt something else too.

Expectation.

The news of our union had spread through the rebellion like wildfire licking through a dry forest, and though I held no doubts about the choices we made, trepidation about their reactions gripped my throat.

They hadn't accepted me as one of them, and I doubted that they ever would. But Dacre was the rebellion, and he always had been.

It didn't matter that he had broken their trust, that he had betrayed them in some of their eyes, he was still one of them.

And now, he was a part of me.

Dacre exhaled, his shoulders relaxing slightly when he saw me. The mark that tethered us together burned once his eyes met mine, and I could feel his restlessness through our magic as I moved beside him.

His hand found mine, his fingers pressing against my palm, before he moved them higher, absently running them along my mark.

"Is everything okay?" I asked him quietly, and when he looked at me, I already knew the answer.

"You're late." His voice was low, a subtle thread of amusement woven beneath the seriousness of his tone.

I arched my brow, a playful smirk tugging at the corner of my lips as I slowly slid my arms around his waist. "I didn't realize this was a scheduled event."

He let his arms fall, relaxing instantly before wrapping them around me and drawing me into his chest. "I was talking to her," he said softly, before he nodded to his sister who had just settled at his side.

"Me?" Wren asked, her voice rising to a near shriek as she pointed at her own chest. "First of all, I'm not your errand boy. Second, you try telling Kai you need him for a meeting that you actually have no idea what the meeting is about when he's in one of his moods."

She was right. Kai had been particularly moody today, his temper simmering just beneath the surface as we trained, and he had pushed me harder than I anticipated.

So had Dacre's grandmother.

"Where is he anyway?" Dacre's eyes scanned the room as he peered over my head, looking for his friend.

"He just walked in," Wren replied, her gaze fixed on her brother.

I glanced over my shoulder to catch sight of Kai striding into the chamber. His dark hair was wet and ruffled and his clothes were fresh. He had a look of determination etched on his face, a familiar expression I had come to realize he wore often, and he scanned the room until his gaze finally landed on Wren.

It didn't take him long to reach us, or for him to move to Wren's side.

"Sorry," he muttered, his voice a low, gravelly rumble. "There was something I had to take care of."

Dacre gave him a knowing nod. "Be prepared."

"Always am," Kai answered quickly, positioning himself with such protective intent that he nearly obscured Wren from the view of the rest of the room.

"What does that mean?" I asked, my eyes darting between the two of them.

Dacre, however, simply brushed a stray lock of hair away from my face before leaning down to plant a soft, lingering kiss at the corner of my mouth.

"Dacre." I uttered his name as a gentle warning, yet his smile lingered against my lips, warm and teasing.

"Yes, wife?" he replied, his voice carrying a playful note.

A deep ache settled in my stomach, twisting with longing and unease. This was everything I wanted, him and me, entwined in each other's arms, teasing and playing with one another, free from the burdens of the world. But even as a soft smile played on his lips, I could feel the tension twisting inside him and his magic humming with vigilance and poised to strike.

Around us, the room buzzed with a chorus of murmurs, like an unsettling symphony of ghosts that clawed at the edges of the dream I clung to desperately.

His lips remained pressed against mine, and I dug my hands into his back, my fingers trembling.

His lips then traveled to my ear, where he pressed another gentle kiss just below it, sending chills cascading across my skin.

"Everything is going to be okay," he whispered softly, his arms tightening around me. I squeezed my eyes shut and let myself feel him, allowing his words to soothe over me. "You and me. Nothing else matters beyond that."

He was right, I knew he was, but even as I held him against me, I couldn't shake the unease that crept along my skin.

Dacre pulled back slightly, enough to peer into my eyes, searching for something intangible. Then he leaned down again, capturing my lips in a tender kiss before pulling away completely. I settled next to Wren, letting my shoulder press against hers, and Dacre stepped forward.

Dacre's voice was calm, but there was an edge to it when he finally spoke. "We've received word."

The room fell into silence. A heavy pause as if we were all waiting for something to drop.

"Some of you have already heard whispering, but it's true." His voice did not waver. "They are true."

He glanced back at me once, only for a moment.

"The king is preparing for something," he continued. "And if we don't make our move now, it may be too late."

A low murmur spread through the room, but I could hardly hear any of them over the roar of my magic in my ears.

"What does that mean?" a man called out, someone I didn't recognize. "What's he preparing for?"

Dacre's jaw tightened, but before he could speak again, Eiran stepped forward. "Word came from the city this morning. The city is burning."

He looked to Dacre, and I was surprised when Dacre gave him a small nod. I glanced between them, unease prickling at my skin. Dacre had told me he once trusted Eiran like a brother, but not anymore.

And it was clear where Eiran's loyalty had lain.

Why was he speaking now? Why was Dacre listening?

"The king has started raiding homes, dragging people from their beds in the dead of night. They're being taken to the dungeons, or worse." He exhaled sharply. "Bodies are hanging from the palace walls."

A cold, sharp chill rippled through me, prickling my skin like icy needles. The walls seemed to close in, pressing against me, making the air feel dense and suffocating until my breaths came in short, shallow gasps.

The mark on my wrist burned as if it were aflame.

"He's looking for me." The words fell from my lips before I even realized I had spoken them.

A murmur rushed through the crowd, but I couldn't hear what they were saying; I couldn't focus on anything except the magic that moved inside me. Not just mine. Dacre's was there too, it skated over my own, as if it were trying to calm it, calm me.

Eiran nodded once, his jaw tight. "And he's willing to burn his own city to the ground to find you."

I felt the shift before I saw it, the way the younger rebels stiffened, the way the older members exchanged glances, uncertain.

Dacre turned back to the room, his voice measured. "You all know what this means. What we've prepared for."

There was another pause before another voice rang out. I couldn't even tell where it came from. "Then maybe we should give her to him. Give the king what he wants."

The words slammed into me, and for a moment, I didn't breathe.

A pained grunt cut through the room. A boot scraped against the stone floor. Someone cursed under their breath.

Dacre's magic lashed through the air, his body going rigid in front of me. I felt him, not just through the bond, but through the raw force of his fury, seeping into every inch of me. His rage curled like a living thing, wild and angry.

His voice was low, lethal. "Say that again."

The room fell deathly still, and in that silence, I knew.

This was it. This was the moment they would either choose to fight with us—or against us.

I could feel him so clearly through our bond, as if his

fingers were wrapping around mine. It wasn't just a phantom touch, it was an anchor, a claim, a warning. His magic surged through the bond, slamming into mine like a shield.

Not her. The unspoken words vibrated through me, through the air between us, through the crackling tension of the room.

"If any of you think for a damn second that I would ever hand her over..." His voice shook with his anger. "Then you have forgotten exactly who the hell I am."

The weight of him filled the room, his fury a tangible thing, pressing against every rebel who stood before him. A muscle in Dacre's jaw flexed as his gaze swept the gathered rebels. "She is not a bargaining chip. She is not a pawn to be moved in your war. She is the war."

Their gazes turned to me, and I forced myself to stand straighter beneath the weight of it.

Then, Eiran's voice cut through the tension once again. "The king is moving fast." He looked toward Dacre, then at me. "And if we don't act now, he'll force our hands before we're ready."

Dacre nodded as he dragged a hand through his hair, and I could feel it then, his desperation to keep me from the palace. To keep me from my father.

To keep me.

A ripple of unease spread through the room, the tension thickening like a storm about to break.

I looked across the room, and I spotted Dacre's father for the first time. He stood stiff and unmoving near the far wall, but his silence was louder than anything else in the room.

And he was staring at Eiran with his eyes narrowed.

"You're all worried about the wrong thing," Eiran said, and his voice shook with desperation.

I turned back to him as he stepped farther into the room, farther in front of the entire rebellion. There was something about his posture, about the way his hands wrapped around his arms and his fingers dug into his skin that made my stomach tighten.

"Enlighten us then, Eiran," Dacre's father drawled, and everyone turned to look at him.

Eiran shifted on his feet, his fingers twitching. His gaze flickered toward Dacre for a brief second, before he looked at the gathered rebels. "You're all sitting here debating whether or not she's the real threat." Finally, his gaze landed on me. "When the actual threat is already on the move."

The air seemed to shift.

"The tithe is meant to fuel this kingdom, but the king is using it to drain it dry." Eiran's gaze burned into mine. "He's starving us."

It was as if poison had been injected into my veins, the venom coursing through me with a nauseating intensity. Each pulse was a drumbeat of discomfort, making my magic feel twisted and foreign beneath my skin. My stomach churned violently, threatening to expel its contents with every agonizing throb.

"The king is cutting off the kingdom's lifeline," Kai muttered, his expression darkening.

Dacre's father looked to Kai, his mouth a hard line. "And he won't stop until he has her back."

The mark on my wrist continued to burn, but my body

went numb. The blood flowing through my veins turned to icy rivulets, the frigid chill seeping out from my core and spreading like frost through my limbs.

I would not go back to my father. I would fight him; I would fight them all, but I would never go back to being in his cage.

I could hear muffled noises around me, though I couldn't make out a thing they were saying. My vision blurred, edges softening and merging into one another, and in a desperate attempt to anchor myself, I grasped for something to hold on to. It landed on something solid, and I dug my fingers in hard.

"Verena." The sound of my name was distant and distorted, as though I were submerged underwater and couldn't get to the source.

I wasn't sure how long it lasted. Whether it was a fleeting second or an eternity of moments strung together, I couldn't be certain. But gradually, the world around me began to sharpen and come back into focus. I felt firm, reassuring hands gripping me, keeping me upright as I fought for each breath.

Dacre's face slowly came into view, his eyes wide and brimming with concern.

"Breathe, Verena," he urged gently, leaning down until his face was level with mine, his voice a lifeline amidst the chaos swirling in my mind.

I nodded weakly, trying desperately to quell the rising panic that was consuming me.

"No one is going to touch you." The words spoken didn't fall from Dacre's lips, and I blinked as I turned my head toward the sound. My gaze landed on my own fingers, clenching Kai's forearm with such intensity that I'd almost drawn blood. "We will never let him touch you again."

His promise hung in the air, and I nodded slowly because I believed him.

If Kai had a choice, if Dacre did, neither of them would ever let my father near me again.

But it was the lack of choice, the iron grip of my fate, that caused my fear to still flow through my veins like a raging current. Even as my breath gradually steadied and my vision cleared, the dread remained.

"He won't stop," I said for them all to hear, shaking my head slowly, feeling the weight of their gazes settling on me. "No matter what you offer him, no matter what he takes, he will keep demanding more until there is nothing left of your rebellion except the memory of what you once fought for."

Eiran took another step forward. His face was pale, his shoulders stiff, but his voice, his voice was steady.

"I've watched you all prepare for this war for years," he said, his gaze sweeping the rebels. "I've watched you sharpen your blades and count your arrows. I've watched you rally behind the men who led you." His eyes flicked to Dacre's father then to his own father. I hadn't even noticed his father behind him before that moment, but it was impossible to miss him now.

He stood there with a cane in his hand, bearing his weight on it for support, and he watched his son with a wary gaze. He had hunted me through the woods with Dacre's father. He was the man that Dacre had attacked when we finally got free, and I didn't trust him or his son.

"But what if I told you that we've been fighting the wrong war all along?"

Dacre's father scoffed, shaking his head, but there was something in the set of his shoulders, a stiffness that hadn't been there before. "What the hell are you talking about?"

Eiran didn't look at him. He looked at Dacre.

"Do you remember everything from that night?" Eiran's voice was quieter now, but Dacre's emotion raged through our bond.

His power pulsed against mine as if I were the only thing keeping his contained.

Eiran's throat bobbed as he searched Dacre's eyes, and I had never seen Eiran look so vulnerable before, so fearful. "The night of the palace raid."

The room stilled, and Dacre said nothing. But his pulse, his breath, the bond between us tightened until I felt like I couldn't breathe.

"You were trying to save your mother," Eiran continued, his voice barely more than a whisper. "I was trying to save myself."

A flicker of pain crossed Dacre's face, and Wren gasped beside me, but I didn't dare look away.

Eiran exhaled shakily, and his father moved, his steps unsteady as he used his cane to help him forward toward his son.

"Son." His voice was hard, desperate, a warning.

But Eiran didn't stop. "I saw what happened that night. I saw who killed her."

Dacre's breath hitched, and he took the smallest step back as if he had been hit.

Eiran glanced back at his father once before his voice cracked. "It wasn't the king."

A murmur rippled through the room, and Dacre's father took a slow step forward, his expression darkening. "Careful with your next words, boy."

Eiran's gaze snapped to him, and for the first time, I saw it. The raw fury barely held in check, the guilt that was eating him alive.

"I watched your wife die," Eiran whispered. "And I watched my father stand beside you all these years after he drove the blade through her chest."

There was a beat of silence, a breath that seemed to be ripped from all our chests, then chaos.

Dacre's father staggered back as if Eiran had struck him across the face. His breath shuddered, his fingers clenching at his sides.

"You're lying." His voice was low, rough, but there was something in it, something that cracked.

Eiran didn't move. "I wish I was."

Dacre's father's gaze snapped to Eiran's father, Reed. "Tell him he's lying."

There was a tense, horrible silence before Reed, the man who had stood at Dacre's father's side for years, tightened his grip on his cane and slowly shook his head.

"I did what had to be done."

Dacre's father lunged, and the room erupted.

His hands slammed into Reed's chest, knocking him backward, sending his cane clattering against the stone. Reed hit the ground hard, breath rushing from his lungs, his hands trembling as he tried to brace himself.

"You killed her?" Dacre's father's voice shook with fury. "You murdered my wife?"

The room was spiraling. The rebels were yelling, bodies shifting, some surging forward, others frozen in place.

Eiran's father gasped for breath. "She was helping the enemy."

Dacre's father's fist connected with his face. A sickening crack echoed through the cavern.

Then magic snapped through the air. A force so sharp and sudden it threw Dacre's father backward. I gasped, feeling that power rush through me.

Dacre's eyes were wild. His magic lashed out, curling through the room, the torches bending toward him as if they were drawn to his rage.

He was breathing too hard, his hands trembling at his sides, and I could taste his anger, feel it pulling my own magic through our tether.

"Dacre." I reached for him, grasping his wrist. His pulse slammed against mine, his magic surging toward me, gripping onto me like a lifeline.

"Dacre," I whispered his name again, pulling him back.

He gasped, his chest heaving, but he wouldn't look at me. He was still looking at them.

Dacre's father braced himself with his hands on his knees, his breath coming too fast, his fists still clenched.

"Why?" His voice cracked. A demand, a plea, an accusation all tangled into one.

Reed spat blood onto the stone floor, his lip curled in disgust. "Because she wasn't fighting for us." Then his chin lifted, and for the first time, his gaze cut directly to me. "She was fighting for her."

The breath ripped from my lungs, and Dacre went deathly still. His body was coiled so tight, and I could feel the tremor in his magic, the barely contained violence waiting to be unleashed.

"What?" Dacre's voice was raw, hoarse with disbelief.

Reed let out a bitter, rattling breath. "I saw her." He wiped at his jaw, but his hands still trembled. "I saw her trying to get the princess out."

The words struck like a blade. The princess.

Me.

I staggered back, my shoulder colliding with someone behind me as a memory slammed into me. A flicker of movement, a hand grasping mine, a voice whispering *"Run."*

A voice I hadn't recognized before. A voice that had been hers.

Dacre turned toward me, his breath shallow, his hands trembling at his sides. "Verena—"

But I barely heard him because I remembered.

I remembered running. I remembered guards shouting, the palace halls blurring past me. I remembered a woman, dark hair, brown eyes with a hint of silver, her fingers tight around my wrist as she pulled me through the corridors, her voice low and urgent.

"You have to go. You have to get out."

I sucked in a sharp breath, my vision swimming. Dacre's mother had saved me.

And she had died for it.

Eiran's shaky voice drew me back, made me see what was right in front of me. "I didn't understand it at the time," he said, his voice hoarse. "I was just a kid, barely older than Verena. I thought we were there to kill the king. To end it."

His eyes flicked to Dacre, and something broke in his expression.

"But your mother...she had her own mission."

Dacre's magic lashed out again, heat pulsing through the cavern, but it didn't attack, it hovered.

Eiran swallowed hard, his hands clenching at his sides. "We were supposed to breach the palace and get to the throne room. But then—" He exhaled sharply, as if just saying the words burned. "She wasn't with us anymore."

Dacre's hands curled into fists, and his father looked as if he wasn't breathing.

"She wasn't fighting," Eiran continued, his voice gaining strength. "She wasn't cutting down guards or leading rebels. She was running. Pulling someone behind her."

His eyes flicked to me, and I felt the world tilt. I could barely breathe.

"She was getting the princess out."

The words ripped through the room like a blade slicing through flesh. Murmurs rose from the rebels, some quiet gasps, others angry, disbelieving.

"You're lying. She fought for this rebellion," Dacre's father snarled, but his voice shook. "She would never—"

"She did," Eiran cut him off, his voice raw. "I saw it. I saw her pull Verena through the halls, saw her shove her into the tunnels."

He dragged in a ragged breath. "And my father saw it too." He hesitated, his gaze flicking back to his father.

Dacre's eyes narrowed. Dangerous. Out of control. "What?"

Eiran gritted his teeth.

"He tried to stop her. He tried to rip Verena from her hands, to use her against her father, but your mother fought him." His gaze jumped around, his body shifting uncomfortably. "She wouldn't let him through the doors, into the tunnels, and I saw him raise his sword and drive it into her chest."

Dacre swayed. His breaths came too fast, too ragged. His hands trembled at his sides, his magic choking the air.

Someone cursed. Others moved, but it was Dacre's father who I couldn't take my eyes off of. His head snapped toward Reed, pure, unfiltered rage in his eyes. "You—"

"I was fighting for our people. For this rebellion," Reed spat, his voice shaking. "And she was a traitor."

Dacre moved so fast the air cracked. He slipped from my hands and he shot past his father. He didn't stop until he reached Reed's side, until his fist collided with the man's jaw.

Dacre's chest heaved. His knuckles were slick with blood, but he didn't stop. He slammed his fist into Reed again and again.

I could feel the storm raging inside him through our bond—grief, fury, betrayal.

Kai moved for his friend, for his brother, but Dacre's father was already there. He pulled Dacre back, pulling him off Reed, and he whispered something to Dacre that none of the rest of us could hear.

A rough, wet cough rattled from Reed's lips as he crumpled to the ground. Blood pooled beneath his nose, and his breaths came in short, wheezing gasps.

No one moved to help him. No one spoke. The rebels stared. Some with horrified realization. Others with pure rage.

"You…" Reed wheezed, his voice garbled. He spat more blood onto the ground. "I tell you how she betrayed us and you…"

"She was saving a child, you bastard." Liya's voice ripped through the silence, and when I turned toward her, her eyes were wild with fury.

She shoved herself away from the wall, stepping forward, her fingers curling like she wanted to wrap them around Reed's throat herself.

"You call her a traitor?" she hissed, her own magic snapping through the air like static before a storm. "She was a mother, protecting a child, and you cut her down for it."

Reed opened his mouth, but before he could speak, another voice rose from the crowd.

"She was one of us."

A murmur rippled through the gathered rebels. A spark. A shift.

"She fought for us." Someone else. Louder.

Dacre's father hadn't moved. His hands still fisted in his son's shirt, holding him back, but his face was ashen. His gaze locked on to Reed as if he was looking at a stranger.

"You killed her." The words weren't loud. They weren't angry. They were ruined.

Reed's lips parted. "She—"

"You killed my wife." Dacre's father let go of his son without looking away from the man he had trusted for decades. His hands shook.

"She was trying to protect her from the king." His voice sounded like gravel grinding together. Like it hurt him to say it, like he regretted the decisions he had made.

Reed's gaze darted to the rebels. Some still stood in shock. Some were shaking their heads. Others…others looked away from him instead of meeting his gaze.

And that's when he panicked.

"She was supposed to fight for us!" he snarled, scrambling to his feet. "For our cause! Not for the enemy—"

Dacre's father moved so fast, so violently, that I flinched. His hand wrapped around Reed's throat before I even saw him move.

"You were my brother," he growled, voice shaking. "And you slaughtered my wife."

Reed gasped, clawing at his grip, but Dacre's father's rage had finally found its outlet.

This was the moment. The moment that shattered everything. Reed's voice choked in his throat.

"I trusted you," Dacre's father whispered. "I built this rebellion with you. And all this time, you—"

A raw, shuddering breath. Then, Reed's next words were a death sentence.

"You are no brother of mine." Reed was still gasping, still clawing at the hand around his throat, but no one moved to stop Dacre's father.

Eiran stared at the ground, stared down at his father. He hadn't moved since his confession, since he had ripped the truth from his chest and thrown it into the fire.

Dacre's breath was still ragged, and I could feel his
magic roiling, burning against mine through our bond, but
his eyes were locked on Eiran.

"You were my friend," Dacre rasped, his voice raw,
shaking. Accusing.

Eiran's throat bobbed. "I know."

"I trusted you."

A muscle in Eiran's jaw ticked. "I know."

Dacre took a single, sharp step forward. "Then why?"

Eiran finally looked at him, and I saw it. Not just guilt.
Grief.

"I didn't understand then," he admitted, his voice
barely above a whisper. "All I had seen was your mother's betrayal, what my father told me. And I…" He
exhaled sharply. "I could barely look at you without
seeing what your mother had done. What my father
had."

Dacre shook his head, his magic snapping like a live
wire. "And now?"

Eiran hesitated before his gaze flickered to me.

"Then you brought her here," he said. "And I didn't see
it at first, didn't recognize her." He let out a slow, shaking
breath. "And when I did, it was too late."

I stiffened.

"That's why my father sent me after her when she ran,"
Eiran continued, his eyes locked on mine. "Why I went into
those woods."

My stomach dropped.

Oh gods.

The moment Eiran had found me, when I thought he
had been there to help me, but he knew.

Dacre lunged, but Kai was there, shoving between them.

"Move," Dacre growled, voice like shattered glass.

"No," Kai snapped, shouldering him back, his hands wrapping around his friend. "Think, Dacre."

Eiran's hands shook. "I should have told you. I should have told you what I knew that night."

"Then why didn't you?" Dacre growled, looking past Kai who was still shoving him back.

Eiran's jaw clenched. "Because I trusted my father, because I was a coward."

His father let out a strangled sound from where Dacre's father still held him pinned against the ground. "Eiran—"

"I let him tell me who to be." Eiran's voice rose, cracking like thunder. "I let him tell me what to believe, what to do. I let him turn me into him." His hands curled into fists. "And I regret all of it."

Everyone was watching. Everyone held their breath.

"I know it's too late to fix it," he said quietly. "But I had to say it now. Because she's the answer." His throat bobbed. "Verena is the one who will end this war."

A murmur rippled through the room before Dacre's father moved. He dropped his grip on Reed, let him fall to the floor, and then he straightened.

Then he turned. His face was ashen, his hands shaking at his sides. His entire body seemed heavier. As if something had been ripped from his chest.

His voice was low, gravelly. "This rebellion was never meant for this."

His shoulders dropped, and his gaze fell to me.

"My wife died fighting for you," he said, his voice

rough. "And I let her murderer stand by my side all this time."

"You do not speak for this rebellion," Reed growled from where he was trying to scramble to his feet. "You never did."

But Dacre's father didn't look back at him, instead, he looked to his son, then past him to Wren, before he finally looked back to me.

"I have been wrong about a great many things." His voice didn't shake, not anymore. "And I was wrong about you."

His words slammed into my chest.

"I was wrong about this rebellion."

The mark on my wrist felt like it was going to burn me alive, but I didn't dare look away from Dacre's father. Not as he moved forward, not as he bent a knee.

A gasp ripped through the room as he pressed a fist to the ground and dropped his head slightly. "I will follow you into war."

I didn't breathe. I didn't think anyone in the room did.

"And I will fight beside you until the king is dead." He lifted his head slightly, his gaze burning into mine. "He has already taken too much, too much of you, too much of us, and we will not allow him to take any more."

Then, one by one, the rebels began to kneel.

Some moved quickly, heads bowed without hesitation. Others faltered, exchanging wary glances, but still, they dropped to the ground.

They weren't kneeling for fate.

They weren't kneeling for a prophecy.

They were kneeling for a choice.

A choice to fight for us all, a choice to end this war.

I swallowed, my chest tight, full, burning. The weight of it, of all of it, pressed against my ribs, but I forced my shoulders back.

I took a step forward, toward Dacre's father, toward all of them. Dacre moved to my side, his hand wrapping around mine, and I couldn't look anywhere else as he brought my hand to his mouth and pressed a kiss to my mark, to our bond.

There was no hesitation left in me, no more wavering over what I would do.

I dropped to one knee, and Dacre's father's gaze snapped to mine.

Dacre's fingers tightened around my wrist. The mark throbbed between us, pulsing unlike I had ever felt before.

"I will fight beside you." My voice was steady. Strong. "Until the king is dead."

The tides had turned.

And I knew when tomorrow dawned, we would march.

Tomorrow, my father would fall.

CHAPTER 24
DACRE

The tunnels twisted in endless, winding paths beneath the hidden city. The stone was cool against my fingertips as I ran my palm along the wall, following Verena deeper into the cavern. I could barely hear the movement around us anymore, the rebels making their final preparations, sharpening their blades, preparing for war.

Here, it was silent.

Only the soft scuff of our boots against the ground, only the sound of her breathing, steady and controlled, as she led me forward.

I didn't ask where we were going. I already knew.

She didn't look back at me, not yet, but her grip on my wrist tightened, as if she could feel the weight pressing into my chest. As if she knew what I wasn't saying.

The air grew warmer, the damp scent of stone and earth giving way to something softer, something familiar. The springs.

The first place I had ever seen her clearly. A place that had once been a refuge. The place where she had first let me heal her, touch her.

When she had still been wary of me, still guarded and sharp-tongued, and I had been more than uncertain of her. I had thought her to be my enemy, and she had embraced the role with precision. Until neither of us could resist the undeniable force that simmered, pulling us toward the truth of what we really were, of what we were always destined to be.

What neither of us could ever imagine was forcing us together.

Verena stepped forward, releasing my wrist as she moved toward the edge of the water. She reached for the laces of her leathers, her fingers working them loose until each piece came away from her body with a soft rustle, revealing her skin as she shed the layers of clothes that still clung to her skin.

The warm glow of the moss bathed her bare skin in warm light, flickering over the ridges of her spine as she turned.

She still hadn't spoken. She didn't have to.

The moment she let her armor fall away, the moment she stepped into the water, I felt it. The tremor in her magic. The weight in her chest. The fear she wasn't saying aloud.

"I need you," she whispered as she settled into the water, her voice soft with vulnerability, and gods, there was nothing in this world or the next that I wouldn't give her.

My hands were already moving before I could think,

unfastening my own leathers, each piece falling away as I discarded them, my focus solely on her.

I followed her with a singular purpose, the world around us fading into insignificance, and by the time I reached her, the surface of the water was rippling gently around her.

The heat curled around my skin as I sank into the water, the steam rising between us, twisting through the silence.

Verena turned to me, lifting her arms beneath the surface, letting her fingers skim over my ribs, her touch soft and trembling. I let her touch settle me, but it did nothing to quiet the war raging inside me.

Her fingers traced slow, careful circles against my ribs, her body warm where she pressed against me, the steam curling in thick ribbons around us.

But I felt her waiting.

I had felt it since we left the training grounds, since she pulled me away from the rebellion, away from the eyes watching me too closely, waiting for me to fall apart.

But she was waiting, too.

I pressed my face into her neck, inhaling her scent, the soft mix of salt and wildflowers that was so uniquely her. My arms tightened around her waist, pulling her body flush with mine.

But it wasn't enough.

She must have felt it, how I was barely holding on, because when she spoke there was so much caution in her voice, so much sadness.

"You haven't said a word about her."

An exhale punched from my lungs.

Verena didn't pull away, but she lifted her head slightly, enough for her lips to brush against my temple. "Dacre," she whispered. "Talk to me."

I closed my eyes, pressing my forehead against her shoulder. "There's nothing left to say."

She stiffened then she pushed. Gently at first, her hands moving to cup my face, lifting me so I had no choice but to look at her.

But I wasn't ready for what I saw in her eyes.

There was no pity, no hesitation, just understanding, and a sudden ache sliced through my chest.

Her voice was barely above a whisper. "You lost her twice."

Her words hit me. They haunted me. "I never even got to say goodbye."

She didn't look away. Didn't let me.

"You were just a boy," she murmured, her thumbs sweeping along my jaw, soft, steady. "And you tried to save her."

I let out a hollow laugh. "And I failed."

"No." Her voice was unyielding. "You didn't fail her, Dacre."

I turned my head slightly, pressing my lips against her palm. "Then why does it feel like I did?"

Verena exhaled slowly, her forehead pressing against mine. "Because you loved her. Because people who you trusted took her from you."

A muscle jumped in my jaw, and I refused to allow my thoughts to go to Eiran, refused to let his betrayal settle back deep inside me again until I couldn't find my breath. "She would have loved you."

Verena's breath hitched, but she didn't pull away. "You think so?"

"I know so," I rasped. "You're what she wanted for this kingdom. She died trying to save you." My fingers tightened against her waist, and I could feel the ache in her chest as I said the words, feel her guilt. "And I will finish what she started."

The air between us shifted, thickened, the weight of what we were about to do settling over us.

I let my hands slide to her lower back, pressing her more firmly against me, reminding myself that she was still there. "Tell me," I murmured, my voice rough. "Tell me what you need me to do when we get inside the palace."

Her breaths came unsteady, but she met my gaze without hesitation.

"We find my father." Her fingers curled against my ribs. "We kill him."

The words settled between us, but she didn't move. She didn't blink.

I let my other hand skim up her spine, over the curve of her shoulder, tracing a path to her jaw. Soft. Careful. "How can I do it without you?"

Her throat bobbed. "What?"

"I don't want you anywhere near him. I don't want him to ever be able to hurt you again." This wasn't what we had already talked about, it wasn't what we had planned, but every part of me screamed to never let her set foot back in that palace again.

A flicker of doubt crossed her face, but it was gone in an instant. She squared her shoulders, pulling herself straighter in my arms. "He is connected to the vessel, that's where he gets his power, that's his only source." She looked away from me, beyond me, and I hated the fear that snaked into my veins. Her fear. "If I can sever its hold, he won't have anything left. It's already killing him." She swallowed before she looked back to me. "But it has to be me."

She sounded so detached. So resigned.

Like she had already accepted that it would cost her.

And that same feeling sank into my gut because I knew too. No matter what happened, no matter what we did, it was going to cost us far more than I would ever be willing to give.

I dragged my knuckles along the curve of her cheek, watching her carefully. "And if you can't sever it?"

She hesitated, and her eyes shuddered, her lashes fluttering rapidly against her cheeks.

I clenched my jaw and tried to control the storm of emotions that raged through me. "Verena."

She exhaled slowly, pressing her forehead to mine. "Then I'll take it from him."

My stomach turned. "Like you did with me?" I whispered.

She nodded, her grip tightening around my hands. "But I'll be ready this time. I won't let it control me."

She said it as if she was trying to convince herself, as if her words could wrap around her and strengthen her spine.

I swallowed hard. "And what if you can't?"

Her silence was deafening. My magic surged. My anger. My fear.

"I have to try. All of this can't have been for nothing."

She looked around before her eyes paused on her mark, our mark. "Our mothers cannot have died for nothing."

She didn't look at me; she looked anywhere else, clung to anything else. "And if I'm unable to do what needs to be done, if I can't, then you have to promise me you'll leave."

I pushed back from her just enough to see her face, to force her to look at me with my hand on her chin. "You truly believe I would ever do that?"

"No." She shook her head quickly. "No, but I need you to promise. I need to know that he won't be able to get to you."

She blinked up at me, and there were tears in her eyes.

"I will promise you anything, Verena." I let my fingers trail along her cheeks. "But I can't promise you that."

Verena's fingers traced slow, steady circles along my wrist, and I could still feel the tension in her. The moment we left this cavern, the moment we stepped out of the hidden city, there would be no turning back.

She inhaled softly, her cheek pressing against my palm as she whispered, "Tell me everything one more time."

I didn't hesitate. We had already gone over the plan, the strategy my father had been working toward and searching for, for years.

My father had helped as we traced over the routes we would take, the positions we would hold, but he hadn't said a word about my mother. Even as Reed was dragged to the tunnels, he hadn't looked back at him. He hadn't met my eyes.

"We will take the outer districts," I murmured, my lips brushing against her hair. "We'll be in place by nightfall.

Kai will lead the first wave, keep the king's forces distracted, keep them fighting in the streets."

She nodded against me. "That gives us the time we need."

"To get inside."

My grip on her waist tightened slightly, but I forced myself to keep my voice steady. "The tunnels lead directly to the lower chambers beneath the throne room, directly to the dungeons. Once we're in, we split. You, Wren, and my grandmother go for the vessel."

Her breath hitched, but she didn't argue.

"And you?"

"I go for your father."

Her fingers stilled on my wrist. I felt her shift, tilting her head up to meet my gaze. Her eyes searched mine, filled with something deep, something raw.

Everything in me rebelled against the idea. The thought of letting her out of my sight, of leaving her alone in the same palace where she had been tortured, it felt like a mistake. But we didn't have a choice. She needed to get to the vessel, and I needed to get to him.

I exhaled slowly. "I will do whatever it takes to keep him from getting to you."

A shiver ran through her, and I knew what she was thinking: he would come for her. If the king knew she was in his palace, if he could feel her magic even a fraction of the way I could, he would hunt her down before she could sever the vessel's power.

She swallowed. "Dacre…"

I brushed a damp strand of hair from her face. "We go

in. We do what we must. And we walk out of there together."

I needed her to believe that because I needed to believe it too.

I gently tucked my fingers beneath her chin, lifting it until I could brush my lips over the curve of her jaw and across her cheek before I rested my forehead against hers.

"This isn't goodbye," I murmured softly, the words barely audible over the gentle lapping of the water around us. "Promise me."

Her grip tightened against my body, a silent plea in her touch.

I swallowed hard, struggling with the weight of the moment.

"Not goodbye." She shook her head softly against mine, her voice edged with enough vulnerability to break me.

I kissed her before either of us could utter another word.

Not soft. Not careful. I couldn't be either of those things when I was so desperate for her, so desperate to remind both of us that we were together.

Her lips parted beneath mine, her nails digging into my skin with a fervent urgency, as if she could anchor us in this moment, as if she could keep me from slipping through her fingers.

I sensed it in the way she clung to me, her body melding seamlessly into mine, every movement charged with a frantic, aching intensity.

I moved us, gently pressing her back against the smooth rocks of the springs, the heat of the water rising around us like a warm, embracing mist, licking at our skin. But it paled in comparison to the flames that burned inside me. Her touch was like a match being struck against my skin, igniting a wildfire of desire that consumed me from the inside out.

"Verena," I groaned against her mouth, my hands roaming down her sides, gripping her hips, pulling her closer.

She gasped, tilting her head back, her throat exposed to me, and I didn't hesitate.

I worshiped her.

My lips traced her neck, over her collarbone, down the slope of her shoulder. I tasted her skin, memorized every shiver, every breathy sound that escaped her lips.

"I love you," she whispered, her voice breaking as she pressed her forehead against my shoulder.

Gods. The mark between us, the soul-bond flared. It swirled between us, our powers merging into one.

I lifted her into my arms, the water cradling us as I moved deeper into the spring, until we were surrounded by nothing but warmth, nothing but each other.

Her legs wrapped around my waist, her hands tangling in my hair, her lips everywhere.

I needed her. Not just like this. Not just in body. I needed to exist in this moment, to breathe her in, to let her consume me.

I let her.

I let her take what she needed, and I gave her everything.

I settled into the seat in the warm springs, feeling the soothing water lap gently around my shoulders. She remained astride me, her body pressed close, and I gazed up at her in sheer awe.

She was my mate, my wife, and the thought of losing this connection was unimaginable.

She steadied herself on her knees, her delicate hand reaching to guide my cock against her, aligning our bodies. Slowly, she descended, sliding down onto me, and a broken sound escaped my lips as I felt the heat of her sink onto me, enveloping me in a way that shattered every last shred of control I had left.

Verena gasped, her fingers trembling where they rested against my shoulders. She clung to me, her breath hitching as she took me deeper, and I felt it, the slow stretch of her body adjusting to mine, the way her thighs tensed and trembled, the way her nails bit into my skin.

I ran my hands up the length of her spine, fingers pressing into the damp heat of her body. Her chest rose and fell in unsteady, shallow breaths, her lips parting slightly as her lashes fluttered, her eyes locking on to mine.

She was stunning.

Her flushed skin, the curve of her lips, the way the water beaded along her collarbones, trailing lower, catching in the valley between her breasts.

She was ruinous.

And she was mine.

I lifted my hands to cradle her face, my thumbs sweeping over her cheekbones as I guided her mouth back to mine. The kiss unfolding slowly, unhurriedly, each moment drawn out with the desperation to have her feel me, truly feel me and how hopelessly in love with her I was.

I tilted my hips upward, filling her completely, and she gasped into my mouth, her fingers tangling in my hair, pulling, as if she wanted to sink even deeper, as if she wanted to drown in me.

And gods, I would let her.

I wanted to submerge myself in the depths of her, to immerse myself in every part of her until we were one.

No war. No prophecy. No fate that threatened to take her from me. Just the two of us forgetting everything outside these cavern walls, even if only for a little while.

Her hips rocked, slow, teasing. A roll of her body that had my breath catching in my throat, my fingers tightening against her waist.

Her pace was torturous. She was savoring every second, carving this moment into her bones so that no matter what came tomorrow, she would still feel this.

Still feel me.

A soft whimper escaped her lips, and I felt her tighten around me, felt the way her body clenched, the way she trembled in my arms, her control slipping.

I dropped my head back against the rock, my chest heaving, my grip tightening as I fought against the primal need to take control, to pin her beneath me and devour her.

But this moment was hers.

I let her take.

I surrendered to her rhythm, allowing her to dictate the pace, her movements slow and devastating, her body rolling against mine in a way that had my teeth grinding, my muscles coiling beneath her touch.

She was killing me.

Soft gasps spilled from her lips, her forehead pressing to mine, our breaths mingling, hot and uneven.

I love you.

She didn't say it, but I felt it in every touch, every kiss, every desperate pull of her body against mine. I felt it screaming at me through our bond.

It was as if I could feel the warmth of the sun, even as far underground as we were. It was all-encompassing and inescapable. It heated every parted of me, and I gasped as I felt the way she was choosing every part of me, the way she trusted me fully.

And I hoped that she could feel me as well, because I needed her to know. She was not just my mate, not just my wife.

She was everything, and I would worship her until my dying breath.

I thrust up into her, pulling a sharp gasp from her throat. Her eyes widened, her fingers gripping my arms as I did it again, harder this time, my pace matching the frantic rhythm of my heartbeat.

Her moan shattered against my lips, and I swallowed the sound, drinking her in, devouring her. Her body arched, her back bowing as she rode me, her nails dragging down my chest, leaving faint, stinging trails in their wake.

I slid my hand between us, my fingers finding her clit, pressing, teasing, until she gasped, her head falling back, her body tightening around me. Her thighs quivered, her grip turning bruising, her lips parting on a broken sound that sent a violent shudder through me.

I wasn't going to last. Not like this. Not when she

looked like that, like the gods themselves had carved her from stardust and set her ablaze just for me.

Just for this.

I buried my face against her neck, my teeth grazing her pulse point, biting down just enough to remind her that she was mine, and I was hers.

She cried out, her body trembling, her release hitting her in waves that sent me spiraling. I held her tight, crushing her against me as I let go, let myself fall with her, let the pleasure rip through me like a storm.

It was blinding, and her name tore from my lips as I buried myself deep inside her, as I lost myself completely in her warmth, in her scent, in the fucking feel of her.

The world blurred at the edges, the cavern walls, the glowing moss, the water lapping at our bodies, none of it existed.

Only her.

Only us.

I held her there, her body still shaking, her breath still uneven, her heart hammering against mine. Neither of us spoke. We just breathed. Just held on.

Her hands slid into my hair, soft and reverent, and I closed my eyes, exhaling slowly. I felt her lips press against my temple, a whisper of warmth, of love. Of a promise.

"I love you," she murmured, her voice thick, hoarse, fractured.

I pulled back just enough to look at her, to study every inch of her face, every flushed detail, every lingering trace of pleasure in her gaze.

"And I love you," I rasped, brushing my lips over hers.

She curled against me, resting her head against my

shoulder, and for a moment, just one perfect, fleeting moment, there was nothing but warmth, nothing but her.

Nothing but this.

But even as I held her, my body ached, my muscles trembling with the exhaustion I had been ignoring. I knew she felt it too. Her arms slackened slightly where they had been locked around my shoulders, her breathing deepening as if she were already on the edge of sleep.

Neither of us spoke about it. Neither of us let go, and I would hold on to it for as long as the gods allowed.

But when the sun set and rose again, the war would begin, and I didn't know if we'd ever have this again.

The night stretched before us, endless and waiting. The rebels moved in near silence, boots pressing into damp earth, blades strapped to their backs, eyes locked ahead toward the towering walls of the capital. This was the moment they had trained for.

The moment they had spent their lives dreading.

The wind howled through the trees, carrying the distant sound of city bells tolling the final hours before midnight.

By sunrise, the kingdom would be drenched in blood.

By sunrise, my father would fall.

I stood at the edge of the forest, the soft cascade of the waterfall echoing in the distance, its waters spilling over the jagged cliffs that hid the tunnels leading beneath the palace. The path we had planned for. The path that would lead me straight to the vessel and Dacre straight to *him*.

But despite everything, despite the weight of the night pressing down on me, I wasn't alone.

Dacre was beside me, his fingers brushing against mine,

a tether between us as he scanned the tree line. His face was stoic, but through the bond, I could feel his magic moving with mine, restless and waiting.

Wren and Kai stood close, their postures rigid, their weapons secured against their bodies.

Everything was in place.

Dacre turned to me, his voice steady, but there was something else beneath it. Something unspoken. "Once we reach the palace, you make sure to stay with Wren and my grandmother."

I nodded. We had already gone over this so many times already, but he hadn't calmed the anxiety in either of us. "We go to the vessel."

"Verena—"

"I can do this." I said the words out loud, but I needed to hear them too. Needed to feel them inside me until I could force myself to believe them.

His jaw tightened, and I knew what he was thinking. What we were both thinking, but I refused to let all of the fears that screamed at me to take root.

Wren moved closer to my side, and I watched as her throat bobbed. She looked between me and Dacre, a flicker of hesitation in her gaze, and her fingers curled tightly around the strap of the bow across her chest.

"You keep her with you," Dacre spoke before she could. "Keep each other within your sights at all times. Do not separate. Do not leave the other."

She nodded once, but he wasn't satisfied.

"I need to know that you're both safe. You will protect Verena, and she will protect you."

"Dacre," she whispered his name, and I could feel the tension rolling off Kai as he moved closer to Wren's side.

"You are my family." Dacre looked at each of us. "We are all each other has, and we will fight together. We will fight for each other."

Wren shifted, her anxiety evident in the tense lines of her posture. "And if we don't come back?"

Dacre's fingers curled around mine as he looked at his sister, really looked at her, and I could feel the warmth in my chest, the aching love he had for her. His voice was low, but it didn't waver. "Then I will find you in the next life. All of you."

His words were a vow; they were a promise.

"In the next life." Kai nodded before he took Wren's hand in his. He laced their fingers together, and he lifted her hand to his mouth, pressing a kiss to her knuckles.

My chest ached as I watched them, but I couldn't tell if it came from me or from Dacre.

Wren exhaled shakily, her gaze lingering on Kai for a long moment. "In the next life."

I swallowed hard, my fingers tightening around Dacre's, and I forced myself to look at each of them. To take in their features, the lines of their skin, the freckles on Wren's nose. I took in every little detail that I wasn't willing to forget. "In the next life."

But I didn't want the next life.

I wanted this one.

Dacre lifted my hand, pressing it against his chest. I wanted to stay in this moment, to linger in the warmth of him, of our family, but there was no more time.

We turned, preparing to move toward the tunnel entrance below the falls, and everything went wrong.

A sharp rustling in the trees behind us made me turn.

Dacre's father emerged from the darkness, his posture rigid, his steps slow, his eyes panicked. He was alone. His usual commanding presence felt heavier, weighted by something none of us had braced for.

Dacre stiffened at my side. "You should be with the others."

His father didn't answer immediately. His gaze swept over us, landing on me, then Wren, then back to Dacre.

"There's a problem." His voice was rough, lined with exhaustion.

There was a beat of silence then Dacre took a single step forward. "What problem?"

His father exhaled sharply. "The tunnels." He shook his head once, as if still trying to process his own words. "They've been collapsed."

My stomach plummeted.

"What?" Dacre's voice betrayed his panic.

"They're gone." His father's fists clenched at his sides. "Your plan, our plan, it's not going to work."

A breath left my lips as I turned to the cliffside.

Kai cursed under his breath. "How?"

Dacre's father's jaw locked. "The king knew." His gaze flicked to me, to the mark hidden beneath my sleeve. "He knew that's how we got inside to get to Verena."

I swallowed against the tightness in my throat. My father had destroyed the only way we could have made it inside without walking directly into his trap.

"They are filled with stone," Dacre's father growled. "He's made sure that we'll never use them again.

Dacre ran a hand through his hair, his shoulders rising and falling with his uneven breathing. I could feel the weight of his frustration, his magic churning beneath his skin.

He turned toward his father. "Then tell me how the hell we get inside."

His father's expression darkened, but I could see it in his face, the rebellion leader he had always been. "There's only one way now. We'll have to go through the city."

The words settled over us like a death sentence, and I felt Wren shift beside me, could feel the ripple of unease that spread through us all.

Dacre inhaled sharply. "We should turn back."

His father nodded.

But I wasn't going back. I wasn't willing to stop until we finally brought this to an end. "I'm not turning back."

I felt Dacre's magic surge again, felt the undeniable fear settle into his chest through our bond. This changed everything. It shifted everything.

There was no more sneaking. No more careful strategy.

"Verena," he pleaded with me, but there was no choice to make.

I couldn't go back into hiding; I couldn't spend even one more day waiting for my father to come, waiting for him to find me again.

Dacre's jaw tightened, his nostrils flaring as he turned fully to face me. "Verena, this could be a trap." His voice was low, but through the bond, I felt the panic beneath his anger. "He will be waiting for us."

"I know that." My voice didn't waver. "But he always will be. He'll be waiting or hunting, and I can't go another day with the fear of him hovering over me."

His hands curled into fists at his sides, his magic rippling against mine, demanding and desperate.

"He wants you." His voice was strained, hoarse. "I'm not going to recklessly risk you by charging in there."

I took a step closer, my fingers brushing against his wrist, against the mark that bound us. "And if we turn back? If we wait?" I swallowed hard. "How many more will he kill? How long before he gets his hands on me again?"

His breath hitched.

I lifted my chin. "We don't have a choice, Dacre."

His pulse hammered through the bond, his heartbeat erratic, his magic a storm barely contained beneath his skin.

I turned to Dacre's father. "How many men do you already have inside the city?"

He looked back and forth between his son and me, but I could see the calculation in his gaze. "Enough to hold a fight, but not enough to win one." His jaw clenched. "We were relying on those tunnels."

I nodded once. "Then we change the plan."

Dacre exhaled sharply, dragging a hand down his face before turning to Kai, his voice clipped. "What do you think?"

Kai crossed his arms, shifting his weight. "The outer districts are already waiting for us. They'll need a signal to move in. If we don't give it to them—"

"They'll be slaughtered," Wren finished, her voice

tight. "Once the king realizes they are there, he will never let them leave."

Dacre's father let out a slow breath. "We go through the city," he muttered, as if the words themselves made him sick. "Straight through the bridge and the palace gates."

Dacre shook his head once, tension radiating from him. "We'll never make it inside before reinforcements surround us."

"We will." Dacre's father's gaze locked on to me, his lips pressing into a grim line. "Because we have her."

All eyes turned to me. A sharp breath left my lips. "You want me on the front lines."

His expression didn't shift. "We need you there if we want to stand a chance." His voice was even, controlled.

"No." Dacre's voice was a command, something none of us should have been willing to go against, but we had no other choice.

"He's not wrong, Dacre." Kai let out a breath. "I'll lead the front line as planned, and Verena will stick with you. She will stay behind us until we need her."

Wren stepped closer, shaking her head. "If Verena takes the front, she'll be the target."

"She already is," Dacre muttered. His eyes met mine, dark and burning. "She always has been."

I stepped forward, pressing my hand against his chest, feeling the rapid beat of his heart beneath my palm. "We do this together."

Dacre's breath shuddered against my skin just as a scream cut through the night.

It wasn't close. It was from the capital city. A warning. A promise of what was already happening there.

Dacre's father reacted first, his body going rigid. "It's started."

My breath caught in my throat as I turned toward the looming walls of the capital. The flickering glow of torches burned from within, but they were burning brighter now, something was burning.

Dacre's grip on my arm tightened. "We go now."

Kai let out a sharp breath. "We stay together. As close as we can."

The plan they had been crafting crumbled to dust and carried through the wind just as another scream rang out. This one more terrifying, more guttural than the one before.

No more careful strategies. No tunnels. No secret passageways.

Just war.

Dacre's father turned, lifting a hand toward the trees behind us, toward the rebels waiting in the shadows. "Form ranks!"

A ripple of movement swept through the forest, boots shifting, blades unsheathing, quiet murmurs carrying through the still air. They were ready.

Dacre exhaled sharply, turning to me. His jaw was tight, his magic rippling between us. He wasn't ready for this, wasn't prepared to send me into it.

But we had no more time.

I reached up, brushing my fingers over his jaw, then over the mark that tethered us together. "We do this together."

His hand curled over mine.

A breath. A moment.

Then the city bells began to ring, and we ran.

The first arrow flew as we inched closer to the city. It barely missed Kai's shoulder, sinking into the earth beside him with a sharp thud.

Shouts erupted from the darkness. The king's soldiers were waiting.

Kai didn't hesitate. "Go!"

The rebellion surged forward, and I ran alongside them, my pulse hammering in my throat. The trees gave way to open ground, the bridge stretching before us like a death sentence.

And beyond it, the gates of the palace.

A solid wall of armored soldiers stood across the bridge, their swords pointed outward, their ranks unwavering. Their polished armor glinted beneath the torchlight, a sea of steel standing between us and the throne.

This was the only way in. My father had made sure of that.

Kai reached the front line first, his twin swords flashing as he met the nearest guard. Steel clashed against steel. We had just been talking, just been promising each other what our futures would hold, and it had slipped from our hands so easily.

There was no more time for vows, no more time to decide who we were going to be. The war had begun, whether we were ready for it or not.

Dacre was beside Kai in an instant, cutting through the enemy with brutal efficiency. Wren moved swiftly beside me, sending arrows into the thick of the soldiers.

I could barely think, barely breathe. I looked around for Dacre's grandmother, but she was nowhere to be seen.

Everything was a blur of movement and chaos, of snarled commands and desperate cries.

A guard lunged at me, sword raised, and I twisted, stepping into his attack rather than away from it. My blade met his ribs, slicing through the gaps in his armor.

Another came at me before I had a chance to catch my breath. I ducked, spun, struck.

The fight moved faster than thought, faster than fear.

My magic roared inside me, as did Dacre's, but I needed to save it. I had no idea what I would face once we got inside, once I got to the vessel, but I knew that I would need every bit of power I had to fight him.

Another scream split through the night, a rebel cut down just feet from me.

I turned toward the sound, my chest tightening, and I tried to breathe as I watched more rebels fall.

I slammed my dagger into another guard, the bones in my arm, aching with the impact, but Wren was already there, her blade slicing through the man's throat before he could fight back.

I turned, looking for Dacre, looking for Kai, then I saw it.

A building to my right, directly across the bridge, had flames licking at its walls. A deep, relentless ache settled in my stomach as I watched the fire greedily engulfing the side of the familiar building, one that had been a constant fixture outside my bedroom window for as long as I could remember.

Then my gaze settled on the rebellion mark, freshly painted across the brick facade, its dark color still glistening even as the flames ate at it with the same hunger my father had to kill this rebellion.

My breath caught in my throat as my eyes traveled down the wall, where a line of four figures hung lifelessly. The ropes, cruelly taut, had snapped their necks, leaving them to dangle from the building's roof and the flames licked up against their feet, threatening to consume them next.

Three were men, men I didn't know, but it was the presence of the fourth that shattered my composure. A young boy, innocent and ignorant of the world's harsh burdens, suspended alongside them.

This was my father.

I had known my father would retaliate. I had known the lengths he would go to in order to find me, in order to make sure that every one of his people realized that none of us were safe.

But seeing it, seeing the proof of his cruelty displayed so openly, I broke. A deep, relentless ache settled in my stomach before it turned to rage.

The magic inside me roared to life, writhing and desperate to be unleashed.

"Don't." A hand clamped down on my shoulder, stopping my advance, and I turned to the voice, tears already burning in my eyes. Micah shook his head solemnly before his gaze flickered up to where I knew the boy still hung. I hadn't even known Micah was here. I hadn't seen him...

"That's where he wants your attention. That's all he wants you to see." He let his hand fall away from my shoulder. "We both know how he works."

I knew he was right. Of course, I did, but in that

moment, all I could see was that boy, all I could think of was everything my father had done.

I took a step away from Micah, then another, and I didn't stop as I pushed through the lines of warriors who were tearing each other down.

I moved as quickly as I could, and I could feel power stirring within me. It grew ravenous and desperate, mirroring my own hunger and desperation to destroy.

I raised my hands, palms turned outward toward the waiting enemy soldiers as I moved closer to the front line. A deep, primal energy coursed through me, a mixture of my own and something else, and I allowed my power to draw from the soldiers' strength, siphoning their magic until I was brimming with it, threatening to overflow.

I could hear my name being called, could hear someone shouting for me. Dacre. I couldn't tell if it was from behind me or through the bond, but it was too late.

I let go.

Power exploded from me in an unrelenting wave. The black inky force slammed into the soldiers, knocking them back as if struck by an invisible weapon. Some collapsed outright, their bodies crumpling to the ground, weapons slipping from lifeless fingers.

I didn't stop.

I couldn't.

The magic kept coming, demanding, taking, burning. I felt it seep into me, siphoning their strength, their life. I could feel their magic trembling beneath my fingertips, could feel the way my body wanted to devour even more.

A soldier in front of me fell to his knees, gasping for

breath, his energy draining before my eyes. He would die here because of me.

I took a slow step forward, my heart hammering wildly in my chest, my power desperate to make the man pay.

A hand gripped my wrist.

Dacre.

His magic collided with mine, cutting through the chaos, through the hunger, and I gasped.

The bond between us flared, throbbed, screamed.

"Enough," he whispered.

The word cracked through my ribs, slicing through the power clawing at my skin, pulling me back before I lost myself completely.

I blinked rapidly, trying to clear the haze of power, the world spinning wildly around me.

Dacre was so close, his chest heaving against me, and he didn't let go.

He wasn't going to.

I sucked in a sharp breath, my magic slowly pulling back, but the damage had been done.

The soldiers were staring as they retreated. Not just the king's men. The rebels.

They had seen.

A murmur rippled through the rebellion, voices whispering, but not with fear. They were no longer afraid of me. They were in awe.

I let my gaze run through them, looked at these people who now fought alongside me, and I tried to breathe, let myself remember exactly what we were fighting for.

Someone called out, voice rough and raw with emotion. "The queen is here! The queen has come!"

It echoed through the bridge, through the army behind me.

"The heir has returned. The queen has come."

I barely had time to process their words before Dacre turned me toward him completely, forcing me to look at him, but I couldn't. Instead, my eyes fixated on the boy. His lifeless body swayed above those crackling flames, the fire hungrily reaching for his small frame.

"Verena," Dacre whispered, his voice rough, his fingers pleading.

I could smell it then, the burning flesh as the fire had already overtaken the others.

My hands curled into fists, my power still swirling in the air as if it, too, couldn't manage to slow its breath, to quell the deathly urge inside it.

"Dacre, I…"

His fingers tightened against my arms, pulling me closer, pressing his forehead against mine. "You need to save your power." His breath was ragged, his own fury barely contained. "You're going to burn yourself out before the real fight even begins."

I knew I should be listening to him, but I didn't feel like I was going to burn out; I didn't feel anything except the need to take, to make them all pay for what they had done.

"The boy," I whispered, my voice cracking, and Dacre followed my gaze to where I looked at the boy who was now burning.

Thick plumes of smoke curled into the night sky, starting to block the boy from my view.

His jaw clenched, his entire body going taut beneath my hands.

He closed his eyes for the briefest moment before exhaling sharply. "We fight for him. We end this for them all."

I lifted my chin, inhaling one last, shaky breath, and Dacre's hands moved into my hair, anchored on each side of my face as he stared down at me.

He didn't need to say a word. I could feel everything through our bond, his fear, his longing, his love.

I wrapped one of my hands around his, and I turned my head just enough to press my lips against the base of his palm. Then I turned my gaze toward the palace gates, standing untouched beyond the chaos.

We were going to take the palace.

And we were going to end this.

CHAPTER 26
VERENA

The halls of the palace felt eerily still despite the chaos that still rang out around us.

It was unlike anything I had every felt before.

Not in all my years behind these walls. Not in all the nights I had curled beneath my blankets, listening for the distant sounds of music from the ballroom, the hurried footsteps of servants, the faint cries of people he was hurting. Not in all the nights when I had begged for him to stop, to leave me, to let me go.

Dacre's fingers curled around mine as we carefully moved inside. Beside us, Kai and Wren stood close, their blades drawn, their breaths steady but sharp. Dacre's father and Eiran moved ahead of us, but I still hadn't seen Dacre's grandmother. None of us had.

"She should be here," I murmured, scanning the empty corridor.

The plan had been simple. Get to the vessel first. Cut

my father off from his power before we faced him. But something was wrong. She should already be with us.

A rustle in the shadows made me tense, and all of us braced as a figure stepped into view.

Dacre's grandmother moved swiftly, her long skirt billowing behind her. But there was blood smeared across her sleeve. Her silver hair had come loose from its usual bun, strands clinging to her face.

She had been fighting.

Dacre exhaled sharply, stepping forward. "Where have you been?"

She lifted a hand, her breathing measured but strained.

"We tried," she murmured. "We tried to reach the vessel."

Micah moved behind her, just as breathless.

My pulse quickened. "What do you mean?"

Her sharp silver eyes locked on to mine. "Micah used his magic to get us across the bridge, and the gates were empty when we arrived. The entrance to the vessel is blocked. He was waiting."

A cold weight settled in my gut. Of course he was. He would protect the vessel over everything else.

"How many guards?" Dacre asked, his grip tightening on his sword.

"Too many," she admitted. "The mass of his guards was protecting the bridge and protecting the vessel. I tried to fight my way through them, but there are too many. They didn't follow as we retreated. They are not leaving their guard of the vessel." She looked at me. "There's no way to the vessel except through the throne room. There is a path just behind his dais. A stairwell that leads directly down." She lifted her hand, running it over her mouth, and I was shocked to see how badly it shook. "The others?"

"They are right behind us." A muscle in Dacre's jaw twitched. I could feel his magic coiling, restless, the same fear curling inside me.

But then there was *something else*.

A pounding. A deep, thrumming beat. Not from the castle walls, not from the rebellion still clashing outside the gates. From within me.

My breath hitched. My knees nearly buckled as the sensation rippled through me, a call, a whisper, a pull. It wasn't magic, not in the way Dacre and I shared magic. This was something older. Something deeper.

I gasped, pressing a hand against my stomach as the sensation clawed inside me.

Dacre's head snapped toward me, his hands catching my arms. "What is it?"

He couldn't feel it, not through me, not through our bond. I tried to answer, but the words died on my tongue as it pushed harder against me until pain thrummed in my temples.

Dacre couldn't feel this because it was tied to me.

The vessel was calling me.

Not like before, when I had felt its power, its vast emptiness, when my father had assaulted me with its power. This was different. This wasn't just the vessel lying deep beneath the palace.

This was the piece of it that lived inside me now.

A fragment of its magic buried inside my bones, inside my blood. A piece that I hadn't even realized was there.

A shudder racked through me, threatening to buckle my knees.

I recognized the feel of it. I had felt it when he connected me to it. When he tore through my body and left his power inside my veins, when he had tried to bind me to him forever.

I thought he had failed.

But the vessel had never let me go.

"Verena?" Dacre's voice was urgent now, low and rough. He could feel me shaking, feel my magic reacting to the unseen force, as he ran his hands over me.

"The vessel," I whispered, voice hoarse. I lifted my head, my gaze locking on to the doors ahead. The throne room.

It was waiting. He was waiting, and I couldn't stop my feet from moving forward.

I barely felt the marble beneath my boots as I stepped forward. The doors stood ahead, massive, dark, waiting.

Somewhere behind me, Dacre was calling my name, but the sound was muffled, like I was slipping beneath deep waters.

I pressed my hands against the doors, and they opened. A slow, groaning creak, the ancient wood bowing inward. Not pushed. Not pulled.

The vessel was welcoming me inside. It was calling me.

I stepped into the throne room, and the air became suffocating. The walls stretched high, the familiar tapestries that once draped over the stone now hung in ruins, moth-eaten and crumbling. The chandeliers above, once gleaming with golden light, flickered weakly, their flames barely clinging to life.

Decay.

That was what filled the room, what clung to my skin, what made my stomach turn as my gaze landed on the throne.

There were guards in the room, but not many and each of them looked *drained.* My father hadn't expected me to make it this far. There were a few others there too, people who I didn't recognize.

And I saw *him.*

My father sat slouched in his seat, a shell of the man he had been when I last saw him. His skin, once golden with power, was gray, his cheekbones hollowed, his lips cracked.

But it was his eyes that made everything inside me revolt.

Still sharp. Still cruel.

He was still watching me as if I were something to devour.

"You've finally returned home, daughter."

I flinched at his words, and his expression shifted, the corners of his mouth lifting into a sickening smile.

"This isn't my home." The power inside me reacted, it coiled and bent, and I didn't know if it was my power, the vessel, or my bond.

"No? Then why did you come back?" He cocked his head, and I stilled, my entire body reacting to him. "Is it me you missed or the power I let you feel?"

He studied me, his gaze flickering over the leather armor strapped to my body, the weapons that adorned my chest. Then he sighed. "You look like your mother when I first saw her."

Rage flared inside me, burning away everything else I

could feel. "You mean when you stole her away from her kingdom, before you destroyed Veyrith?"

His eyes narrowed, a slow, almost imperceptible movement. "Your mother came willingly."

A sharp laugh scraped against my throat, bitter and cold. "You took everything from her, her home, her magic, her choices." My breath shuddered. "Just like you tried to do to me."

Something flickered in his eyes. Something almost human.

"It's what I did to you." His words were poison, and I could feel them infecting me. "It's what I'm still doing."

"What happened to your guards?" I nodded toward the men who looked to be barely standing on their feet.

"My men serve me." He narrowed his eyes. "And they sacrificed to fuel me with what I need."

The shadows near his throne shifted, and the Sight stepped forward.

She stood beside him, her long white hair falling in waves down her back, her skin as pale as the moon. Her eyes—white, cloudy, endless.

I remembered those eyes. I remembered her hands pressed against my skull when I was locked in my cell. I felt the sting of my father's magic. Felt the vessel crawl inside me all over again.

A ghost of pain rippled through my veins.

She tilted her head, her expression vacant, and yet, I knew she was seeing me in ways no one else could.

"She knew you were coming," my father murmured, standing from his throne. His steps were slow, measured, as he moved down the dais. "She warned me of your plans for the tunnels."

I clenched my fists at my sides, forcing my magic to still, begging the vessel to stop whispering in my mind.

"She has seen the future, Verena." His voice was almost soft. "And she has seen the end."

The Sight finally lifted her chin, finally spoke. "You will kneel before him."

My blood turned to ice just as I felt someone move behind me. Dacre's chest pressed against my back, and I tried to breathe, tried to feel him.

His breath was warm against the back of my neck, his presence steady even as the weight of my father's words pressed into my ribs.

"I will never kneel to you," I said, my voice like steel, but the Sight's blank, white eyes bore into me.

"You already have."

A chill raced through me as she took a slow step forward, her movements eerily graceful, as if she wasn't fully of this world.

"I have seen you in a thousand lives, Verena," she whispered. "And in every one, you kneel."

Dacre's magic surged, wild and furious, and it raced through every inch of me. The Sight tilted her head, her lips parting just slightly as though she were listening, not to me, but to something inside me. Her white eyes flicked down, landing on the golden mark on my wrist.

It burned under her gaze before she murmured, "You carry more than his mark."

Her words radiated through my wrist, and my breath caught. "What?"

She exhaled slowly. "The vessel you seek is not the only one that calls your name. The blood of Veyrith sings inside you."

Then she turned, and her eerie gaze landed on someone else. "And it sings in another."

A gasp rang out from the other side of the throne room, and I turned my head just in time to see Micah go rigid, his body coiling like a predator poised to strike.

Then I saw her.

The woman stood just behind the king, hidden behind a small line of guards with two other courtesans. Her hair fell in waves down her back, and even beneath the dim torch-light, I could see it, her resemblance to Micah.

It was his sister.

"Maliah!" Micah's voice was a snarl, a battle cry of pure desperation as he shoved through the rebels, his sword already drawn, already moving.

He barreled toward the throne, toward his sister, his sword already raised, and my father snapped his fingers.

Power lashed from his palm, a sudden, violent burst of magic that sent Micah flying across the room. His body slammed into the marble, skidding across the floor with a sickening thud. He tried to climb back to his knees, but he fell back to his stomach.

I barely had time to react before my father's head jerked toward me. His eyes darkened then he moved.

I didn't see it. I barely felt it. One second he was standing at the foot of the dais, then the next he was right in front of me.

I gasped, stumbling back into Dacre, but his hand snapped around my wrist.

A cruel, sick smile curved his lips. "My daughter," he breathed before his gaze landed on Dacre at my back. "Is this the one you cried out for?"

Dacre tensed for only a second before his roar filled the room, and before I could react, steel flashed through the air.

Dacre's sword sliced down, so fast it was nothing but a blur. My father jerked away from me at the last second, dodging the blade, but only just. Dacre's sword sliced through the fabric of my father's robes, leaving a thin, bleeding cut along his ribs.

My father snarled, his lips curling in disgust as he watched Dacre move between us, his chest heaving, his body coiled. His sword was dripping with a trace of my father's blood.

"She had cried for you, you know." His voice was a low, taunting drawl as he locked eyes with Dacre, a predatory gleam lighting up his gaze.

My magic surged within me, a wild, rabid beast desperate to do anything to get my father's attention back on me, away from my mate. But I held on to it as tightly as I could, forcing it to simmer beneath the surface.

"So many of those scars on her body," he continued, his tone dripping with disdain, "could have been prevented if you had only come when she called." He clicked his tongue in mock disappointment, his eyes sweeping over Dacre with a scrutinizing glare. "I hope the scars aren't too much for you, that I haven't ruined her beyond your desire."

His words hit Dacre exactly where he wanted them to, provoked him until he lunged forward, his movement sudden and charged with emotion. It was a trap, meticulously laid by my father, but I moved. I reached out and snatched Dacre's hand in mine before he could take another step forward.

My father laughed, the sound slithering over my skin, as he looked back at me. "I think I'll kill him first," he declared with a chilling calm. "I'll hang him in the city streets, gently, though, ensuring he fights for each breath until death mercifully claims him. Slower than the others."

The others. *The boy.*

"You'll be able to watch from your window," he added, lifting his finger to point ominously to the floor above us. "Once you get settled back in."

Fury ignited within me like a wildfire, fueled by his words and the grotesque image he painted in my mind. It was provoked by the image of the boy that I couldn't get out of my mind, the one who likely still burned in the flames outside.

I was consumed by my anger, so lost in it completely, that I didn't see it coming.

He raised his hand, and a sudden, searing pain followed, enveloping me. It ripped through me like a thousand blades, twisting, searing, burning.

My father's magic slammed into my chest, but it wasn't his at all. It was the vessel that surged inside me.

Not just the piece buried in my veins, the power deep beneath the palace. It recognized me, claimed me, and suddenly, I wasn't just standing in the throne room anymore.

I was falling.

A rush of memories, of visions, spilled through my mind.

A throne room before this one, walls carved from white

stone, vines curling through the cracks. A golden-haired queen standing with a crown of silver and sapphire resting against her brow. A king with eyes like mine pressing his hand against a glowing vessel, binding his blood to it.

The vessel of Veyrith.

I gasped, my body locking up as I saw my mother. She stood near the king and queen that I didn't recognize, her hand held out to me, and I reached for her as I fell. Pried through the fog in my mind as I tried to touch my fingers to hers, and the moment they did, the moment the warmth of her skin pressed against mine, another ancient power crashed through me.

It filled me, flooded me, and I had no power to stop it.

The heir.

The words weren't my own. They flowed through my veins, whispered in my bones.

A throne carved from white stone. The queen's hands outstretched. A vessel humming with life.

My breath caught, my chest rising and falling in sharp, desperate gasps.

And I wasn't alone.

A sound ripped through the air, not a scream, but something else. A chorus of gasps.

I pressed my hands against my temples as my vision came back to me, as my father's throne room came back into view.

Wren fell to her knees, a strangled noise escaping her lips.

Dacre's head jerked back, his breath coming in short, sharp bursts.

Micah staggered, his hand clamping over his chest.

His sister let out a choked cry, her eyes going wide as she looked at me.

Dacre's grandmother stared in shock, her silver brows drawing together as she clutched the pendant at her throat.

It was inside all of us. *The blood of Veyrith.*

And it had answered.

The Sight's lips parted as she shuffled back, her cloudy eyes bouncing throughout the room. "The tideborn has come. The vessel of Veyrith rises."

The Sight stumbled, her gaze darting to my father. "The vessel of Veyrith rises," she whispered again, her voice trembling.

My father stiffened, his hand releasing me. His entire body jerked, his lips pulling back from his teeth as his fingers curled into fists. The veins along his neck darkened, pulsing with magic, and then the throne room shook.

The torches along the walls flared, shadows stretching high, flickering wildly as if caught in a storm. The floor beneath us groaned under the weight of power, power he could not control.

"This is mine!" he snarled, his voice splitting through the chaos, his magic lashing outward.

I staggered back as his fury hit me like a wave. The magic plowed into me, it struck me in a way I had never felt before. He was trying to reclaim control, trying to silence the power that had awakened inside me.

But he couldn't.

Panic twisted across his face, warring with rage as his eyes darted through the room, searching, calculating, desperate. His body trembled, the gray hue of his skin deepening, as if the power inside him was rotting him from the inside out before my very eyes.

His gaze snapped to the Sight. "Do something."

But the Sight only shook her head.

"I warned you," she whispered, stepping farther back into the shadows. "You tried to claim what was never meant to be yours."

My father let out a feral roar, and then he moved. Not toward me. Not toward Dacre, but toward Wren. His power struck before I could react, a vicious whip of dark magic lashing out and slamming into Wren's chest.

She choked on a scream as the force of it sent her skidding to the ground. She hit the ground hard, gasping, her limbs twitching, the mark of his magic burning like black veins along her skin.

Dacre's magic detonated.

"No!" His roar shattered the air, and I felt the rage inside him snap, his control breaking apart as he lunged forward, his sword aimed for the king's throat.

But before he could reach him, my father yanked Wren upright, his hand wrapped in the back of her hair.

"Enough." His single word rang through the throne room, and everything stopped.

Dacre froze. Kai's chest heaved beside me, his magic a raging storm inside him. The rebels halted their fight, watching in horror as the king held Dacre's sister in front of him, her body limp, her breath ragged.

His gaze slid to me, a slow, venomous smile curling across his face. "Let's see if your mother's blood is as powerful as they say."

His fingers tightened around her, and Wren screamed.

Her body jerked violently, her back arching as power ripped from her. He was siphoning from her.

I lunged forward, but a stumbling guard blocked my path. I hadn't noticed him, hadn't even paid attention as the guards looked far too weakened by my father's siphoning to even begin to fight.

My attention had been solely on my father, and even though I still didn't look away from him, I could hear it now, the others fighting around us.

Dacre snapped. His sword sank through the soldier's ribs before I could even blink, and I heard Kai's voice, raw and wild.

"Wren!"

Kai's blade was already flying. He was already moving like a shadow weaving through the room as my father lifted his other hand.

But Wren wasn't the one who fell.

Eiran was.

A sickening crack filled the air as Eiran's body slammed into Wren, knocking her free from the king's grip, shielding her just as my father's magic struck once more.

Wren slammed into the marble, and Eiran's back arched violently, his mouth opening in a scream as the siphoning power meant for Wren hit him instead.

I gasped, I could feel it pulling, feel it taking. It was killing him.

Eiran's body convulsed as my father drained the life from him.

His hands clawed at the ground; his breath became shallow. Staggering.

I tried to reach out, tried to stop it, but the power my father slammed into him was too strong, too cruel.

Dacre's father shouted his name, but Eiran was already stilling. He was already gone.

Kai moved to Wren's side, and he pulled her into his arms, his chest heaving, her gasping for air.

And my father—my father laughed.

He wiped a hand over his mouth, stepping over Eiran's lifeless body like it was nothing. Then he looked at me, his smile razor sharp.

"You cannot stop this," he whispered.

And I felt it again, the vessel snarling beneath the palace, rising to meet me.

My father's magic crashed into me. Not like before. Not like the searing, consuming heat of his siphoning. This was cold.

It dug into my ribs like shards of ice, pressing, twisting, pulling at something inside me.

I gasped, my knees buckling as the sensation ripped through my chest, as if invisible hands were trying to pry me open, trying to dig deep and pull something free.

The vessel was inside me. Not just its power. Its will.

It curled through my veins, dragging me toward him, toward my father. I could feel its tether, the invisible chain he had forged when he had forced its magic into me. He was trying to summon me back to him, trying to bind me completely.

A breath shuddered from my lips.

No.

I dug my heels into the ground, my body trembling

under the weight of it, but another force rose inside me, something equal in power, something opposite.

Veyrith.

Its presence slammed into me, its power pushing against the vessel like a crashing tide. It did not bind. It did not chain. It called, and I answered.

A sound tore from my throat as my power lashed outward, white-hot and blinding. The very air cracked, and suddenly, I was not just inside the throne room.

I was inside the vessels.

Marmoris and Veyrith.

The two of them clashed inside me; one built on power hoarded, the other built on power shared. One built on taking, the other on giving.

The vessel of Veyrith had awakened, and it had chosen me.

The last daughter of Veyrith. My mother's blood sang in my veins.

A voice filled my mind. "It was never lost, Verena. It was only waiting."

I opened my eyes, my vision fractured, split between two worlds, the throne room fading in and out like a flickering candle.

The Sight stood frozen where she hovered near the wall, her white eyes wide, her mouth slightly parted as if she could see it too.

Dacre's fingers dug into my arm, his voice distant, fraying, as he called my name.

But my father looked at me and staggered back.

He was afraid.

I felt them both.

The vessel of Marmoris. A gaping void, endless and consuming.

The vessel of Veyrith. A storm, an untamed current.

They warred inside me, the magic tearing through my veins, fighting for dominance, pulling me in two.

Too much. It was too much. I couldn't hold them both, I couldn't control either. A hand slammed over my wrist. Pressed hard against my skin.

I blinked up at Dacre, tried to focus on the details of his face. His grip on me was tight, his voice a roar through the storm. "Verena."

The vessels surged, but his presence held steady, his soul twining with mine, our bond flaring within me.

Not just a tether. A balance. Our bond rushed through my veins, raced alongside the vessels within me. It coaxed them, calmed them, helped me breathe.

I gasped, my vision snapping clearer, the throne room sharpening back into focus. The Sight was watching me, lips parted, awed. My father was still staggering back. His face was ashen, his body trembling. He could feel it.

I wasn't just wielding one vessel. I wasn't tied to it as he had tried to force me to be. I was wielding both.

I lifted my hand, and he fell to his knees.

His head snapped up, panic bleeding into his gaze, and I knew that he had never truly feared before this moment.

Because he had never believed I could break him.

But I reached inside myself for that power, for the bond he had forged between himself and the vessel of Marmoris. The one that had made him a god.

I could see it now. The magic wrapped around him like

a leash. A chain. I tightened my fist, wrapping my hand around it, and I tugged.

My father shot forward, his hands slamming down against the marble as he looked up at me with so much fear in his eyes.

I could hear the others fighting around us, could hear the clang of metal and grunts of pain. I paid them no attention.

I tightened my hold on the chain, wrapped it securely around my hand, and this time, when I wrenched it back, the chain snapped.

A scream ripped from my father's throat, his body convulsing as he clutched his chest. I felt the vessel pull away from him, severing its hold, its power twisting free, twisting into something completely different.

The Sight gasped, her voice a whisper of prophecy. "The tideborn's gift, bound in chain. To break the bond or bind again."

I lifted my gaze, and I could feel it.

Not just in my veins. Not just in the magic thrumming beneath my skin, but everywhere.

The palace walls shuddered. The marble beneath my feet trembled. The entire kingdom quaked.

The vessel of Marmoris was no longer a thing to be wielded, to be controlled. It was breathing. It was alive, and it saw me.

A rush of something ancient, something vast and unknowable, coiled inside my chest.

Not a king. Not a tyrant. Not a god. It had been waiting for me. They both had.

A breath left my lips, and suddenly, I saw the kingdom.

The land greening, the rivers running fuller, the weight of something unseen lifting from the air.

I saw Veyrith. Not just lost ruins, not a broken kingdom, but something stirring. Something awakening.

It was like standing at the edge of two worlds, Marmoris and Veyrith, and for the first time, they both belonged to me.

Born of two kingdoms.

I gasped, my knees threatening to buckle, but Dacre's grip tightened.

Stay with me, his magic whispered through the bond, steadying me. *You are still here. You are still mine.*

I blinked, my vision snapping back to my father. His body shook, hollowed, crumbling as he climbed to his knees. The power he had hoarded for so long was gone.

And without it, he was nothing.

Dacre's fingers tightened against me. His voice was quiet. "End it."

The magic coiled inside me, a storm waiting to break. I could feel it all.

My mother's screams. The kingdom's suffering. The weight of a thousand lives crushed beneath his rule.

And I saw him for what he was.

A man who had stolen power that was never his. A man who had called himself a king while he let the kingdom wither.

A man who had tried to break me, tried to make me his weapon.

But I was never his. I was hers.

I was Marmoris. I was Veyrith.

I was the heir.

My father staggered back, his body trembling, magic he no longer controlled dripping from his fingertips like something rotten, something decayed. His chest heaved, his skin gray and cracking as the power he had hoarded for so long rejected him.

"You…" His voice was nothing more than a rasp, a shadow of the man who had once ruled. "You think you can take my throne?"

I lifted my chin, magic burning in my veins, the two vessels surging, pulsing, a rhythm that would shake the world.

"You never deserved it."

He lurched toward me, hands outstretched, but he had nothing left. No power. No kingdom. Not even fear.

"You destroyed Veyrith." My voice rang through the throne room, loud enough to make the walls tremble. "You corrupted Marmoris."

His eyes widened as I took a step, the magic inside me rising, screaming. Dacre's hold slipped from my arm.

"You stole my mother; you tried to steal me."

Magic roared to life inside me, a storm ready to break, but I didn't reach for it.

Instead, I reached for the dagger.

I didn't need magic for this. I wanted him to feel it. He had called me powerless for years. So when I took his life, it would be at my hand, and my hand alone.

His powerless heir.

His eyes widened as my dagger plunged into his chest. Straight to his heart.

His lips parted, a choked, gasping sound escaping him,

his hands grasping for me, but there was nothing left to take.

No power. No kingdom. No more control.

"You wanted a weapon," I whispered, twisting the blade. "And you got one."

A shudder tore through his body before his weight sagged, the dagger still buried in his chest, and I watched as the great King of Marmoris crumbled.

Like dust. Like nothing.

A sharp, rattling breath left my lips, and Dacre was there before I could fall, his arms steady, sure.

And somewhere, someone whispered, "The king is dead."

A breath. A murmur.

Then, "Long live the queen!"

The words slammed into my chest, shot into the magic that still moved within me.

I turned, and one by one, the room fell to their knees.

CHAPTER 27
VERENA

The battle was over, but the weight of it was just beginning.

I stood in the throne room, surrounded by the bodies of men and women who had fought for a tyrant, men and women who had fought for me. The air was thick with the scent of blood and burning oil, the torches flickering against cracked stone. The world was quieter now, but the silence felt wrong.

It didn't feel like victory.

It felt like too much.

My chest rose and fell in shallow, uneven breaths. I could still feel the magic inside me, Marmoris, Veyrith, the balance between them. But now, instead of pulling me in different directions, instead of battling for control, they were settling. A storm that had finally stilled.

My father was dead.

I had killed him. I had torn him apart, stripped him of his throne, shattered the power he had stolen. And yet, as I stood there, my dagger still slick with his blood, the world hadn't changed the way I thought it would.

I thought I would feel free, but instead, I felt everything else.

Relief. Sadness. Happiness. Fury. Grief. Numb.

I didn't know which feeling to hold on to. I didn't know how to hold onto any of them for longer than a few moments before it would shift to something else.

But warm hands found me. Steady hands.

Dacre.

He moved in front of me, and his fingers wrapped around mine and his magic slid against my veins. His voice was rough, hoarse. "Breathe, Verena."

I did. I pulled in a breath, and I felt him, felt our bond threading between us like a lifeline. He hadn't let go of me once, and he never would.

I looked up into his eyes, and for the first time since I stepped into this palace, since I walked into this throne room, I felt as if I might find it again, the steadiness, the calm.

But the world was still breaking around us.

A ragged gasp echoed from across the room, and I turned. Micah was staggering to his feet, his chest still heaving from where my father had thrown him. His eyes were locked on to the far side of the throne room.

And then I saw her too, his sister. She was standing among my father's courtesans, still shadowed against the wall. Her face was ashen, her hands trembling where they clutched the fabric of her dress.

She didn't look at Micah. She was looking at me.

Micah shoved past the people filling the room, his sword clattering to the ground as he ran to her.

"Maliah." His voice cracked, raw and desperate as he reached for her, but she flinched.

Micah's face twisted, agony and relief warring in his expression as he stood in front of her. "It's me." His words faltered, his voice shook.

I swallowed past the lump in my throat, dropped Dacre's hands and stepped forward. I moved across the room before I could talk myself out of it. I stopped beside Micah, beside the man who had been my savior, my enemy, my betrayal.

"Maliah." I spoke her name gently, carefully. Her wide, frightened gaze flicked to mine, and I kept my voice steady. "It's over. You're safe now."

She hesitated, and I looked at Micah. At the torment in his face, and even though I didn't owe him anything, I took the smallest step forward. "You are safe with Micah."

Maliah's gaze flicked back and forth between us before she took a small step forward and collapsed into his arms. He let out a strangled, broken sound as he wrapped himself around her, his body shaking against hers. His hands clutched at her back, his forehead pressing against her shoulder.

"I'm sorry," he choked. "I'm so sorry, Maliah."

And I saw it. The guilt that had been eating him for years, the weight of everything he had done, everything he had been forced to become, finally breaking him.

I moved beside him, and when he lifted his head, his gaze bloodshot, his lips parted as if to speak, I said it for him.

"Go back to Veyrith." The words slipped from my lips so easily.

His breath hitched. Maliah stiffened in his arms.

"The kingdom is waking, Micah," I continued. "It needs someone to watch over it. To help it grow again."

He stared at me as if I had just struck him.

"Marmoris has brought you nothing but pain. Both of you." I nodded to his sister. "You are welcome to stay, but you are also welcome to go."

"You would trust me with that?" His voice was barely above a whisper, thick with disbelief, thick with guilt.

"Veyrith belongs to you just as much as it does to me." I met his gaze steadily. "You were never meant to be trapped here, trapped into what they made you become. Neither of you."

Tears slipped down his face, but he didn't wipe them away. He just nodded as he squeezed his sister tighter against him.

I turned my head to give them space, to give them a moment that they hadn't had in a very long time, and my breath caught at what I saw.

Wren was on her knees, her body trembling, her arms braced against the marble as if she couldn't hold herself up, but she wasn't alone.

Kai was there. He was always there.

His hands framed her face, his dark eyes searching, pleading. His forehead pressed against hers, and I could see the way his fingers shook where they held her. The way his chest rose and fell in uneven, fractured breaths.

Her breath was shaking, but she was breathing.

And that was all he needed.

A sharp, choked sound escaped his lips, his fingers sliding into her hair as he exhaled. "You're here," he whispered, his voice breaking. His lips brushed her temple, once, twice, and then again as if he couldn't stop, as if he needed to keep touching her to believe it. "You're here."

Wren's hands fisted in the front of his tunic, her knuckles stark white, her body trembling as she whispered words I couldn't hear.

Kai made a noise in the back of his throat, something between a laugh and a sob.

His fingers slid down to her throat, to the pulse beating beneath her skin. He pressed his thumb there, as if to feel it beneath his hands, as if to prove to himself that she was real. That she was alive. He was speaking to her for only her to hear.

She tilted her face up, staring at him for a long moment, and he kissed her.

Not careful. Not soft.

He kissed her like he needed her, like he couldn't breathe without her, like she was the only thing that tethered him to this world.

I exhaled sharply, something deep in my chest twisting as I watched them. I had seen Wren fight. I had seen her strong, and I had never been so scared as when my father had her in his hands.

She was breaking, and Kai, Kai was breaking with her.

I felt Dacre's magic at my back before I felt the warmth of his skin.

We had survived. We had all survived.

A low huff of laughter vibrated against my back, warm and familiar. I turned just enough to see Dacre's lips curve slightly, the exhaustion lining his face doing nothing to dull the sharp amusement in his eyes.

"Well," he murmured, voice rough, "I suppose they're done pretending."

I let out a breath, something fragile and aching unraveling inside me.

"I guess they are," I whispered.

Dacre's expression softened. He lifted a hand, brushing his knuckles gently along my cheek before letting his fingers trace down to my jaw. His touch was warm, the only thing in this room that still felt whole.

I leaned into it, into him.

His thumb swept slowly across my skin before he exhaled, something shifting in his gaze.

"She's gone."

I frowned. "Who?"

His jaw tightened slightly. "The Sight."

A chill curled down my spine. I pulled back just enough to look up at him fully, but his expression was unreadable.

"She vanished before anyone could stop her," he continued. "No one saw where she went."

A flicker of unease curled low in my stomach, but I forced myself to breathe through it. I swallowed, pushing thoughts of her away, and forced my focus back on Dacre.

"What about your grandmother? Is she okay?"

His fingers twitched against my jaw. "She's already begun tending to the wounded."

I nodded, relief settling in my chest.

"And my father," Dacre added, voice quieter now. "He…" A muscle in his jaw jumped. "He's checking the streets for the wounded and the fallen."

I nodded. "Is he okay?"

"I think he's shaken." Dacre swallowed and brushed hair off my face. "I think he was still shaken about Reed, and after what Eiran did." He hesitated, and his expression faltered. Guilt and sadness both battling to settle within him.

"He saved Wren," I muttered as I faced him fully and leaned into him. "But he also did really bad things." I slid my fingers into his hair and pulled him down until his forehead pressed against mine. "It's okay to feel both of those things. It's okay to feel whatever it is that's battling inside you."

"And you?" His question fell against my lips. "Do you know that as well?"

My breath hitched. He was looking at me, really looking at me, his eyes dark, something unspoken lingering between us.

The bond hummed.

"I do." I nodded and tightened my hold on him. "We'll get through it together. All of it."

I settled myself in the weight of his hands, in the warmth of his skin.

He held me tighter, like he was afraid to let go, like if he did, the weight of everything would pull us both under. His fingers traced slow, steady patterns against my back.

I exhaled, pressing into him, feeling the tremble in his breath, the way it shuddered through him.

His voice was rough when he finally spoke. "You were never supposed to bear this alone."

A lump formed in my throat. "I didn't."

His hand moved to my jaw, his thumb brushing just

beneath my bottom lip. His touch was warm, careful, reverent, but his eyes, gods, his eyes burned. "You changed everything," he murmured. "You changed me."

I swallowed, my throat tight. "And you saved me."

His fingers slid into my hair, his grip tightening as if he needed to hold on to something real. "I wanted to tear him apart, Verena. When he touched you, when he hurt you, I wanted..." He broke off, his voice raw.

I reached for him, pulling him closer, pressing my lips to his jaw, to the corner of his mouth. "He's gone," I whispered. "He's gone, Dacre."

His breath hitched, and I felt it, the relief, the grief, the love, the rage, all of it tangled together. I lifted a hand, brushing his damp hair from his forehead, letting my fingers linger.

A sound escaped his lips, something between a laugh and a breath of disbelief, and then he kissed me.

It was slow, deep, aching. Like he was learning me all over again. Like he needed to feel every part of me, memorize every inch of me, just in case the gods tried to steal me from him again.

I melted into him, letting the world fall away, letting the bond between us hum, warm and steady beneath my skin.

"You are mine," he whispered against my lips, his hands shaking where they held me.

"I'm yours," I murmured. "And you are mine."

His lips ghosted over mine, his voice nothing more than a breath. "In this life and every life after."

CHAPTER 28
VERENA

The sea was still that night.

Not a ripple stirred its darkened surface, no wind to carry the scent of salt through the city's battered streets. It was as if the ocean itself was holding its breath, waiting, watching, as we prepared to send the dead home.

Torches lined the shore, their flickering flames casting light over the gathered crowd. The rebels stood in solemn ranks, their armor battered, their faces streaked with soot and grief. Those who had once fought for my father stood farther back, their expressions unreadable.

And in the water, drifting silently beyond the shallows, the boats waited.

Dozens of them.

Eiran, the rebels who had fallen, the innocents my father had slaughtered.

And the boy.

The hanged child who had burned in the streets, his lifeless body swaying as the flames swallowed him. His mother had been waiting when we found him, clutching his toy he'd left behind against her chest, her screams raw.

She stood beside me now, her fingers clutching the edge of the boat that bore him. She hadn't spoken, not since she had laid him inside, smoothing back what was left of his burned hair with shaking hands.

I felt her grief like a physical thing. It pressed against me, wrapped around my throat.

He should have had more time.

I swallowed past the sharp ache in my chest, my breath shuddering as I stepped forward.

The torch in my hand flickered, the heat licking against my fingers, but I barely felt it. My legs trembled as I waded into the water, my dress clinging to my legs, heavy with seawater and grief.

I pressed a hand against the edge of his boat.

Then I pushed.

The tide caught him, pulled him into its embrace.

His mother let out a broken, keening sob, her knees buckling beneath her. Someone caught her before she could fall.

I did not turn to see whom.

My fingers were trembling as I lifted the torch, as I let the flames kiss the wood.

Fire bloomed, a golden glow against the night, and then the boy was gone, drifting toward the horizon, carried beyond my reach.

Tears streaked down my face and the wind picked up, whispering against my skin, against my heart.

I turned my head to see Dacre where he stood just

beyond the water's edge, watching me, his torch still burning in his hand.

His lips parted, and though he didn't say the words, I felt them.

We will honor them.

I swallowed against the lump in my throat, my fingers tightening around my torch.

A few feet away, another boat waited. Eiran's body lay atop it, arms crossed over his chest, his face shadowed beneath the glow of the flames.

Dacre moved forward, stepping into the water beside me. He hesitated only for a moment then he set the boat aflame.

Neither of us spoke as we watched the fire spread, licking at the edges of the wood, curling over the man who had once been his brother and his enemy.

He had betrayed Dacre. He had saved Wren.

Dacre's father stood on the beach, his lips pressed into a thin line, and his eyes never leaving the flames as Eiran's body was carried out to sea.

I didn't know if Dacre and his father's relationship would ever heal. Even now, I could feel Dacre's hesitation through our bond. I could feel his desperation and confusion over whether they could ever repair what they had lost.

Dacre exhaled sharply, lowering the torch to his side. His knuckles were white where they gripped the handle.

I looked at him then, really looked at him. At the war still raging inside him, at the grief that tangled with his fury.

His throat bobbed as he swallowed, and I reached for him, my fingers brushing against his wrist.

He let out a breath. Then another.

Then he turned away, his torch falling into the shallows with a soft hiss.

I looked back at the boats, at the flames now drifting farther and farther into the dark, until they were only distant specks of light, swallowed by the horizon.

And I wasn't sure if the ache inside me would ever fade.

I tried to breathe, tried to force air into my lungs where guilt had taken root, but I didn't think it would ever let go of me.

The fires burned, the sea carried the ashes, and still, the weight remained.

They would never see this kingdom rise. Never see what we would build from the ruin left behind. But I would carry them with me, in every stone, in every whisper, in every breath.

Their names would not be forgotten.

A sharp wind carried over the sea, stirring the flames, sending embers dancing across the waves until they danced above, carrying over my face, and whipping through my hair.

I lifted my chin, and I let them crown me.

EPILOGUE
DACRE

The kingdom had begun to heal.

Marmoris was no longer the fractured, broken land it had been under the king's rule. Flowers bloomed where there had once been only ash. Children laughed in the streets, their voices carrying through the air like bird-song. The weight of oppression that had once smothered this place had started to lift, and yet, even as the palace thrived, Verena had refused her coronation for weeks.

She had given herself to rebuilding first.

I had watched her spend long nights among our people. She would kneel in the dirt alongside farmers, Wren with her, their fingers deep in the soil as they tested its fertility and sowed the seeds of new crops. With blacksmiths and weavers, she stood shoulder to shoulder, the rhythmic clink of metal and the soft whisper of threads weaving tales of our kingdom and of Veyrith, dispelling shadows of fear that had once loomed over them because of her father's legacy.

She did not sit upon the throne as her predecessor had before; instead, she worked side by side with them to rebuild.

And her people, our people, had come to love her for it.

It was only after she had seen the magic return to the land, seen the tithe restructured by the hands of her and my grandmother in a way that let the kingdom flourish, that she had finally agreed to take the throne.

But it wasn't just Marmoris that was changing.

Across the sea, Veyrith had begun to stir.

I had heard the whispers from Micah's letters, his careful words painting a picture of a land long thought to be lost. The ruins had begun to breathe again, its once barren rivers filling, its magic uncoiling from centuries of slumber. Just as Marmoris was finding its balance, so too was the kingdom my mate's mother had once called home.

And today, Verena stood before her kingdom as the queen of them both.

I stood just beyond the curved balcony doors, watching her with awe.

The wind carried the scent of the sea, lifting the delicate silks of her gown. Deep sapphire blue, the color of a Marmoris sky before a storm. It was the first time I had seen her wear something that was truly befitting of a queen.

Her mother's dress.

A crown now rested upon her head, delicately woven gold twisted in intricate patterns, the centerpiece a single dark sapphire that captured the fading light of the sun with a mesmerizing gleam. Her hair was pulled back out of her face, long curls cascading over her bare shoulders, and the

THE RIVALED CROWN
435

gown's intricate embroidery sweeping across her collarbones like trailing ivy.

She was breathtaking.

And she was mine.

I stepped toward her, unable to restrain myself any
longer, drawn to her like the tides to the moon. My fingers
brushed against her lower back, and I felt the slow, steady
rise and fall of her breath beneath my palm.

"You were staring," she murmured, her voice laced with
quiet amusement.

"I will never stop staring at you."

A soft exhale left her lips, a gentle whisper in the quiet
air, and she finally turned to face me. The sunlight poured
over her like liquid gold, casting warm, golden hues across
her face and illuminating her features with a delicate glow.
Her deep blue eyes shimmered like a forest at twilight, rich
and full of burdens.

She was still carrying so much weight, the invisible
duty pressing down on her shoulders: the strains of her new
role, heavy with responsibility, and the hardship of caring
so deeply for the people she felt she had previously failed.

"I was never meant for this," she whispered, her doubts
filling her words as if they were secrets she could no longer
hold. "I was never meant to be queen."

"That's a lie." I brushed my fingers along her cheek,
feeling the warmth of her skin beneath my touch. With
gentle insistence, I tilted her chin upward until her eyes,
deep and tumultuous like a stormy sea, locked with mine.
"You were meant to be exactly this. You are the future our
mothers fought for, the one they sacrificed everything for."

She swallowed hard, her throat moving beneath my

fingertips like a fragile, delicate bird caught in a moment of vulnerability when it had forgotten how to use its wings. "And if I fail them?"

"You won't." My voice was as firm as tempered steel, unwavering and resolute. "You have already given them more than your father ever did. You are rebuilding a kingdom, not from power, but from love. They follow you because they believe in you. I believe in you."

Her lips parted slightly, as if she wanted to argue, but no words came forth.

Instead, she leaned forward on her tiptoes and kissed me.

It was slow, lingering, filled with an ache that I could feel in my bones.

I groaned softly against her lips, my hands gliding around the curve of her waist, drawing her closer until there was not even a whisper of space between us. Her body melded into mine with an effortless grace, as if she had always been destined to be there, as if there had never existed a world where we didn't fit together so perfectly.

"Verena," I murmured against her mouth, my grip tightening as heat coursed through me. "I am bewitched by you."

Her fingers curled against my chest, my shirt crumbling in her hold.

"And I you," she murmured breathlessly.

I shook my head because she didn't understand. She would never grasp the power she held, the hold she had over me that had nothing to do with the crown that sat upon her head.

I peppered gentle kisses along the curve of her neck,

savoring the taste of her skin, lavishing in the feel of her beneath my tongue. I let my lips wander lower, tracing a path to the soft valley between her breasts, feeling her shiver against me.

Slowly, I descended farther, lowering myself to my knees before her.

She hesitated, her fingers curling and slipping into my hair "Dacre, I…"

"Please," I cut her off, pressing my forehead to her trembling stomach. "Let me remind you that you are more than this crown. More than what they expect you to be. That you are still mine."

She closed her eyes, a gentle sigh escaping her lips as she allowed the tenderness of the moment to wash over her. Her fingers delicately trailed over the back of my neck, the touch as soft as a feather, sending shivers down my spine.

"The kingdom is right behind me," she whispered, her voice trailing off with a laugh. "They cannot see their queen like this."

I grinned as I looked past her, my hands settling firmly on her hips. "No one will see us as long as you're quiet."

Her gaze flicked behind her to the view of the city below us, and I let my hands fall down her body, beneath the soft hem of her dress.

"Tell me you're mine," I whispered as I eased her dress upward, allowing my fingertips to glide over the smooth, warm skin of her knees.

Her breath caught, a subtle hitch that rippled through me. She turned her gaze back to me, her eyes locking on to mine. "You know that I'm yours."

I cocked my head slightly just as her supple thighs came into view. "And do you know that?"

She laughed softly, but her body was coiled with tension as she widened her thighs just the slightest bit. "You're very demanding. Has anyone ever told you that?"

I smiled as I leaned forward and pressed a kiss against her inner thigh. "They have. I think it might have been you now that I think of it."

"And what if I said I didn't like it?" she practically purred, a soft challenge that lingered in the air.

I slowly lifted her dress higher, the silky fabric sliding upward until it gathered in delicate folds against her hips.

I glided my thumb over the lace of her underwear, tracing the intricate line of her pussy as she squirmed beneath my touch, her breaths quickening.

"Then I would tell you that you're a liar." I looked up at her, at how beautiful she looked above me.

"I don't think you're supposed to speak to your queen that way." She grinned, a fucking traitorous little grin, and I knew that I was going to devour her. "I could call for my guards right now and have you carried away."

I pressed my thumb hard against her clit through her underwear, and her hips surged forward, betraying her. "You wouldn't dare."

"Wouldn't I?" she asked so breathlessly.

I smirked, dragging my thumb in slow, lazy circles over the lace covering her, feeling her body tremble beneath my hands. Her breath hitched, her fingers tightening in my hair. "Dacre…"

I pressed a kiss to the inside of her thigh, right at the

edge of where she wanted me most, deliberately slow, savoring the way she shivered beneath me. "I should have known," I murmured, my lips brushing against her skin, "that even as my queen, you would still be a little traitor."

BEFORE YOU GO

Please consider leaving an honest review.

THANK YOU

Thank you so much for reading The Rivaled Crown! I was so emotional writing this book, and I can't believe that Verena and Dacre's story has come to an end.

I hope that you loved them as much as I did.

Ready to fall in love with another world that I have created? A Kingdom of Stars and Shadows is a sexy, enemies-to-lovers fantasy romance that will have you begging for more!

I would love for you to join my reader group, Hollywood, so we can connect and talk about all of your thoughts on The Veiled Kingdom! This group is the first place to find out about cover reveals, book news, and new releases!

Xo,

Holly Renee
www.authorhollyrenee.com

Before You Go

Please consider leaving an honest review.

MORE FROM HOLLY RENEE

Stars and Shadows Series:

A Kingdom of Stars and Shadows

A Kingdom of Blood and Betrayal

A Kingdom of Venom and Vows

A Kingdom of Fire and Fate

The Good Girls Series:

Where Good Girls Go to Die

Where Bad Girls Go to Fall

Where Bad Boys are Ruined

The Boys of Clermont Bay Series:

The Touch of a Villain

The Fall of a God

The Taste of an Enemy

The Deceit of a Devil

The Seduction of Pretty Lies

The Temptation of Dirty Secrets

The Rock Bottom Series:

Trouble with the Guy Next Door

Trouble with the Hotshot Boss

Trouble with the Fake Boyfriend

The Wrong Prince Charming

ACKNOWLEDGMENTS

Thank you to all the readers who have loved this series from the very beginning. I'll never be able to put in words how much your support means to me.

Thank you to my husband, Hubie. *In this life and the next.*

To Lauren Cox- My baby, my boo. I couldn't make it through a single day without you. Thank you endlessly for everything you do, and for, you know, just being the best friend ever.

To Amber Palmer- You are one of the greatest friends I've ever known. Thank you for always being my biggest cheerleader. (Oh, and letting me cry in voice notes when your girl is stressed.)

To Brandi and Kenie Marie- Thank you for being the best sisters and employees ever. ;)

To Rachel Brookes- Thank you for always being there and always be willing to help. I appreciate you more than you know.

Thank you to my entire team who I couldn't do this without. Lauren, Regan, Savannah, Ellie, Rumi, Cynthia, Lo, Rebecca: thank you, thank you, thank you.

CONTINUE READING FOR A LOOK AT

A KINGDOM OF STARS AND SHADOWS

CHAPTER 1

I tried to swallow as the smoke from the burning embers encircled me in a cruel, slow torture. The royal army had been camped outside the cleave between our world and theirs for a total of three days. Three excruciatingly long days.

The grim tick of the clock echoed throughout the room, and my heart raced it before the next beat could sound.

My fingers trembled as I pulled my boot on my foot and tied up the laces. The room was as black as the starless night inside our home, but I didn't mind it. I welcomed it, honestly, because it was the only time I could do anything without everyone watching my every move.

"Where are you going?"

I clamped my eyes closed before quickly tucking my father's dagger into the side of my boot before she could see.

"I just need some air." I stood and pulled the hood of my worn-out cloak over my head. "Go back to sleep."

My mother wrapped her thin arms around herself and avoided my gaze. "Sleep alludes me." She shook her head. "You shouldn't be going out there tonight."

"I can take care of myself."

"I know that." Her dark brown eyes finally met my own. "But it won't be long now until they come, and..."

"And I should be able to enjoy my last few hours of freedom however I choose."

Her jaw clenched at my words. "They aren't taking you as a prisoner, Adara. Being the chosen Starblessed is a blessing from the gods."

"Of course." I bowed in front of her dramatically. "Look at the life it has afforded you."

She sucked in a shocked breath, but this wasn't a new argument. My fate had never been mine, and my mother had accepted many luxuries in exchange for her daughter. Luxuries that my father fought against. That he lost his life over.

I walked to the door and hesitated when my mother's trembling voice called back out to me. "Do not run. They will find you, and we will both pay the price for your treason."

I let her words skate over me and reminded myself of exactly who she was. My heart ached as dread filled me. My fate lay in the hands of the soldiers who waited for me outside the cleave, but I would mourn for no one that I left behind.

The cool night air danced along my skin as if it had been waiting for me to open the door and slide outside. I pulled my hood tighter around my face to hide my curse as I stepped onto the cobblestone street and headed directly toward the place I should have been avoiding.

The streets were bare and quiet. Even the small pub that was usually overflowing with ale and unfaithful husbands was locked down tightly and not a flicker of candlelight shone through the window.

A chill ran down my spine, but I wouldn't allow myself to be fearful like they were. The Achlys family was powerful, but they weren't gods. If they were, then they would have no need for me.

I had never seen a single one of them. Not the king, the queen, or the crowned prince to whom I was sworn to marry. All I knew was that they were high fae and that the blood that coursed through my veins was somehow the key to unlocking their dormant power.

Lethal power they longed to possess.

To my knowledge, none of the royals had ever crossed over the cleave. They had men for that, and those low-ranked guards were the only ones I had encountered. If they had magic, I had never seen it.

My mother said they didn't use it here because they didn't have to, but part of me wondered if they still had any powers at all. If they didn't have magic, then I had no real reason to fear them. I could run, and my mother would be the one left to face the consequences.

Without powers, I doubted any of them would be able to find me. Only the twin moons knew my secrets as they watched me shift through the shadows. Everyone thought they knew exactly who I was, and that meant they all believed that I was the key to some blessing they thought the royals would bestow on them once I was sacrificed.

My fingers trailed across the bricks as I passed the last building and stepped onto the damp grass. I knew the path that led into the woods better than I knew my own home, and I let my feet lead the way as I looked around me for signs of anyone watching.

The edge of our town was only a few minutes' walk to the perimeter of the cleave, and I often liked to come here just to watch and imagine what life was like on the other side. It didn't look any different from the Starless realm.

The trees grew tall and heavy on both sides, and the only indication that the cleave existed was the thin veil that could hardly be seen at night. It reminded me of the mist that coated our land in the early morning hours, but the cleave never left. I crouched low and ran my fingers through the magic and a thrill of excitement rushed through me. I stared up as I watched the magic recoil from my touch, but it went on for as far as I could see.

It was hard to explain, but the divide between our worlds had felt more familiar to me than my own home. It felt like an old friend that I didn't even know. A familiar stranger that always greeted me.

Tonight, though, it felt different. Darker somehow as if it was warning me away. I pulled my hand back and searched through the gleam.

There were at least fifty soldiers camped in the woods about twenty yards from the cleave, and I watched the one who was standing guard at this edge of the camp.

His gaze was searching the tree line, looking for a threat, but he hadn't noticed me. I could easily cross the cleave and slit his throat if I dared. It would be far too effortless if he were only a man, but I didn't know what powers lay beneath his clueless stare.

My fingers edged toward my dagger as I looked past him and scanned the camp. There were several tents, all bearing the royal seal proudly, and a few soldiers sat by a large fire, laughing as they spoke to one another. I clenched my jaw as I watched them so at ease.

Soldiers sent here to take a human girl against her will, but that fate didn't seem to weigh heavily on any of them.

They were nothing but fools of a crooked kingdom, and my heart pounded in my chest as I watched them.

None of them sensed a threat. Not a single one of them worried about what the Starless could do to them.

But I wasn't Starless.

The twin moons shined brightly above me as my fingers traced over the rough metal handle of my dagger I had memorized years ago, but they tensed as my spine bristled. I turned to look behind me just as a gloved hand clamped down around my mouth.

Panic ensnared me as I searched the dark eyes behind me. His hand flexed against my mouth harder as if he was worried I would scream, but I wouldn't. None of these people would help me, and I didn't want to draw any attention from the fae soldiers.

They were already after me, and I didn't want them to know that I was watching them so closely.

"What the fuck are you doing?" his deep, sensual voice that I didn't recognize growled at me before he dropped his hand from my mouth and jerked my own away from my dagger and tugged it out of my boot.

"Give that back."

I reached out for my blade, but he quickly moved out of my reach. He opened his hand and my dagger was enveloped in black smoke that dripped from his fingers. It floated in the air as if nothing was holding it but his magic. My breath rushed out of me as my marks hummed against my skin. It was as if the stranger in front of me had roused them from a deep slumber that I hadn't realized they were in.

"That's not going to happen." He lowered his hood, and my face flushed with warmth as I looked up at him. His jaw was sharp and his cheekbones high. His hair was black as the night sky and cut short. And gods, he was beautiful. High fae, I was absolutely certain. His ears came to the slightest point that always gave the fae away, but it was his unnatural beauty that divulged what he was so easily. That and his domineering boldness. "What are you doing on the edge of the cleave with nothing but a dagger to protect you?"

"I can handle myself." I had become tired of repeating that sentiment, but I still said it regardless of the fact that I didn't owe this fae any explanation.

"Can you?" His hand shot out and wrenched me forward. I flinched and barely noticed his hand as he pulled my hood back with a harsh tug.

His head jerked back as his gaze flicked rapidly over my face, and I knew exactly what he was seeing.

"You're the Starblessed?" His hand tightened around my arm almost to the point of pain, and my pulse raced beneath his touch.

"Starcursed." I lifted my chin as I corrected him. "You are a fae soldier?"

He didn't look like the other soldiers I had seen walking around the camp. His clothes were all black and held no marking of the royal guard.

He hesitated for a second before a small smile appeared on his full lips. "You could say that."

I didn't trust him. Whoever this man was, I knew that he was someone I should stay far away from.

"Let me go." I jerked my arm out of his hold, and his smile widened until his teeth were bared.

"What is the Starblessed doing in the woods in the middle of the night by herself? Shouldn't you be getting rest to meet your new husband tomorrow?"

Tomorrow. I was going to meet the crowned prince of Citlali tomorrow.

"I have a name." I turned away from him and looked back toward the camp. The soldiers there seemed none the wiser that either one of us stood in the woods just outside their tents.

"Adara." My name sounded like a plea from his lips.

I spun back toward him and searched his face. "I seem to be at a disadvantage. You know me, but I have no damn clue who you are."

That only made him smile harder.

"I'm no one important."

His answer grated on my nerves. It was nothing more than a distraction. "So, you won't tell me your name then?"

His eyes narrowed and he cocked his head to the side as

he studied me with a slow gaze over every inch of me. I wouldn't know the difference between the truth and a lie regardless of what he told me, but no matter who he was, he was strong. He screamed power without uttering a word. He could be the crowned prince standing in front of me, and I wouldn't know him.

"My name is Evren."

"Evren," I said his name aloud and savored the way it felt across my lips. "Are you going to be the one who escorts me to my prison?"

He jerked back as if I had slapped him. "You consider your betrothal to the crowned prince a prison?"

"I've never met the man, and yet my hand has been forced in marriage simply because he craves the power he believes my blood possesses. If that is not walking into a prison, what would you call it?"

He stepped forward, coming close enough to me that I could smell the hint of leather and something I couldn't quite put my finger on. I tensed as his eyes darkened and he clenched his jaw.

"You should watch the way you speak about the royal family."

Threatening. Everything about him felt like a threat.

"Or what?" I challenged and stared straight up at him as my breath rushed in and out of me. "They'll imprison me? They'll kill me? My blood is no good to them if it runs cold."

"You've lived a charmed life off the royal coin, have you not?" His tone was sharp and his gaze steady.

The urge to smack him was overwhelming, but I

refused to let this fae see how badly his words affected me. "You know nothing of the life I've lived."

He was fae, and he couldn't possibly imagine the horrors that happened in our world. The Starless lived in poverty and fear. My family had been blessed by the starlight markings on my face and back, but we had also been cursed.

The royal favor had provided us with water and food to ensure I didn't starve, a roof over our heads to keep me safe, but it also stole my father from me. It stole my fate.

My cheeks and nose were covered in what looked like freckles if it weren't for their unnatural light golden color that seemed to flow against my skin. But it was my back that always shocked people. Those same markings cascaded down my spine in row after row of starlight, and it shot out at the edges as if it couldn't be controlled. Some edges stayed tightly against my spine while others touched the curve of my ribs.

Markings that almost felt like nothing to me, but they meant the world to everyone else.

"Perhaps, I don't." He lifted his hand, and for a second, I thought he was going to touch the markings on my cheek, but his hand balled into a fist and dropped back to his side. "Perhaps you are nothing like I thought you would be."

"But you have thought of me?" I questioned, my curiosity eating at me.

"We have all thought of you, Adara." He took a step back, putting some space between us before clutching my dagger back in his hand and holding it in my direction. "You will determine the future of our world."

My heart raced at his words, and my fingers trembled

as I took my weapon back from this stranger who so easily stole it. "And what if you're wrong about that? What if I am nothing like what you all thought I would be?"

He took another step back into the shadows of the trees, but I could feel his gaze still roaming over every inch of me. "I'm counting on that."

CHAPTER 2

The sun blinked into my window, and I groaned. It was far too early to be awoken by the false promise of a bright new day. Especially when I had spent far too long into the night watching the army and imagining what today would bring.

I had watched Evren as he left my side and made his way back to the camp. He moved stealthily through the soldiers who waited there, and when I took my eyes off of him for only a moment, he disappeared. No matter how long I scoured those campgrounds, I was not able to find him again.

It didn't matter, though. Evren was nothing more than a soldier who was there to do his job, and it was a job I hated him for.

Because today I would be seized from my home and taken to Citlali.

I tugged on my quilt until it completely covered my head, and I pinched my eyes closed against the reality of the day. I just needed a few more minutes to dream. A few more moments to think about what life might have been like if I wasn't born with a few spots on my face and down my back.

Starblessed.

What a damn joke. The stars hadn't blessed me. They had cursed me and my future, and I wasn't prepared for what was to come.

Last night was my first experience with fae magic, but I knew they were capable of so much more. I had been told stories throughout my childhood, but every one felt like a dark fairy tale. I had been told of how they drank the blood of the Starblessed to fuel their powers. A custom they had adopted from the vampyres before they had been banished from their lands. None of it had ever felt real, but today I would find out the truth.

Evren hadn't looked like the monster I had imagined in my head. He looked nothing like I expected of the high fae at all.

"Adara, it's time to get up." My mother barged into my small room and jerked the blanket from my body. She was dressed in her finest pink dress that fell over her body as if it were made just for her. Her dark hair was pulled out of her face and showed off the gleam that lay in her eyes.

"Mother," I growled as I reached out for my quilt, but she was already ripping open my curtains.

"It's reported that the royal guards have already packed up camp and are soon to breach the cleave. You need to get up and get dressed. Today is your destiny."

My destiny. My mother was foolish if she truly believed that today was anything other than my death sentence. She was willingly handing me over to the fae, and she smiled as she moved about my room with no hesitation.

For a moment, I wondered what she would have done if it had been the vampyres who had come to claim me. She had told me many legends of the Blood Court that was beyond the kingdom of Citlali. Would she have given me over so willingly then too?

I knew deep down that she would have still sacrificed me for the life she now lived. The people of this town worshipped my mother. She had birthed the Starblessed with the largest mark in over a century.

She thought that made her special, blessed somehow, and I guess the reality of it was that she was right. Birthing me had afforded my mother a life she would never have been able to have on her own, and all that it cost her was her daughter and a husband she had supposedly loved.

"I'm up." I swung my legs over the side of my small bed and rubbed at my eyes. I was still wearing the same outfit from last night, and I figured my mother would complain about the dirt that I had managed to track into my bed.

But she didn't say a word.

Instead, she stared at me as she swallowed hard. "You need a bath, then I will do your hair. You can't arrive at the palace like this."

"I don't want to arrive at the palace at all." I pleaded with my eyes even as I felt my heartbeat pounding through me.

My mother shook her head, but I didn't feel like begging her to choose me. There was nothing I could say that would ever make her change her mind about the decision she was making. Even if I could, both of us knew that the royals would do the exact same thing to her that they did to my father when he had tried to deny them.

And my life wasn't worth losing hers.

I pushed past her and into the washroom. She already had a bath drawn for me, and I quickly stripped out of my clothes before sinking into the lukewarm water. Tension eased from my body, but it couldn't stop the way my heart raced in panic with every passing second.

I slipped under the water and drowned out the world for a few short moments. I tried to reach for that feeling I got when I stood at the edge of the cleave far above the town where no one could see me. There was a sense of freedom there that I never felt anywhere else, but that comfort eluded me today.

Instead, all I could imagine was Evren's face and the way his dark eyes had studied me.

You will determine the future of our world.

Damning words that I wasn't ready to face.

I pushed out of the water and gasped for breath. I didn't know what Evren thought of me, but whatever it was, he was wrong.

"Here." My mother handed me a bar of soap and gave no heed to giving me any privacy.

She didn't leave my side again. Not until after I was bathed and my tangled wet hair combed. She sat on my bed as we argued about the dress she had set out for me and how I decided to wear my pair of dark trousers instead.

She was angry when I tucked my black button-down shirt that had belonged to my father into the trousers, but I didn't care. She had made every choice for me, but I was going to wear what I wanted.

She offered to braid my hair and add a few flowers that she had picked from the field, and even though I wanted to argue, the anguish in her eyes made me sit down in front of her and bite my tongue until she was finished.

"You look beautiful." She tucked in the last flower, and I looked away from her before I did something foolish like begging her once again not to do this.

It was only a second later when a loud chime of the town bell rang out throughout the town and dread filled me.

"They're here," my mother whispered the thing no one needed to say. We all knew what today was, and we all knew what they came for.

I stood and grabbed my father's dagger from my dresser before tucking it down into my boot. My mother watched my every move, but she didn't dare say a word against it.

She led me back through our house, and I tried to take in every little detail as I followed her. The walls were worn and stained with years of life, and there were fresh flowers set on the small table only big enough for the two of us. I wouldn't particularly miss anything about it because it had never really felt like home to me, but it was the only real home I had ever had.

The place we lived before this, the home we had with my father, it was such a distant memory that I couldn't recall a single detail of it. It was nothing more than a feeling now, but it was stronger than anything I felt here.

My mother opened the front door, and I swallowed a

deep breath as I heard whispers and some cheers from our neighbors. They had all been awarded just as handsomely as my mother for living with and protecting the Starblessed.

As if any one of them could ever protect me.

They were all filled with fear, and that fear had every last one of them bowing their heads as the royal guard rode along our dirt road that led to me.

I held up my head in defiance as I stared straight ahead. I would not bow to some fake royals who thought they were gods in our world because they possessed a bit of magic.

They would take from me as they saw fit, but they would do so against my will. I was Adara Cahira of Starless, and even though I feared them more than most, I refused to bend the knee to them.

I would rather die.

The royal guards stopped directly in front of us, and my mother fell to her knees before them. I swallowed down my disgust as I stared ahead at the guard who rode in the lead.

He watched me carefully, and his gaze dropped to my knees before his jaw clenched. He didn't reprimand me as he dismounted from his horse and moved around to stand in front of me.

"Adara Cahira." His gruff voice sounded as if he had spent far too many years with a pipe in his mouth.

I nodded my head once but didn't speak. My heart felt like it was lodged in my throat. I searched through the guards for Evren, but he wasn't anywhere to be seen.

"I am here on behalf of the house of Achlys to claim you for your betrothal to the crowned prince of Citlali."

I scoffed and looked down the line of the other royal guards. "They were too busy to come themselves?"

Shocked gasps rang out around me, but the guard's stern face carved into the slightest smile. "That they were, Starblessed."

I rolled my eyes at the name. I hated that name as much as the fate it damned me with.

"We are expected to arrive in Citlali by nightfall." He motioned toward the carriage that rode between the swarm of guards, and the dark black wood made me shudder with dread.

"How long is the trip?" I tried not to allow him to sense my fear.

"Several hours." He nodded toward my mother who still hadn't climbed from her knees. "You should say your goodbyes."

I looked down at her, and only after the guard took a step back did she rise. Emotion choked me as I stared at her, and I wasn't prepared for how affected I was by this moment. I had been angry with her for as long as I could remember, but I still wasn't ready to leave her.

I didn't want to say goodbye.

"Be smart, Adara." She reached out for me and gripped my hands in her own trembling ones. "Do what is expected of you."

I loathed her words. Every single one of them felt like a dagger to the chest, but I shouldn't have been surprised. That was all my mother ever wanted from me.

I nodded my head toward her once before pulling her into my arms. I didn't whisper words of love or fears of missing her because I didn't know if either were true. But she was all I had.

She clung to me before pulling away and tucking a stray hair behind my ear so nothing was out of place. Her dark brown eyes that were a mirror of my right one searched my face, but there were no more words to waste between us.

Part of me wondered if she regretted the decisions she had made as she looked up at me and saw the reminder of my father staring back at her in my ice-blue eye.

She had always told me that I was equal parts him and her. Half my father and half the woman who was so easily watching me leave, but she was wrong. I was nothing like her.

I stepped away and turned back to the guard who tilted his head in the direction of the carriage. I took the few short steps and ignored his hand when he held it out in my direction.

I climbed into the carriage and took a deep breath as the door closed behind me and surrounded me with the fear of my future. The interior was far nicer than anything I had ever seen in my entire life. The seat a supple black leather with satin red pillows against the wooden backrest.

I pressed against them before looking back out the open window. One of the guards was loading my small trunk onto the carriage while my mother gazed in longingly with unshed tears in her eyes.

The sight ripped at my chest until I noticed her hands clinging to a piece of parchment that was sealed with the blood-red royal crest.

I knew what that piece of parchment held without her

even opening it. That was what she had traded me for. That was whatever she had been promised all those years ago when she had so willingly accepted my betrothal to our enemy.

The guards didn't linger, and they had no reason to. They had gotten what they came for, but I still clung to the seat as the horses lurched forward and the carriage began to move.

With panicked eyes, I looked back to my mother, but I could barely see her through the crowd of people that had gathered on the street. Most of them were waving at me with smiles on tired faces while others were tossing white wildflowers in my direction.

It was a sign of respect, something we usually only did to honor those who had passed to the gods, and dread filled me as I watched them hit the ground.

I traced the outline of my dagger as we began to pass by them in a blur. It was only a couple minutes' ride until we hit the cleave, and I anxiously watched my world fly by as I tried to steady my racing heart.

With every turn of the wooden wheels of our carriage, my fear spiked higher and higher.

I had never seen a single human pass through the cleave besides my father, and I was far too young to truly remember it. It is legend that passing through the cleave alters the Starless, changed forever by the magic that slumbered there, but there were very few stories about the Starblessed. The only thing I knew for sure was that it was said once you passed through, you shall never return.

It didn't matter how they were changed after they passed through the magic, because they were never going to return. I was never going to come back here after today.

I held my breath as we neared the edge of my world, and I slowly blinked them open once I knew we should have passed through. The horses didn't slow. They continued in their punishing rhythm.

I searched out the window, but the world around me didn't look much different from the one I had just given up. But it felt different. It was hard to explain, but it made me feel similar to the way I had with Evren the night before.

The smattering of marks across my cheeks and spine felt like they were alive, and my skin buzzed. It was as if the magic in this land sparked something inside of my curse to life. But it was duller than when Evren touched me. The magic of this world felt like a watered-down version of him.

I ran my fingers over my cheek as I tried to trace that feeling with my fingertips. It was foreign, but it also felt like it belonged.

I spent a long time tracing over those marks I had been born with before I switched over to staring out the window. The scenery that passed us was so like that back home, and I soon became bored of the lush fields and dense forests.

I hadn't even realized I had fallen asleep until I was awoken by the stopping of the carriage. My hand shot out to catch myself on the seat across from me, and my heart raced as I realized I had let down my guard so easily with these fae males.

It was already dark outside, and as I stepped outside of the carriage, I realized that the fae sky was as starless as my own.

Only the twin moons shined high in the sky and provided what little light that they allowed. We were still near the forest edge, and I saw no signs of Citlali City.

"Where are we?" I asked one of the passing guards as I wrapped my arms around myself. Nightfall brought a chill along with it. Another thing that hadn't changed between worlds.

"We're about an hour outside of the capital, ma'am." He tilted his head down as if he was showing me honor, as if I was one of the royals that he served. "We tried to make it the entire distance, but the horses require water."

I nodded in understanding before stepping away from him and looking down the line of guards. There were far too many guards for the task at hand, in my opinion, but I assumed giving up this many men was nothing to the royals.

I stepped into the line of the dark forest and a chill ran down my back. The moonlight seemed to disappear with that one simple step, and I searched the line of black trees as my mark felt like it was flaring against my skin.

"Whoa there." A strong arm wrapped around my middle and jerked me back against his hard body and a step outside of the forest.

Evren.

My curse knew it was him before I could manage to put even an inch between us.

"The Onyx Forest is no place for a Starblessed. Especially not alone."

I looked back at him over my shoulder, and my stomach fluttered under his hold. "I didn't see you."

"That's because you were staring out into the trees."

"No." I shook my head softly. "Before."

"Were you looking for me?" A half smile formed on his lips.

"No." I told a lie we could both easily see through.

His hand tightened around me, almost involuntarily, as he stared down at me, and for a moment, we said nothing.

Evren had given me no reason to, but something deep inside me told me that I should fear this male. Everything inside of me felt tense and my heart hammered against my chest. But I couldn't bring myself to look away from his dark eyes even as that feeling sank into my gut.

"Don't go near the forest again without someone accompanying you." His voice was a hard warning.

"Why?" My gaze finally flicked away from him to look back to the quiet woods. "What's in there? Why are the leaves black? Are the vampyres this close to Citlali?"

My spine straightened at the thought. As much as I hated the fae, I was far more fearful of the vampyres. Every story I had ever been told of them had been of their cruelty. While the highest of fae fed from the Starblessed to garner their powers, the vampyres fed from anyone they chose.

For food, for power, for pleasure.

"You have no reason to fear the vampyres here." Evren spoke softly above me and brought my attention back to him. "There are far worse things that lurk in those trees."

A chill coursed through me at his words.

"I am surrounded by enemies then?" I took a step out of his hold and tried to clear my head.

"You are surrounded by threats." He nodded his head once as if in warning and took a small step closer to me. He searched my eyes for a long moment before he lowered his tone. "You shouldn't trust anyone here."

"Even you?"

"Especially me." His eyes darkened and my stomach became heavy with yearning that made me feel like a traitor. This man was no different from the rest of them, and I would do well to remember that.

"Captain!" one of the guards called out, and Evren's jaw tensed. "We're ready to push on."

He looked over his shoulder toward the guard, and I watched as the young guard flinched. I wasn't sure if it was from respect or true fear, but my hands trembled as I watched the guard lower his head.

I couldn't trust him. He had just warned me of that himself.

"The future queen needs a moment." His voice was pure power, and it sent shivers down my spine.

It took a moment for his words to really hit me. I had known almost my entire life that I was betrothed to the future king of Citlali, but I had never imagined myself as anything other than his property. To hear someone call me the future queen, it messed with my head.

"Of course, Captain." The guard quickly backed away from where we stood, and Evren brought his attention back to me.

His gaze was still dark and domineering, but I couldn't bring myself to look away.

"We'll arrive at the Achlys palace shortly. You should prepare yourself."

"And how am I supposed to do that?" I asked breathlessly. "How am I supposed to prepare myself for what lies inside that castle?"

I didn't know why I was asking him these questions. Evren was one of them. He was a high fae and loyal to the house of Achlys. But part of me was still desperate for his answer.

"You are the future queen of Citlali. Those who reside behind those castle walls will fall to their knees when they see you, as will all of Citlali."

"You didn't." I lifted my chin as I stared up at him.

A small smile played on his lips as he searched my face, and I could see his gaze roaming over every inch of the starlight that marked my face. "Trust me, princess. It took everything inside of me not to fall to my knees before you."

He slipped his hands into his pockets, and even though I knew I should have retreated, his words made me fall impossibly closer to him.

"Don't call me that."

He lifted his fingers until they were only an inch away from my jaw before he slowly pulled them away. "You should get back to your carriage. The night is still young, and as the chosen Starblessed, you have much to face."

Made in United States
Troutdale, OR
03/21/2025